The Indian in the Cupboard

•

Return of the Indian

•

The Secret of the Indian

•

Three bestselling stories about Omri,
and his friend Patrick, who turns his plastic
Red Indian, Little Bull,
into a real miniature person.

Lynne Reid Banks

The Indian in the Cupboard

•

Return of the Indian

•

The Secret of the Indian

Collins
An Imprint of HarperCollins *Publishers*

The Indian in the Cupboard and Return of the Indian
were first published in Great Britain by
J. M. Dent & Sons Ltd in 1981 and 1986
The Secret of the Indian was first published
in Great Britain by Collins 1989
This three-in-one edition first published by Collins 1993
5 7 9 10 8 6

Collins is an imprint of
HarperCollinsPublishers Ltd,
77-85 Fulham Palace Road,
Hammersmith, London W6 8JB.

ISBN 0 00 674952-6

The author asserts the moral right to be
identified as the author of this work.

Printed and bound in Great Britain by Caledonian
International Book Manufacturing Ltd, Glasgow, G64

Contents

The Indian in the Cupboard

For Omri – who else?

Contents

Chapter 1
Birthday Presents

It was not that Omri didn't appreciate Patrick's birthday present to him. Far from it. He was really very grateful – sort of. It was, without a doubt, *very* kind of Patrick to give Omri anything at all, let alone a secondhand plastic Red Indian which he himself had finished with.

The trouble was, though, that Omri was getting a little fed up with small plastic figures, of which he had loads. Biscuit-tinsful, probably three or four if they were all put away at the same time, which they never were because most of the time they were scattered about in the bathroom, the loft, the kitchen, the breakfast-room, not to mention Omri's bedroom and the garden. The compost heap was full of soldiers which, over several autumns, had been raked up with the leaves by Omri's mother, who was rather careless about such things.

Omri and Patrick had spent many hours together playing with their joint collections of plastic toys. But now they'd had about enough of them, at least for the moment, and that was why, when Patrick brought his present to school on Omri's birthday, Omri was disappointed. He tried not to show it, but he was.

'Do you really like him?' asked Patrick as Omri stood silently with the Indian in his hand.

'Yes, he's fantastic,' said Omri in only a slightly flattish voice. 'I haven't got an Indian.'

'I know.'

'I haven't got any cowboys either.'

'Nor have I. That's why I couldn't play anything with him.'

Omri opened his mouth to say, 'I won't be able to

either,' but, thinking that might hurt Patrick's feelings, he said nothing, put the Indian in his pocket and forgot about it.

After school there was a family tea, and all the excitement of his presents from his parents and his two older brothers. He was given his dearest wish – a skateboard complete with kick-board and cryptonic wheels from his Mum and Dad, and from his eldest brother, Adiel, a helmet. Gillon, his other brother, hadn't bought him anything because he had no money (his pocket-money had been stopped some time ago in connection with a very unfortunate accident involving their father's bicycle). So when Gillon's turn came to give Omri a present, Omri was very surprised when a large parcel was put before him, untidily wrapped in brown paper and string.

'What is it?'

'Have a look. I found it in the alley.'

The alley was a narrow passage that ran along the bottom of the garden where the dustbins stood. The three boys used to play there sometimes, and occasionally found treasures that other – perhaps richer – neighbours had thrown away. So Omri was quite excited as he tore off the paper.

Inside was a small white metal cupboard with a mirror in the door, the kind you see over the basin in old-fashioned bathrooms.

You might suppose Omri would once again be disappointed, because the cupboard was fairly plain and, except for a shelf, completely empty, but oddly enough he was very pleased with it. He loved cupboards of any sort because of the fun of keeping things in them. He was not a very tidy boy in general, but he did like arranging things in cupboards and drawers and then opening them later and finding them just as he'd left them.

'I do wish it locked,' he said.

'You might say thank you before you start complaining,' said Gillon.

'It's got a keyhole,' said their mother. 'And I've got a whole boxful of keys. Why don't you try the smaller ones and see if any of them fit?'

Most of the keys were much too big, but there were half a dozen that were about the right size. All but one of these were very ordinary. The un-ordinary one was the most interesting key in the whole collection, small with a complicated lock-part and a fancy top. A narrow strip of red satin ribbon was looped through one of its curly openings. Omri saved that key to the last.

None of the others fitted, and at last he picked up the curly-topped key and carefully put it in the keyhole on the cupboard door, just below the knob. He did hope very much that it would turn, and regretted wasting his birthday-cake-cutting wish on something so silly (or rather, unlikely) as that he might pass his spelling test the next day, which it would take real magic to bring about as he hadn't even looked at the words since they'd been given out four days ago. Now he closed his eyes and unwished the test-pass and wished instead that this little twisty key would turn Gillon's present into a secret cupboard.

The key turned smoothly in the lock. The door wouldn't open.

'Hey! Mum! I've found one!'

'Have you, darling? Which one?' His mother came to look. 'Oh, *that* one! How very odd. That was the key to my grandmother's jewel-box, that she got from Florence. It was made of red leather and it fell to bits at last, but she kept the key and gave it to me. She was most terribly poor when she died, poor old sweetie, and kept crying because she had nothing to leave me, so in the end I said I'd rather have this little key than all the jewels in the world. I threaded it on that bit of ribbon – it was much longer then – and hung it round my neck and told her I'd always wear it and remember her. And I did for a long time. But then the ribbon broke and I nearly lost it.'

'You could have got a chain for it,' said Omri.

She looked at him. 'You're right,' she said. 'I should have done just that. But I didn't. And now it's your cupboard key. Please don't lose it, Omri, will you.'

Omri put the cupboard on his bedside table, and opening it, looked inside thoughtfully. What would he put in it?

'It's supposed to be for medicines,' said Gillon. 'You could keep your nose-drops in it.'

'No! That's just wasting it. Besides, I haven't any other medicines.'

'Why don't you pop this in?' his mother suggested, and opened her hand. In it was Patrick's Red Indian. 'I found it when I was putting your trousers in the washing-machine.'

Omri carefully stood the Indian on the shelf.

'Are you going to shut the door?' asked his mother.

'Yes. And lock it.'

He did this and then kissed his mother and she turned the light out and he lay down on his side looking at the cupboard. He felt very content. Just as he was dropping off to sleep his eyes snapped open. He had thought he heard a little noise...but no. All was quiet. His eyes closed again.

In the morning there was no doubt about it. The noise actually woke him.

He lay perfectly still in the dawn light staring at the cupboard, from which was now coming a most extraordinary series of sounds. A pattering; a tapping; a scrabbling; and – surely? – a high-pitched noise like – well, almost like a tiny voice.

To be truthful, Omri was petrified. Who wouldn't be? Undoubtedly there was something alive in that cupboard. At last, he put out his hand and touched it. He pulled very carefully, the door was tight shut. But as he pulled the cupboard moved, just slightly. The noise from inside instantly stopped.

10

He lay still for a long time, wondering. Had he imagined it? The noise did not start again. At last he cautiously turned the key and opened the cupboard door.

The Indian was gone.

Omri sat up sharply in bed and peered into the dark corners. Suddenly he saw him. But he wasn't on the shelf any more, he was in the bottom of the cupboard. And he wasn't standing upright. He was crouching in the darkest corner, half hidden by the front of the cupboard. And he was alive.

Omri knew that immediately. To begin with, though the Indian was trying to keep perfectly still – as still as Omri had kept, lying in bed a moment ago – he was breathing heavily. His bare, bronze shoulders rose and fell, and were shiny with sweat. The single feather sticking out of the back of his headband quivered, as if the Indian were trembling. And as Omri peered closer, and his breath fell on the tiny huddled figure, he saw it jump to its feet; its minute hand made a sudden, darting movement towards its belt and came to rest clutching the handle of a knife smaller than the shaft of a drawing-pin.

Neither Omri nor the Indian moved for perhaps a minute and a half. They hardly breathed either. They just stared at each other. The Indian's eyes were black and fierce and frightened. His lower lip was drawn down from shining white teeth, so small you could scarcely see them except when they caught the light. He stood pressed against the inside wall of the cupboard, clutching his knife, rigid with terror, but defiant.

The first coherent thought that came into Omri's mind as he began to get over the shock was, 'I must call the others!' – meaning his parents and brothers. But something (he wasn't sure what) stopped him. Maybe he was afraid that if he took his eyes off the Indian for even a moment, he would vanish, or become plastic again, and then when the others came running they would all laugh and accuse Omri of making things up. And who could blame anyone for not believing *this* unless they saw it with their own eyes?

Another reason Omri didn't call anyone was that, if he was not dreaming and the Indian had really come alive, it was certainly the most marvellous thing that had ever happened to Omri in his life and he wanted to keep it to himself, at least at first.

His next thought was that he must somehow get the Indian in his hand. He didn't want to frighten him any further, but he *had* to touch him. He simply had to. He reached his hand slowly into the cupboard.

The Indian gave a fantastic leap into the air. His black pigtail flew and the air ballooned out his loose-fitting leggings. His knife, raised above his head, flashed. He gave a shout which, even though it was a tiny shout to match his body, was nevertheless loud enough to make Omri jump. But not so much as he jumped when the little knife pierced his finger deeply enough to draw a drop of blood.

Omri stuck his finger in his mouth and sucked it and thought how gigantic he must look to the tiny Indian and how fantastically brave he had been to stab him. The Indian stood there, his feet, in mocassins, planted apart on the white-painted metal floor, his chest heaving, his knife held ready and his black eyes wild. Omri thought he was magnificent.

'I won't hurt you,' he said. 'I only want to pick you up.'

The Indian opened his mouth and a stream of words, spoken in that loud-tiny voice, came out, not one of which Omri could understand. But he noticed that the Indian's strange grimace never changed – he could speak without closing his lips.

'Don't you speak English?' asked Omri. All the Indians in films spoke a sort of English; it would be terrible if his Indian couldn't. How would they talk to each other?

The Indian lowered his knife a fraction.

'I speak,' he grunted.

Omri breathed deeply in relief. 'Oh, good! Listen, I don't know how it happened that you came to life, but it must be something to do with this cupboard, or perhaps the key – anyway, here you are, and I think you're great, I don't mind that you stabbed me, only please can I pick you up? After all, you are my Indian,' he finished in a very reasonable tone.

He said all this very quickly while the Indian stared at him. The knife-point went down a little further, but he didn't answer.

'Well? Can I? Say something!' urged Omri impatiently.

'I speak *slowly*,' grunted the miniature Indian at last.

'Oh.' Omri thought, and then said, very slowly, 'Let – me – pick – you – up.'

The knife came up again in an instant, and the Indian's knees bent into a crouch.

'No.'

'Oh, *please*.'

'You touch – I kill!' the Indian growled ferociously.

You might have expected Omri to laugh at this absurd threat from a tiny creature scarcely bigger than his middle finger, armed with only a pin-point. But Omri didn't laugh. He didn't even feel like laughing. This Indian – *his* Indian – was behaving in every way like a real live Red Indian brave, and despite the vast difference in their sizes and strengths, Omri respected him and even, odd as it sounds, feared him at that moment.

'Oh, okay, I won't then. But there's no need to get angry. I don't want to hurt you.' Then, as the Indian looked baffled, he said, in what he supposed was Indian-English, 'Me – no – hurt – you.'

'You come near, I hurt *you*,' said the Indian swiftly.

Omri had been half lying in bed all this time. Now, cautiously and slowly, he got up. His heart was thundering in his chest. He couldn't be sure why he was being cautious. Was it so as not to frighten the Indian, or because he was frightened himself? He wished one of his brothers would come in, or better still, his father... But no one came.

Standing in his bare feet he took the cupboard by its top corners and turned it till it faced the window. He did this very carefully but nevertheless the Indian was jolted, and, having nothing to hold on to, he fell down. But he was on his feet again in a second, and he had not let go of his knife.

'Sorry,' said Omri.

The Indian responded with a noise like a snarl.

There was no more conversation for the next few minutes. Omri looked at the Indian in the early sunlight. He was a splendid sight. He was about seven centimetres tall. His blue-black hair, done in a plait and pressed to his head by a coloured headband, gleamed in the sun. So did the minuscule muscles of his tiny naked torso, and the reddish skin of his arms. His legs were covered with buckskin trousers which had some decoration on them too small to see properly, and his belt was a thick hide thong twisted into a knot in front. Best of all, somehow, were his mocassins. Omri found himself wondering (not for the first time recently) where his magnifying glass was. It was the only way he would ever be able to see and appreciate the intricate embroidery, or beadwork, or whatever it was which encrusted the Indian's shoes and clothes.

Omri looked as closely as he dared at the Indian's face. He expected to see paint on it, war-paint, but there was none. The turkey-feather which had been stuck in the headband had come out when the Indian fell and was now lying on the floor of the cupboard. It was about as big as the spike on a conker, but it was a real feather. Omri suddenly asked,

'Were you always this small?'

'I no small! You, big!' the Indian shouted angrily.

'No – ' began Omri, but then he stopped.

He heard his mother beginning to move about next door.

The Indian heard it too. He froze. The door of the next room opened. Omri knew that at any moment his mother would come in to wake him for school. In a flash he had bent down and whispered, 'Don't worry! I'll be back.' And he closed and locked the cupboard door and jumped back into bed.

'Come on, Omri. Time to get up.'

She bent down and kissed him, paying no attention to the cupboard, and went out again, leaving the door wide open.

The Door is Shut

Omri got dressed in a state of such high excitement that he could scarcely control his fumbling fingers enough to do up buttons and tie his shoe-laces. He'd thought he was excited yesterday, on his birthday, but it was nothing compared to how he felt now.

He was dying to open the cupboard door and have another look, but the landing outside his bedroom door was like a railway station at this hour of the morning – parents and brothers passing continually, and if he were to close his door for a moment's privacy somebody would be sure to burst in. He'd nip up after breakfast and have a quick look when he was supposed to be cleaning his teeth...

However, it didn't work out. There was a stupid row at the breakfast table because Adiel took the last of the Rice Krispies, and although there were plenty of cornflakes, not to mention Weetabix, the other two fairly set upon Adiel and made such an awful fuss that their mother lost her temper, and the end of it was nobody got to clean their teeth at all.

They were all bundled out of the house at the last minute – Omri even forgot to take his swimming things although it was Thursday, the day his class went to the pool. He was an excellent swimmer and he was so annoyed when he remembered (halfway to school, too late to go back) that he turned on Adiel and shouted, 'You made me forget my swimming stuff!' and bashed him. That naturally led to them all being late for school, and furthermore, arriving in a very grubby condition.

All this actually pushed the Indian right out of Omri's

mind. But the minute he set eyes on Patrick, he remembered. And not for one single second for the rest of the day was that Indian out of Omri's thoughts.

You may imagine the temptation to tell Patrick what had happened. Several times Omri very nearly did tell him, and he couldn't help dropping a number of tantalizing hints.

'Your present was the best thing I got.'

Patrick looked rather astonished. 'I thought you got a skateboard!'

'Ye-es...But I like yours better.'

'Better than a skateboard? Are you having me on?'

'Yours turned out to be more exciting.'

Patrick just stared at him. 'Are you being sarcastic?'

'No.'

Later, after they'd had the spelling test and Omri had been marked three right out of ten, Patrick joked, 'I bet the plastic Indian could have done better.'

Unwarily, Omri replied, 'Oh, I don't think he can *write* English, he can only just speak –'

He stopped himself quickly, but Patrick was giving him a very odd look. 'What?'

'Nothing.'

'No, what did you say about him speaking?'

Omri wrestled with himself. He wanted to keep his secret; in any case Patrick wouldn't believe him. Yet the need to talk about it was very strong. 'He can speak,' he said slowly at last.

'Beard,' said Patrick, which was their school slang for 'I don't believe you.'

Instead of insisting, Omri said nothing more, and that led Patrick to ask, 'Why did you say that, about him speaking?'

'He does.'

'*Itchy* beard.' (Which of course means the same only more so.)

Omri refused to get involved in an argument. He was somehow scared that if he talked about the Indian, something bad would happen. In fact, as the day went on and he longed more and more to get home, he began to feel certain that the whole incredible happening – well, not that it hadn't happened, but that something would go wrong. All his thoughts, all his dreams were centred on the miraculous, endless possibilities opened up by a real, live, miniature Indian of his very own. It would be too terrible if the whole thing turned out to be some sort of mistake.

After school Patrick wanted him to stay in the school grounds and skateboard. For *weeks* Omri had longed to do this, but had never had his own skateboard till now. So it was quite beyond Patrick's understanding when Omri said, 'I can't, I have to get home. Anyway, I didn't bring it.'

'Why not? Are you crazy? Why do you have to get home, anyway?'

'I want to play with the Indian.'

Patrick's eyes narrowed in disbelief. 'Can I come?'

Omri hesitated. But no, it wouldn't do. He must get to know the Indian himself before he thought of introducing him to anyone else, even Patrick.

Besides, the most awful thought had come to him during the last lesson which had made it almost impossible for him to sit still. If the Indian *were* real, and not just – well, moving plastic, as Pinocchio had been moving wood, then he would need food, and other things. And Omri had left him shut up in the dark all day with nothing. Perhaps – what if there were not enough air for him in that cupboard? The door fitted very tight... How much air would such a very small creature need? What if – what if the Indian were – what if he'd *died*, shut up there? What if Omri had killed him?

At the very best, the Indian must have passed a horrible day in that dark prison. Omri was dismayed at the thought of it. Why had he allowed himself to be drawn into that silly row at breakfast instead of slipping away and making sure the Indian was all right? The mere thought that he might be dead was frightening Omri sick. He ran all the way home, burst through the back door, and raced up the stairs without even saying hallo to his mother.

He shut the door of his bedroom and fell on his knees beside the bedside table. With a hand that shook, he turned the key in the lock and opened the cupboard door.

The Indian lay there on the floor of the cupboard, stiff and stark. Too stiff! That was not a dead body. Omri picked it up. It was an 'it', not a 'he' any more.

The Indian was made of plastic again.

Omri knelt there, appalled – too appalled to move. He *had* killed his Indian, or done something awful to him. At the same time he had killed his dream – all the wonderful, exciting, secret games that had filled his imagination all day. But that was not the main horror. His Indian had been real – not a mere toy, but a person. And now here he lay in Omri's hand – cold, stiff, lifeless. Somehow through Omri's own fault.

How had it happened?

It never occurred to Omri now that he had imagined the whole incredible episode this morning. The Indian was in a completely different position from the one he had been in when Patrick gáve him to Omri. *Then* he had been standing on one leg, as if doing a war-dance – knees bent, one mocassined foot raised, both elbows bent too and with one fist (with the knife in it) in the air. Now he lay flat, legs apart, arms at his sides. His eyes were closed. The knife was no longer a part of him. It lay separately on the floor of the cupboard.

Omri picked it up. The easiest way to do this, he found, was to wet his finger and press it down on the tiny knife, which stuck to it. It, too, was plastic, and could no more have pierced human skin than a twist of paper. Yet it had pierced Omri's finger this morning – the little mark was still there. But this morning it had been a real knife.

Omri stroked the Indian with his finger. He felt a painful thickness in the back of his throat. The pain of sadness, disappointment, and a strange sort of guilt, burnt inside him as if he had swallowed a very hot potato which wouldn't cool down. He let the tears come, and just knelt there and cried for about ten minutes.

Then he put the Indian back in the cupboard and locked the door because he couldn't bear to look at him any longer.

That night at supper he couldn't eat anything, and he couldn't talk. His father touched his face and said it felt very hot. His mother took him upstairs and put him to bed and oddly enough he didn't object. He didn't know if he was ill or not, but he felt so bad he was quite glad to be made a fuss of. Not that that improved the basic situation, but it was some comfort.

'What is it, Omri? Tell me,' coaxed his mother. She stroked his hair and looked at him tenderly and questioningly, and he nearly told her everything, but then he suddenly rolled over on his face.

'Nothing. Really.'

She sighed, kissed him, and left the room, closing the door softly after her.

As soon as she had gone, he heard something. A scratching – a muttering – a definitely *alive* sound. Coming from the cupboard.

Omri snapped his bedside light on and stared wide-eyed at his own face in the mirror on the cupboard door. He stared at the key with its twisted ribbon. He listened to the sounds, now perfectly clear.

Trembling, he turned the key and there was the Indian, on the shelf this time, almost exactly level with Omri's face. Alive again!

Again they stared at each other. Then Omri asked falteringly, 'What happened to you?'

'Happen? Good sleep happen. Cold ground. Need blanket. Food. Fire.'

Omri gaped. Was the little man giving him orders? Undoubtedly he was! Because he waved his knife, now back in his hand, in an unmistakable way.

Omri was so happy he could scarcely speak.

'Okay – you stay there – I'll get food – don't worry – ' he gasped as he scrambled out of bed.

He hurried downstairs, excited but thoughtful. What could it all mean? It was puzzling, but he didn't bother worrying about it too much. His main concern was to get downstairs without his parents hearing him, get to the kitchen, find some food that would suit the Indian, and bring it back without anyone asking questions.

Fortunately his parents were in the living-room watching television, so he was able to tiptoe to the kitchen along the dark passage. Once there, he dared not turn on a light; but there was the fridge light and that was enough.

He surveyed the inside of the fridge. What did Indians eat? Meat, chiefly, he supposed – buffalo meat, rabbits, the sort of animals they could shoot on their prairies. Needless to say there was nothing like that.

Biscuits, jam, peanut butter, that kind of thing was no problem, but somehow Omri felt sure these were not Indian foods. Suddenly his searching eyes fell on an open tin of sweetcorn. He found a paper plate in the drawer where the picnic stuff lived, and took a good teaspoon of corn. Then he broke off a crusty corner of bread. Then he thought of some cheese. And what about a drink? Milk? Surely, Indian braves did not drink milk? They usually drank something called 'fire-water' in films, which was presumably a hot drink, and Omri dared not heat anything. Ordinary non-fire water would have to do, unless... What about some Coke? That was an American drink. Lucky there was a bit in a big bottle left over from the birthday party, so he took that. He did wish there were some cold meat, but there just wasn't.

Clutching the Coke bottle by the neck in one hand and the paper plate in the other, Omri sneaked back upstairs with fast-beating heart. All was just as he had left it, except that the Indian was sitting on the edge of the shelf dangling his legs and trying to sharpen his knife on the metal. He jumped up as soon as he saw Omri.

'Food?' he asked eagerly.

'Yes, but I don't know if it's what you like.'

'I like. Give, quick!'

But Omri wanted to arrange things a little. He took a pair of scissors and cut a small circle out of the paper plate. On this he put a crumb of bread, another of cheese, and one kernel of the sweetcorn. He handed this offering to the Indian, who backed off, looking at the food with hungry eyes but trying to keep watch on Omri at the same time.

'Not touch! You touch, use knife!' he warned.

'All right, I promise not to. Now you can eat.'

Very cautiously the Indian sat down, this time cross-legged on the shelf. At first he tried to eat with his left hand keeping the knife at the ready in his right, but he was so hungry he soon abandoned this effort, laid the knife close at his side and, grabbing the bread in one hand and the little crumb of cheese in the other, he began to tear at them ravenously.

When these two apparently familiar foods had taken the edge off his appetite, he turned his attention to the single kernel of corn.

'What?' he asked suspiciously.

'Corn. Like you have –' Omri hesitated. 'Where you come from,' he said.

It was a shot in the dark. He didn't know if the Indian 'came from' anywhere, but he meant to find out. The Indian grunted, turning the corn about in both hands, for it was half as big as his head. He smelt it. A great grin spread over his face. He nibbled it. The grin grew wider. But then he held it away and looked again, and the grin vanished.

'Too big,' he said. 'Like you,' he added accusingly.

'Eat it. It's the same stuff.'

The Indian took a bite. He still looked very suspicious, but he ate and ate. He couldn't finish it, but he evidently liked it.

'Give meat,' he said finally.

'I'm sorry, I can't find any tonight, but I'll get you some tomorrow,' said Omri.

After another grunt, the Indian said, 'Drink!'

Omri had been waiting for this. From the box where he kept his Action Man things he had brought a plastic mug. It was much too big for the Indian but it was the best he could do. Into it, with extreme care, he now poured a minute amount of Coke from the huge bottle.

He handed it to the Indian, who had to hold it with both hands and still almost dropped it.

'What?' he barked, after smelling it.

'Coca-Cola,' said Omri, enthusiastically pouring some for himself into a toothmug.

'Fire-water?'

'No, it's cold. But you'll like it.'

The Indian sipped, swallowed, gulped. Gulped again. Grinned.

'Good?' asked Omri.

'Good!' said the Indian.

'Cheers!' said Omri, raising his toothmug as he'd seen his parents do when they were having a drink together.

'What cheers?'

'I don't know!' said Omri, feeling excessively happy, and drank. His Indian – eating and drinking! He *was* real, a real, flesh-and-blood person! It was too marvellous. Omri felt he might die of delight.

'Do you feel better now?' he asked.

'I better. You not better,' said the Indian. 'You still big. You stop eat. Get right size.'

Omri laughed aloud, then stopped himself hastily.

'It's time to sleep,' he said.

'Not now. Big light. Sleep when light go.'

'I can make the light go,' said Omri, and switched out his bedside lamp.

In the darkness came a thin cry of astonishment and fear. Omri switched on again.

The Indian was now gazing at him with something more than respect – a sort of awe.

'You spirit?' he asked in a whisper.

'No,' said Omri. 'And this isn't the sun. It's a lamp. Don't you have lamps?'

The Indian peered where he was pointing. 'That lamp?' he asked unbelievingly. 'Much big lamp. Need much oil.'

'But this isn't an oil lamp. It works by electricity.'

'Magic?'

'No, electricity. But speaking of magic – how did you get here?'

The Indian looked at him steadily out of his black eyes.

'You not know?

'No, I don't. You were a toy. Then I put you in the cupboard and locked the door. When I opened it, you were real. Then I locked it again, and you went back to being plastic. Then –'

He stopped sharply. Wait! What if – he thought furiously. It was possible! In which case...

'Listen,' he said excitedly. 'I want you to come out of there. I'll find you a much more comfortable place. You said you were cold. I'll make you a proper tepee –'

'Tepee!' the Indian shouted. 'I not live tepee! I live longhouse!'

Omri was so eager to test his theory about the cupboard that he was impatient. 'You'll have to make do with a tepee tonight,' he said. Hastily he opened a drawer and took out a biscuit tin full of little plastic people. Somewhere in here was a plastic tepee... 'Ah, here!' He pounced on it – a small, pinkish, cone-shaped object with designs rather badly painted on its plastic sides. 'Will this do?'

He put it on the shelf beside the Indian, who looked at it with the utmost scorn.

'*This* – tepee?' he said. He touched its plastic side and made a face. He pushed it with both hands – it slid along the shelf. He bent and peered in through the triangular opening. Then he actually spat on the ground, or rather, on the shelf.

'Oh,' said Omri, rather crestfallen. 'You mean it's not good enough.'

'Not want toy,' said the Indian, and turned his back, folding both arms across his chest with an air of finality.

Omri saw his chance. With one quick movement he had picked up the Indian by the waist between his thumb and forefinger. In doing this he pinned the knife, which was in the Indian's belt, firmly to his side. The dangling Indian twisted, writhed, kicked, made a number of ferocious and hideous faces – but beyond that he was helpless and he evidently knew it, for after a few moments he decided it was more dignified to stop struggling. Instead, he folded his tiny arms across his chest once again, put his head back, and stared with proud defiance at Omri's face, which was now level with his own.

For Omri, the feeling of holding this little creature in his fingers was very strange and wonderful. If he had had any doubts that the Indian was truly alive, the sensation he had now would have put them to rest. His body was heavier now, warm and firm and full of life – through Omri's thumb, on the Indian's left side, he could feel his heart beating wildly, like a bird's.

Although the Indian felt strong, Omri could sense how fragile he was, how easily an extra squeeze could injure

him. He would have liked to feel him all over, his tiny arms and legs, his hair, his ears, almost too small to see – yet when he saw how the Indian, who was altogether in his power, faced him boldly and hid his fear, he lost all desire to handle him; he felt it was cruel, and insulting to the Indian, who was no longer his plaything but a person who had to be respected.

Omri put him down gently on the chest-of-drawers where the cupboard stood. Then he crouched down till his face was again level with the Indian's.

'Sorry I did that,' he said.

The Indian, breathing heavily and with his arms still folded, said nothing, but stared haughtily at him, as if nothing he did could affect him in any way.

'What's your name?' asked Omri.

'Little Bull,' said the Indian, pointing proudly to himself. 'Iroquois brave. Son of Chief. You son of Chief?' he shot at Omri fiercely.

'No,' said Omri humbly.

'Hm!' snorted Little Bull with a superior look. 'Name?'

Omri told him. 'Now we must find you another place to sleep – outside the cupboard. Surely you sleep in tepees sometimes?'

'Never,' said Little Bull firmly.

'I've never heard of an Indian who didn't,' said Omri with equal firmness. 'You'll have to tonight, anyway.'

'Not this,' said the Indian. 'This no good. And fire. I want fire.'

'I can't light a real fire in here. But I'll make you a tepee. It won't be very good, but I promise you a better one tomorrow.'

He looked round. It was good, he thought, that he never put anything away. Now everything he needed was strewn about the floor and on tables and shelves, ready to hand.

Starting with some pick-up-sticks and a bit of string, he made a sort of cone-shape, tied at the top. Around this he draped, first a handerchief, and then, when that didn't seem firm enough, a bit of old felt from a hat that had been in the dressing-up crate. It was fawn coloured, fortunately, and looked rather like animal hide. In fact, when it was pinned together at the back with a couple of safety-pins and a slit cut for an entrance, the whole thing looked pretty good, especially with the poles sticking up through a hole in the top.

Omri stood it up carefully on the chest-of-drawers and anxiously awaited Little Bull's verdict. The Indian walked round it four times slowly, went down on hands and knees and crawled in through the flap, came out again after a minute, tugged at the felt, stood back to look at the poles, and finally gave a fairly satisfied grunt. However, he wasn't going to pass it without any criticism at all.

'No pictures,' he growled. 'If *tepee*, then need pictures.'

'I don't know how to do them,' said Omri.

'I know. You give colours. I make.'

'Tomorrow,' said Omri, who, despite himself, was beginning to feel very sleepy.

'Blanket?'

Omri fished out one of the Action Man's sleeping-rolls.

'No good. No keep out wind.'

Omri started to object that there was no wind in his bedroom, but then he decided it was easier to cut up a square out of one of his old sweaters, so he did that. It was a red one with a stripe round the bottom and even Little Bull couldn't hide his approval as he held it up, then wrapped it round himself.

'Good. Warm. I sleep now.'

He dropped on his knees and crawled into the tent. After a moment he stuck his head out.

'Tomorrow talk. You give Little Bull meat – fire – paint – much things.' He scowled fiercely up at Omri. 'Good?'

'Good,' said Omri, and indeed nothing in his life had ever seemed so full of promise.

Chapter 3
Thirty Scalps

Within a few minutes, loud snores – well, not loud, but loud for the Indian – began to come out of the tepee, but Omri, sleepy as he was himself, was not quite ready for bed. He had an experiment to do.

As far as he had figured it out so far, the cupboard, or the key, or both together, brought plastic things to life, *or if they were already alive, turned them into plastic*. There were a lot of questions to be answered, though. Did it only work with plastic? Would, say, wooden or metal figures also come to life if shut up in the cupboard? How long did they have to stay in there for the magic to work? Overnight? Or did it happen straight away?

And another thing – what about objects? The Indian's clothes, his feather, his knife, all had become real. Was this just because they were part of the original plastic figure? If he put – well, anything you like, the despised plastic tepee for instance, into the cupboard and locked the door, would that be real in the morning? And what would happen to a real object, if he put that in?

He decided to make a double trial.

He stood the plastic Indian tent on the shelf of the cupboard. Beside it he put a Matchbox car. Then he closed the cupboard door. He didn't lock it. He counted slowly to ten.

Then he opened the door.

Nothing had happened.

He closed the door again, and this time locked it with his great-grandmother's key. He decided to give it a bit longer this time, and while he was waiting he lay down in bed. He began counting to ten slowly. He got roughly as far as five before he fell asleep.

29

He was woken at dawn by Little Bull bawling at him.

The Indian was standing outside the felt tepee on the edge of the table, his hands cupped to his mouth as if shouting across a measureless canyon. As soon as Omri's eyes opened, the Indian shouted:

'Day come! Why you still sleep? Time eat – hunt – fight – make painting!'

Omri leapt up. He cried, 'Wait' – and almost wrenched the cupboard open.

There on the shelf stood a small tepee made of real leather. Even the stitches on it were real. The poles were twigs, tied together with a strip of hide. The designs were real Indian symbols, put on with bright dyes.

The car was still a toy car made of metal, no more real than it had ever been.

'It works,' breathed Omri. And then he caught his breath. 'Little Bull!' he shouted. 'It works, it works! I can make any plastic toy I like come alive, come real! It's real magic, don't you understand? Magic!'

The Indian stood calmly with folded arms, evidently disapproving of this display of excitement.

'So? Magic. The spirits work much magic. No need wake dead with howls like coyote.'

Omri hastily pulled himself together. Never mind the dead, it was his parents he must take care not to wake. He picked up the new tepee and set it down beside the one he had made the night before.

'Here's the good one I promised you,' he said.

Little Bull examined it carefully. 'No good,' he said at last.

'What? Why not?'

'Good tepee, but no good Iroquois brave. See?' He pointed to the painted symbols. 'Not Iroquois signs. Algonquin. Enemy. Little Bull sleep there, Iroquois spirits angry.'

'Oh,' said Omri, disappointed.

'Little Bull like Omri tepee. Need paint. Make strong pictures - Iroquois signs. Please spirits of ancestors.'

Omri's disappointment melted into intense pride. He had made a tepee which satisfied his Indian! 'It's not finished,' he said. 'I'll take it to school and finish it in handcrafts lesson. I'll take out the pins and sew it up properly. Then when I come home I'll give you poster-paints and you can paint your symbols.'

'I paint. But must have longhouse. Tepee no good for Iroquois.'

'Just for now?'

Little Bull scowled. 'Yes,' he said. 'But very short. Now eat.'

'Er . . . Yes. What do you like to eat in the mornings?'

'Meat,' said the Indian immediately.

'Wouldn't you like some bread and cheese?'

'Meat.'

'Or corn? Or some egg?'

The Indian folded his arms uncompromisingly across his chest.

'Meat,' said Omri with a sigh. 'Yes. Well, I'll have to see what I can do. In the meantime, I think I'd better put you down on the ground.'

'Not on ground now?'

'No. You're high above the ground. Go to the edge and look – but don't fall!'

The Indian took no chances. Lying on his stomach he crawled, commando-fashion, to the edge of the chest-of-drawers and peered over.

'Big mountain,' he commented at last.

'Well . . .' But it seemed too difficult to explain. 'May I lift you down?'

Little Bull stood up and looked at Omri measuringly. 'Not hold tight?' he asked.

'No. I won't hold you at all. You can ride in my hand.'

He laid his hand palm up next to Little Bull, who, after

only a moment's hesitation, stepped on to it and, for greater stability, sat down cross-legged. Omri gently transported him to the floor. The Indian rose lithely to his feet and jumped off on to the grey carpet.

At once he began looking about with suspicion. He dropped to his knees, felt the carpet and smelt it.

'Not ground,' he said. 'Blanket.'

'Little Bull, look up.'

He obeyed, narrowing his eyes and peering.

'Do you see the sky? Or the sun?'

The Indian shook his head, puzzled.

'That's because we're not outdoors. We're in a room, in a house. A house big enough for people my size. You're not even in America. You're in England.'

The Indian's face lit up. 'English good! Iroquois fight with English against French!'

'Really?' asked Omri, wishing he had read more. 'Did *you* fight?'

'Fight? Little Bull fight like mountain lion! Take many scalps.'

Scalps? Omri swallowed. 'How many?'

Little Bull proudly held up all ten fingers. Then he closed his fists, opening them again with another lot of ten, and another.

'I don't believe you killed so many people!' said Omri, shocked.

'Little Bull not lie. Great hunter. Great fighter. How show him son of Chief without many scalps?'

'Any white ones?' Omri ventured to ask.

'Some. French. Not take English scalps. Englishmen friends to Iroquois. Help Indian fight Algonquin enemy.'

Omri stared at him. He suddenly wanted to get away. 'I'll go and get you some – meat,' he said in a choking voice.

He went out of his room, closing the bedroom door behind him.

For a moment he did not move, but leant back against the door. He was sweating slightly. This was a bit more than he had bargained for!

Not only was his Indian no mere toy come to life; he was a real person, somehow magicked out of the past of over two hundred years ago. He was also a savage. It occurred to Omri for the first time that his idea of Red Indians, taken entirely from Western films, had been somehow false. After all, those had all been actors playing Indians, and afterwards wiping their war-paint off and going home for their dinners, not in tepees but in houses like his. Civilized men, pretending to be primitive, pretending to be cruel...

Little Bull was no actor. Omri swallowed hard. Thirty scalps...phew! Of course things were different in those days. Those tribes were always making war on each other, and come to that the English and French (whatever they thought they were doing, fighting in America) were probably no better, killing each other like mad as often as they could...

Come to *that*, weren't soldiers of today doing the same thing? Weren't there wars and battles and terrorism going on all over the place? You couldn't switch on television without seeing news about people killing and being killed...Was thirty scalps, even including some French ones, taken hundreds of years ago, so very bad after all?

Still, when he tried to imagine Little Bull, full size, bent over some French soldier, holding his hair in one hand and running the point of his scalping-knife...Yuk!

Omri pushed away from the door and walked rather unsteadily downstairs. No wonder he had felt, from the first, slightly afraid of his Indian. He asked himself, swallowing repeatedly and feeling that just the same he might be sick, whether he wouldn't do better to put Little Bull back in the cupboard, lock the door and turn him back into plastic, knife and all.

Down in the kitchen he ransacked his mother's store-cupboard for a tin of meat. He found some corned beef at last and opened it with the tin-opener on the wall. He dug a chunk out with a teaspoon, put it absently into his own mouth and stood there chewing it.

The Indian hadn't seemed very surprised about being in a giant house in England. He had shown that he was very superstitious, believing in magic and good and evil spirits. Perhaps he thought of Omri as – well, some kind of genie, or whatever Indians believed in instead. The wonder was that he wasn't more frightened of him then, for genies, or giants, or Great Spirits, or whatever, were always supposed to be very powerful and often wicked. Omri supposed that if one happened to be the son of an Indian Chief, one simply didn't get scared as easily as ordinary people. Especially, perhaps, if one had taken thirty scalps...

Maybe Omri ought to tell someone about Little Bull.

The trouble was that although grown-ups usually knew what to do, *what* they did was very seldom what children wanted to be done. What if he took the Indian to – say, some scientists, or – whoever knew about strange things like that, to question him and examine him and probably keep him in a laboratory or something of that sort? They would certainly want to take the cupboard away too, and then Omri wouldn't be able to have any more fun with it at all.

Just when his mind was seething with ideas, such as putting in plastic bows and arrows, and horses, and maybe even other little people – well, no, probably that was too risky, who knew what sort you might land up with? They might start fighting each other! But still, he knew for certain he didn't want to give up his secret, not yet, no matter how many Frenchmen had been scalped.

Having made his decision, for the moment anyway, Omri turned to go upstairs, discovering only halfway up that the tin of corned beef was practically empty. Still, there was a fair-sized bit left in the bottom. It ought to do.

Little Bull was nowhere to be seen, but when Omri called him softly he ran out from under the bed, and stood waving both arms up at Omri.

'Bring meat?'

'Yes.' Omri put it on the miniature plate he'd cut the night before and placed it before the Indian, who seized it in both hands and began to gnaw on it.

'Very good! Soft! Your wife cook this?'

Omri laughed. 'I haven't got a wife.'

The Indian stopped and looked at him. 'Omri not got wife? Who grow corn, grind, cook, make clothes, keep arrows sharp?'

'My mother,' said Omri, grinning at the idea of her sharpening arrows. 'Have you got a wife then?'

The Indian looked away. After a moment he said, 'No.'

'Why not?'

'Dead,' said Little Bull shortly.

'Oh.'

The Indian finished eating in silence and then stood up, wiping his greasy hands on his hair. 'Now. Do magic. Make things for Little Bull.'

'What do you want?'

'Gun,' he answered promptly. 'White man's gun. Like English soldier.'

Omri's brain raced. If a tiny knife could stab, a tiny gun could shoot. Maybe it couldn't do much harm, but then again, maybe it could.

'No, no gun. But I can make you a bow and arrows. I'll have to buy plastic ones, though. What else? A horse?'

'Horse!' Little Bull seemed surprised.

'Don't you ride? I thought all Indians rode.'

Little Bull shook his head.

'English ride. Indians walk.'

'But wouldn't you like to ride, like the English soldiers?'

Little Bull stood quite still, frowning, wrestling with this novel idea. At last he said, 'Maybe. Yes. Maybe. Show horse. Then I see.'

'O.K.'

Again Omri rummaged in the biscuit tin. There were a number of horses here. Big heavy ones for carrying armoured knights. Smaller ones for pulling gun-carriages in the Napoleonic wars. Several cavalry horses – those might be the best. Omri ranged five or six of various sizes and colours before Little Bull, whose black eyes began to shine.

'I have,' he said promptly.

'You mean all of them?'

Little Bull nodded hungrily.

'No, that's too much. I can't have herds of horses galloping all over my room. You can choose one.'

'One?' said Little Bull sadly.

'One.'

Little Bull then made a very thorough examination of every horse, feeling their legs, running his hands over their rumps, looking straight into their plastic faces. At last he selected a smallish, brown horse with two white feet which had originally (as far as Omri could remember) carried an Arab, brandishing a curved sword at a platoon of French Foreign Legionnaires.

'Like English horse,' grunted Little Bull.

'And he's got a saddle and bridle, which will become real too,' gloated Omri.

'Little Bull not want. Ride with rope, bare-back. Not like white soldier,' he added contemptuously, having another spit. 'When?'

'I still don't know how long it takes. We can start now.'

Omri lifted the cupboard onto the floor, shut the horse in and turned the key. Almost at once they could hear the clatter of tiny hooves on metal. They looked at each other with joyful faces.

'Open! Open door!' commanded Little Bull.

Omri lost no time in doing so. There, prancing and pawing

the white paint, was a lovely, shiny-coated little brown Arab pony. As the door swung open he shied nervously, turning his face and pricking his ears so far forward they almost met over his forelock. His tiny nostrils flared, and his black tail plumed over his haunches as he gave a high, shrill neigh.

Little Bull cried out in delight.

In a moment he had vaulted over the bottom edge of the cupboard and, as the pony reared in fright, jumped into the air under its flying hooves and grasped the leather reins. The pony fought to free its head, but Little Bull hung on with both hands. Even as the pony plunged and bucked, the Indian had moved from the front to the side. Grasping the high pommel of the saddle he swung himself into it. He ignored the swinging stirrups, holding on by gripping with his knees.

The pony flung himself back on his haunches, then threw himself forward in a mighty buck, head low, heels flying. To Omri's dismay, Little Bull, instead of clinging on somehow, came loose and flew through the air in a curve, landing on the carpet just beyond the edge of the cupboard.

Omri thought his neck must be broken, but he had landed in a sort of somersault, and was instantly on his feet again. The face he turned to Omri was shining with happiness.

'Crazy horse!' he cried with fierce delight.

The crazy horse was meanwhile standing quite still, reins hanging loose, looking watchfully at the Indian through wild, wide-apart eyes.

This time Little Bull made no sudden moves. He stood quite still for a long time, just looking back at the pony. Then, so slowly you could scarcely notice, he edged towards him, making strange hissing sounds between his clenched teeth which almost seemed to hypnotize the pony. Step by step he moved, softly, cautiously, until he and the pony stood almost nose to nose. Then, quite calmly, Little Bull reached up and laid his hand on the pony's neck.

That was all. He did not hold the reins. The pony could have jumped away, but he didn't. He raised his nose a little, so that he and the Indian seemed to be breathing into each other's nostrils. Then, in a quiet voice, Little Bull said, 'Now horse mine. Crazy horse mine.'

Still moving slowly, though not as slowly as before, he took the reins and moved alongside the pony. After a certain amount of fiddling he found out how to unbuckle the straps which held the Arabian saddle, and lifted it off, laying it on the floor. The pony snorted and tossed his head, but did not move. Hissing gently now, the Indian first leant his weight against the pony's side, then lifted himself up by his arms until he was astride. Letting the reins hang loose on the pony's neck, he squeezed with his legs. The pony moved forward, as tame and obedient as you please, and the pair rode once round the inside of the cupboard as if it had been a circus arena.

Suddenly Little Bull caught up the reins and pulled them to one side, turning the pony's head. At the same time Little Bull kicked him sharply. The pony wheeled, and bounded forward towards the edge of the cupboard.

This metal rim, about two centimetres high, was up to the pony's chest – like a five-barred gate to a full-sized horse. There was no room to ride straight at it, from the back of the cupboard to the front, so Little Bull rode diagonally –a very difficult angle, yet the pony cleared it in a flying leap.

Omri realised at once that the carpet was too soft for him – his feet simply sank into it like soft sand.

'Need ground. Not blanket,' said Little Bull sternly. 'Blanket no good for ride.'

Omri looked at his clock. It was still only a little after six in the morning – at least another hour before anyone else would be up.

'I could take you outside,' he said hesitantly.

'Good!' said Little Bull. 'But not touch pony. You touch, much fear.'

Omri quickly found a small cardboard box which had held a Matchbox lorry. It even had a sort of window through which he could see what was happening inside. He laid that on the carpet with the end flaps open.

Little Bull rode the pony into the box, and Omri carefully shut the end up and even more carefully lifted it. Then, in his bare feet, he carried the box slowly down the stairs and let himself out through the back door.

It was a lovely fresh summer morning. Omri stood on the back steps with the box in his hands, looking round for a suitable spot. The lawn wasn't much good – the grass would be over the Indian's head in most places. The terrace at the foot of the steps was no use at all, with its hard uneven bricks and the cracks between them. But the path was beaten earth and small stones – real riding-ground if they were careful. Omri walked to the path and laid the Matchbox carton down.

For a moment he hesitated. Could the Indian run away? How fast could such a small pony run? As fast as, say, a mouse? If so, and they wanted to escape, Omri wouldn't be able to catch them. A cat, on the other hand, would. Omri knelt on the path in his pyjamas and put his face to the cellophane 'window'. The Indian stood inside holding the pony's head.

'Little Bull,' he said clearly, 'we're outdoors now. I'm going to let you out to ride. But remember – you're not on your prairie now. There are mountain lions here, but they're big enough to swallow you whole and the pony too. Don't run away, you wouldn't survive. Do you understand?'

Little Bull looked at him steadily and nodded. Omri opened the flap and Indian and pony stepped out into the morning sunlight.

Chapter 4
The Great Outdoors

Both horse and man seemed to sniff the air, tasting its freshness and testing it for danger at the same time. The pony was still making circles with his nose when Little Bull sprang onto his back.

The pony, startled, reared slightly, but this time Little Bull clung on to his long mane. The pony's front feet had no sooner touched the path than he was galloping. Omri leapt to his feet and gave chase.

The pony's speed was remarkable, but Omri found that by running along the lawn beside the path he could keep up quite easily. The ground was dry and as Indian and pony raced along, a most satisfying cloud of dust rose behind them so that Omri could easily imagine that they were galloping across some wild, unbroken territory...

More and more, he found, he was able to see things from the Indian's point of view. The little stones on the path became huge boulders which had to be dodged, weeds became trees, the lawn's edge an escarpment twice the height of a man... As for living things, an ant, scuttling across the pony's path, made him shy wildly. The shadow of a passing bird falling on him brought him to a dead stop, crouching and cowering as a full-sized pony might if some huge bird of prey swooped at him. Once again, Omri marvelled at the courage of Little Bull, faced with all these terrors.

But it was not the courage of recklessness. Little Bull clearly recognized his peril and, when he had had his gallop, turned the pony's head and came trotting back to Omri, who crouched down to hear what he said.

'Danger,' said the Indian. 'Much. I need bow, arrows, club. Maybe gun?' he asked pleadingly. Omri shook his head. 'Then Indian weapons.'

'Yes,' said Omri. 'You need those. I'll find them today. In the meantime we'd better go back in the house.'

'Not go shut-in place! Stay here. You stay, drive off wild animals.'

'I can't. I've got to go to school.'

'What school?'

'A place where you learn.'

'Ah! Learn. Good,' said Little Bull approvingly. 'Learn law of tribe, honour for ancestors, ways of the spirits?'

'Well...something like that.'

Little Bull was clearly reluctant to return to the house, but he had the sense to realize he couldn't cope outside by himself. He galloped back along the path, with Omri running alongside, and, dismounting, re-entered the carton.

Omri was just carrying it up the back steps when the back door suddenly opened and there was his father.

'Omri! What on earth are you doing out here in your pyjamas? And nothing on your feet, you naughty boy! What are you up to?'

Omri clutched the box to him so hard in his fright that he felt the sides bend and quickly released his hold. He felt himself break into a sweat.

'Nothing – I – couldn't sleep. I wanted to go out.'

'What's wrong with putting on your slippers, at least?'

'Sorry. I forgot.'

'Well, hurry up and get dressed now.'

Omri rushed upstairs and, panting, laid the box on the floor. He opened the flap. The pony rushed out alone, and stood under the table, whinnying and trembling – he had had a rough ride. Full of foreboding, Omri bent down and peered into the box. Little Bull was sitting in a corner of it, hugging his leg, which Omri saw, to his horror, was bleeding right through his buckskin leggings.

'Box jump. Pony get fear. Kick Little Bull,' said the Indian, who, though calm, was clearly in pain.

'Oh, I'm sorry!' cried Omri. 'Can you come out? I'll see what I can do.'

Little Bull stood up and walked out of the box. He did not let himself limp.

'Take off your leggings – let me see the cut,' said Omri. The Indian obeyed him and stood in his breech-cloth. On his tiny leg was a wound from the pony's hoof, streaming blood onto the carpet. Omri didn't know what to do, but Little Bull did.

'Water,' he ordered. 'Cloths.'

Omri, through his panic, forced himself to think clearly. He had water in a toothmug by his bed, but that would not be clean enough to wash a wound. His mother had some Listerine in her medicine cupboard; when any of the boys had a cut she would add a few drops to some warm water and that was a disinfectant.

Omri dashed to the bathroom, and with trembling hands did what he had seen his mother do. He took a small piece of cotton-wool. What could be used as a bandage he had no idea at all. But he hurried back with the water, and poured some into the Action Man's mess-tin. The Indian tore off a minute wisp of cotton-wool and dipped it into the liquid and applied it to his leg.

The Indian's eyes opened wide though he did not wince. 'This not water! This fire!'

'It's better than water.'

'Now tie,' said the Indian next. 'Hold in blood.'

Omri looked round desperately. A bandage small enough for a wound like that! Suddenly his eyes lighted on the biscuit tin. There, lying on top, was a First-World-War soldier with the red armband of a medical orderly. In his hand was a doctor's bag with a red cross on it. What might that not contain if Omri could make it real?

Not stopping to think too far ahead, he snatched the figure up and thrust it into the cupboard, shutting the door and turning the key.

A moment later a thin English voice from inside called: 'Here! Where am I? Come back you blokes – don't leave a chap alone in the dark!'

Chapter 5
Tommy

Omri felt himself grow weak. What an idiot he'd been! Not to have realized that the man and not just the medical bag would be changed! Or had he? After all, what did he need more just then than a bandage of the right size for the Indian? *Someone* of the right size to put it on! And, unless he was sadly mistaken, that was just what was waiting inside the magic cupboard.

He unlocked the door.

Yes, there he was – pink cheeked, tousle-headed under his army cap, his uniform creased and mud-spattered and blood-stained, looking angry, frightened and bewildered.

He rubbed his eyes with his free hand.

'Praise be for a bit of daylight, anyway,' he said. 'What the – '

Then he opened his eyes and saw Omri.

Omri actually saw him go white, and his knees gave way under him. He uttered a few sounds, half curses and half just noises. He dropped the bag and hid his face for a moment. Omri said hastily:

'Please don't be afraid. It's all right. I –' Then he had an absolute inspiration! 'I'm a dream you're having. I won't hurt you, I just want you to do something for me, and then you'll wake up.'

Slowly the little man lowered his hands and looked up again.

'A dream, is it? Well...I should've guessed. Yes, of course. It would be. The whole rotten war's nightmare enough, though, without giants and – and –' He stared round Omri's room. 'Still and all, perhaps it's a change for the better. At least it's quiet here.'

'Can you bring your bag and climb out? I need your help.'

The soldier now managed a rather sickly smile and tipped his cap in a sort of salute. 'Right you are! With you in a tick,' he said, and picking up the bag, clambered over the edge of the cupboard.

'Stand on my hand,' Omri commanded.

The soldier did not hesitate a moment, but swung himself up by hooking his free arm round Omri's little finger. 'Bit of a lark, this,' he remarked. 'I won't half enjoy telling the fellows about this dream of mine in the trenches tomorrow!'

Omri carried him to the spot where Little Bull sat on the carpet holding his leg which was still bleeding. The soldier stepped down and stood, knee-deep in carpet-pile, staring.

'Well, I'll be jiggered!' he breathed. 'A bloomin' redskin! This is a rum dream and no mistake! And wounded, too. Well, I suppose that's my job, is it? – to patch him up?'

'Yes, please,' said Omri.

Without more ado, the soldier put the bag on the floor and snapped open its all-but-invisible catches. Omri leant over to see. Now he really did need a magnifying glass, and so badly did he want to see the details of that miniature doctor's bag that he risked sneaking into Gillon's room (Gillon always slept late, and anyway it wasn't seven o'clock yet) and pinching his from his secret drawer.

By the time he got back to his own room, the soldier was kneeling at Little Bull's feet, applying a neat tourniquet to the top of his leg. Omri peered through the magnifying glass into the open bag. It was amazing – everything was there, bottles, pill-boxes, ointments, some steel instruments including a tiny hypodermic needle, and as many rolls of bandages as you could want.

Omri then ventured to look at the wound. Yes, it was quite deep – the pony must have given him a terrific kick.

That reminded him – where was the pony? He looked

round in a fright. But he soon saw it, trying forlornly to eat the carpet. 'I must get it some grass,' thought Omri, meanwhile offering it a small piece of stale bread which it ate gratefully, and then some water in a tin lid. It was odd how the pony was not frightened of him. Perhaps it couldn't see him very well.

'There now, he'll do,' said the soldier, getting up.

Omri looked at the Indian's leg through his magnifying glass. The wound was bandaged beautifully. Even Little Bull was examining it with obvious approval.

'Thank you very much,' said Omri. 'Would you like to wake up now?'

'Might as well, I suppose. Not that there's much to look forward to except mud and rats and German shells coming over . . . Still. Got to win the war, haven't we? Can't desert, even into a dream, not for long that is – duty calls and all that, eh?'

Omri gently picked him up and put him into the cupboard.

'Goodbye,' he said. 'Perhaps, some time, you could dream me again.'

'A pleasure,' said the soldier cheerfully. 'Tommy Atkins, at your service. Any night, except when there's an attack on – none of us gets any sleep to speak of then.' And he gave Omri a smart salute.

Regretfully Omri shut and locked the door. He was tempted to keep the soldier, but it was too complicated just now. Anyway he could always bring him back to life again if he liked . . . A moment or two later he opened the door again to check. There was the orderly, bag in hand, standing just as Omri had last seen him, at the salute. Only now he was plastic again.

Little Bull was calmly pulling on his blood-stained leggings.

'Good magic,' he remarked. 'Leg better.'

'Little Bull, what will you do all day while I'm at school?'

'You bring bark of tree. Little Bull make longhouse.'

'What's that?'

'Iroquois house. Need earth, stick posts in.'

'*Earth*? *Posts*?'

'Earth. Posts. Bark. Not forget food. Weapons. Tools. Pots. Water. Fire –'

There were no quarrels at breakfast that morning. Omri gulped down his egg and ran. In the greenhouse he found a seed-tray already full of soil, well pressed down. He carried that secretly upstairs and laid it on the floor behind the dressing-up crate, which he was pretty sure his mother wouldn't shift even if it was her cleaning day. Then he took his penknife and went out again.

Fortunately one of the trees in the garden had the sort of bark which came off easily – a silvery, flaky kind. He cut off a biggish strip, and then another to make sure (how long *was* a longhouse?). He pulled some grass for the pony. He cut a bundle of thin, strong, straight twigs and stripped off their leaves. Then he went back to his room and laid all these offerings beside Little Bull, who was seated cross-legged outside his tepee, arms folded, eyes closed, apparently saying his prayers.

'Omri!' came his mother's call from downstairs. 'Time to go!'

Omri took out of his pocket the corner of toast he'd saved from breakfast and cleaned out the last of the corned beef from the tin. There was some corn left as well, though it was getting rather dry by now. He filled up the Action Man's beaker with water from the bathroom, pouring a little into the pony's drinking-lid. The pony was munching the fresh grass with every sign of enjoyment. Omri noticed its bridle had been replaced with a halter, cleverly made of a length of thread.

'Omri!'

'Just coming!'

'The others have gone! Hurry up, you'll be late!'

One last thing! Little Bull couldn't make a longhouse without some sort of tool beside his knife. He'd need an axe. Frantically Omri rummaged in the biscuit tin. Ah! A knight, wielding a fearsome-looking battle-axle. It wasn't right, but it was better than nothing and would have to do. In a second the knight was locked in the cupboard.

'*Omri*!'

'One second!'

'What are you *doing*?'

Crash! The axe was being used on the inside of the cupboard door!

Omri wrenched it open, snatched the axe from the startled hands of the knight, who had just time for one horrified look before he was reduced to plastic again by the slamming of the door. Never mind! He had looked most unpleasant, just as knights must have looked when they were murdering the poor Saracens in Palestine. Omri had very little time for knights.

The axe was a beauty, though. Shining steel, with a sharp edge on both sides of the head, and a long heavy steel handle. Omri laid it at Little Bull's side.

'Little Bull –'

But he was still in a trance – communicating with his ancestors, Omri supposed. Well, he would find everything when he came to. There was quite a trail of spilt earth leading behind the crate. Omri flashed down the stairs, grabbed his anorak and his lunch-money and was gone.

Chapter 6
The Chief is Dead, Long Live the Chief

He got to school early by running all the way. The first thing he did was to head for the upper school library shelves. He felt that a Ladybird book on Indian tribes would not meet the situation; he wanted a much more grown-up book. And to his joy, he soon found one, under the section labelled 'Peoples of the World' – a book called *On the Trail of the Iroquois*.

He couldn't take it out because there was nobody there to write him down for it; but he sat down then and there on a bench and began to read it.

Omri was not what you'd call a great reader. He couldn't get into books, somehow, unless he knew them already. And how, as his teacher never tired of asking, was he ever going to get to know any more books until he read them for the first time?

And this *On the Trail of the Iroquois* was not exactly a comic. Tiny print, hardly any pictures, and no fewer than three hundred pages 'Getting into' it was obviously out of the question, so Omri just dipped.

He managed to find out one or two fairly interesting things straight away. Iroquois Indians were sometimes called 'The Five Nations'. One of the five were the Mohawks, a tribe Omri had heard of. They had indeed lived in longhouses, not wigwams, and their main foods had been maize and squash (whatever they were) and beans. These vegetables had, for some strange reason, been called 'The Three Sisters'.

There were many mentions of the Algonquins as the Iroquois' enemies, and Omri confirmed that the Iroquois had fought beside the English while the Algonquins fought for the French some time in the 1700s, and that both sides had scalped like mad.

At this point he began to get really interested. The book, in its terribly grown-up way, was trying to tell him something about *why* the Indians had done such a lot of scalping. Omri had always thought it was just an Indian custom, but the book seemed to say that it wasn't at all, at least not till the White Man came. The White Man seemed to have made the Iroquois and the Algonquin keen on scalping each other, not to mention scalping White Men, French or English as the case might be, by offering them money and whisky, and guns....Omri was deep in the book, frowning heavily, several minutes after the bell had rung. Someone had to tap him on the shoulder and tell him to hurry in to Assembly.

The morning lasted forever. Three times his teacher had cause to tell Omri to wake up. At last Patrick leant over and whispered, 'You're even dreamier than usual today. What's up?'

'I'm thinking about your Indian.'

'Listen,' hissed Patrick. 'I think you're having me on about that Indian. It was nothing so marvellous. You can buy them for a few p. in Yapp's.' (Yapp's was their local newsagent and toyshop.)

'I know, and all the equipment for them! I'm going shopping at lunchbreak; are you coming?'

'We're not allowed out of school at lunch unless we eat at home, you know that!'

'I'm going anyway. I've got to.'

'Go after school.'

'No, I've got to go home after school.'

'What? Aren't you staying to skateboard?'

'*Omri and Patrick*! Will you kindly stop chattering?'

They stopped.

At long last lunchtime came.

'I'm going. Are you coming?'

'No. There'll only be trouble.'

'I can't help that.'

'You're a twit.'

Twit or not, Omri sneaked out, ran across the playground, through a hole in the fence (the front gate was locked to keep the infants from going in the road) and in five minutes, by running all the way, had reached Yapp's.

The selection of plastic figures there was good. There was one whole box of mixed cowboys and Indians. Omri searched till he found a Chief wearing a cloak and a full feather headdress, with a bow in his hand and a quiverful of arrows slung across his back. Omri bought it with part of his lunch money and rushed back to school before he could be missed.

He showed the Chief to Patrick.

'Why get another Indian?'

'Only for the bow and arrows.'

Patrick was now looking at him as if he'd gone completely screwy.

In the afternoon, mercifully, they had two periods of handicrafts.

Omri had completely forgotten to bring the tent he'd made, but there were plenty of scraps of felt, sticks, needles and thread lying about the handicrafts room and he'd soon made another one, much better than the first. Sewing had always bored him rigid, but now he sat for half an hour stitching away without even looking up. He was trying to achieve the patched look of a real tepee made of odd-shaped pieces of hide, and he also found a way of bracing the sticks so that they didn't fold up every time they were nudged.

'Very good, Omri!' remarked his teacher several times. 'What patience all of a sudden!' Omri, who usually liked praise as much as anyone, hardly heard her, he was concentrating so hard.

After a long time he became aware that Patrick was

standing over him, breathing through his nose rather noisily to attract his attention.

'Is that for my Indian?'

'*My* Indian. Yes.'

'Why are you doing it in bits like that?'

'To be like a real one.'

'Real ones have designs on.'

'So will this. He's going to paint proper Iroquois ones.'

'Who is?'

'Little Bull. That's his name.'

'Why not call him Running Nose?' asked Patrick with a grin.

Omri looked up at him blankly. 'Because his name's Little Bull,' he said. Patrick stopped grinning. He frowned.

'I wish you'd stop this stupid business,' he said peevishly. 'Going on as if it weren't a joke.'

Omri went on looking at him for a moment and then went back to his bracing. Each pair of sticks had to have another, short stick glued between them with Airfix glue. It was quite tricky. Patrick stood a minute and then said, 'Can I come home with you *today*?'

'No. I'm sorry.'

'Why not?'

'Mum's having guests,' Omri mumbled. He didn't tell lies very well, and Patrick knew at once it was a lie and was hurt.

'Oh, all right then, be like that,' he said, and stalked off furiously.

The afternoon ended at last. Omri accomplished the walk home, which with normal dawdling took half an hour, in a little over ten minutes. He arrived sorely out of breath and greeted his surprised mother ('Have you developed a jet-engine, or have you been expelled?') with a lot of gasping and a request to eat tea in his room.

'What have you been up to, up there? There's an awful

mess on the floor – looks like bits of grass and bark. And where *did* you get that beautiful little Indian tepee? I think it's made of real leather.'

Omri looked at her, speechless. 'I –' he began at last. Telling lies to Patrick was one thing. Lying to his mother was quite something else and he never did it unless the emergency was dire. But mercifully the phone rang just then, so he was spared – for the moment. He dashed upstairs.

There was indeed a fair old mess, though no worse than he often left himself when he'd been working on something. Little Bull and the pony were nowhere to be seen, but Omri guessed where to look – behind the dressing-up crate.

A wonderful sight met his eyes. A longhouse – not quite finished, but no less interesting and beautiful for that – stood on the seed-box, whose smooth surface was now much trampled over. There were hoof- as well as mocassin-prints. Omri saw that a ramp, made of part of the bark, had been laid against the wooden side of the box, up which the pony had been led – to Omri's delight (odd as it may seem) a tiny pile of horse-manure lay on the ramp as proof of the pony's passing. And there he was, tied by a thread to an upright twig hammered (presumably) into the ground, munching a small pile of grass which the Indian had carried up for him.

Little Bull himself was still working, so intently that he did not even notice he was not alone. Omri watched him in utter fascination. The longhouse was about half finished. The twigs, which had been pliant ones taken from the weeping-willow on the lawn, had been stripped of their bark, leaving them shining white. Each one had then been bent into an arch, the ends thrust into the earth, and cross-pieces lashed to the sides with thread. More and more twigs (which were stout poles to the Indian) had been added, with never a nail or a screw needed, to strengthen the structure, and now Little Bull had begun to fix flakes of bark, like tiny tiles, on to the cross-pieces.

He was seated on the roof itself, his feet locked round the main roof-pole which ran the length of the house, hanging these bark-tiles, each of which he would first carefully shape with his knife. The knight's battle-axe lay on the ground beside an unused pile of twigs. It had clearly been used to chop and strip them and had been made to serve Little Bull's purpose very well.

At last Omri saw him straighten up, stretch his arms towards the ceiling, and open his mouth in a tremendous noisy yawn.

'Tired?' he asked him.

Little Bull got such a fright he almost fell off the longhouse roof, and the pony neighed and tugged at his rope. But then Little Bull looked up and saw Omri hanging over the crate far above him, and grinned.

'Little Bull tired. Work many hour. Look! Make longhouse. Work for many braves. I make alone. Also not good tools. Axe Omri give heavy. Why no tomahawk?'

Omri was getting used to his Indian's ungrateful ways and was not offended. He showed him the tepee he'd made. 'I suppose you won't want this, now you've got your longhouse,' he said rather sadly.

'Want! Want!' He seemed to have decided tepees had their uses after all. He circled it. 'Good! Give paints. Make pictures.'

Omri unearthed his poster paints. When he came back with them, he found Little Bull sitting cross-legged on the earth, facing the figure of the Chief which Omri had put next to the tepee. Little Bull was clearly puzzled.

'Totem?' he asked.

'No! It's plastic.'

'Plass-tick?'

'Yes. I bought it in a shop.'

Little Bull stared at the figure with its big feather head-dress.

'You make magic, get bow and arrows from plass-tick?'

'Yes.'

'Also make feathers real?' he asked, with a gleam in his eye.

'You like that headdress?'

'Little Bull like. But that for Chief. Little Bull not Chief till father die. Little Bull wear feathers of Chief now, spirits angry.'

'But you could just try it on?'

Little Bull looked doubtful but he nodded.

'Make real. Then see.'

Omri shut the Indian Chief into the cupboard. Before he turned the key, he leant down to where Little Bull was examining the (to him) enormous pots of paint.

'Little Bull, are you lonely?'

'Huh?'

'Would you like a – friend?'

'Got friend,' said the Indian, jerking his head towards the pony.

'I meant, another Indian.'

Little Bull looked up swiftly, his hands still. There was a long silence.

'Wife?' he asked at last.

'No, it's a man,' said Omri. 'The – Chief.'

'Not want,' said Little Bull immediately, and went back to his work with a bent head.

Omri was disappointed. He had thought it might be fun to have two Indians. But somehow he couldn't do anything Little Bull didn't want. He would have to treat this Chief as he had treated the knight – grab the weapons and turn him back into plastic again at once.

Only this time it wasn't quite so easy.

When he opened the cupboard, the Chief was sitting on the shelf, looking about him in bewilderment, blinking as the light struck his eyes. Omri saw at once that he was a very old man, covered in wrinkles. He took the bow out of his hands quite easily. But the quiverful of arrows was hung round him on a leather thong, and as for actually lifting the feathered headdress off his grey old head, Omri found he just couldn't bring himself to do it. It seemed so rude.

The old man gazed up at him, blankly at first, and then with dawning terror. But he didn't get up and he didn't speak, though Omri saw his lips moving and noticed he had hardly any teeth.

Omri somehow felt he should offer the old Chief some friendly word to reassure him. So he held up one hand, as white men sometimes did in films when they were treating Indian Chiefs with politeness, and said, 'How.'

The old Indian lifted a trembling hand, and then suddenly he slumped on to his side.

'Little Bull! Little Bull! Quick, get on to my hand!'

Omri reached down and Little Bull climbed on to his hand from the longhouse roof.

'What?'

'The old Indian – I think he's fainted!'

He carried Little Bull to the cupboard and Little Bull stepped off on to the shelf. He stooped beside the crumpled figure. Taking the single feather out of the back of his own headband he held it in front of the old man's mouth. Then he shook his head.

'Dead,' he said. 'No breath. Heart stop. Old man. Gone to ancestors, very happy.' Without more ado, he began to strip the body, taking the headdress, the arrows, and the big, richly-decorated cloak for good measure.

Omri was shocked.

'Little Bull, stop. Surely you shouldn't –'

'Chief dead; I only other Indian here. No one else to be chief. Little Bull Chief now,' he said, whirling the cloak about his own bare shoulders and clapping the splendid circle of feathers on to his head with a flourish. He picked up the quiver.

'Omri give bow!' he commanded. And it was a command. Omri obeyed it without thinking. 'Now! You make magic. Deer for Little Bull hunt. Fire for cook. Good meat!' He folded his arms, scowling up at Omri.

Omri was quite taken aback by all this. While giving Little Bull every respect as a person, he was not about to be turned into his slave. He began to wonder if giving him those weapons, let alone letting him make himself into a Chief, was such a good idea.

'Now look here, Little Bull –' he began, in a teacherish tone.

'OMRI!'

It was his father's voice, fairly roaring at him from the foot of the stairs. Omri jumped, bumping the cupboard. Little Bull fell over backwards, considerably spoiling his dignity.

'Yes?'

'COME DOWN HERE THIS INSTANT!'

Omri had no time for courtesies. He snatched Little Bull up, set him down near his half-finished longhouse, shut and locked the cupboard and ran downstairs.

His father was waiting for him.

'Omri, have you been in the greenhouse lately?'

'Er –'

'And did you, while you were there, remove a seed-tray planted out with marrow seeds, *may I ask*?'

'Well, I –'

'Yes or no.'

'Well, yes, but –'

'And is it possible that in addition you have been hacking at the trunk of the birch and torn off strips of bark?'

'But Dad, it was only –'

'Don't you know trees can *die* if you strip too much of

their bark off? It's like their skin! As for the seed-tray, that is *mine*. You've no business taking things from the greenhouse and you know it. Now I want it back, and you'd better not have disturbed the seeds or heaven help you!'

Omri swallowed hard. He and his father stared at each other.

'I can't give it back,' he said at last. 'But I'll buy you another tray and some more seeds. I've got enough money. *Please*.'

Omri's father had a quick temper, especially about anything concerning the garden, but he was not unreasonable, and above all he was not the sort to pry into his children's secrets. He realized at once that his seed-tray, as a seed-tray, was lost to him forever and that it was no use hectoring Omri about it.

'All right,' he said. 'You can go to the hardware shop and buy them, but I want them today.'

Omri's face fell.

'Today? But it's nearly five o'clock now.'

'Precisely. Be off.'

Chapter 7
Uninvited Brothers

Omri was not allowed to ride his bicycle in the road, but then he wasn't supposed to ride it on the pavement either, not fast at any rate, so he compromised. He rode it slowly on the pavement as far as the corner, then bumped down off the curb and went like the wind.

The hardware shop was still open. He bought the seed-tray and the seeds and was just paying for them when he noticed something. On the seed packet, under the word 'Marrow' was written another word in brackets: 'Squash'.

So one of the 'three sisters' was marrow! On impulse he asked the shopkeeper, 'Do you know what maize is?'

'Maize, son? That's sweetcorn, isn't it?'

'Have you some seeds of that?'

Outside, standing by Omri's bike, was Patrick.

'Hi.'

'Hi. I saw you going in. What did you get?'

Omri showed him.

'More presents for the Indian?' Patrick asked sarcastically.

'Well, sort of. If –'

'If what?'

'If I can keep him long enough. Till they grow.'

Patrick stared at him and Omri stared back.

'I've been to Yapp's,' said Patrick. 'I bought you something.'

'Yeah? What?' asked Omri, hopefully.

Slowly Patrick took his hand out of his pocket, held it in front of him and opened the fingers. In his palm lay a cowboy on a horse, with a pistol in one hand pointing upward, or what would have been upward if it hadn't been lying on its side.

Omri looked at it silently. Then he shook his head.

'I'm sorry. I don't want it.'

'Why not? Now you can play a proper game with the Indian.'

'They'd fight.'

'Isn't that the whole idea?'

'They might hurt each other.'

There was a pause, and then Patrick leaned forward and asked, very slowly and loudly, '*How can they hurt each other? They are made of plastic*!'

'Listen,' said Omri, and then stopped, and then started again. 'The Indian isn't plastic. He's real.'

Patrick heaved a deep, deep sigh and put the cowboy back in his pocket. He'd been friends with Omri for years, ever since they'd started school. They knew each other very well. Just as Patrick knew when Omri was lying, he also knew when he wasn't. The only trouble was that this was a non-lie he couldn't believe.

'I want to see him,' he said.

Omri debated with himself. He somehow felt that if he didn't share his secret with Patrick, their friendship would be over. He didn't want that. And besides, the thrill of showing his Indian to someone else was something he could not do without for much longer.

'Okay. Come on.'

Going home they broke the law even more, riding on the road *and* with Patrick on the crossbar. They went round the back way by the alley in case anyone happened to be looking out of a window.

Omri said, 'He wants a fire. I suppose we can't make one indoors.'

'You could, on a tin plate, like for indoor fireworks,' said Patrick.

Omri looked at him.

'Let's collect some twigs.'

Patrick picked up a twig about a foot long. Omri laughed.

'That's no good! They've got to be tiny twigs. Like this.' And he picked some slivers off the privet hedge.

'Does he want the fire to cook on?' asked Patrick slowly.

'Yes.'

'Then that's no use. A fire made of those would burn out in a couple of seconds.'

Omri hadn't thought of that.

'What you need,' said Patrick, 'is a little ball of tar. That burns for ages. And you could put the twigs on top to look like a real campfire.'

'That's a brilliant idea!'

'I know where they've been tarring a road, too,' said Patrick.

'Come on, let's go.'

'No.'

'Why not?'

'I don't believe in him yet. I want to see.'

'All right. But first I have to give this stuff to my dad.'

There was a further delay when his father at first insisted on Omri filling the seed-tray with compost and planting the seeds in it then and there. But when Omri gave him the corn seed as a present he said, 'Well! Thanks. Oh, all right, I can see you're bursting to get away. You can do the planting tomorrow before school.'

Omri and Patrick rushed upstairs. At the top Omri stopped, cold. His bedroom door, which he always shut automatically, was wide open. And just inside, crouching side by side with their backs to him, were his brothers.

They were so absolutely still that Omri knew they were watching something. He couldn't bear it. They had come into his room without his permission, and they had seen his Indian. Now they would tell everybody! His secret, his precious secret, his alone to keep or share, was a secret no more. Something broke inside him and he heard himself scream: 'Get out of my room! Get out of my room!'

Both boys spun round.

'Shut up, you'll frighten him,' said Adiel at once. 'Gillon came in to look for his rat and he found it, and then he saw this absolutely fabulous little house you've made and he called me in to look at it.'

Omri looked at the floor. The seed-tray, with the longhouse now nearly finished, had been moved into the centre of the room. It was *that* they had been looking at. A quick glance all round showed no sign of Indian or pony, but Gillon's tame white rat was on his shoulder.

'I can't get over it,' Adiel went on. 'How on earth did you do it, without using any Airfix glue or anything? It's all done with tiny little threads, and pegs, and – look, Gillon! It's all made of real twigs and bark. It's absolutely *terrific*,' he said with such awe-struck admiration in his voice that Omri felt ashamed.

'I didn't –' he began. But Patrick, who had been gaping at the longhouse in amazement, gave him a heavy nudge which nearly knocked him over.

'Yes,' said Omri. 'Well. Would you mind pushing off now? And take the rat. You're not to let him in here! This *is* my room, you know.'

'And this *is* my magnifying glass, you know,' echoed Gillon, but he was obviously too overcome with admiration to be angry with Omri for pinching it. He was using it now to examine the fine details of the building. 'I knew you were good at making things,' he said. 'But this is amazing. You must have fingers like a fairy to tie those *witchy* little knots. What's that?' he asked suddenly.

They'd all heard it – a high, faint whinny coming from under the bed.

Omri was galvanized into action. At all costs he must prevent their finding out now! He flung himself on his knees and pretended to grope under the bed. 'It's nothing, only that little clockwork dolphin I got in my Christmas stocking,' he burbled. 'I must have wound it up and it suddenly started clicking, you know how they do, it's quite creepy sometimes when they suddenly start – clicking –'

By this time he'd leapt up again and was almost pushing the two older boys out of the room.

'Why are you in such a hurry to get rid of us?' asked Gillon suspiciously.

'Just *go*, you know you have to get out of my room when I ask you –' He could hear the pony whinnying again and it didn't sound a bit like the dolphin.

'That sounds just like a pony,' said Adiel.

'Oh, *beard* it's a pony, a tiny witchy pony under my bed!' said Omri mockingly.

At last they went, not without glancing back suspiciously several times, and Omri slammed the door, bolted it, and leaned against it with closed eyes.

'*Is* it a pony?' whispered Patrick, agog.

Omri nodded. Then he opened his eyes, lay down again, and peered under the bed.

'Give me that torch from the chest-of-drawers.'

Patrick gave it to him and lay beside him. They peered together as the torch-beam probed the darkness.

'Crumbs!' breathed Patrick reverently. 'It's true!'

The pony was standing, seemingly alone, whinnying. When the torchlight hit him he stopped and turned his head. Omri could see a pair of leggings behind him.

'It's all right, Little Bull, it's me!' said Omri.

Slowly a crest of feathers, then the top of a black head, then a pair of eyes appeared over the pony's back.

'Who they others?' he asked.

'My brothers. It's okay, they didn't see you.'

'Little Bull hear coming. Take pony, run, hide.'

'Good. Come on out and meet my friend Patrick.'

Little Bull jumped astride the pony and rode proudly out, wearing his new cloak and headdress. He gazed up imperiously at Patrick, who gazed back in wonder.

'Say something to him,' whispered Omri. 'Say "How". That's what he's used to.'

Patrick tried several times to say 'How' but his voice just came out as a squeak. Little Bull solemnly raised an arm in salute.

'Omri's friend, Little Bull's friend,' he said magnanimously.

Patrick swallowed. His eyes seemed in danger of popping right out of his head.

Little Bull waited politely, but when Patrick didn't speak he rode over to the seed-tray. The boys had brought it out from behind the crate; they'd been careful, but the ramp had got moved. Omri hurried to put it back, and Little Bull rode the pony up it, dismounted and tied it by its halter to the post he had driven into the compost. Then he went calmly on with his work on his longhouse, hanging the last few tiles.

Patrick licked his lips, swallowed twice more, and croaked out, 'He's real. He's a real live Indian.'

'I told you.'

'How did it happen?'

'Don't ask me. Something to do with this cupboard, or maybe it's the key – it's very old. You lock plastic people inside, and they come alive.'

Patrick goggled at him. 'You mean – it's not only him? You can do it with any toy?'

'Only plastic ones.'

An incredulous grin spread over Patrick's face.

'Then what are we waiting for? Let's bring loads of things to life! Whole armies –'

And he sprang towards the biscuit tins. Omri grabbed him.

'No, wait! It's not so simple.'

Patrick, his hands already full of soldiers, was making for the cupboard. 'Why not?'

'Because they'd all – don't you see – they'd be *real*.'

'Real? What do you mean?'

'Little Bull isn't a toy. He's a real man. He really lived. Maybe he's still – I don't know – he's in the middle of his life – somewhere in America in seventeen-something-or-other. He's from the *past*,' Omri struggled to explain as Patrick looked blank.

'I don't get it.'

'Listen. Little Bull has told me about his life. He's fought in wars, and scalped people, and grown stuff to eat like marrows and stuff, and had a wife. She died. He doesn't know how he got here but he thinks it's magic and he accepts magic, he believes in it, he thinks I'm some kind of spirit or something. What I mean,' Omri persisted, as Patrick's eyes strayed longingly to the cupboard, 'is that if you put all those men in there, when they came to life they'd be real men with real lives of their own, from their own times and countries, talking their own languages. You couldn't just – set them up and make them do what you wanted them to. They'd do what *they* wanted to, or they might get terrified and run away or – well, one I tried it with, an old Indian, actually died of – of fright. When he saw me. Look, if you don't believe me!' And Omri opened the cupboard.

There lay the body of the old Chief, now made of plastic, but still unmistakably dead, and not dead the way some plastic soldiers are made to look dead but the way real people look – crumpled up, empty.

Patrick picked it up, turning it in his hand. He'd put the soldiers down by now.

'This isn't the one you bought at lunchtime?'

'Yes.'

'Crumbs.'

'You see?'

'Where's his headdress?'

'Little Bull took it. He says he's a Chief now. It's made him even more bossy and – *difficult* than before,' said

Omri, using a word his mother often used when he was insisting on having his own way.

Patrick put the dead Indian down hurriedly and wiped his hand on the seat of his jeans.

'Maybe this isn't such fun as I thought.'

Omri considered for a moment.

'No,' he agreed soberly. 'It's not *fun*.'

They stared at Little Bull. He had finished the shell of the longhouse now. Taking off his headdress he tucked it under his arm, stooped, and entered through the low doorway at one end. After a moment he came out and looked up at Omri.

'Little Bull hungry,' he said. 'You get deer? Bear? Moose?'

'No.'

He scowled. 'I say get. Why you not get?'

'The shops are shut. Besides,' added Omri, thinking he sounded rather feeble, especially in front of Patrick, 'I'm not sure I like the idea of having bears shambling about my room, *or* of having them killed. I'll give you meat and a fire and you can cook it and that'll have to do.'

Little Bull looked baffled for a moment. Then he swiftly put on the headdress, and drew himself to his full height of seven centimetres (nearly eight with the feathers). He folded his arms and glared at Omri.

'Little Bull Chief now. Chief hunts. Kills own meat. Not take meat others kill. If not hunt, lose skill with bow. For today, you give meat. Tomorrow, go shop, get bear, plasstick. Make real. I hunt. Not here,' he added, looking up scornfully at the distant ceiling. 'Out. Under sky. Now fire.'

Patrick, who had been crouching, stood up. He, too, seemed to be under Little Bull's spell.

'I'll go and get the tar,' he said.

'No wait a minute,' said Omri. 'I've got another idea.'

He ran downstairs. Fortunately the living-room was

empty. In the coal-scuttle beside the open fireplace was a packet of firelighters. He broke a fairly large bit off one and wrapped it in a scrap of newspaper. Then he went to the kitchen. His mother was standing at the sink peeling apples.

Omri hesitated, then went to the fridge.

'Don't eat now, Omri, it's nearly suppertime.'

'Just a tiny bit,' he said.

There was a lovely chunk of raw meat on a plate. Omri sniffed his fingers, wiped them hard on his sweater to get the stink of the firelighter off them, then took a big carving-knife from the drawer and, with an anxious glance at his mother's back, began sawing a corner off the meat.

Luckily it was steak and cut easily. Even so he nearly had the whole plate off the fridge shelf and onto the floor before he'd cut his corner off.

His mother swung round just as he closed the fridge door.

'A tiny bit of what?' she asked. She often reacted late to things he said.

'Nothing,' he said, hiding the raw bit of meat in his hand. 'Mum, could I borrow a tin plate?'

'I haven't got such a thing.'

'Yes you have, the one you bought Adiel to go camping.'

'That's in Adiel's room somewhere, I haven't got it. A tiny bit of *what*?'

But Omri was already on his way upstairs. Adiel was in his room (he would be!) doing his homework.

'What do *you* want?' he asked the second Omri crept in.

'That plate – you know – your camping one.'

'Oh, that!' said Adiel, going back to his French.

'Well, can I have it?'

'Yeah, I suppose so. It's over there somewhere.'

Omri found it eventually in an old knapsack, covered with disgusting bits of baked beans, dry and hard as cement. He hurried across to his own room. Whenever he'd been away from it for even a few minutes, he felt his heart beating in panic as he opened the door for fear of what he might find (or not find). The burden of constant worry was beginning to wear him out.

But all was as he had left it this time. Patrick was crouching near the seed-tray. Little Bull was directing him to take the tops off several of the jars of poster paint while he himself fashioned something almost too small to see.

'It's a paintbrush,' whispered Patrick. 'He cut a bit off his own hair and he's tying it to a scrap of wood he found, about the size of a big splinter.'

'Pour a bit of paint into the lids so he can reach to dip,' said Omri.

Meanwhile he was scraping the dry beans off the plate with his nails. He took the fragment of firelighter and the privet-twigs out of his pocket and arranged them in the centre of the plate. He washed the bit of meat in his bed-side water glass. He'd had a wonderful idea for a spit to cook it on. From a flat box in which his first Meccano set had once been neatly laid out, but which was now in chaos, he took a rod, ready bent into a handle shape, and pushed this through the meat. Then, from small bits of Meccano, he quickly made a sort of stand for it to rest on, with legs each side of the fire so that the meat hung over the middle of it.

'Let's light it now!' said Patrick, who was getting very excited again.

'Little Bull – come and see your fire,' said Omri.

Little Bull looked up from his paints and then ran down the ramp, across the carpet and vaulted onto the edge of the plate. Omri struck a match and lit the firelighter, which flared up at once with a bluish flame, engulfing the twigs and the meat at once. The twigs gave off a gratifying crackle while they lasted, but the firelighter gave off a very ungratifying stench which made Little Bull wrinkle up his nose.

'Stink!' he cried. 'Spoil meat!'

'No it won't!' Omri said. 'Turn the handle of the spit, Little Bull.'

Evidently he wasn't much used to spits, but he soon got the hang of it. The chunk of steak turned and turned in the flame, and soon lost its raw red look and began to go grey and then brown. The good juicy smell of roasting beef began to compete with the reek of the firelighter.

'Mmm!' said Little Bull appreciatively, turning the handle till the sweat ran off his face. 'Meat!' He had thrown off his Chief's cloak and his chest shone red. Patrick couldn't take his eyes off him.

'Please Omri,' he whispered, 'couldn't I have one? Couldn't I choose just one – a soldier, or anything I liked – and make him come to life in your cupboard?'

Chapter 8
Cowboy!

Omri gaped at him. He hadn't thought of this, but of course now that he did it was obvious – no boy who knew the secret could possibly rest until he had a little live person of his own.

'Patrick – it's not like you think – just something to play with –'

'Of course not, you've explained all about it, now just let me put –'

'But you have to think about it first. No, no, stop, you can't yet! And anyway I don't agree to you using one of mine!' Omri didn't know why he was so reluctant. It wasn't that he was mean. He just knew, somehow, that something awful would happen if he let Patrick have his own way. But it wasn't easy to stop him. Omri had grabbed him, but he wrenched free.

'I've got to –' he panted. 'I've got to –'

He stretched out his hand towards the pile of soldiers again. They struggled. Patrick seemed to have gone a bit crazy. Suddenly Omri felt the rim of the tin plate under his shifting feet.

He shoved Patrick out of the way and they both stared downward. The plate had tipped, the fire slipped off on to the carpet. Little Bull, with a yell, had leapt clear, and was now waving his arms and shouting horrible things at them. His roast meat had disappeared under Omri's foot, which instinctively stamped down on the fire to put it out. Omri felt the Meccano crunching under his school shoe, and a squishy feeling...

'Now look! We've spoilt the meat!' he shouted at Patrick. 'If all you can do is fight, I wish I'd never brought you!'

70

Patrick looked mulish. 'It was your fault. You should have let me put something in the cupboard.'

Omri lifted his shoe. Underneath was a nasty mess of burnt stuff, squashed meat and bent Meccano. Little Bull let out a wail.

'You no great spirit! Only stupid boy! Fight, spoil good meal! You feel shame!'

'Maybe we can rescue it –'

He crouched down and disentangled the meat from the mess, burning his fingers. He tried to brush it clean but it was no use – it was all mixed up with the smelly stuff of the firelighter, and stuck with bits of carpet hairs.

'I'm terribly sorry, Little Bull,' he mumbled.

'No good sorry! Little Bull hungry, work all day, cook meat – now what eat? I chop you down like tree!' And to Omri's horror he saw Little Bull run to where the battle-axe was lying, pick it up and advance towards his leg, swinging it in great circles as he came.

Patrick fairly danced with excitement. 'Isn't he fantastically brave, though! Much more than David with Goliath!'

Omri felt the whole thing was going too far. He removed his leg from harm's way. 'Little Bull! Calm down,' he said. 'I've said I'm sorry.'

Little Bull looked at him, blazing-eyed. Then he rushed over to the chair Omri used at his table and began chopping wedges out of the leg of it.

'Stop! Stop! Or I'll put you back in the cupboard!'

Little Bull stopped abruptly and dropped the axe. He stood with his back to them, his shoulders heaving.

'I'll get you something to eat – right now – something delicious. Go and paint. It'll make you feel better. I won't be long.' To Patrick he said, 'Hang on. I can smell supper cooking, I'll go and get a bit of whatever we're having,' and he rushed downstairs without stopping to think.

His mother was dishing up a nice hot stew.

'Can I have a tiny bit of that, Mum? Just a little bit, in a spoon. It's for a game we're playing.'

His mother obligingly gave him a big spoonful. 'Don't let it drip,' she said. 'Does Patrick want to stay for supper?'

'I don't know – I'll ask,' said Omri.

'Were you two fighting up there? I heard thumps.'

'No-o – not really. It was just that he wanted to do something that I –'

Omri stopped dead, as if frozen to the ground. He might have been frozen, his face went so cold. Patrick was up there – with the cupboard – and two biscuit-tinsful of little plastic figures – alone!

He ran. He usually won the egg-and-spoon race at the school sports, which was just as well – it's hard enough to carry an egg in a spoon running along a flat field; it's a great deal harder to carry a tablespoonful of boiling hot stew steady while you rush up a flight of stairs. If most of it was still there when he got to the top it was more by good luck than skill because he was hardly noticing the spoon at all – all he could think of was what might be – no, *must* be happening in his room, and how much more of it would happen if he didn't hurry.

He burst in through the door and saw exactly what he'd dreaded – Patrick, bent over the cupboard, just turning the key to open it.

'What –' Omri gasped out between panting breaths, but he had no need to go on. Patrick, without turning round, opened the cupboard and reached in. Then he did turn. He was gazing into his cupped hands with eyes like huge marbles. He slowly extended his hands towards Omri, and whispered, 'Look!'

Omri, stepping forward, had just time to feel intensely glad that at least Patrick had not put a whole handful of figures in but had only changed one. But which? He leant over, then drew back with a gasp.

It was the cowboy. And his horse.

The horse was in an absolute panic. It was scrambling about wildly in the cup of Patrick's hand, snorting and pawing, up one minute and down on its side the next, stirrups and reins flying. It was a beautiful horse, snow-white with a long mane and tail, and the sight of it acting so frightened gave Omri heart-pains.

As for the cowboy, he was too busy dodging the horse's flying feet and jumping out of the way when he fell to notice much about his surroundings. He probably thought he was caught in an earthquake. Omri and Patrick watched, spellbound, as the little man in his plaid shirt, buckskin trousers, high-heeled leather boots and big hat, scrambled frantically up the side of Patrick's right hand and, dodging through the space between his index finger and thumb, swung himself clear of the horse – only to look down and find he was dangling over empty space.

His hat came off and fell, slowly like a leaf, down, down, down to the floor so infinitely far below. The cowboy gave a yell, and scrabbled with his feet against the back of Patrick's hand, hanging on for dear life to the ridge beside his thumb-nail.

'Hold your hands still!' Omri commanded Patrick, who in his excitement was jerking them nervously about. There was a moment of stillness. The horse stood up, trembling all over, prancing about with terror. Beside his hooves was some tiny black thing. Omri peered closer. It was the pistol.

The cowboy had now recovered a little. He scrambled back through the finger-gap and said something to the horse which sounded like 'Whoaback, steady, fella.' Then he slid down and grabbed the reins, holding them just below the horse's nose. He patted its face. That seemed to calm it. Then, looking round swiftly but not apparently noticing the enormous faces hanging over him, he reached cautiously down and picked the pistol up from between the horse's hooves.

'Whoa there! Stand – '

Omri watched like a person hypnotized. He wanted to cry out to Patrick that it was a real gun, but somehow he couldn't. He could only think that the sound of his voice would throw the horse once more into a panic and that horse or man would get hurt. Instead he watched while the cowboy pointed the gun in various directions warily. Then he lowered it.

Still holding the reins he moved until he could press his hand against Patrick's skin. Then he let his eyes move upward towards the curved fingers just level with the top of his head.

'What the dawggone heck –' he said. 'It sure looks like a great big – Aw, what'm Ah talkin' about? It cain't be. Hell, it just ain't possible!' But the more he looked, the more certain he must have become that he was, indeed, in a pair of cupped hands. And finally, after scratching his gingery head for a moment, he ventured to look right up past the fingers, and then of course he saw Patrick's face looking a him.

There was a petrified moment when he couldn't move. Then he raised his pistol in a flash.

'Patrick! Shut your eyes!'

Bang!

It was only a little bang, but it was a real bang, and a puff of real, gun-smelling smoke appeared. Patrick shouted with pain and surprise and would have dropped the pair if Omri hadn't thrust his hand underneath to catch them. Patrick's own hand had clapped itself to his cheek.

'Ow! Ow! He's shot me!' Patrick screamed.

Omri was not much bothered about Patrick at that moment. He was furious with him, and very anxious about the little man and his horse. Quickly he put them down on the bed, saying, like the cowboy himself, 'Steady! Whoa! I won't hurt you! It's okay!'

'Ow!' Patrick kept yelling. 'It hurts! Ow!'

'Serve you right, I warned you,' said Omri. Then he felt sorry and said, 'Let's have a look.'

Gingerly Patrick took his hand down. A drop of blood had been smeared on his cheek, and by peering very close Omri could see something very like a bee's sting embedded in his skin.

'Hang on! I see it – I'll squeeze it out –'

'OW!'

A quick squeeze between his thumbnails and the almost invisible speck of black metal, which had only just penetrated the skin, popped out.

'He – shot me!' Patrick got out again in a shocked voice.

'I *told* you. My Indian stuck a knife in me,' said Omri, not to be outdone. 'I think we ought to put him back – your cowboy I mean, of course, not my Indian.'

'Put him back where?'

Omri explained how the cupboard could change him back to plastic again, but Patrick wasn't having any of that.

'Oh no! I want him! He's terrific. Look at him now –'

Patrick feasted his eyes admiringly on the little cowboy. Ignoring the 'giants', whom he clearly thought he must have imagined, he was doggedly dragging his horse across Omri's quilt as if he were wading through the dunes of some infinite pale-blue desert.

Omri reached for him determinedly, but Patrick stepped into his path.

'Don't you touch him! I bought him, I changed him – he's mine!'

'You bought him for me!'

'You said you didn't want him.'

'Well, but the cupboard's mine, and I told you not to use it.'

'And so what if I did? Anyway, it's done, he's alive now and I'm keeping him. I'll bash you right in if you try to take him. Wouldn't you bash me if I took your Indian?'

Omri was silent. That reminded him! Where was Little Bull? He looked round. He soon spotted him at the other side of the room, busy with his paints. Some beautiful, minute designs, showing turtles and herons and beavers, mainly in red and yellow, had appeared on the side of the tepee Omri had made. As Omri crouched beside him to admire them, Little Bull, without looking at him, said, 'You bring food? I very soon die if not eat.'

Omri looked around. What had he done with the spoonful of stew? But he soon saw that he'd put it down on the table without thinking. There it sat, tilting slightly and spilling a few drops of gravy, but still steaming. He hurried to get Little Bull's – or rather the Action Man's – mess-tin (the paper plate had got all soggy) and carefully filled it with the hot savoury stuff.

'Here you are.'

Little Bull stopped work, laid down his paintbrush, and sniffed eagerly.

'Ah! Good!' He sat down cross-legged among the paint lids to eat, dipping some of yesterday's stale bread in as a spoon. 'Your wife cook? Ah. No. Little Bull forgot. Omri not got wife.' He ate ravenously for a few moments and then said, 'Not want?'

'I'm having mine downstairs in a minute,' Omri said.

'Mean, Omri not want wife,' said Little Bull, who was now in a much better mood.

'I'm not old enough.'

Little Bull looked at him for a moment. 'No. I see. Boy.' He grinned. 'Big boy, but boy.' He went on eating. 'Little Bull want,' he said finally, not looking up.

'Another wife?'

'Chief needs wife. Beautiful. Good cook. Act as told.' He put his face into the mess-tin and licked it clean. Then he looked up.

'With Iroquois, mother find wife for son. But Little Bull's mother not here. Omri be mother and find.'

Omri couldn't quite see himself as Little Bull's mother, but he said, 'I might try. I think there were some Indian women in Yapp's. But what if I get one and make her real and then you don't fancy her?'

'Fancy?'

'Like her.'

'I like. Young. Beautiful. Act as told. I like. So you get.'

'Tomorrow.'

Little Bull grinned at him happily, his face smeared with gravy.

Patrick had come up behind him.

'Let's put them together and see what they do!'

Omri jumped up quickly.

'No!'

'Why *not*?'

'You idiot, because yours has got a gun and mine's got a bow and arrow and one of them's sure to kill the other!'

Patrick considered this. 'Well, we could take their weapons away from them. Come on, I'm going to!' And he reached towards the bed.

Just at that moment there was the sound of steps on the stairs. They froze. Then Omri swiftly moved the dressing-up crate enough to hide Little Bull, and Patrick sat down on the end of the bed, masking the poor cowboy who was still toiling along over the lumps in the quilt.

Just in time! Omri's mother opened the door next second and said, 'Patrick, that was your mum on the 'phone. She wants you to come home right away. And Omri – it's supper.' And she went.

Omri opened his mouth to protest, but Patrick at once said, 'Oh, okay.' With one quick movement he had scooped up cowboy and horse in his left hand and thrust them into his blazer pocket. Omri winced – he could easily imagine the horse's legs being injured by such rough treatment, not to mention the matter of fright. But Patrick was already halfway out of the door.

Omri jumped up and grabbed his arm.

'Patrick!' he whispered. 'You must be careful! Treat them carefully! They're *people* – I mean they're alive – what will you do with them? How will you hide them from your family?'

'I won't, I'll show them to my brother anyway, he'll go out of his mind.'

Omri began to think he might go out of his. He shook Patrick's arm. '*Will you think*? How are you going to explain? What will happen? If you say you got him from me I'll do worse than bash you – you'll ruin everything – they'll take the cupboard away – '

That got through to Patrick at last. He put his hand slowly back into his pocket.

'Listen then. You can look after them. But remember – they're mine. If you put them back in the cupboard, I'll tell everyone. I'm warning you. I will. Bring them to school tomorrow.'

'To school!' cried Omri aghast. 'I'm not bringing Little Bull to school!'

'You can do what you like about Little Bull, he's yours. The cowboy's mine, and I want him at school tomorrow, otherwise I'll tell.'

Omri let go of his arm and for a moment they looked at each other as if they'd been strangers. But they weren't strangers; they were friends. That counts for a lot in this life. Omri gave in.

'All right,' he said, 'I'll bring them. Now give them to me. *Gently*.' And Patrick brought man and horse out of his pocket and tipped them very carefully into Omri's waiting hand.

Chapter 9
Shooting-Match

Omri put the cowboy and horse in his shirt drawer while he had the quickest supper on record. Then he raced upstairs again, stopping only to pinch a few grains of Gillon's rat feed for the two horses.

Shut up in his room, he took stock. A room this size was like a sort of indoor national park to the cowboy and the Indian. It should be easy enough to keep them apart for one night. Omri thought first of putting the new pair straight back in the cupboard, and then bringing them back to life next morning in time for school, but he had promised Patrick not to. So he decided to empty out the dressing-up crate and put the cowboy and his horse in there for the night.

The crate was a metre square, made of planks. There was certainly no visible way out of it for the cowboy. Omri put him carefully down into it. Looking at him, he felt curious – about his name, where he came from and so on; but he decided it was better not to talk to him. The cowboy had clearly decided that Omri was not really there at all. When his big hands reached down, carrying some cold stew, grain for the pony, some fragments of apple for them both and, later, some cottonwool and scraps of material for bedding, the cowboy deliberately covered his eyes by pulling down his big hat brim. It was only when Omri reached in one final time to give him a drink of water in a minute green glass bottle that he had found in the bathroom cupboard, that the cowboy spoke a word.

'Take that filthy stuff outa here!' he suddenly shouted, in his strong Texas accent. 'Ah ain't aimin' to drink no more o' that as lawng as Ah live!' And he heaved the bottle (which was almost as big as himself) up by its base and tipped its contents out onto the boards at the bottom of the crate.

'It's only water,' Omri ventured to say.

'You shet yer mouth!' shouted the little man. 'Ah won't take no lip from no gol-darned hallucy-nation, no sir! Mebbe Ah do drink too much, mebbe Ah cain't hold m'likker like some o' them real tough guys do. But if'n Ah'm gittin' the dee-lirium tremens, and startin' in to see things, why couldn't Ah see pink elly-fants and dancin' rats and all them purty things other fellas see when they gits far gone? It ain't fair fer me to see giants and blue deserts and git put in boxes the size of the Grand Canyon with no one but m'little hoss for comp'ny!' He sat down on the pile of hay, took the horse's nose in his arms, put his face against it and began to sob.

Omri was shattered. A cowboy – crying! He didn't know what to do. When his mother cried, as she did sometimes when things got too much, she only asked to be left alone till she felt better. Maybe all grown-ups were like that. Omri turned away and got slowly into his pyjamas, and then went to see how Little Bull was getting along on the far side of the crate.

He'd finished the painting. The tepee looked really good. Little Bull was now in the longhouse, arranging his blanket for the night. The pony was tethered to his post on a long rope. Omri took out the rat food and gave it to him. Then he called Little Bull out.

'Are you okay? Anything you need?'

He should have known better than to ask.

'Plenty! Want fire in longhouse, keep warm, keep wild animals away. Want tomahawk –'

'So you can chop bits out of my leg?'

'Little Bull angry when say that. Sorry now. Use tomahawk cut down trees, chop firewood, kill bird –'

'What bird?'

Little Bull replied with a very good imitation of a cock crowing. Then he did a mime of catching it, putting its neck on to a block, and, with a whirl of his arm, chopping off its head with gleeful relish.

'I don't know about that!'

'You get. Tomorrow. Birds from plass-tick. Good tools. But fire – now. Chief Little Bull say!'

Omri sighed. He went to the waste paper basket and picked out the remains of the other fire that he'd thrown away in there. There was quite a lot of the firelighter left. He gathered up some of the bits of willow-bark and twigs from where Little Bull had been working.

'You're not having it inside, though – far too dangerous!'

He arranged the fire on the packed earth of the seed-tray, about fifteen centimetres from the entrance to the longhouse, first moving the tepee to safety. Then he struck a match and soon there was a cosy blaze.

Little Bull crouched beside it, his red skin glowing and his eyes bright with pleasure.

'Little Bull, can you dance?'

'Yes. War dance, wedding dance, many kind.'

'Would you do one now so I can see?'

He hesitated, then he shook his head once.

'Why not, though?'

'No make war, no make wedding. No reason dance.'

'Maybe if I got you a wife –'

The Indian looked up eagerly. 'You get? Give word?'

'I only said I'd try.'

'Then Little Bull dance. Then do best dance – love dance.'

Omri turned off his light and drew back from the scene. It looked amazingly real, with the fire making shadows, the little horse munching his grain and the Indian sitting on his heels warming himself, wearing his colourful headdress and the Chief's cloak. Omri wished he himself were small enough to join Little Bull by the fire.

'Om - ri! Are you in bed? I'm coming up in five minutes to kiss you goodnight!'

Omri felt panicky. But it was all right. The fire was going out. Already Little Bull was standing up, yawning and stretching. He peered up through the darkness.

'Hey, Omri! Paintings good?'

'Great!'

'You sleep now?'

'Yes.'

'Peace of great spirits be on you.'

'Thanks, same to you.'

Omri peered quickly into the crate. The poor cowboy had crawled away into his makeshift bed and was snoring loudly. He hadn't eaten a thing. Omri sighed. He hoped Patrick was making plans and arrangements. After all, if Omri could keep his Indian secret, Patrick might be able to do the same. All might yet be well. But Omri certainly wasn't going to try the experiment again. It was all just too much worry.

He climbed into bed, feeling unusually tired. His mother came in and kissed him, and the door was shut. He felt himself drifting off almost right away.

When suddenly, a piercing whinny sounded. And was answered by another.

The horses had smelt each other!

They were not so far apart – and the cowboy's wasn't tied up. Omri could hear his little hooves clattering on the bare boards of the crate, and then the whinnies began again, high, shrill – almost questioning. Omri thought of putting on his light, but he was awfully tired – besides, what could he do? They couldn't possibly reach each other through the planks of the crate wall. Let them whinny their heads off, they'd soon get fed up.

Omri rolled over and fell asleep.

He was woken just after dawn by shots.

He was out of bed in about one-fifth of a second. One

glance into the crate showed him all too clearly that the cowboy and his horse had escaped. The second glance showed how – a knot in the wood had been pushed out (or perhaps kicked out by the horse) leaving an oval-shaped hole like an arched doorway, just big enough to let horse and rider through.

Omri looked round wildly. At first he could see nothing. He dropped to his knees beside the seed-box and peered into the longhouse. Little Bull was not there – nor was his pony.

Suddenly some tiny thing whizzed past Omri's ear and struck the crate beside him with a ping! Twisting his head, Omri saw it – a feathered arrow the size of a pin, still quivering from its flight.

Was Little Bull shooting at *him*?

'Little Bull! Where are you?'

No answer. But suddenly, a movement, like that of a mouse, caught the corner of his eye. It was the cowboy. Dragging his horse behind him, he was running, half bent over, from behind one chair-leg to another. He had his revolver in his hand, his hat on his head. Another arrow flew, missing the crate this time and burying itself in the carpet – just ahead of the running cowboy, who stopped dead, jumped backwards till his horse hid him, and then fired another two shots from behind the horse's shoulder.

Omri, following his aim, spotted Little Bull at once. He and his pony were behind a small heap of cloth which was like a snow-covered hill to them but was actually Omri's vest, dropped carelessly on the floor the night before. Little Bull, safe in the shelter of this cotton mountain, was just preparing to shoot another arrow at the cowboy, one which could hardly fail to hit its mark. The poor fellow was now scrambling desperately on to his pony to try and ride away and was in full sight of the Indian as he drew back his bowstring.

'Little Bull! Stop!'

Omri's voice rang out frenziedly. Little Bull did not stop; but his surprise spoilt his aim, and the arrow sped over the cowboy, doing no worse than sweep away his big hat and pin it to the skirting-board behind the chair.

This infuriated the little man, who, forgetting his fear, stood up in his stirrups and shouted, 'Tarnation take ya, ya red varmint! Wait'll Ah ketch ya. Ah'll have yer stinkin' red hide for a sleeping' bag!'

With that he rode straight towards the vest-hill at full gallop, shouting out strange cowboy-like war cries and waving his gun, which, by Omri's count, still had two bullets in it.

Little Bull had not expected this, but he was only outfaced for a moment. Then he coolly drew another arrow from his quiver and fitted it to his bow.

'Little Bull, if you shoot I'll pick you up and *squeeze* you!' Omri cried.

Little Bull kept his arrow pointing towards the oncoming horseman.

'What you do if he shoot?' he asked.

'He won't shoot! Look at him.'

Sure enough, the carpet was too soft for much galloping, and even as Omri spoke the cowboy's horse stumbled and fell, pitching its rider over its head.

Little Bull lowered his bow and laughed. Then, to Omri's horror, he laid down the bow among the folds of the vest, reached for his knife, and began to advance on the prostrate cowboy.

'Little Bull, you are not to touch him, do you hear?'

Little Bull stopped. 'He try to shoot Little Bull. White enemy. Try take Indian's land. Why not kill? Better dead. I act quick, he not feel, you see!' And he began to move forward again.

When he was nearly up to the cowboy Omri swooped on him. He didn't squeeze him of course, but he did lift him high and fast enough to give him a fright.

'Listen to me now. That cowboy isn't after your land. He's got nothing to do with you. He's Patrick's cowboy, like you're my Indian. I'm taking him to school with me today, so you won't be bothered by him any more. Now you take your pony and get back to your longhouse and leave him to me.'

Little Bull, sitting cross-legged in the palm of his hand, gave him a sly look.

'You take him to school? Place you learn about ancestors?'

'That's what I said.'

He folded his arms offendedly. 'Why you not take Little Bull?'

Omri was startled into silence.

'If white fool with coward's face good enough, Indian Chief good enough.'

'You wouldn't enjoy it –'

'If him enjoy, I enjoy.'

'I'm not taking you. It's too risky.'

'Risky! Fire-water?'

'Not *whisky* – risky. Dangerous.'

He shouldn't have said that. Little Bull's eyes lit up.

'Like danger! Here too quiet. No hunting, no enemy, only *him*,' he said scornfully, peering over the edge of Omri's hand at the cowboy, who, despite the softness of his landing-place, was only just scrambling to his feet. 'Look! Him no use for fight. Little Bull soon kill, take scalp, finish. Very good scalp,' he added generously. 'Fine colour, look good on belt.'

Omri looked across at the cowboy. He was leaning his ginger head against his saddle. It looked as if he might be crying again. Omri felt very sorry for him.

'You're not going to hurt him,' he said to the Indian, 'because I won't let you. If he's such a coward, it wouldn't do your honour any good anyway.'

Little Bull's face fell, then grew mulish. 'No tell from

scalp on belt if belong to coward or brave man,' he said slyly. 'Let me kill and I do dance round campfire,' he coaxed.

'No –' Omri began. Then he changed his tactics. 'All right, you kill him. But then I won't bring you a wife.'

The Indian looked at him a long time. Then he slowly put his knife away.

'No touch. Give word. Now you give word. Take Little Bull to school. Take to Plass-tick. Let Little Bull choose own woman.'

Omri considered. He could keep Little Bull in his pocket all day. No need to take any chances. If he were tempted to show the other children, well, he must resist temptation, that was all.

And after school he could take him to Yapp's. The boxes with the plastic figures in them were in a corner behind a high stand. Provided there weren't too many other kids in the shop, he might be able to give Little Bull a quick look at the Indian women before he bought one, which would be a very good thing. Otherwise he might pick an old or ugly one without realizing it. It was so hard to see from their tiny plastic faces what they would be like when they came to life.

'Okay then, I'll take you. But you must do as I tell you and not make any noise.'

He put him down on the seed-tray and gently shooed the pony up the ramp. Little Bull tied it to its post and Omri gave it some more rat food. Then he crawled on hands and knees over to where the cowboy was now sitting dolefully on the carpet, his horse's rein looped round his arm, looking too miserable to move.

'What's the matter?' Omri asked him.

The little man didn't look up. 'Lost muh hat,' he mumbled.

'Oh, is that all?' Omri reached over to the skirting-board and pulled the pin-like arrow out of the wide brim of the hat. 'Here it is,' he said kindly, laying it in the cowboy's lap.

The cowboy looked at it, looked up at Omri, then stood up and put the hat on. 'You shore ain't no reg'lar hallucynation,' he said. 'I'm obliged to ya.' Suddenly he laughed. 'Jest imagine, thankin' a piece o' yor dee-lirium tremens fer givin' you yer hat back! Ah jest cain't figger out what's goin' on around here. Say! Are you real, or was that Injun real? 'Cause in case you ain't noticed, you're a danged sight bigger'n he is. You cain't both be real.'

'I don't think you ought to worry about it. What's your name?'

The cowboy seemed embarrassed and hung his head. 'M'name's Boone. But the fellas all call me Boohoo. That's on account of Ah cry so easy. It's m'soft heart. Show me some'n sad, or scare me just a little, and the tears jest come to mah eyes. Ah cain't help it.'

Omri, who had been somewhat of a cry-baby himself until very recently, was not inclined to be scornful about this, and said, 'That's okay. Only you needn't be scared of me. And as for the Indian, he's my friend and he won't hurt you, he's promised. Now I'd like you and your horse to go back into that big crate. I'll stick the knot back in the wood, you'll feel safer. Then I'll get you some breakfast.' Boone brightened visibly at this. 'What would you like?'

'Aw shucks, Ah ain't that hungry. Coupla bits o' steak and three or four eggs, sittin' on a small heap o' beans and washed down with a jug o' cawfee'll suit me just dandy.'

'You'll be lucky,' thought Omri.

Chapter 10
Breakfast Truce

He crept downstairs. The house was still asleep. He decided to cook breakfast for himself and his cowboy and Indian. He was quite a good cook, but he'd mostly done sweet stuff before; however, any fool, he felt sure, could fry an egg. The steaks were out of the question, but beans were no problem. Omri put frying-pan over gas and margarine in pan. The fat began to smoke. Omri broke an egg into it, or tried to, but the shell, instead of coming cleanly apart, crumpled up somehow in his hand and landed in the hot fat mixed up with the egg.

Hm. Not as easy as he'd thought. Leaving the mess to cook, shell and all, he got a tin of beans out of the cupboard and opened it without trouble. Then he got a saucepan and began pouring the beans in. Some of them got into the egg-pan somehow and seemed to explode. The egg was beginning to curl and the pan was still smoking. Alarmed, he turned off the gas. The centre of the egg still wasn't cooked and the beans in the pan were stone cold but the smell in the kitchen was beginning to worry him – he didn't want his mother coming down. He tipped the whole lot into a bowl, hacked a lopsided slice off the loaf, and tiptoed up the stairs again.

Little Bull was standing outside his longhouse with hands on hips, waiting for him.

'You bring food?' he asked in his usual bossy way.

'Yes.'

'First, Little Bull want ride.'

'First, you must eat while it's hot, I've been to a lot of trouble to cook it for you,' Omri said, sounding like his mother.

Little Bull didn't know how to take this, so he burst into a rather forced laugh and pointed at him scornfully. 'Omri cook – Omri woman!' he teased. But Omri wasn't bothered.

'All the best cooks are men,' he retorted. 'Come on, you're going to eat with Boone.'

Little Bull's laughter died instantly.

'Who Boone?'

'You know who he is. The cowboy.'

The Indian's hands came off his hips and one of them went for his knife.

'Oh, knock it off, Little Bull! Have a truce for breakfast, otherwise you won't get any.'

Leaving him with that thought to chew over, Omri crossed to the crate, in which Boone was grooming his white horse with a wisp of cloth he'd found clinging to a splinter. He'd taken off the little saddle, but the bridle was still on.

'Boone! I've brought something to eat,' said Omri.

'Yup. Ah thought Ah smelt some'n good,' said Boone. 'Let's git to it.'

Omri put his hand down. 'Climb on.'

'Ah, shucks – where'm Ah goin'? Why cain't Ah eat in mah box, where it's safe?' whined Boone. But he clambered up into Omri's palm and sat grumpily with his back against his middle finger.

'You're going to eat with the Indian,' said Omri.

Boone leapt up so suddenly he nearly fell off, and had to grab hold of a thumb to steady himself.

'Hell, no, Ah ain't!' he yelled. 'You jest put me down, son, ya hear? I ain't sharin' m'vittles with no lousy scalp-snafflin' Injun and that's m'last word!' It was, as it happened, his last word before being set down within a few centimetres of his enemy on the seed-tray.

They both bent their legs into crouches, as if uncertain whether to leap at each other's throats or turn and flee. Omri hurriedly spooned up some egg and beans and held it between them.

'Smell that!' he ordered them. 'Now you eat together or you don't get any at all, so make up your minds to it. You can start fighting again afterwards if you must.'

He took a bit of clean paper and laid it, like a tablecloth, under the spoon. Then he broke off some crumbs of bread crust and pushed a little into each of their hands. Still with their eyes fixed on each other's faces, Indian and cowboy sidled towards the big, steaming 'bowl' of food from opposite sides. Little Bull, after hesitating, was first to shoot his arm out and dip the bread into the egg. The sudden movement startled Boone so much he let out a yell and tried to run, but Omri's hand was blocking the way.

'Don't be silly, Boone,' he said firmly.

'Ah ain't bein' silly! Them Injuns ain't jest ornery and savage. Them's *dirty* . And Ah ain't eatin' from the same bowl as no – '

'Boone,' said Omri quietly. 'Little Bull is no dirtier than you. You should see your own face.'

'Is that mah fault? What kinda hallucy-nation are ya, anyways, tellin' me Ah'm dirty when ya didn't bring me no washin' water?'

This was a fair complaint, but Omri wasn't about to lose the argument on a side issue.

'You can have some after breakfast. But if you don't agree to eat with my Indian, I'm going to tell him your nickname.'

The cowboy's face fell. 'Now that ain't fair. That plumb ain't no ways fair,' he muttered. But hunger was getting the better of him anyway, so, grumbling and swearing under his breath, he turned back and marched to his side of the spoon. By this time Little Bull was seated cross-legged on the piece of paper, a hunk of bean in one hand and a mess of egg in the other, eating heartily. Seeing this, Boone lost no time in tucking in, eyeing the Indian, who ignored him.

'Whur's muh cawfee?' he complained after he'd eaten a

few bites. 'Ah cain't start the day till Ah've had muh jug o' cawfee!'

Omri had completely forgotten about coffee, but he was beginning to be pretty well fed up with being bossed around by ungrateful little men, so he settled down to eat the remains of the food and simply said, 'Well, you'll have to start this one without any.'

Little Bull finished his breakfast and stood up.

'Now we fight,' he announced, and reached for his knife.

Omri expected Boone to leap up and run, but he didn't. He just sat there munching bread and beans.

'Ah ain't finished yit,' he said. 'Ain't gonna fight till Ah'm plumb full o' vittles. So you kin jest sit down and wait, Redskin.'

Omri laughed. 'Good for you, Boone! Take it easy, Little Bull. Don't forget your promise.'

Little Bull scowled. But he sat down again.

Boone ate and ate. It was hard not to suspect, after a while, that he was eating as much and as slowly as possible, to put off the moment when he would have to fight.

At last, very reluctantly, he scraped the last bit of egg from the spoon, wiped his hands on the side of his trousers, and stood up. Little Bull was on his feet instantly. Omri stood ready to part them.

'Looka here, Injun,' said Boone. 'If we're gonna fight, we're gonna fight fair. Probably ain't even a word for "fair" in your language, but Ah'm here to tell ya, with me it's fight fair or don't fight a-tall.'

'Little Bull fight fair, kill fair, scalp fair.'

'You ain't gonna scalp nobody. Less'n ya take it off with yer teeth.'

For answer, Little Bull raised his knife, which flashed in the morning light. Omri, his hands on his knees, waited.

'Yeah, Ah see it. But you ain't gonna have it much longer. And why aincha? Because Ah ain't got one. Ah only got m'gun, and m'gun's run plumb outa bullets. What Ah got, and all Ah got, is m'fists. Oh – and one other thing. Ah got mah hallucy-nation here.' He waved a hand at Omri without taking his eyes off Little Bull for a second. 'And Ah know he don't want to see this here purty red scalp o' mine hangin' from no stinkin' redskin's belt. So if Ah fight, it's gonna be fist to fist, face to face – man to man, Injun! D'ja hear me? No weapons! Jest us two, and let's see if a white man cain't lick a red man in a fair fight. Less'n mebbe – jest mebbe – you ain't red a-tall, but yeller?' And Boone stepped round the bowl of the spoon, threw his empty gun on the ground, and put up his fists like a boxer.

Little Bull was nonplussed. He lowered his knife and stared at Boone. Whether Little Bull had completely understood the cowboy's strange speech was doubtful, but he couldn't mistake the gesture of throwing the gun away. As Boone began to dance round him, fists up, making little mock jabs towards his face, Little Bull was getting madder and madder. He made a sudden swipe at him with his knife. Boone jumped back.

'Oh, you naughty Injun! Ah see Ah'll have to set mah hallucy-nation on to you!'

But Omri didn't have to do anything. Little Bull had got the message. Throwing down the knife in a fury, he hurled himself on to Boone.

What followed was not a fist fight, or a wrestling match, or anything so well organized. It was just an all-in, no-holds-barred two-man war. They rolled on the ground, pummelling, kicking and butting with their heads. At one point Omri thought he saw Boone trying to bite. Maybe he succeeded, because Little Bull suddenly let him go and Boone rolled away swift as a barrel down a slope and on to his legs and then, with a spring, like a bow-legged panther, on to the Indian again. Feet first.

Little Bull let out a noise like 'OOOF!' – caught Boone by

both ankles, and heaved him off. Little Bull picked up a clod of compost and flung it after him, catching him full in the face. Then Little Bull got up and ran at him, holding both fists together and swinging them as he had swung the battle-axe. They caught the cowboy a heavy whack on the ear which sent him flying to one side. But as he flew, he caught Little Bull a blow in the chest with one boot. That left them both on the ground.

The next moment each of the men found himself pinned down by a giant finger.

'All right, boys. That's enough,' said Omri, in his father's firm end-of-the-fight voice. 'It's a draw. Now you must get cleaned up for school.'

School

He brought them a low type of egg-cup full of hot water, and a corner of soap cut off a big cake, to wash with. They stood one on each side of it. Little Bull, already naked to the waist, lost no time in plunging his arms in and began energetically rubbing the whole of the top part of his body with his wet hands, throwing water everywhere. He made a lot of noise about it and seemed to be enjoying himself, though he ignored the soap.

Boone was a different matter. Omri had already noticed that Boone was none too fussy about being clean, and in fact didn't look as if he'd washed or shaved for weeks. Now he approached the hot water gingerly, eyeing Omri as if to see how little washing he could actually get away with.

'Come on, Boone! Off with that shirt, you can't wash your neck with a shirt on,' said Omri briskly, echoing his mother.

With extreme reluctance, shivering theatrically, Boone dragged off his plaid shirt, keeping his hat on.

'I should think your hair could do with a wash too,' said Omri.

Boone stared at him.

'Wash mah *hair*?' he asked incredulously. 'Washin' hair's fur *wimmin*, ''tain't fer men!' But he did consent to rub his hands lightly over the piece of soap, although grimacing hideously as if it were some slimy dead thing. Then he rinsed them hastily, smeared some water on his face, and reached for his shirt without even drying himself.

'Boone!' said Omri sternly. 'Just look at Little Bull! You called him dirty, but at least he's washing himself thoroughly! Now you just do something about your neck and – well, under your arms.'

Boone's look was now one of stark horror.

'Under mah arms!'

'*And* your chest I should think. I'm not taking you to school all sweaty.'

'Hell! Don't you go runnin' down sweat! It's sweat that keeps a man clean!'

After a lot of bullying, Omri managed to get him to wash at least a few more bits of himself.

'You'll have to wash your clothes some time, too,' he said.

But this was too much for Boone.

'Ain't nobody gonna touch muh duds, and that's final,' he said. 'Ain't bin washed since Ah bought 'em. Water takes all the stuffin' outa good cloth. Without all the dust 'n' sweat they don't keep ya warm no more.'

At last they were ready, and Omri pocketed them and ran down to breakfast. He felt tense with excitement. He'd never carried them around the house before. It was risky, but not so risky as taking them to school – he felt that having family breakfast with them secretly in his pocket was like a training for taking them to school.

Breakfast in his house was often a dicey meal anyway, with everybody more or less bad-tempered. Today, for instance, Adiel had lost his football shorts and was blaming everybody in turn, and their mother had just discovered that Gillon, contrary to his assurances the night before when he had wanted to watch television, had not finished his homework. Their father was grumpy because he had wanted to do some gardening and it was raining yet again.

'I *know* I put them in the laundry basket,' Adiel was saying fretfully.

'If you did, I washed them, in which case they're back in your top drawer,' said his mother. 'But you didn't, because I didn't, and they're not. Now listen to me, Gillon –'

'It's only a tiny bit of history, one mini little castle to draw and a mouldy paragraph on mottes and bailies to write,' said Gillon. 'I can do it at school.'

'Stinking climate,' muttered their father. 'Those onion-sets will rot if I don't get them in soon.'

'Gillon, did you borrow them?' put in Adiel.

'I've got my own.'

'You actually told me a lie last night –' said their mother.

'I did not! I said I'd *nearly* finished.'

'There was no mention of "nearly"!'

'You probably didn't hear.'

'Probably not,' retorted their mother. 'With the row going on from *The Water Margin*.'

Omri ate his cereal in silence, grinning to himself, hugging his secret. He slipped a couple of cornflakes into his pockets.

'I bet Omri took them!' said Adiel suddenly.

Omri looked up. 'Took what?'

'My *shorts*.'

'What on earth would I want your shorts for?'

'It might be your idea of a joke to hide them,' Adiel retorted.

This was not as outrageous as it sounds. It had, until very recently, been a common form of revenge, when Adiel or Gillon had been specially unbearable, for Omri to sneak some valuable possession and hide it.

Now, however, Omri felt very far away from such babyishness, and was quite insulted.

'Don't be stupid,' he said.

'So you did,' said Adiel in triumph.

'I did not!'

'You're red in the face – that's proof you're guilty!'

'I swear!' said Omri.

'They're probably under your bed,' said their mother to Adiel. 'Go up and have a look.'

'I have looked! I've looked everywhere.'

'Oh, my God, it's starting to hail now,' said their father despairingly. 'So much for the apple blossom.'

Under cover of the moans that went up about the prospect of no apples in the autumn, and the exclamations about the size of the hailstones, Omri slipped his coat on and ran through the bouncing ice-lumps to school. On the way he stopped under a protecting yew tree and took the little men out. He showed them each a large hailstone, which, to them, was the size of a football.

'Now, when we get to school,' said Omri, 'you must lie very still and quiet in my pockets. I'm putting you in separate ones because I can't risk any fighting or quarrelling. If you're seen I don't know what will happen.'

'Danger?' asked Little Bull, his eyes gleaming.

'Yes. Not of death so much. You might be taken away from me. Then you'd never get back to your own time.'

'You mean we'd never wake up outa this here drunken dream,' said Boone.

But Little Bull was staring at him very thoughtfully. 'Own time,' he said musingly. 'Very strange magic.'

Omri had never arrived at school with more apprehension in his heart, not even on spelling-test days. And yet he was excited too. Once he had taken a white mouse to school in his blazer pocket. He'd planned to do all sorts of fiendish things with it, like putting it up his teacher's trouser leg (he had had a man teacher then) or down the back of a girl's neck, or just putting it on the floor and letting it run around and throw the whole class into chaos. (He hadn't actually dared do anything with it except let it peep out and make his neighbours giggle.) This time he had no such plans. All he was hoping was that he could get through the day without anybody finding out what he had in his pockets.

Patrick was waiting for him at the school gate.

'Have you got him?'

'Yes.'

His eyes lit up. 'Give! I want him.'

'All right,' said Omri. 'But you have to promise that you won't show him to *anybody*.'

Omri reached into his right-hand pocket, closed his fingers gently round Boone, and passed him into Patrick's hand.

The moment he'd let go of him, things started to happen.

A particularly nasty little girl called April, who had been playing across the playground at the moment of the transaction, was at Patrick's side about two seconds later.

'What've you got there then, what did he give you?' she asked in her raucous voice like a crow's.

Patrick flushed red. 'Nothing! Push off!' he said.

At once April pointed her witchy finger at him. 'Look at Patrick blu-shing, look at Patrick blu-shing!' she squawked. Several other children speedily arrived on the scene and soon Patrick and Omri found themselves surrounded.

'What's he got? Bet it's something horrid!'

'Bet it's a slimy toad!'

'A little wriggly worm, more like.'

'A beetle!'

'Like him!'

Omri felt his blood begin to get hot in his head. He longed to bash them all one by one, or better still, all at once – Bruce Lee, knocking down hordes of enemies like skittles. He imagined them all rolling backwards down a long wide flight of steps, in waves, bowled over by his flashing fist and flying feet.

The best he could manage in reality, though, was to lower his head and, keeping his hand cupped stiffly over his left pocket, barge through the chanting circle. He caught one of them a good butt in the stomach which was rather satisfying. Patrick was hot on his heels, and they belted across the playground and in through the double doors, which fortunately had just been opened.

Once inside, they were relatively safe. There were teachers all over the place, and any kind of fighting or taunting, above a sly pinch or a snide whisper, was out. Patrick and Omri slowed to a walk, went to their places and sat down, trying to look perfectly calm and ordinary so as not to attract their teacher's attention. Their breathing gave them away, though.

'Well, you two, what are you puffing about? Been running?'

They glanced at each other and nodded.

'So long as you've not been fighting,' she said, giving them a sharp look. She always behaved as if a little fight was a long step along the road to hell.

Neither of the boys got much work done during the morning. They couldn't concentrate. Each of them was too aware of the passenger in his pocket. Both Little Bull and Boone were restless, particularly Little Bull. Boone was naturally lazier; he kept dozing off in the dark, and then waking with a little jump that made Patrick very nervous. But Little Bull was scrambling about the whole time.

It was during the third period – when they were all in the main hall listening to the headmaster, whose name was Mr Johnson, announcing plans for the end-of-year show – that Little Bull got really sick and tired of being imprisoned, and started to take drastic action.

The first thing Omri knew was a sharp prick in his hip, as if an insect had stung him. For a moment he was silly enough to think an ant or even a wasp had somehow got into his clothes, and he only just stopped himself from slapping his hand instinctively against his side to squash it. Then there came another jab, sharper than the first, sharp enough in fact to make Omri let out a short yelp.

'Who did that?' asked Mr Johnson irritably.

Omri didn't answer, but the girls sitting near him began giggling and staring.

'Was that you, Omri?'

'Yes. I'm sorry, something stuck into me.'

'Patrick! Did you stick a pencil into Omri?' (Such a thing was not unknown during assemblies when they were bored.)

'No Mr Johnson.'

'Well, be quiet when I'm talking!'

Another jab, and this time Little Bull meant business and kept his knife embedded. Omri shouted 'Ouch!' and jumped to his feet.

'Omri! Patrick! Leave the hall!'

'But I didn't –' began Patrick.

'Out, I said!' shouted Mr Johnson furiously.

They left, Patrick walking normally and Omri dancing about like a flea on a hot stove, shouting 'Ow! OW!' at every step as Little Bull continued to dig the needle-point of his knife in. The whole school was in hysterics of laughter (and Mr Johnson was frothing with rage) by the time they reached the swing-doors and departed.

Outside, they ran (well, Patrick ran and Omri performed a series of sideways leaps) to the far end of the playground. On the way Omri plunged his hand into his pocket, seized Little Bull, and dragged him out. The agony stopped.

Safe in a sheltered corner behind some privet bushes, Omri held his persecutor at eye-level and shook him violently, the way you shake a bottle of medicine. He called him the worst names he could possibly think of. When he'd run out of swear-words (which was not for some time) he hissed, like Mr Johnson, 'What do you mean by it? How dare you? How dare you stick your knife into me?'

'Little Bull dare! Omri keep in dark many hours! Little Bull want see school place, not lie in hot dark! No breathe, no see! Want *enjoy!*'

'I warned you you wouldn't, it's not my fault you made me bring you! Now you've got me into trouble.'

Little Bull looked mulish, but he stopped shouting. Seeing this evidence that a truce was on its way, Omri calmed down a bit too.

'Listen. I can't let you see because I can't take you out. You have no idea what would happen if I did. If any of the other children saw you they'd want to grab you and mess you about – you'd hate it, and it would be terribly dangerous too, you'd probably get hurt or killed. You've *got* to lie quiet till school's over. I'm sorry if you're bored but it's your own fault.'

Little Bull thought this over and then he said a most astonishing thing.

'Want Boone.'

'What? Your enemy?'

'Better enemy than alone in dark.'

Patrick had taken Boone out of his pocket. The little cowboy was sitting on his hand. They were gazing at each other. Omri said, 'Boone, Little Bull says he wants you. He's lonely and bored.'

'Well, ain't that jest too bad!' said Boone sarcastically. 'After he tried to kill me, now he's come over all lovey-dovey. Listen, you redskin!' he shouted through cupped hands across the yawing gulf between Patrick and Omri. 'I don't care how lonesome y'are! Ah don't care if'n ya drop down daid! Th' only good Injun's a daid Injun, d'ya hear me?'

Little Bull turned his head haughtily away.

'I think he's lonely too, really,' said Patrick in a whisper. 'He's been crying.'

'Oh no, not again!' said Omri. 'Honestly, Boone – at your age –'

Just then they heard their teacher calling them from the school door.

'Come on, you two! You've not got the day off, you know!'

'Give me your knife,' said Omri to Little Bull on a sudden impulse. 'Then I'll put you together.' With only a moment's hesitation, Little Bull handed over his knife. Omri slipped it into the small breast-pocket of his shirt which was empty and where it wouldn't easily get lost. Then he said to Patrick, 'Let me have Boone.'

'No!'

'Just for the next lesson. Then at lunchtime you can have both of them. They'll keep each other company. They can't do each other much damage in a pocket.'

Reluctantly Patrick handed Boone over. Omri held them one in each hand so they were face to face.

'Be good, you two. Try talking to each other instead of fighting. But whatever you do, don't make any noise.' And he slipped them both into his left-hand pocket and he and Patrick ran back to the school buildings.

Chapter 12
Trouble with Authority

What was left of the morning passed uneventfully. Omri even got a few sums done. By the time the first whiffs of school dinner were beginning to flood through the classrooms, Omri was congratulating himself on a stroke of genius in putting the two little men together. There had not been another peep out of either of them, and when Omri took an opportunity (when the teacher's back was turned) to open his pocket stealthily and peer down into it, he was pleased to see them, sitting in the bottom of it, face to face, apparently having a conversation. They were both gesticulating with their arms – there was too much noise all round for Omri to be able to hear their tiny voices.

He had given some thought to the matter of their dinner. He would separate them for that, one into each pocket, and slip some dry bits of food down to them. Omri let himself play with the wonderful fantasy of what the other kids' reaction would be if he casually brought them out and sat them on the edge of his plate...Funny to think that he would certainly have done it, only a week ago, without thinking about the dangers.

The bell rang at last. There was the usual stampede, and Omri found himself in the queue next to Patrick.

'Come on then, hand them over,' Patrick whispered over his tray as they shuffled towards the fragrant hatches.

'Not *now*, everyone'd see.'

'You said at lunchtime.'

'After lunch.'

'Now. *I* want to feed them.'

'Well, you can have Boone, but I want to feed Little Bull.'

'You said I could have them both!' said Patrick, no longer in a whisper. Others in the queue began to turn their heads.

'Will you shut up?' hissed Omri.

'No,' said Patrick in a loud clear voice. He held out his hand.

Omri felt trapped and furious. He looked into Patrick's eyes and saw what happens even to the nicest people when they want something badly and are determined to get it, come what may. Omri slammed his empty tray down on the floor and, taking Patrick by the wrist, pulled him out of the queue and into a quiet corner of the hall.

'Listen to me,' he grated out between teeth clenched in anger. 'If you let anything happen to Little Bull, I will bash you so hard your teeth will fall out.' (This, of course, is the sort of thing that happens even to the nicest people when they are in a trap.) With that, he groped in his pocket and brought the two little men out. He didn't look at them or say goodbye to them. He just put them carefully into Patrick's hand and walked away.

He had lost his appetite, so he didn't get back in the queue; but Patrick did. He even pushed a bit, he was so eager to get some food to give to the cowboy and the Indian. Omri watched from a distance. He wished now he hadn't been too angry to give Patrick some pretty clear instructions. Like telling him to separate them. Now he thought about it, perhaps it wasn't a good idea to feed them in a pocket. Who wants to eat something that's descended between two layers of cloth and collected bits of dust and fluff? If he'd still had them, he would have taken them to some private place and taken them out to eat properly. Why had he ever brought them to school at all? The dangers here were too awful.

Watching, he suddenly stiffened. Patrick had reached the hatch now, and received his dinner. He almost ran with it to a table – he did try to go to one in the outside row near the windows, but a dinner-lady stopped him and made him sit in the middle of the hall. There were children all round him and on either side. Surely, thought Omri, surely he wasn't going to try to feed them there?

He saw Patrick take a pinch of bread and slip it into his pocket. He wasn't wearing a jacket; the men were in his jeans pocket. Fortunately the jeans were new and loose, but still he had to half stand up to get the bit of bread in; when he was sitting down the people in his pocket must be pretty well squashed against his leg. Omri imagined them trying to eat, held down flat by two thick layers of cloth. He could almost see Patrick imagining it, too. He was frowning uneasily and shifting around in his chair. The girl next to him spoke to him. She was probably telling him not to wriggle. Patrick said something sharp in reply. Omri sucked in his breath. If only Patrick wouldn't draw attention to himself!

Suddenly he gasped. The girl had given Patrick a hard push. He pushed her back. She nearly went off her chair. She stood up and pushed him with all her might, using both hands. He went flying over backwards, half on to the boy on the other side of him, who jumped from his place, spilling part of his dinner. Patrick landed on the floor.

Omri didn't stop to think. He raced towards him across the hall, dodging in and out among the tables. His heart was hammering with terror. If Patrick had fallen on them! Omri had a terrible, fleeting vision of the pocket of Patrick's jeans, with bloodstains spreading – he clamped down on his imagination.

By the time he got there, Patrick was back on his feet, but now the other boy was angry and clearly looking for a fight. The girl on his other side looked ready to clobber him too. Omri pushed between them, but a stout dinner-lady was ahead of him.

''Ere, 'ere, what's goin' on?' she asked, barging in with her big stomach and sturdy arms. She grabbed Patrick in one hand and the boy with the other and kind of dangled them at arm's length and shook them. 'No fighting in 'ere, thank you very much, or it'll be off to the 'ead master's orfice before you can say knife, the 'ole bloomin' pack of you!' She dumped them down,in their separate chairs as if they'd been bags of shopping. They were both thoroughly tousled and red-faced. Omri's eyes shot down to Patrick's thigh. No blood. No movement either, but at least no blood.

Everyone began to eat again as the stout dinner-lady stamped away, tut-tutting as she went. Omri leaned over the back of Patrick's chair and whispered out of a dry mouth, 'Are they all right?'

'How do I know,' said Patrick sulkily. But his hand crept down and delicately explored the slight bump on the top of his leg where his pocket was. Omri held his breath. 'Yeah, they're okay. They're moving,' he muttered.

Omri went out into the playground. He felt too jumpy to stay indoors, or eat, or anything. How would he get them back from Patrick, who, quite obviously, was not a fit person to have charge of them? Nice as he was, as a friend, he just wasn't fit. It must be because he didn't take them seriously yet. He simply didn't seem to realize that they were *people*.

When the bell rang Omri still hadn't come to any decision. He hurried back into school. Patrick was nowhere to be seen. Omri looked round for him frantically. Maybe he'd gone into the washroom to be private and give the men something to eat. Omri went in there and called him softly, but there was no answer. He returned to his place in the classroom. There was no sign of Patrick. And there was no further sign of him till about halfway through the lesson – not one word of which Omri took in, he was so worried.

At last, when the teacher turned her back to write on the board, Patrick slipped round a partition, rushed across the room silently and dropped into his chair.

'Where the *hell* have you been?' asked Omri under his breath.

'In the music-room,' said Patrick smugly. The music-room was not a room at all, but a little alcove off the gym in which the musical instruments were stored, together with some of the bulkier apparatus like the jumping horse. 'I sat under the horse and fed them,' he muttered out of the side of his mouth. 'Only they weren't very hungry.'

'I bet they weren't!' said Omri, 'after all they'd been through!'

'Cowboys and Indians are used to rough treatment,' Patrick retorted. 'Anyway, I left some food in my pocket for later if they want it.'

'It'll get all squashy.'

'Oh, so what? Don't fuss so much, they don't mind!'

'How do you know what they mind?' said Omri hotly, forgetting to whisper. The teacher turned round.

'Oh ho, so there you are, Patrick! And where have you been, may I enquire?'

'Sorry Miss Hilton.'

'I didn't ask if you were sorry. I asked where you'd been.'

Patrick coughed and lowered his head. 'In the wash-room,' he mumbled.

'For nearly twenty minutes? I don't believe you! Are you telling me the truth?' Patrick mumbled something. 'Patrick, answer me. Or I'll send you to the headmaster.'

This was the ultimate threat. The headmaster was very fierce and could make you feel five centimetres high. So Patrick said, 'I was in the music-room, and that's true. And I forgot the time.'

And that's not true, added Omri silently. Miss Hilton was nobody's fool. She knew it too.

'You'd better go and see Mr Johnson,' she said. 'Omri, you go too, chattering away there as usual. Tell him I said you were both disturbing the class and that I'm tired of it.'

They got up silently and walked through the tables, while all the girls giggled and the boys smirked or looked sorry for them, according to whether they liked them or not. Omri glanced at Patrick under his eyebrows. They were for it now.

Outside the headmaster's office they stopped.

'You knock,' whispered Omri.

'No, you,' retorted Patrick.

They dithered about for a few minutes, but it was useless to put it off, so in the end they both knocked together.

'Yes?' came a rather irritable voice from inside.

They edged round the door. Mr Johnson was seated at his large desk, working at some papers. He look up at once.

'Well, you two? What was it this time – fighting in the playground or talking in class?'

'Talking,' they said, and Patrick added, 'And I was late.'

'Why?'

'I just was.'

'Oh, don't waste my time!' snapped Mr Johnson. 'There must have been a reason.'

'I was in the music-room, and I forgot the time,' Patrick repeated.

'I don't remember you being especially musical. What were you doing in the music-room?'

'Playing.'

'Which instrument?' asked Mr Johnson with a touch of sarcasm.

'Just – playing.'

'*With what?*' he asked, raising his voice.

'With a – with –' he glanced at Omri. Omri threw him a warning grimace.

'What are you pulling faces about, Omri? You look as if someone's just stuck a knife into you.'

Omri started to giggle, and that set Patrick off.

'Somebody just did!' spluttered Patrick.

Mr Johnson was in no such jolly mood, however. He was scowling horribly.

'What are you talking about, you silly boy? Stop that idiotic noise!'

Patrick's giggles were getting worse. If they hadn't been where they were, Omri thought, Patrick would have folded up completely.

'Someone – did – stick a knife into him!' hiccupped Patrick, and added, 'A very small one!' His voice went off into a sort of whinny.

Omri had stopped giggling and was staring in awful anticipation at Patrick. When Patrick got into this state he was apt to do and say anything, like someone who's drunk. He took hold of his arm and gave it a sharp shake.

'Shut up!' he hissed.

Mr Johnson got up slowly and came round his desk. Both boys fell back a step, but Patrick didn't stop giggling. On the contrary, it got worse. He seemed to be getting completely helpless. Mr Johnson loomed over him and took him by the shoulder.

'Listen here, my lad,' he said in fearsome tones. 'I want you to pull yourself together this moment and tell me what you meant. If there is any child in this school who so far forgets himself as to stick knives into people, or even pretend to, I want to know about it! Now, who was it?'

'Little – Bull!' Patrick squeaked out. Tears were running down his cheeks.

Omri gasped. 'Don't!'

'Who?' asked Mr Johnson, puzzled.

Patrick didn't answer. He couldn't. He was now speechless with nervous, almost hysterical laughter.

Mr Johnson gave him a shake of his own that rocked him back and forth on his feet like one of those weighted dolls that won't fall down. Then, abruptly, he let him go and strode back to his desk.

'You seem to be quite beyond yourself,' he said sharply. 'I think the only thing I can do is telephone your father.'

Patrick stopped laughing instantly.

110

'Ah, that's better!' said Mr Johnson. 'Now. *Who* did you say had stabbed Omri?'

Patrick stood rigid, like a soldier at attention. He didn't look at Omri, he just stared straight at Mr Johnson.

'I want the truth, Patrick, and I want it now!'

'Little Bull,' said Patrick very clearly and much louder than necessary.

'Little Who?'

'Bull.'

Mr Johnson looked blank, as well he might. 'Is that somebody's nickname, or is this your idea of a joke?'

Patrick gave his head one stiff shake. Omri was staring at him, as if paralysed. Was he going to tell? He knew Patrick was afraid of his father.

'Patrick. I shall ask you once more. Who is this – Little Bull?'

Patrick opened his mouth. Omri clenched his teeth. He was helpless. Patrick said, 'He's an Indian.'

'A what?' asked Mr Johnson. His voice was very quiet now. He didn't sound annoyed any more.

'An Indian.'

Mr Johnson looked at him steadily for some seconds, his chin resting on his hand.

'You are too old to tell those sort of lies,' he said quietly.

'It's not a lie!' Patrick shouted suddenly, making both Omri and Mr Johnson jump. 'It's not a lie! He's a real live Indian!'

To Omri's utter horror, he saw that Patrick was beginning to cry. Mr Johnson saw it too. He was not an unkind man. No headmaster is much good if he can't scare the wits out of children when necessary, but Mr Johnson didn't enjoy making them cry.

'Now then, Patrick, none of that,' he said gruffly. But Patrick misunderstood. He thought he was still saying he didn't believe him.

He now said the words Omri had been dreading most.

'It's true and I can prove it!'

And his hand went to his pocket.

Omri did the only thing possible. He jumped at him and knocked him over. He sat on his chest and pinned his hands to the ground.

'You dare – you dare – you dare –' he ground out between clenched teeth before Mr Johnson managed to drag him off.

'Get out of the room!' he roared.

'I won't!' Omri choked out. He'd be crying himself in a minute, he felt so desperate.

'OUT!'

Omri felt his collar seized. He was almost hiked off his feet. The next thing he knew, he was outside the door and hearing the key turning.

Without stopping to think, Omri hurled himself against the door, kicking and banging with his fists.

'Don't show him, Patrick, don't show him! Patrick, don't, I'll kill you if you show him!' he screamed at the top of his lungs.

Footsteps came running. Through his tears and a sort of red haze, Omri just about saw Mrs Hunt, the headmaster's elderly secretary, bearing down on him. He got in a couple more good kicks and shouts before she had hold of him and, with both arms round his waist, carried him, shrieking and struggling, bodily into her own little office.

The minute she put him down he tried to bolt, but she hung on.

'Omri! Omri! Stop it, calm down, whatever's come over you, you naughty boy!'

'Please don't let him! Go in and stop him!' Omri cried.

'Who? What?'

Before Omri could explain he heard the sound of footsteps from the next room. Suddenly Mr Johnson appeared, holding Patrick by the elbow. The headmaster's face was dead white, and his mouth was partly open. Patrick's head was hung down and his shoulders were heaving with sobs. One look at him told Omri the worst. Patrick had shown the headmaster.

Chapter 13
Art and Accusation

Mr Johnson opened and shut his mouth for several seconds without a sound coming out. At last he croaked: 'Mrs Hunt...I'm afraid I'm unwell...I'm going home to bed...Will you take charge of this child...' His voice dropped to a mumble like an old man's. Omri just caught the words,'...back to their lessons...' Then Mr Johnson let go of Patrick's arm, turned, walked most unsteadily to the door, and then put his hand on it and swayed as if he might fall over.

'Mr Johnson!' said Mrs Hunt in a shocked tone. 'Shall I call a taxi...?'

'No...No...I'll be all right...' And the headmaster, without looking back, tottered out into the corridor.

'Well!' exclaimed Mrs Hunt. 'What*ever* have you been doing to the poor man?'

Neither of them answered. Omri was staring at Patrick, or rather, at his pocket. Patrick's shoulders were heaving and he was not looking at anybody. Mrs Hunt was obviously flummoxed.

'Well. You'd better go to the wash-room and wash your faces, both of you, and then go back to your classroom as fast as you can toddle,' she said in her funny old-fashioned way. 'Run along!'

They needed no second telling. Neither of them said a word until they were in the boys' wash-room. Patrick went straight to a basin and began running the cold water. He splashed some on to his face, getting his collar soaked. Omri stood watching him. Obviously he was as upset as Omri, if not more so. Once again Omri felt their friendship trembling on the edge of destruction. He drew a deep breath.

'You showed him,' he said at last in a trembling voice.

Patrick said nothing. He dried his face on the roller-towel. He was still gasping the way one does when one has been crying.

'Give them back to me. Both of them.'

Patrick reached slowly into his pocket. He put his closed hand backwards. Omri looked as his fingers slowly opened. Little Bull and Boone were sitting there, absolutely terrified. They were actually clinging to each other. Even Little Bull was hiding his face and they were both trembling.

With infinite slowness and care, so as not to frighten them more, Omri took them into his own hand. 'It's all right,' he whispered, bringing them near to his face. 'Please. It's all right.' Then he put them carefully in his pocket and said to Patrick in a low voice, 'You bloody, stupid fool.'

Patrick turned. His face gave Omri more of a jolt than Mr Johnson's had. It was white-mottled-red, with swollen eyes.

'I had to!' he said. 'I had to! He'd have phoned my dad! They'd have made me tell in the end. Anyhow, he didn't believe in them. He thought he was seeing things. He just stood there, gaping at them. He didn't even touch them. When they moved he gave a yell and then I thought he was going to fall over. He went white as a ghost. You saw. He didn't believe his eyes, Omri, honest! He'll think he dreamed it!' Omri went on looking at him stonily. 'Can't I – can't I have Boone?' asked Patrick in a small voice.

'No.'

'Please! I'm sorry I told – I *had* to!'

'They're not safe with you. You *use* them. They're people. You can't use people.'

Patrick didn't ask again. He gave one more hiccupping sob and went out.

Omri took the little men out of his pocket again and

lifted them to his face. Boone was lying flat on his front, holding his big hat down over his ears as if trying to shut out the world. But Little Bull stood up.

'Big man shout. Give fear!' he said angrily. 'Small ears – big noise – no good!'

'I know. I'm sorry,' said Omri. 'But it's okay now. I'm going to take you home.'

'What about wife?'

His promise! Omri had forgotten all about that.

Another Indian! Another live little person to worry about...Omri had heard about people going grey-haired almost overnight if they had too much worry. He felt it might easily happen to him. He thought back to the time, only a few days ago, when this had all started and he had fondly imagined it was going to be the greatest fun anybody had ever had. Now he realized that it was more like a nightmare.

But Little Bull was looking at him challengingly. He *had* promised.

'Right after school,' he said, 'we'll go to the shop.'

There was still another hour of lessons to be got through. Fortunately it was two periods of art. In the art-room you could go away into a corner and even sit with your back turned to the teacher if you liked. Omri went to the furthest and darkest corner.

'Omri, don't try to draw there,' said the art teacher. 'You're in your own light – it's bad for your eyes.'

'I'm going to draw something huge anyway,' said Omri.

All the others sat near the long windows. He was quite alone, and if the teacher approached him he would hear her feet on the bare floor. He suddenly felt he must – he simply *must* get a little fun out of this somehow. He cautiously fished Little Bull and Boone out of his pocket.

They stood on the sheet of white drawing paper as if on a stretch of snow, and looked about them.

'This school place?' asked Little Bull.

'Yes. Sshhh!'

'Sure don't look much like the school Ah went to!' exclaimed Boone. 'Whar's the rows o' desks? Whar's the slate 'n' bit o' chalk? Why ain't the teacher talkin'?'

'We're doing art. We can sit where we like. She doesn't talk much, she just lets us get on with it,' replied Omri in the softest whisper he could possibly manage.

'Art, eh?' asked Boone, brightening up. 'Say, that wuz mah best subject! Ah wuz allus top in art, on'y thing Ah wuz any good at! Still draw a mite when Ah gits a chance, if'n ain't nobody around t'laugh at me.' He reached into the pocket of his own tiny jeans and fished out a stub of pencil almost too small to see. 'Kin Ah draw a mite on yor paper?' he asked.

Omri nodded. Boone strode to the very centre of the paper, looked all round at the white expanse stretching away from him in every direction, and gave a deep sigh of satisfaction. Then he knelt down and began to draw.

Little Bull and Omri watched. From the microscopic point of Boone's pencil there developed a most amazing scene. It was a prairie landscape, with hills and cactus and a few tufts of sage-brush. Boone sketched in, with sure strokes, some wooden buildings such as Omri had often seen on cowboy films – a saloon with a swinging sign reading 'Golden Dollar Saloon' in twirly writing; a post-office and general store, a livery stable, and a stone house with a barred window and a sign saying 'Jail'. Then, moving swiftly on his knees, as it were from one end of his 'street' to another, Boone drew in the foreground – figures of men and women, wagons, horses, dogs, and all the trappings of a little town.

From Boone's point of view, he was drawing something quite large, making the best use of his vast piece of paper; but from Omri's, the drawing was minute, perfect in its detailing but smaller than any human hand could possibly have made it. He and Little Bull watched, fascinated.

'Boone, you're an artist!' Omri breathed at last, when Boone had even made the mud on the unpaved street look real. Little Bull grunted.

'But not like real place,' he said.

Boone didn't trouble to answer, in fact he was so absorbed he probably didn't hear. But Omri frowned. Then he understood. Of course! Boone's town was part of an America which was not thought of during Little Bull's time.

'Boone,' he whispered, bending his head down. 'What year is it – your town – your time?'

'Last time Ah saw a newspaper it was 1889,' said Boone. 'There! that's muh drawin'. Not bad, huh?'

'It's absolutely brilliant,' said Omri, enthralled.

'Omri!'

Omri jumped. His two hands instantly cupped themselves over the two men.

From the other side of the room, the teacher said, 'I see it's no use trying to stop you chattering. You even do it when you're alone! Bring me your picture.'

For a moment Omri hesitated. But it was too marvellous to be passed up! He scooped the men into his pocket and picked up the sheet of paper. For once he wouldn't stop to think. He'd just enjoy himself.

He carried Boone's drawing to the teacher and put it innocently into her hand.

What happened then made up for a good deal of the worry and general anxiety the little men had caused him. First she just glanced. At a *glance,* the drawing in the middle of the paper just looked like a scribble or a smudge.

'I thought you said you were going to do something huge,' she said with a laugh. 'This isn't much more than a –'

And then she took a second, much closer, look.

She stared without speaking for about two minutes, while Omri felt inside him the beginnings of a huge, gleeful, uncontrollable laugh. Abruptly the teacher, who had been perched on a desk, stood up and went to a cupboard. Omri was not surprised when she turned round to see a magnifying glass in her hand.

She put the paper down on a table and bent over it, with the glass poised. She examined the drawing for several minutes more. Her face was something to see! Some of the nearest children had become aware that something unusual was going on, and were also craning to see what the teacher was looking at so attentively. Omri stood with the same innocent look on his face, waiting, the laugh slowly rising inside him. Fun? This *was* fun, if you liked! *This* was what he'd been imagining!

The teacher looked at him. Her face was not quite as stunned as Mr Johnson's had been, but it was an absolute picture of bafflement.

'Omri,' she said. 'How in the name of all that's holy did you *do* this?'

'I like drawing small,' said Omri quite truthfully.

'*Small!* This isn't small! It's tiny! It's infinitesimal! It's microscopic!' Her voice was rising higher with every word. Several of the other children had now stood up and were crowding round the paper, peering at it in absolute stupefaction. Small gasps and exclamations of wonder were rising on all sides. Omri's held-in laugh threatened to explode.

The teacher's eyes were now narrow with astonishment – and doubt.

'Show me,' she said, 'the pencil you used.'

This took Omri aback, but only for a second.

'I left it over there. I'll just go and get it,' he said sweetly.

He walked back to his table, his hand in his pocket. With his back turned he bent over, apparently searching the top of the table. Then he turned round, smiling, holding something cupped in his hand. He walked back.

'Here it is,' he said, and held out his hand.

Everyone bent forward. The art teacher took hold of his hand and pulled it towards her. 'Are you having me on, Omri? There's nothing there!'

'Yes there is.'

She peered close until he could feel her warm breath on his hand.

'Don't breathe hard,' said Omri, his laugh now trembling on his very lips. 'You'll blow it away. Maybe you'd see it better through the magnifying glass,' he added kindly.

Slowly she raised the glass into position. She looked through.

'Can I see? Is it there? Can I look?' clamoured the other children. All except Patrick. He was sitting by himself, not paying attention to the crowd around Omri.

The art teacher lowered the glass. Her eyes were dazed.

'I don't believe it.'

'It's there.'

'How did you pick it up?'

'Ah. Well, that's a bit of a secret method I have.'

'Yes,' she said. 'Yes, it must be. And you wouldn't feel like telling us?'

'No,' said Omri in a trembly voice. His laugh was on the very brink – it was going to burst out – 'May I go to the loo?'

'Yes,' she said in a dazed voice. 'Go on.'

He took the drawing back and tottered to the door. He managed to get outside before the laugh actually blew out. But it was so loud, so overpowering that he was obliged to go right out into the playground. There he sank on to a bench and laughed till he felt quite weak. Her face! He had never enjoyed anything so much in his whole life. It had been worth it.

The bell rang. School was over. Omri brought out the men and held them up.

'Guys,' he said (after all, they were both Americans), 'I enjoyed that. Thank you. Now we're going to the shop.'

Omri ran all the way to Yapp's and was there before most other children had even left the school. In ten minutes the place would be full of them, buying crisps and sweets and toys and comics. Just now he had it to himself, and he had to make the most of the few minutes he had.

He went directly to the corner where the boxes of plastic figures were kept, and stood with his back to the main counter. He was still holding Little Bull and Boone in his hand, and he put them down among the figures in the cowboys-and-Indians box. He hadn't reckoned on Boone's sensitive nature, however.

'Holy catfish! Look at all them dead bodies!' he squeaked, hiding his eyes. 'There musta bin a massacree!'

'Not dead,' said Little Bull scornfully. 'Plass-tick.' He kicked a plastic cowboy aside. 'Too many,' he said to Omri. 'You find women. I choose.'

'You'll have to be quick,' said Omri in a low voice. He was already rummaging through the box, picking out the Indian women. There were very few. Of the five he found, one was clearly old, and two had babies tied on their backs in parcels laced up like boots.

'You don't fancy one with a baby, I suppose?'

Little Bull gave him a look.

'No – I thought not,' said Omri hastily. 'Well, what about these?'

He stood the two other figures on the edge of the table. Little Bull jumped down and faced them. He looked carefully first at one, then at the other. They both looked the same to Omri, except that one had a yellow dress and the other a blue. Each had a black pigtail and a headband with a single feather, and mocassins on her feet.

Little Bull looked up. His face showed furious disappointment.

'No good,' he said. 'This one from own tribe – taboo. This one ugly. Chief must have beautiful wife!'

'But there aren't any others.'

120

'Many, many plass-tick! You look good, find other!'

Omri rummaged frantically, right to the bottom of the box. Kids were beginning to come into the shop.

He had almost despaired when he saw her. She lay face down on the very bottom of the box, half-hidden by two cowboys on horses. He pulled her out. She was the same as the others (apparently) except that she wore a red dress. They obviously all came out of the same mould, because they were all in the same position, as if walking. If the others were ugly, so would this one be.

Without much hope, he set her before Little Bull.

He stood staring at her. The shop was getting busy now. At any moment somebody would come up behind him, wanting to buy a plastic figure.

'Well?' asked Omri impatiently.

For another five seconds Little Bull stared. Then, without speaking a word, he nodded his head.

Omri didn't wait for him to change his mind. He scooped him and Boone back into his pocket and, picking up the approved figure, made his way to the counter.

'Just this one, please,' he said.

Mr Yapp was looking at him. A very odd look.

'Are you sure you only want the one?' he asked.

'Yes.'

Mr Yapp took the plastic figure, dropped it into a bag, and gave it back to Omri.

'Ten p.'

Omri paid and left the shop. Suddenly he felt a hand on his shoulder. He spun round. It was Mr Yapp. The look on his face was now not odd at all, but red and angry.

'Now you can hand over the two you stole.'

Omri stood aghast. 'I didn't steal any!'

'Don't add lying to your faults, my lad! I watched you put them in your pocket – a cowboy and an Indian.'

Omri's mouth hung open. He thought he was going to be sick.

'I didn't – ' he tried to say, but no words came out.

'Turn out your pockets.'

'They're mine!' Omri managed to gasp.

'A likely story! And I suppose you brought them out to help you choose the new one?'

'Yes!'

'Ha, ha, ha,' said Mr Yapp heavily. 'Come on, stop playing around. I lose hundreds of pounds' worth of stuff a year to you thieving kids. When I do catch one of you red-handed, I'm not likely to let it pass – I know your sort – if I let you off, you'd be boasting to your pals at school how easy it is to get away with it, and most likely back you'd come tomorrow for another pocketful!'

Omri was now fighting back tears. Quite a crowd had collected, much like the crowd in the art-room – some of the same people, even – but his feelings were no longer so pleasant. He wished he could die or disappear.

'It's no good trying to get round me by crying!' shouted Mr Yapp. 'Give me them back – right now, or I'll call the police!'

All at once Patrick was beside him.

'They're his,' he said. 'I know they're his because he showed them to me at school. A cowboy with a white stetson hat and an Indian in a Chief's headdress. He told me he was coming to buy a new one. Omri wouldn't steal.'

Mr Yapp let go of Omri and looked at Patrick. He knew Patrick quite well, because it happened that Patrick's brother had once been his paper-boy.

'Will you vouch for him, then?'

'Course I will!' said Patrick staunchly. 'I'm telling you, I saw 'em both this afternoon.'

But still the shopkeeper wasn't convinced. 'Let's see if they fit your description,' he said.

Omri, who had been staring at Patrick as at some miraculous deliverer, felt his stomach drop into his shoes once more. But then he had an idea.

He reached both hands into his pockets. Then he held out one hand slowly, still closed, and everyone looked at it, though it was actually empty. The other hand he lifted to his mouth as if to stifle a cough, and whispered into it, 'Lie still! Don't move! *Plastic*!' Then he put both hands before him and opened them.

The men played along beautifully. There they lay, side by side, stiff and stark, as like lifeless plastic figures as could possibly be. In any case Omri was taking no chances. He gave Mr Yapp just long enough to see that they were dressed as Patrick had said before closing his fingers again.

Mr Yapp grunted.

'Those aren't from my shop anyhow,' he said. 'All my Indian Chiefs are sitting down, and that sort of cowboy is always on a horse. Well, I'm sorry, lad. You'll have to excuse me, but you must admit, it did look suspicious.'

Omri managed a sickly smile. The crowd were melting away. Mr Yapp shuffled back into the shop. Omri and Patrick were left alone on the pavement.

'Thanks,' said Omri. It came out as croaky as a frog.

'That's okay. Have a Toffo.'

They had a Toffo each and walked along side by side. After a while Omri said, 'A man's gotta chew what a man's gotta chew.'

They gave each other a quick grin.

'Let's give them some.'

They stopped, took the men out, and gave them each some bits of the chocolate covering on the Toffo.

'That's a reward,' said Patrick, 'for playing dead.'

Little Bull then naturally demanded to know what it had all been about, and the boys explained as well as they could. Little Bull was quite intrigued.

'Man say that Omri steal Little Bull?'

'Yes.'

'And Boone?'

Omri nodded.

'Omri fool to steal Boone!' roared Little Bull, laughing. Boone, stuffing himself with chocolate, gave him a dirty look.

'Where woman?' Little Bull asked eagerly.

'I've got her.'

'When make real?'

'Tonight.'

Patrick gave him a look of pure longing. But he didn't say anything. They walked along again. They were getting near Omri's house.

Omri was thinking. After a while he said, 'Patrick, what about you staying the night?'

Patrick's face lit up like a bulb.

'Could I? And see –'

'Yes.'

'Wow! Thanks!'

They ran the rest of the way home.

Chapter 14
The Fateful Arrow

Omri's brothers were already sitting at the tea-table when the two boys rushed in.

'Hi! What's for tea?' Omri asked automatically.

Gillon and Adiel didn't answer. Adiel had a funny smirk on his face. Omri hardly noticed.

'Let's make a sandwich and eat it upstairs,' he suggested to Patrick.

They slapped some peanut butter on bread, poured mugs of milk, and hurried up the stairs to Omri's room, whispering all the way.

'How long does it take?'

'Only a few minutes.'

'Can I see her?'

'Wait till we get upstairs!'

Omri opened the door – and stopped dead.

The white medicine-cupboard was gone.

'Wh – where is it?' gasped Patrick.

Omri didn't say a word. He turned and rushed downstairs again, with Patrick behind him.

'Okay, where've you hidden it?' he shouted as soon as he burst into the kitchen.

'I don't know what you're referring to,' said Adiel loftily.

'Yes you damn well do! You've nicked my cupboard!'

'And supposing I did. It was only to teach you a lesson. You're always nicking my things and hiding them. Now you'll see how funny it *isn't.*'

'When did I last take anything of yours? Tell me one thing in the last *month!*'

'My football shorts,' said Adiel promptly.

'I never touched your lousy shorts, I already swore I hadn't!'

'I had to miss games again today because I didn't have them, *and* I got a detention for it, so you can be grateful I'm only punishing you tit-for-tat and not bashing you in,' said Adiel with maddening calm.

Omri felt so furious he even wondered, for a moment, whether it was worth bashing *Adiel* in. But Adiel was enormous and it was hopeless. So after gazing at him for another moment with hate-filled eyes, Omri turned and dashed upstairs again, almost falling over Patrick on the way.

'What'll you do?'

'Look for it, of course!'

He was turning Adiel's room upside down like a madman when Adiel, slowly mounting the stairs in the direction of his homework, heard the racket and came running.

He stood in the doorway looking at the shambles of pulled-out drawers, degutted cupboards and furniture pulled awry.

'You LITTLE SWINE!' he howled, and dived at Omri. Omri fell to the ground with Adiel on top.

'I'll tear everything – you've got to pieces – till you give it back to me!' he shouted in jerks as Adiel shook and pummelled him.

'Then cough up my shorts!'

'I HAVEN'T GOT YOUR BLOODY SHORTS!' screamed Omri.

'Are these them?' asked a small voice in the background.

Adiel and Omri stopped fighting, and Adiel, sitting astride, twisted his neck to see. Patrick was just lifting a crumpled navy-blue object from behind a radiator.

Omri felt the anger go out of Adiel.

'Oh... Yes. It is, as a matter of fact. How did they get there..?' But Omri knew perfectly well how; Adiel had hung them there to dry and they'd dropped off backwards.

Adiel scrambled up looking distinctly sheepish. He even helped Omri to his feet.

'Well, but you have hidden things in the past,' he mumbled. 'How was I to know?'

'Can I have my cupboard now?'

'Yeah, it's up in the attic. I piled a whole lot of stuff on it.'

Omri and Patrick took the stairs to the attic two at a time.

They found the cupboard quite quickly, under a heap of bits and pieces. But Omri had carried it down to his room again before he made the fatal discovery.

'The key!'

The little twisted key with its red satin ribbon was missing.

Once again Omri ran into Adiel's room, to find Adiel uncomplainingly putting things straight.

'What happened to the key?'

'What key?'

'There was a key in the cupboard door – with a red ribbon!'

'I didn't notice.'

They went out and closed the door. Omri was now feeling desperate.

'We've got to find it. It doesn't work without the key.'

They searched the attic till suppertime. Never had Omri so clearly seen the point of all his mother's urgings to tidy up and keep everything in its proper place. The attic was just a sort of glory-hole, where they could play and leave a total mess, and that was what they always did, only clearing spaces when they needed them for a new layout or for some special game. And their way of clearing was just to shove things aside into ever-more-chaotic heaps.

Underneath the heaps were all the myriad little oddments which were small enough to filter through the bigger things – marbles, wheels of Matchbox cars, bits of Leggo, small tools, parachute men, cards, and so on and so on, plus all sorts of fragments which could have been almost anything. At first they just raked through everything. But after a while Omri realized that they would have to clear up systematically. Otherwise it was like the old saying about looking for a needle in a haystack.

He found some boxes and they began sorting things into them – Leggo here, parts of games there, water-pistols, tricks and novelties in another. Bigger things they stacked neatly on to what his father rather sarcastically called 'the shelves provided', which normally stood empty since everything was on the floor.

In an amazingly short time the floor was clear except for a few odd things they hadn't found homes for, and a great deal of mud, dust and sand.

'Where did all this come from?' asked Patrick.

'Oh, Gillon brought up boxes of it from the garden to make a desert scene,' said Omri. 'Months ago. We might as well sweep it up.' He looked round. Despite his anxiety about the key, he felt a certain pride. The room looked entirely different – there was real playing-space now.

He went downstairs and fetched a broom, a dustpan and a soft brush.

'We'll have to do this carefully,' he said. 'It'd be terrible if we threw it away with the sand.'

'We could sieve it,' suggested Patrick.

'That's a good idea! In the garden.'

They carried the sand out in a cardboard box and Omri borrowed his father's large garden sieve. Omri held it and Patrick spooned in the sand and earth with a trowel. Several small treasures came to light, including a ten p. piece. But no key.

Omri was in despair. He and Patrick sat down on the lawn under a tree and he took the two little men out of his pocket.

'Where woman?' Little Bull asked instantly.

'Never mind the wimmin, whur's the vittles?' asked the every-hungry Boone grumpily.

Omri and Patrick fed them some more Toffo, and, with a deep sense of misery, Omri produced the plastic Indian woman from his pocket. Little Bull stopped chewing chocolate crumbs the moment he saw her and gazed in rapture. It was obvious he was half in love with her already. He reached out a hand and tenderly touched her plastic hair.

'Make real! Now!' he breathed.

'I can't,' said Omri.

'Why can't?' asked Little Bull sharply.

'The magic's gone.'

Now Boone stopped eating too, and he and Little Bull exchanged a frightened look.

'Ya mean – ya cain't send us back?' asked Boone in an awe-stricken whisper. 'Never? We got to live in a giants' world for *ever?*'

It was clear that Little Bull had been explaining matters.

'Don't you like being with us?' asked Patrick.

'Wal...Ah wouldn't want to hurt yer feelin's none,' said Boone. 'But jest think how you'd feel if Ah wuz as big to you as you are to me!'

'Little Bull?' asked Omri.

Little Bull dragged his eyes away from the plastic figure and fixed them – like little bright crumbs of black glass – on Omri.

'Omri good,' he pronounced at last. 'But Little Bull Indian brave – Indian *Chief*. How be brave, how be chief with no other Indians?'

Omri opened his mouth. If he had not lost the key, he might have rashly offered to bring to life an entire tribe of Indians, simply to keep Little Bull contented. Through his mind flashed the knowledge of what this meant. It wasn't the fun, the novelty, the magic that mattered any more.

What mattered was that Little Bull should be happy. For that, he would take on almost anything.

They all sat quietly on the lawn. There seemed nothing more to say.

A movement near the back of the house caught Omri's eye. It was his mother, coming out to hang up some wet clothes. He thought she moved as if she were tired and fed up. She stood for a moment on the back balcony, looking at the sky. Then she sighed and began pegging the clothes to the line.

On impulse Omri got up and went over to her.

'You – you haven't found anything of mine, have you?' he asked.

'No – I don't think so. What have you lost?'

But Omri was too ashamed to admit he'd lost the key she'd told him to be so careful of. 'Oh, nothing much,' he said.

He went back to Patrick, who was showing the men an ant. Boone was trying to pat its head like a dog, but it wasn't very responsive.

'Well,' Omri said, 'we might as well make the best of things. Why not bring the horses out and give the fellows a ride?'

This cheered everyone up and Omri ran up and brought the two ponies down carefully in an empty box. Next Patrick stamped a small patch of the lawn hard to give the horses a really good gallop. Quite a large black beetle alighted on the flattened part, and Little Bull shot it dead with an arrow. This cheered him up a bit more (though not much). While the ponies grazed the fresh grass, he kept giving great love-sick sighs and Omri knew he was thinking of the woman.

'Maybe you'd rather not stay the night now,' Omri said to Patrick.

'I want to,' said Patrick. 'If you don't mind.'

Omri felt too upset to care one way or the other. When

130

they were called in to supper he noticed that Adiel was trying to be friendly, but he wouldn't speak to him. Afterwards Adiel took him aside.

'What's up with you now? I'm trying to be nice. You got your silly old cupboard back.'

'It's no good without the key.'

'Well, I'm sorry! It must have dropped out on the way up to the attic.'

On the way *up* to the attic! Omri hadn't thought of that. 'Will you help me find it?' he asked eagerly. 'Please! It's terribly important!'

'Oh...all right then.'

The four of them hunted for half an hour. They didn't find it.

After that, Gillon and Adiel had to go out to some function at school, so Patrick and Omri had the television to themselves. They took out the two men and explained this new magic, and then they all watched together. First came a film about animals, which absolutely transfixed both the little men. Then a Western came on. Omri thought they ought to switch off, but Boone, in particular, set up such a hullabaloo that eventually Omri said, 'Oh – all right. Just for ten minutes, then.'

Little Bull was seated cross-legged on Omri's knee, while Boone, who had somehow gravitated back to Patrick, preferred to stand in his breast-pocket, leaning his elbows along the pocket top with his hat on the back of his head, chewing a lump of tobacco he had had on him. Patrick, who'd heard something of cowboys' habits, said, 'Don't you dare spit! There are no spittoons here, you know.'

'Lemme listen to 'em talkin', willya?' said Boone. 'Ah jest cain't git over how they *talk*!'

Before the ten minutes was up, the Indians in the film started getting the worst of it. It was the usual sequence in which the pioneers' wagons are drawn into a circle and the Indians are galloping round uttering savage whoops while the outnumbered men of the wagon train fire muzzle-loading guns at them through the wagon wheels. Omri could sense Little Bull was getting restive and tense. As brave after brave bit the dust, he suddenly leapt to his feet.

'No good pictures!' he shouted.

'Watcha talkin' about, Injun?' Boone yelled tauntingly across the chasm dividing him from Little Bull. 'That's how it was! Mah maw and paw wuz in a fight like thet'n – mah paw tole me he done shot near'nuff fifteen-twenny of them dirty savages!'

'White men move on to land! Use water! Kill game!'

'So what? Let the best man win! And we won! Yippee!' he added as another television Indian went down with his horse on top of him.

Omri was looking at the screen when it happened. In a lull on the soundtrack he heard a thin faint whistling sound, and heard Boone grunt. He looked back at Boone swiftly, and his blood froze. The cowboy had an arrow sticking out of his chest.

For a couple of seconds he remained upright in Patrick's breast pocket. Then, quite slowly, he fell forward.

Omri had often marvelled at the way people in films, particularly girls and women, were given to letting out loud screams at dramatic or awful moments. Now he felt one rise in his own throat, and would have let it out only that Little Bull cried out first.

Patrick, who had not noticed anything amiss till now, looked at Little Bull, saw where his bow-arm was still pointing, and looked down at his own pocket. Over the top of it Boone hung, head down, as limp as a piece of knotted string.

'Boone! Boone!'

'No!' snapped Omri. 'Don't touch him!'

Ignoring Little Bull, who tumbled down his trouser-leg to the floor as he moved, Omri very carefully lifted Boone clear between finger and thumb, and laid him across the palm of his hand. The cowboy lay face up with the arrow still sticking out of his chest.

'Is he – dead?' whispered Patrick in horror.

'I don't know.'

'Shouldn't we take the arrow out?'

'We can't. Little Bull must.'

With infinite care and slowness, Omri laid his hand on the carpet. Boone lay perfectly still. With such a tiny body it was impossible to be sure whether the arrow was stuck in where his heart was, or a little higher up towards his shoulder – the arrow-shaft was so fine you could only make it out by the minute cluster of feathers.

'Little Bull. Come here.'

Omri's voice was steely, a voice Mr Johnson himself might have envied – it commanded obedience.

Little Bull, scrambling to his feet after his fall, walked unsteadily to Omri's hand.

'Get up there and see if you've killed him.'

Without a word, Little Bull climbed on to the edge of Omri's hand and knelt down beside the prostrate Boone. He laid his ear against his chest just below the arrow. He listened, then straightened up, but without looking at either of the boys.

'Not killed,' he said sullenly.

Omri felt his breath go out in relief.

'Take the arrow out. Carefully. If he dies now, it'll be doubly your fault.'

Little Bull put one hand on Boone's chest with his fingers on either side of the arrow, and with the other took hold of the shaft where it went into Boone's body.

'Blood come. Need stop up hole.'

Omri's mother kept boxes of tissues in every room, mainly so nobody would have an excuse to sit sniffing. Patrick jumped up and took one, tearing off a tiny corner and rolling it into a wad no bigger than a pinhead.

'Now it's got germs on it from your hand,' said Omri.

'Where's the disinfectant?'

'In the bathroom cupboard. Don't let my mum see you!'

While Patrick was gone, Omri sat motionless and silent, his eyes fixed on Little Bull, still poised to pull out the arrow.

After a very long minute, the Indian muttered something.

Omri bent his head low. 'What?'

'Little Bull sorry.'

Omri straightened up, his heart cold and untouched.

'You'll be a lot sorrier if you don't save him,' was all he said.

Patrick raced back with the bottle of Listerine. He poured a drop into the lid and dipped the little ball of tissue into it. Then he held the cap close to Little Bull.

'Go on,' Omri ordered. 'Pull it out.'

Little Bull seemed to brace himself. Then he began to tremble.

'Little Bull not do. Little Bull not doctor. Get doctor back. He know make wound good.'

'We can't,' said Omri shortly. 'The magic's gone. You must do it. Do it now. Now, Little Bull!'

Again the Indian stiffened, closing his hand tightly around the arrow. Slowly and steadily he drew it out, and threw it aside. Then, as the blood welled out over Boone's check shirt, Little Bull swiftly squeezed the liquid out of the ball of tissue and pressed it against the wound.

'Use your knife now. Cut the dirty shirt away.'

Without hesitating, Little Bull obeyed. Boone lay still. His face under its tan had turned ashy grey.

'We need a bandage,' said Patrick.

'There's nothing we could use, and we can't move him to wrap it round him. We'll have to use a tiny bit of sticking plaster.'

Again Patrick went to the bathroom. Again Omri, Little Bull and Boone were left alone. Little Bull knelt now with his hands loose on his thighs, his head down. His shoulders rose and fell once. Was he sobbing? With shame, or fear? Or – could it be – sorrow?

Patrick returned with the box of Band Aid and a pair of nail scissors. He cut out a square big enough to cover the whole of Boone's chest, and Little Bull stuck it on with great care and even, Omri thought, tenderness.

'Now,' said Omri, 'take off your Chief's cloak and cover him up warmly.'

This, too, Little Bull did uncomplainingly.

'We'll take him upstairs and put him to bed,' said Omri. 'Oh, God, I wish we had that key and I could get that doctor back!'

As they walked slowly upstairs, he told Patrick about the First-World-War soldier he had brought to life to tend Little Bull's leg-wound.

'We've got to find that key!' said Patrick. 'We've just got to!'

Little Bull, still at Boone's side on Omri's hand, said nothing.

In Omri's room, Patrick made a bed for the cowboy from a folded handkerchief and another woollen square cut from Omri's sweater. Omri slipped a bit of thin stiff card between Boone and his own hand and on this, he transferred the wounded man without too much disturbance which might have started the bleeding again. He was still unconscious.

Little Bull silently stood by. Suddenly he moved. Reaching up, he snatched off his Chief's headdress and threw it violently on to the ground. Before Omri could stop him, he began jumping on it, and in a second or two all the beautiful tall turkey-feathers were bent and broken.

Leaving it lying there, Little Bull took off across the carpet, running as hard as he could over the deep woollen tufts, stumbling sometimes but running always in the direction of the seed-box and his home. Patrick moved, but Omri said quietly, 'Let him alone.'

Chapter 15
Underfloor Adventure

Omri and Patrick decided they must take it in turns to sit up all night with Boone. This was going to be tricky because of light showing under the door, but Omri unearthed the lumpy remains of a candle he had made himself from a candle-making kit.

'We can put it behind the dressing-up crate. Then the light won't show.'

They got into their pyjamas. Patrick was supposed to be sleeping on a folding-bed, so they got it ready to avoid arousing suspicion.

When Omri's mother came in to kiss them goodnight, they were both in bed, apparently reading. The fact that Omri was reading in semi-darkness was nothing unusual, she was always on at him about it.

'Oh Omri! Why *won't* you switch your bedside light on? You'll ruin your eyes.'

'It doesn't work,' said Omri promptly.

'Yes it does. Daddy fixed it this morning. You know what was wrong with it?'

'What?' asked Omri impatiently, wishing, for once, that she would go.

'That wretched rat of Gillon's had made a nest under the floorboards and lined it with bits of insulation it gnawed off the wires. It's a wonder it didn't electrocute itself.'

Omri sat up sharply.

'Do you mean it's got loose?'

His mother gave a lopsided smile. 'Where have you been keeping yourself? It's been loose since last night – haven't you noticed Gillon frantically looking for it? It seems to have taken up residence under your bed.'

'Under my bed!' Omri yelled, leaping out of it and dropping to his knees.

'It's no use looking for it. I mean right under – the floor. Daddy caught a glimpse of it today when he had the boards up, but he couldn't catch it, of course. It's a matter of waiting till it comes out for food, and then –'

But Omri wasn't listening. A rat! That was all they needed.

'Mum, we've got to get it! We've got to!'

'Why? You're not scared of it, are you?'

'Me – scared of that stupid rat? Of course not! But we've got to catch it!' said Omri, feebly yet desperately. 'It might run across my face –' He felt wild and furious. How could Gillon have let the thing go? The perils that a rat presented to his little men simply turned his blood cold. And why, of all rooms in the house, should it have chosen his?

He was tearing frantically at the edge of the carpet, trying to pull it back, when his mother hiked him to his feet.

'Omri, that carpet and those floorboards have been taken up once today, they've been put back once and everything tidied up. Rat or no rat, I'm not going through it all again tonight. Now get into bed and go to sleep.'

'But –'

'*Into bed*, I said. Now!'

When she used that tone, there was no arguing with her. Omri got into bed, was kissed, and watched the light go off and the door close. As soon as her footsteps had faded, he leapt up again and so did Patrick.

'Now we must definitely stay awake all night. We mustn't close our eyes for a moment,' said Omri.

He was hunting through his ancient collection of book-matches for one out of which his father had *not* cut the matches. At last he found one, and lit the candle. They very gently moved Boone's bed out of hiding on to the bed-side table, set the candle beside it, and sat one on each side, watching Boone's dreadfully ill-looking face. The pink square of sticking plaster moved fractionally up and down as he breathed – you could hardly see it. It was like watching the long hand of a clock moving – only the strongest concentration enabled them to detect the faint motion.

'Hadn't we better move the seed-box up here too?' whispered Patrick.

In the moment when Little Bull had shot Boone, Omri had almost been angry enough to have *fed* him to the rat; but now, his fury had cooled. He certainly didn't want anything awful to happen to him.

'Yes, let's.'

Between them they cleared a place on the table and lifted the seedbox, with its longhouse, fireplace and hitching posts, up out of reach of prowling rodents.

'Careful. Don't frighten the ponies.'

The ponies, however, were getting used to being carried about, and hardly looked up from munching the little piles of grass-cuttings. There was no sign of life from the longhouse.

There followed a timeless period of just sitting there silently, their eyes fixed on Boone's still figure in the flickering candlelight. Omri began to feel light-headed after a bit: the candle flame went fuzzy and Boone's body seemed to vibrate as he stared at it. At the very back of his mind, something else was nagging, nagging... He didn't ask himself what this was, because he had a superstitious feeling that if he let his mind wander from Boone, even for a minute, Boone would slip away into death. It was as if only Omri's will – and Patrick's – were keeping that tiny, fragile heart beating.

Suddenly, though, a thought – like a landscape lit up by lightning – flashed to the forefront of Omri's brain. He sat up, his eyes wide open and his breath held.

'Patrick!'

Patrick jumped. He'd been half asleep.

'What?'

138

'The key! I know where it is!'

'Where? Where?'

'*Right under my feet*. It must have dropped through the floorboards when Dad opened them. There's nowhere else it could be.'

Patrick gazed at him in admiration, but also in dismay.

'How are we going to get it?' he whispered.

'We'll have to take up the carpet first. Maybe Dad didn't nail all the boards down.'

Moving very quietly, they managed to lift one corner of Omri's bed and kick back the edge of carpet from underneath. Another bit was under the bedside table leg, and that was tricky, but they shifted it between them in the end. Carefully they folded the corner of carpet back on itself, exposing the boards. Omri then stuck his fingers down the narrow crack at the ends of the boards, one after another, testing to see if they could be lifted. Only one of them could. The rest were nailed down to the joists underneath.

Making as little noise as possible – he hadn't heard his parents go to bed yet – Omri prised up the short end of board. A hole, about the size of a man's foot, gaped in the light of the candle Patrick was holding. Even when he put the candle down the hole, they couldn't see much.

'We'll have to risk the bedside light,' Omri said.

They switched it on, and carried it on its flex down to the hole. Kneeling on the floor, they peered into the depths. They could make out the dusty lath-and-plaster several centimetres down – the topside of the ceiling of the room below. The room where Omri's parents were now sitting...

'We'll have to be dead quiet or they'll hear us.'

'Dead quiet doing what?' asked Patrick. 'It's not there. You'd see it if it was.'

'It must be under one of the nailed-down boards,' said Omri despairingly.

At that moment they heard Little Bull calling them, and they stood up.

He was standing outside the longhouse, naked but for his breech-cloth. His hair hung loose, his face and chest and arms were smeared with ashes, his feet were bare.

'Little Bull! What are you doing?' asked Omri, aghast at his appearance.

'Want fire. Want make dance. Call spirits. Make Boone live.'

Omri looked at him for a moment and felt an ache in his throat that reminded him painfully of his babyish days, when he used to cry so much – days he thought he had left behind forever.

'Little Bull, dancing won't do any good. The spirits won't help. We need a doctor. To get the doctor we need the key. Would you help find it?'

Little Bull didn't move a muscle. 'I help.'

Gently Omri picked him up. He knelt on the floor and put his hand down in the hole. Patrick held the light. Omri opened his hand and Little Bull stood on it, looking around into the dusty dark tunnel stretching away under the floor.

'I think it's somewhere down there,' Omri said quietly, 'on the other side of that wooden wall. You'll have to find a way through, a hole or crack or something. We'll give you all the light we can, but it's bound to be awfully dark on the other side. Do you think you can do it?'

'I go,' said Little Bull immediately.

'Right. Start looking for a way through.'

Little Bull, a tiny, vulnerable figure, strode off through the dust into the darkness under the floor.

Omri pulled the lampshade off the bedside lamp and thrust the bulb down into the hole. He couldn't get his head in to watch, and Little Bull went out of sight almost at once.

'Is there a way through?' he whispered down the tunnel.

'Yes,' came Little Bull's voice. 'Big hole. I go through. Omri give light.'

Omri pushed the light down as far as he could, but the base of the lamp made it stick.

'Can you see anything?' he whispered as loudly as he dared.

There was no answer. He and Patrick knelt there for an age. There wasn't a sound. Then Patrick said suddenly, 'Did he take his bow and arrows?'

'No. Why?'

'What if – Omri – what if he meets the rat?'

Omri had totally forgotten about the rat in the excitement of realising what had happened to the key. Now he felt a strange jerk in his chest, as if his heart had hiccupped.

He bent his head till his face was in the hole. He could smell the dust. The bright bulb was between him and the place where Little Bull had presumably gone through a hole in the joist into the next section of the under-floor space. A hole! What could make a hole right through a joist? What else but a rat, gnawing away all day? A rat at this moment out on his night-prowl, a hungry rat who hadn't eaten for twenty-four hours – a pink-eyed, needle-toothed, omniverous, giant rat?

'Little Bull!' called Omri frantically into the blankness. 'Come back! Come back!'

Utter silence. And then he heard something. But it wasn't Little Bull's voice. It was the scuttering sound of a rodent's hard little hairless feet on lath-and-plaster.

'*Little Bull!*'

'Omri!' It was a voice from the room below. 'What are you doing up there?'

It was his mother. Then, quite distinctly, he heard his father's voice. 'I can hear that blasted rat pattering about overhead. It's probably keeping the boys awake.'

'I'd better go up,' said his mother. A door closed below and they heard her coming up the stairs.

Even this dire prospect hardly had power to do more than push Omri's desperation one stage further. He probably wouldn't have moved from his place on the floor if Patrick hadn't acted swiftly.

'Quick! Light off! Into bed!'

He pulled Omri up, snatched the lamp out of his hand and switched it off. The candle was still down the hole. Patrick shoved the floorboard roughly back into position and moved the carpet so that it more or less covered the boards if you didn't look closely. Then he pushed Omri into his bed, covered him up – the footsteps were nearly at the door – and had just flung himself down on the folding bed when the door opened.

Omri lay there with his eyes squeezed shut thinking, 'Don't put the light on! Don't put the light on!' Light was coming into the room from the landing, but not enough to see anything much. His mother stood there for what seemed a hundred years. Finally she whispered, 'Are you boys asleep?' Needless to say, she got no reply. 'Omri?' she tried once more. Then, after another hundred years, during which Omri imagined Little Bull bitten in half by the rat right underneath where he was lying, the door closed again, leaving them in darkness.

'Wait – wait – ' breathed Patrick.

It was torture to wait. The rat had stopped moving when all the scuffling and footsteps had started, that was something; but now it was quiet again, Omri imagined it creeping towards its prey, its pink nose twitching, its albino whiskers trembling hungrily . . . Oh, how, *how* could he have let Little Bull go down there? Boone's death would at least not have been his fault, but if Little Bull was killed Omri knew he would never forgive himself.

At long, long last the living-room door closed and both boys stole out of bed again. Patrick reached the light first. Omri grabbed it, but Patrick insisted on looking first to see if Boone was still breathing. He was . . . They rolled back the carpet and lifted the board again, terrified that each movement would attract the grown-ups below. The home-made candle was burning away in the gloom, like a little torch in a disused mine, throwing its eerie light down the tunnel.

Omri lay down flat. He didn't raise his voice, but he called softly: 'Little Bull! Are you there? Come back! You're in terrible danger!'

Silence.

'Oh God! Why doesn't he come?' Omri whispered frenziedly.

At that moment they did hear something. It was hard to identify the sound – it was the rat all right, but what was it doing? There was no running sound, just a sort of tiny shock, as if it had made one short, sudden movement.

A pounce?

Omri's heart was in his mouth. Then there were other sounds. If he had not got used to straining his ears to catch the voices of the little men, he might not have heard it. But he did hear it, and hope nearly lifted him off the ground. It was a faint, light scrambling sound, the sound of a small body getting through a hole in a hell of a hurry.

Omri pulled the lamp back out of the hole and thrust his arm in instead, his hand open. Almost at once, he felt Little Bull run into it. Omri closed his fingers, just as something warm and furry brushed against their backs. He snatched his arm out, grazing his knuckles against the splintery wood.

There was something else in his hands – something cold and knobbly, twice as heavy as Little Bull. He opened his fingers, and both boys leant over to look.

Sitting on Omri's palm, filthy and bedraggled but triumphant, was Little Bull, and cradled in his arms, trailing cobwebs and a red satin ribbon, was the missing key.

'You've done it! Oh, Little Bull – good for you! Now – quick – Patrick, get the candle up and put the floor back. I'll find the Red-Cross man.'

Reckless now, they switched the top light on. Patrick, being as quiet as he could, replaced the floorboard and the carpet, while Omri looked through the figures jumbled up in the biscuit tin. Luckily the figure of the army medical orderly was right on top, still holding his precious doctor's bag. Little Bull, meanwhile, stood beside the pallet-bed on which Boone was lying, staring down at him, still clutching the key in his arms.

Omri took it from him, thrust the plastic man into the cupboard, and turned the key. He made himself count to ten while Patrick watched, pop-eyed and scarcely breathing. Then he opened the door.

There stood his old friend Tommy, his bag at his feet, rubbing his eyes and frowning around him.

His face cleared as he saw Omri.

'Cor! Well! It's you again. I don't half pick my moments to drop off to sleep, I must say! Thundering great Minnie whining over – thought I was a gonner!'

'What's a Minnie?' asked Patrick in a croaky voice.

'What, another of you?' asked Tommy, gaping. 'I must've eaten too much cheese for me dinner! Shouldn't give us cheese before a big attack...very hard on the stomach, especially when it's churned up anyway, with nerves. What's a Minnie? It's our name for a *minnenwerfer* – that's one of them big German shells. Make an 'orrible row they do, even before they land, a sort of whistle which gets louder and louder, and then – KERBOOM! Then blokes with my job has to pick themselves up and run as quick as you like to where it fell, if it fell in a trench, to take care of the wounded.'

'We've got a wounded man here we want you to take care of,' said Omri quickly.

'Oh, yes? The old redskin again, is it?'

'No, it's another one. Could you step on to my hand?'

Omri lifted him to where Boone lay, and Tommy at once knelt down and began a professional examination.

'He's in a bad way,' he said after a few moments. 'Could do with a blood transfusion really. I'll have to have this plaster off and look at his wound...' He was cutting it off with a minute pair of scissors as he spoke. The anxious watchers saw that the tuft of tissue underneath was now red with blood, but Tommy said, 'Bleeding's stopped, that's one good thing. What was it, a bullet?'

'An arrow,' said Omri, and Little Bull shivered all over.

'Oh yes – of course – I see that now. Well, I'm not much up on arrow-wounds. Head's not still in there, I hope?'

'No, it was pulled out.'

'Good, good. Lucky it missed his heart. Well, I'll see what I can do.' He got the hypodermic out of his bag and fiddled with it for a moment, then plunged the needle into Boone's chest. After that he stitched up the wound, put a field-dressing on it, and got Little Bull to help him peel off the rest of the old, blood-stained plaster.

'You a pal of his, are you?' he asked the Indian.

Little Bull stared at him, but did not deny it.

'Then look here. When he wakes up, you keep giving him these here pills. They're iron, see? Build him up. And these as well, they're for the pain. What we have to hope is that there won't be no infection.'

'We need penicillin for him,' said Patrick, who had once had a bad cut on his foot which had turned septic.

Tommy looked at him blankly. 'Penicillin? What's that when it's at home?'

Omri nudged Patrick. 'They hadn't invented it in his time,' he whispered.

'Best thing I can suggest is a drop of brandy,' said Tommy, and, taking out a flask, poured something down Boone's throat. 'Look there,' he said cheerfully, 'he's getting a better colour already. He'll open his eyes soon, I wouldn't wonder. Keep him warm, that's the ticket. Now I must be getting back – waking up, I mean. If that there Minnie's landed, I'll be in demand, and no mistake!'

Omri carried him back to the cupboard.

'Tommy,' he said. 'What if – what if the Minnie had fallen on *you*?'

'Couldn't a done, could it? If it had've, I wouldn't be having this here dream, would I, I'd be singing with an 'eavenly choir! Cheeribye – cor, hurry up and shut that door, I think I can hear 'em calling "Stretcher-bearer" already!'

Omri smiled gratefully at him. He hated to send him back, but obviously he wanted to go.

'Goodbye, Tommy – thanks. And good luck!' And he shut the door.

From the other end of the table, Little Bull suddenly called, 'Omri come! Boone open eyes! Boone wake up!'

Omri and Patrick turned. Sure enough, there was Boone, staring up into Little Bull's face.

'What happened?' he got out in a faint, shaky voice.

Nobody liked to tell him, but at last Little Bull had to confess.

'Me shoot,' he said.

'Watcha talkin' about, ya crazy Injun? Ah asked ya, what happened in the *picture?* Did them settlers beat the redskins and git to whur they wuz aimin' to git to? Or did the redskins carry off the wimmin and scalp all the men, the dirty low-down savages?'

Little Bull drew in his breath. His head, which had been hanging in shame, came up sharply, and to Omri's horror he actually saw his hand go to his belt for his knife. Luckily it wasn't there. But he jumped to his feet.

'Boone shut mouth! Not say bad words, not insult Indian braves, or Little Bull shoot again, this time kill good, take scalp, hang on pole – Boone scalp too dirty hang on belt of Indian Chief!'

And he snatched his Chief's cloak off Boone's body and swirled it proudly back round his own shoulders.

Omri was shocked, but Patrick was laughing so hard he could scarcely hold it in. But he controlled himself enough to wrap Boone up in the cut-out blanket to keep him warm.

Omri snatched Little Bull up between finger and thumb.

'Oh, so you're a Chief again, are you?' he hissed furiously. 'Chiefs ought to know how to keep their tempers! Here –' He picked the broken headdress off the floor and fitted it lopsidedly on to Little Bull's black hair.

'Now, Chief – have a good look at yourself!' And he held Little Bull up before a mirror. Little Bull took one look, and then hid his face in his hands. 'Just you remember what you did – to your friend!'

'Not friend. Enemy,' muttered Little Bull. But the anger had gone out of him.

'Whatever he is, you've got a job to do. Where are those pills? You're to see that he gets them. We can't – we can't even see them. So it's up to you! And when Boone is better, do you know what you're going to do? You're going to make him your blood-brother!'

Little Bull shot him a quick, startled look. 'Blood-brother?'

'I know all about it,' Omri went on. 'You both make little cuts on your wrists and tie them together so the blood mingles, and after that you can't be enemies ever again. It's an old Indian custom.'

Little Bull looked baffled. 'Not Indian custom.'

'I'm sure it is! It was in a film I saw.'

'White man idea. Not Indian.'

'Well, this Indian's going to do it. And you can smoke a peace-pipe. Don't tell me that's not an Indian custom either!'

'Not Iroquois. Other tribes.'

'Couldn't you do it, just this once?'

Little Bull was silent for a moment, thinking. Then Omri saw that crafty look that he knew of old coming on to the Indian's face.

'Good,' he said. 'Little Bull give Boone medicine, make him my brother when strong. And Omri put plass-tick in box, make real wife for Little Bull.'

'Not tonight,' said Omri firmly. 'We've had enough excitement. Tonight you stand guard over Boone, give him his pills when he needs them, drinks of water and all that. Tomorrow, if everything's all right, I'll bring your woman to life. That's a promise.'

Chapter 16
Brothers

Omri had fully intended to go to sleep – Patrick did, almost immediately – but he couldn't, tired though he was.

Instead, he lay in the candle-light, his head turned towards the table where Boone lay,. and Little Bull sat cross-legged next to him, erect and watchful. Sometimes Omri would close his eyes, but he did no more than doze; each time he opened them, he would meet Little Bull's unblinking stare.

It was partly the rat which kept him awake. It pattered around under the floor for hours, making Omri nervous, but it never came anywhere near the men. No, that wasn't the main thing. The main thing was Omri's thoughts.

What was he going to do?

He would bring Little Bull's woman to life as he had promised. But then what?

It had been hard enough with only one little being to feed, protect and keep secret. Much harder after Boone came. Now, with the woman, there'd be three. Young as he was, Omri knew that one woman and two men spelt trouble.

For all Little Bull's unpredictable moods, his demands, his occasional cruelties, Omri liked him. He wanted to keep him. But he knew, now, that that was impossible. Whichever way he thought about it, the end was the same – disaster of some kind. Whatever magic had brought this strange adventure about must be put to use again, to send the little people back to their own place and time.

Having decided this, however sadly and reluctantly, Omri's stressful thoughts let go their hold on him. He drifted off to sleep. When he opened his eyes again, dawn was breaking; the morning chorus of birds was just beginning. The candle had burnt itself out. The rat had gone to sleep. So had Little Bull, nodding over his bow...Omri peered closely at Boone. The yellow field-dressing on his wound moved steadily up and down; his skin had lost the grey look. He was better...Of course Little Bull shouldn't have gone to sleep, but just the same, he had done his best. Omri slipped out of bed.

His blazer was hanging from a hook at the back of his door. He took the paper-bag with the woman in it out of the pocket. Moving on tiptoe, he went to the cupboard, took out the plastic soldier, put in the plastic Indian girl, and locked the cupboard door again.

When he heard little movements, he unlocked the cupboard and opened the door a crack, so she wouldn't be frightened in the dark. Then he got back into bed, covered himself up all except his eyes, and stayed perfectly still to watch what would happen.

At first nothing did. Then, slowly, stealthily, the door was pushed a little further open. Out crept a beautiful Indian girl. There was enough light in the room now for Omri to see the black of her hair, the chestnut brown of her skin, the bright red of her dress. He couldn't see her expression, but he guessed she was bewildered. She glanced all round, and at once spotted Boone lying on the ground and Little Bull dozing beside him.

She approached them cautiously. For a few moments she lingered behind Little Bull, clearly not sure whether she should touch and wake him or not. She decided against it, and, circling Boone's feet, sat herself cross-legged on his other side, facing Little Bull.

She sat staring at him. The three of them were so utterly still that they might have been plastic again. Then a blackbird outside gave a particularly loud chirrup and Little Bull sat up sharply.

At once he saw her. His whole body gave a jolt. Omri

felt a prickling up the back of his neck. The way they looked at each other! It went on a long time. Then, slowly and both together, they rose to their feet.

Little Bull spoke to her quietly in his strange, rustling language which did not move his lips. She answered. He smiled. Standing there on either side of Boone, not touching, they talked for some minutes in low voices. Then he put out his hand and she put hers into it.

They stood silently. Then their hands dropped. Little Bull pointed at Boone, and began talking again. The girl crouched down, touched Boone gently and expertly. She looked up at Little Bull and nodded. Then Little Bull looked around the room. He saw Omri.

Omri put his finger to his lips and shook his head, as if to say, 'Don't tell her about me.'

Little Bull nodded. He took the girl by the hand and led her to the seed-box, up the ramp and into the longhouse. After a moment or two, he came out again. He ran the length of the table till he stood on its edge, as near to Omri as he could get. Omri leant forward so they could talk quietly.

'Do you like her?'

'Fit wife for Chief.' Omri realized this was as near to a word of thanks as he was likely to get, but he didn't mind. 'Now Omri hear Little Bull. Woman say, Boone good. Not die. Little Bull pleased. Omri take Boone, put in longhouse. Woman take care, give little medicines – ' He held up the pill boxes. 'Omri get food. Make wedding feast.'

'How can you have a wedding feast with only two Indians?'

'Yes...not good. Omri make more Indian, come to feast?' he asked hopefully. When Omri shook his head, Little Bull's face fell.

'Little Bull, wouldn't you rather have your wedding feast at home with your own·tribe?'

Little Bull was no fool. He understood at once. He stood still, staring at Omri.

'Omri put in box. Send back,' he said. His voice was very flat – Omri couldn't tell if he liked the idea or not.

'What do you think? Wouldn't it be better?'

Very slowly, the Indian nodded his head. 'And Boone?'

'Boone too.'

'Make him my brother first.'

'Yes. Then I'll send you all back.'

'When?'

'When Boone's well enough.'

Now that Omri had decided, every day that passed was important because it was one day nearer to the last.

Patrick was as sad as he was, but he didn't argue against Omri's decision.

'It's the only way, really,' Patrick said. After that he didn't talk about it any more, he just tried to be at Omri's house as much as possible.

He couldn't do things with Boone much, of course, even though, in a day or two, Boone was sitting up in the longhouse and demanding to talk to his horse (which was brought to the entrance for the purpose) and whining for all sorts of special food. And drink.

'Ah cain't be expected t'git muh strength back if ya won't gimme some o' the hard stuff,' he nagged. He even pretended to have a relapse. Omri pinched a nose-dropperful of whisky from his parents' drinks cupboard and squeezed two large drops down Boone's throat before the Indian girl (whose name was Twin Stars, a reference to her bright eyes, Omri supposed) succeeded in conveying the fact that Boone was perfectly all right and that his faint was faked.

Still, after he'd had his drink Boone seemed so much better that Omri and Patrick decided it wouldn't do him any harm ('He's used to it, after all!') and thereafter Boone got a liquor ration three times a day. And did very well on it.

'He'll be ready to go back tomorrow,' said Omri on the fourth day, when Boone, having had a leg up from Little Bull, managed to ride his horse round the seedbox at a steady walk. 'They'll probably look after him better than we can, in his own time.'

A thought struck him, and he fished out of his pocket the drawing Boone had done.

'Boone, is this your home town?'

'Shore is!'

Omri studied it closely under the magnifying glass. Away up the street he saw a little sign reading 'Doctor'.

'Is he a good doctor?'

''Bout as good as any out West, Ah reckon. Fish a bullet out of a man's arm or cut his foot off fer snake-bite as neat as kin be. I seen him bring a pal o' mine back from the dead, near enough, by puttin' a hot coal in his belly-button. He never operates till a man's dead drunk, *and* he don't charge extry for the likker neither!'

Omri and Patrick looked at each other. 'You'd feel that you were in good hands, with this – er – doctor looking after you?' Patrick asked worriedly.

'Shore would! Anyhow, don't need no sawbones now, m'wound's healin' up fine. S'long as Ah git mah whisky, Ah'll be as good as new.'

Boone bore not the slightest ill-will towards Little Bull for having shot him.

'That there's a Injun's natural nature. Pore simple critter c'd no more help himself than Ah kin keep away from muh horse and muh bottle!'

The night before Omri had decided to send them back, they held the blood-brotherhood ceremony.

'I wish we could ask *our* brothers!' said Patrick to Omri at school that day. 'Supposing we tell them one day about this – they'll never believe us.'

'Sending them back,' said Omri slowly, 'doesn't mean

the magic won't work any more. I'm going to put the key away somewhere so I won't be tempted; but it will always be there.'

Patrick looked at him wonderingly. 'I never thought of that,' he said slowly. 'So there'd be nothing to stop us – months or even years from now – from bringing Boone and Little Bull back again. To visit.'

'I don't know,' said Omri. 'Maybe their time is different from ours. It would be awful if they were old, or – ' But he couldn't say ' – or dead'. Both Boone and Little Bull came from such dangerous times. Omri shivered and changed the subject.

'As for our brothers coming,' he said, 'all I want of my brothers is to keep that rat in its cage.' The rat had been caught by Omri after a long, patient wait with cheese and a fishing-net, and Omri had threatened Gillon with the worst fate imaginable if he let it get away again.

The two boys went to Yapp's after school and bought feast-food for the ceremony – salted nuts, crisps, Hula Hoops and chocolate. Omri bought a quarter of a pound of best mince at the butcher's for tiny hamburgers (a teaspoonful would have been enough, but the butcher wasn't interested in *that*). They got bread, biscuits, cake and Coke from Omri's mother, and Omri sneaked another dropperful of the 'the hard stuff', without which Boone would certainly not consider it a festive occasion at all.

Omri was rather surprised Boone had agreed to be blood-brother to a 'stinkin' redskin' at all, but he actually seemed rather to fancy the idea.

'T'ain't jest anyone gits ter be blood-brother to an Injun chief, y'know,' he said proudly, as he rolled up his sleeve and Twin Stars carefully swabbed his arm with soap and water. But when he saw Little Bull sharpening his knife on a pebble he turned pale.

'Hell! It'll hurt!' he muttered, but Patrick told him not to be a coward.

'It's only a nick, it's nothing at all!'

'Easy fer you!' retorted Boone. 'I ain't sure this is sich a nice idee, after all...'

But he cheered up when he saw the campfire being kindled, and smelt the meat Twin Stars was cooking on a pointed stick; and when Omri gave him a good swig from the dropper he swaggered up to Little Bull and offered his arm with a drunken flourish.

'Chop away, brother!' he said loudly.

Little Bull went through a whole routine first, cleaning himself, offering up loud chanting prayers to the spirits and performing a marvellous stamping dance round the fire. Then he nicked his own wrist with the point of his knife. The blood welled up. Boone took one look and burst into tears.

'Ah don't wanna! Ah changed m'mind!' he bawled. But it was too late for that. Little Bull seized his arm, and before Boone knew what was happening the deed was done.

Twin Stars bound their wrists together with a strip of hide torn from the hem of her red dress. Boone looked at it in a bemused way and said, 'Gee whiz. We done it! I'm part-Injun! Wal...Ah guess Ah cain't say nothin' 'gainst 'em in future.'

Then the two 'brothers' sat on the ground. Little Bull took out a short-stemmed pipe and some rather evil-smelling tobacco, and he and Boone took it in turns to puff at it. Twin Stars served them the cooked meat, and all the rest of the feast. Patrick and Omri offered their congratulations and tucked into their own food. They kept the campfire going with tiny bits of broken matchsticks and a bit of coal-dust Omri had collected in the outside bunker, which, when sprinkled on the flame, made it spit minute sparks. Looking at it, and the three little figures round it, the boys gradually lost their sense of size altogether.

'I feel as if I were the same as them,' murmured Patrick.

'Me, too,' said Omri.

'I wish we *were* all the same size, then there'd be no problem.'

'Don't be funny! No problems, with two full-grown Indians and a crying cowboy?'

'I meant, if we were small. If we could enter their world – sleep in the longhouse – ride the ponies – '

'I wouldn't mind eating one of those hamburgers,' said Omri.

Twin Stars was now crouched by the fire, tending it, singing softly. One of the horses whinnied. Boone seemed to have dropped off to sleep, leaning on Little Bull's shoulder. Little Bull alone was aware of the boys, watching them. He beckoned to Omri with his free hand.

When Omri bent to hear him, he said, 'Now!'

'Now? You mean, to go back?'

'Good time. All happy. Not wait for morning.'

Omri looked at Patrick. He nodded slowly.

'When you go into the cupboard,' Omri said, 'you must hold Twin Stars. Or she may not go back with you.'

'Woman go back with Little Bull. Little Bull hold, not let go. And horse! Little Bull only Iroquois with horse!'

'But Boone must go separately. Don't drag *him* back to your time, your people would kill him even if you are his new brother.'

Little Bull looked at Boone, asleep at his side, and at their joined wrists. Then he took his knife and cut the thong that bound them together. Patrick gently lifted Boone up.

'Don't forget his hat! He'd never forgive us if we let him leave that behind.'

To be safe, they sat Boone on his horse. Cowboys often ride in their sleep, and he didn't stir as Little Bull led him down the ramp, across the table and up another ramp that Omri stood against the rim of the cupboard. Then Little Bull went back to the seedbox. Carefully he and Twin Stars put out the fire with earth. Little Bull took a last look at his longhouse. Then he put Twin Stars on to his pony's back, and led them after Boone.

They stood all together in the bottom of the cupboard. Nobody spoke. Omri had his hand on the door when Patrick suddenly said, 'I'm going to wake Boone up. I don't care, I've got to say goodbye to him!'

Hearing his name, Boone woke up by himself, so suddenly he nearly fell off his horse and had to clutch the high pommel of his saddle.

'Watcha want, kid?' he asked Patrick, whose face was close to him.

'You're going home, Boone. I wanted to say goodbye.'

Boone stared at him and then his face slowly crumpled.

'Ah cain't stand sayin' goodbye,' he choked out as tears began to stream. He pulled a huge grubby handkerchief from his pocket. 'Ah jest re-fuse t' say it, that's all! Ah'll only bust out cryin' if Ah do.' And he blew a trumpet-blast on his nose.

Omri and Little Bull were staring at each other. Something else was needed – some special farewell. It was Little Bull who thought of it.

'Omri give hand!'

Omri put his hand forward. The pony braced his legs but Little Bull held him steady. He took hold of Omri's little finger, drew his knife and pricked it in the soft part. A drop of blood appeared. Then Little Bull solemnly pressed his own right wrist against the place and held it there.

'Brother,' he said, looking up at Omri with his fierce black eyes for the last time.

Omri withdrew his hand. Little Bull jumped on to the back of his pony behind Twin Stars, holding her round the waist so that he, she and the pony made one unit which could not be separated during whatever kind of unearthly journey they had to make together through the unknown regions of time, space – proportion.

Little Bull raised his arm in the Indian salute.

Omri put his hand on the door. He could hardly bear to do it. He had to set his teeth. Boone and his horse stood patiently, but the Indian's pony started to prance and sidle. It put up its head and gave a long challenging neigh.

'Now!' cried Little Bull.

Omri drew in his breath, closed the door and turned the key.

He and Patrick stood frozen with the sadness, the strangeness of it. The magic was working at this moment...Both of them silently counted ten. Then, very slowly, Omri, whose hand had not left the key, turned it back again and swung open the door.

There they were, the two plastic groups – forms, outlines, shells of the real, real creatures they had been. Each boy lifted out his own and helplessly examined it. The life-giving details were blurred – plastic can't show fine bead-work, the perfection of hair and muscle, the folds of cloth, the sheen of a pony's coat or the beauty of a girl's skin. The figures were there, but the people, the personalities, were gone.

Patrick's eyes met Omri's. Both were wet.

'We could bring them back. Just as quick,' he said huskily.

'No.'

'No...I know. They're home by now.'

Omri put his group, the Indian, the girl and the pony, on the shelf nearest his bed where he could see it easily. Patrick slipped the mounted cowboy into his pocket, cupping his hand round it almost as if to keep it warm.

Then Omri took the key and left the room.

His mother was in the kitchen getting everyone a hot drink before bed. She took one look at Omri's face and her hands became still.

'What's happened? What's wrong?'

'Nothing. Mum, I want you to keep this key. I lost it.

Lucky I found it again, but you told me it was important...Better if you keep it. Please.'

She nearly refused, but then, looking at him, she changed her mind and took the key from him.

'I'll get a chain and wear it,' she said, 'like I always meant to.'

'*You* won't lose it, will you?'

She shook her head, and suddenly reached for him and hugged his face against her. He was shaking. He broke away and ran back to his room, where Patrick was still standing with his hand in his pocket gazing at the cupboard.

'Come on, I'm going to put all sorts of medicines in it,' Omri said loudly. 'Bottles of pills and stuff Mum's finished with. We'll pretend it's a doctor's drug-cupboard, and we can mix lots of them together...'

His voice petered out. Those were silly games, such as he had played – before. He didn't feel the slightest interest in them now.

'I'd rather go for a walk,' said Patrick.

'But what shall I do with the cupboard?' asked Omri desperately.

'Leave it empty,' said Patrick. 'In case.'

He didn't say in case what. But he didn't have to. Just to know you *could*. That was enough.

Return of the Indian

To all those who wrote to me,
giving me ideas!

*And to Omri,
my darling son.*

Contents

Chapter 1
A Defeat

Omri emerged cautiously from the station into Hove Road.

Someone with a sense of humour and a black spray-can had recently added an 'l' to the word 'Hove' on the street sign on the corner, making it 'Hovel Road'. Omri thought grimly that this was much more appropriate than 'Hove' which sounded pleasantly like somewhere by the sea. Omri would have liked to live by the sea, or indeed almost anywhere in the world rather than Hovel Road. He had done his best to understand why his parents had decided to move here from the other house in the other, much nicer, district. True, the new house was larger, and so was the garden. But the area was a slum.

Omri's father objected strongly to Omri calling it a slum. But then *he* had a car. He didn't have to walk half a mile along Hovel Road to the station every day, as Omri did to get to school, and again – as now – to get home in the gloomy afternoon. It was October, and the clocks had gone back. That meant that when he came out of the station it was practically dark.

Omri was only one of many children walking, playing or hanging around in Hovel Road at this hour, but he was the only one who wore school uniform. Of course he took his blazer and tie off in the train and stuffed them into his schoolbag, but that still left his white shirt, black trousers and grey pullover. However he mussed them up, he still stood out among the others he had to pass through.

These others all went to a local school where uniform was not required. Under other circumstances, Omri would have begged his parents to let him change schools. At least, then, he wouldn't have been an obvious outsider. Or maybe he would. He couldn't imagine going to school with these kids. After a term and a half of running the gauntlet of their mindless antagonism every working day, he regarded them as little better than a pack of wolves.

That group waiting for him on the corner by the amusement arcade . . . He knew them by now, and they knew him. They waited for him, if they had nothing better to do. His passing seemed to be one of the highlights of their day. Their faces positively lit up as they saw him approach. It took all his courage to keep walking towards them.

At moments like this, he would remember Little Bull. Little Bull had been only a fraction of Omri's size, and yet he had stood up to him. If he had felt scared, as Omri did now, he never showed it. Omri was not that much smaller than these boys. There were just so many of them, and only one of him. But imagine if they'd been giants, as he was to Little Bull! They were nothing but kids like himself, although several years older. Except that they weren't like him. *They're rats*, he thought, to rouse himself for battle. *Pigs. Toads. Mad dogs.* It would be shameful to let them see he was afraid of them. He gripped his schoolbag tightly by both handles and walked on.

If only he had had Boone's revolver, or Little Bull's knife, or his bow and arrows, or his axe. If only he could fight like a cowboy or an Indian brave! How he would show that crew then!

The boy he had to pass first was a skinhead, like several of the others. The cropped head made him look somehow animal-like. He had a flat, whitish face and about five gold rings in one ear. Omri should perhaps have detoured a bit to be out of range, but he would not swerve from his path. The skinhead's boot shot out, but Omri was expecting that and skipped over it. Then a concerted movement by the others jerked Omri into evasive action. Speed was his only hope. He broke into a run, hampered by his heavy bag.

Several hands reached out to grab him as he passed. One caught and held fast. He swung the bag and it hit home. The boy released his hold, doubled over and said, 'Uuoogh!' It reminded Omri of the time Little Bull had fought Boone, the cowboy, and got kicked in the stomach. He'd made the same noise.

Someone else clutched Omri's flying shirt-tail and he jerked away hard and heard it rip. He swung round with his bag again, missed, and found himself turning in a circle after the bag. There was the sound of jeering laughter. He felt hot rage flood under his skin. He was roused now; he wanted to stop, to fight, but he saw their sneering, idiot faces. That was all they were waiting for. They would beat him up. They'd done it once before and he had stumbled home with a bloody nose and a shoulder bruised from the pavement, and one shoe missing. His schoolbag, too. He'd had to go back (Adiel, his eldest brother, had gone with him), and found all his books scattered, and the bag torn and half-full of filthy rubbish.

An experience like that taught you something. He fled, hating himself, but hating his enemies more. They didn't pursue him. That would have been too much trouble. But their shouts and jeers followed him all the way to his gate.

As he turned into it, he slowed down. He was on safe ground here. It was a different world. The property had a high hedge which shut it off from the street. The house was a nice house. Omri didn't deny that. He could see in to the warm, well-lit living room with its familiar furniture and lamps and ornaments and pictures.

His mother was in there, just putting a match to the open fire. Omri paused in the twilight to watch. He loved to see the flames. These, too, reminded him of Little Bull and the tiny fires he had made outside his tepee, the love-dance he had done around his fire when he had married Twin Stars . . . Omri sighed. It was over a year since that time. But not a single day had passed without his thinking about his Indian and all the astonishing adventures they had had together.

Omri had grown up quite a bit in the meantime. There had been moments when he would almost have liked to believe that he'd made the whole thing up. A plastic Red Indian coming alive – absurd! He had tried to push it to the back of his mind, but it wouldn't be pushed. It was as vividly real to him as if it had happened this morning.

The little bathroom cupboard. His special key that his mother had given him. And magic. The magic that brought plastic people to life . . . It *had* happened, all of it. And yet, three days ago, Patrick had behaved in that peculiar way. It had shaken Omri; shaken his belief in his own memory.

Patrick, too, had moved house. When his parents

divorced, he and his mother and brother had gone right away. This had happened months ago. At first the boys had written to each other, but somehow the letters had petered out. There'd been no more contact between them, until three days ago. Omri had been walking out of the school gate (their old school – Omri was now in his final year before high school) and found Patrick waiting for him.

Patrick had grown. His face looked different as well. They just stood in front of each other, grinning, not knowing what to say.

'How've you been?' said Patrick at last.

'All right,' said Omri, 'Have you moved back?'

'No. We're visiting. I thought I'd come and look at the old school.'

They had begun walking toward the station.

'Do you like where you live now?' Omri had asked.

'Oh yeah, the country's all right. Once you get used to it. I've made a few friends. And the cottage is nice. Seems funny with just the three of us.' Omri didn't press this point. He could hardly imagine life without *his* dad, but then, his dad didn't hit him, or hit his mother.

They chatted on rather awkwardly, with some silences, but it got better. By the time they'd reached the station it was almost as if Patrick had never gone away, as if they were still as close as they used to be. That was why Omri didn't hesitate to say, 'Where do you keep Boone and his horse?'

Patrick seemed to stumble as he walked, like a hiccup with his feet.

'Who?'

A little cold shiver passed down Omri's back. He stopped.

'Boone.'

Patrick stopped too. He stared across Omri's shoulder at the station.

'What are you on about? Who's Boone?'

Omri narrowed his eyes. Could Patrick be serious, or was he teasing? But Patrick wasn't a tease.

'You know perfectly well. Your cowboy.' There was a silence. Patrick was rubbing his thumb against the side of his finger, a quick, dry, nervous sound. 'Like Little Bull was my Indian,' said Omri. He couldn't quite believe what seemed to be happening, so he rattled on, 'I've still got *him*, of course. The plastic figure of him, I mean. Remember? How he sat on his pony with Twin Stars in front of him, and raised his hand to say goodbye just as we shut the cupboard door, when we sent them back?'

The silence went on for what seemed like eternity. Then Patrick snapped his head round and looked into Omri's face.

'You're talking a load of rubbish,' he said loudly. 'I gave you a plastic Indian for your birthday. That's all I remember.' He looked at his watch. 'My mum's waiting,' he said shortly. ''Bye.' And he ran off.

Now as Omri stood outside his new house in the gathering dark, a possible solution to this troubling and incredible episode came to him.

Maybe Patrick doesn't want to remember, he thought. Because a thing like that, well . . . it makes you different from other people. It's a secret you can never tell, not if you don't want everyone to think you're crazy. It's lonely having a secret like that. If Patrick hadn't moved away, if they could have kept talking about it and remembering *together*, then he'd never have denied it, or started trying to pretend it never happened.

Chapter 2

A Victory

Omri entered the house by the side door, which opened into the kitchen. His black-and-white cat, Kitsa, was sitting on the draining-board. She watched him out of her knowing green eyes as he came to get a drink of water.

'You're not supposed to be up there, Kits,' he said. 'You know that.' She continued to stare at him. He flicked some water on her but she ignored it. He laughed and stroked her head. He was crazy about her. He loved her independence and disobedience.

He helped himself to a hunk of bread, butter and Primula, and walked through into the breakfast room. It was their every-meal room actually. Omri sat down and opened the paper to the cartoon. Kitsa came in, and jumped, not on to his knee but on to the table, where she lay down on the newspaper right over the bit he was looking at. She was always doing this – she couldn't bear to see people reading.

It had been a long day. Omri laid his head on his arm, bringing it level with Kitsa's face, and communed with her, eyeball to eyeball. He felt sleepy and catlike. When his mother came bursting in, it gave him a fright.

'Oh, Mum . . . I wish you wouldn't bash about like that!'

'Omri!'

He looked at her. She had a strange look on her face. Her eyes and mouth were wide open and she was staring at him as if she'd never seen him before.

He sat up straight, his heart beating. 'What's up?'

'A letter came for you,' she said in an odd voice to match her goggle-eyed expression.

'A letter? For me? Who from?'

'I – I'm afraid I opened it.'

She came over to him and gave him a long envelope, torn open at the top. It had printing on it as well as his name and address in typing. Omri stared at it. It said, 'Telecom – *Your* Communications Service'. He felt numb inside. It couldn't be. *It couldn't be.* He didn't touch the letter, which lay on the table beside Kitsa. (For once his mother didn't even seem to notice that she was there – normally she chased her off.)

'Why did you open it?' Omri asked at last in a croaky voice.

'Darling, because I didn't look at the name. You boys don't get many letters.' She gave a short, rather hysterical laugh. Omri quite saw how it could happen. He just wished . . . he wished he could have been the first to know.

'Well, go on – read it!'

He picked up the envelope and took out the letter.

Dear Omri,

We are delighted to inform you that your story, *The Plastic Indian*, has won first prize for your age group in our Telecom Creative Writing Competition.

We think it is a superb story, showing extraordinary powers of imagination and invention. Our judges consider it worthy of publication.

Your prize, £300.00, will be presented to you at a party we are giving for all prize-winners on November 25th in the Savoy Hotel.

A special invitation card will be sent to you.
May we congratulate you on your success.
              Yours sincerely,
              Squiggle Squiggle,
              Competition Director for Telecom.

Omri kept his eyes on this letter long after he had
finished reading it. Inside, he was jumping up from his
chair, running round and round the room, hugging his
mother, shouting with triumph. But in reality he just sat
there staring at the letter, a deep glow like hot coals in his
chest, too happy and astonished to move or speak. He
didn't even notice that his free hand was stroking Kitsa
from nose tip to tail tip again and again while she lay on
the newspaper, purring with bliss.

His mother woke him from his trance.

'Darling? Do you realize? Isn't it fantastic? And you
never said a single word!'

At this moment his father came in from outdoors. He'd
been working in the gardcen, as he often did, until it was
actually too dark to see. Now he stamped the mud off his
shoes in the open doorway, but for once his mother didn't
care about the mud, and almost dragged him into the
room.

'Oh, do come and hear the news! I've been bursting to
tell you all day. Omri – tell him. Tell him!'

Wordlessly, Omri handed his father the letter. There
was a silence, then his father whispered reverently, 'God
in Heaven. Three hundred pounds!'

'It's not the *money*!' cried his mother. 'Look, look what
they say about his *story*! He must be *brilliant*, and we
never even knew he had writing talent.' She came to Omri
and smothered him with hugs. 'When can we read it? Oh,
just wait till the boys hear about this . . .'

His brothers! Yes. That would be almost the sweetest

thing of all. They always behaved as if he were too thick to do anything. And telling them at school. His English teacher simply wouldn't believe her senses. Perhaps Mr Johnson, the headmaster, would get him up at Assembly and announce the news, and they would all applaud, and he would be asked to read the story aloud . . . Omri's head began to spin with the incredible excitement of it. He jumped up.

'I'll go and get my copy and you can read it,' he said.

'Oh, did you keep a copy?'

'Yes, that was in the rules.' He stopped in the doorway and turned. 'I typed it on your typewriter when you were out,' he confessed.

'Did you, indeed! That must have been the time I found all the keys jumbled together.' But she wasn't really annoyed.

'And I borrowed paper and carbon paper from Dad's desk. And a big envelope to send it in.'

His mother and father looked at each other. They were both absolutely beaming with pride, as they had when Gillon had come home and announced he'd broken a swimming record at school, and when Adiel had got ten O-levels. Omri, looking at them, knew suddenly that he had never expected them to have that look because of him.

'Well,' said his father, very solemnly, 'now you can pay me back. You owe me the price of the stamp,' His face broke into a great, soppy grin.

Omri raced upstairs. His heart was pounding. He'd won. He'd actually won! He'd never dared to hope he would. Of course, he'd dreamed a little. After all, he had tried his very best, and it *was* a great story to begin with. *Imagination and invention*, eh? That was all they knew. The real work was in the way he'd written it, and re-written it, and checked the spelling until just for once he could be confident that every word was right. He'd persuaded Adiel to help with that part – without telling him, of course, what it was actually for.

'Stirrup? Maize? Iroquois?'

'*Iroquois*!' Adiel had exclaimed.

'It's the name of an Indian tribe,' said Omri. Fancy not knowing that! Omri had now read so many books about American Indians that he'd forgotten that not everyone was as knowledgeable on the subject as himself.

'Well, I haven't a clue how to spell it. I-R-O-K-W-'

'No it's not, it's like French. Never mind, I know that one, I just wanted to see if you did. Whisky?'

Adiel spelt it, and then asked, 'What on earth is this you're writing? What a weird bunch of words!'

'It's a story. I've got to make it as perfect as I can.'

'But what's it about? Let me see it,' said Adiel, making a grab at the notebook.

Omri dodged. 'Leave off! I'll show you when it's finished. Now. Bandage?' Adiel spelt this (actually Omri had spelled it correctly) and then Omri hesitated before saying, 'Cupboard?'

Adiel's eyes narrowed.

'You're not telling about the time I hid your so-called secret cupboard after you'd nicked my football shorts?'

'I didn't . . .'

'The time the key got lost and you made such an idiotic uproar? You're not going to put *me* into any stupid school story.'

'I'm changing the names,' said Omri.

'You'd better. Any more words?'

Omri read on silently to the next longish word. 'Magnanimous.'

'Cor,' said Adiel with heavy sarcasm. 'Bet you don't even know what it means.'

'Yes I do. Generous.'

'Where'd you get it from?'

'"The Iroquois were a tribe ferocious in war, stalwart in alliance, magnanimous in victory,"' quoted Omri.

'You sound like Winston Churchill,' said Adiel, but there was a trace of admiration in his voice this time. 'Don't make it too show-offy, will you? You'll only lose marks if your teacher thinks you've copied it.'

'I haven't *written* that, you *berk*,' said Omri. 'I'm just remembering what I've read in a book.' He was beginning to relish long words, though. Later he went through his story yet again to make sure he hadn't used too many. His teacher was forever saying, 'Keep it simple. Stick to what you know.' Little would anyone guess how closely he had stuck to the truth this time!

And now . . . *Imagination and invention* . . .

He paused on the stairs. Had he cheated? It was supposed to be a made-up story. It said so in the rules. Or had it? 'Creative writing' meant that, didn't it? You couldn't create something that had really happened . . . All you could do was find the best way of writing it down. Of course he had had to make up bits of it. Vivid as his memories of Little Bull and Boone were, he couldn't remember every word they ever spoke. Omri frowned and went on up the stairs. He didn't feel entirely easy in his mind, but on the other hand . . . Nobody had helped him. The way he'd written the story was all his own. Maybe it was okay. There wasn't much he could do about it, anyhow.

He continued more slowly up the stairs to his room, at the very top of the house.

Chapter 3
The Way it Began

Omri was rather a private person. At least he needed to be alone quite a bit of the time. So his room, which was right up under the eaves of the house, was perfect for him.

In the old house, his bedroom had been just one of several opening off the upstairs landing, and at certain times of the day had been like a railway station. His new room was right off the beaten track. No one (in his opinion) had any reason to come up here, or even pass the door. There were times, now he had got it all arranged to suit himself, when he forgot about how awful it was living in Hovel Road, when it seemed worth everything to have a room like this.

It wasn't a very large room, so his father had built a shelf high up under the skylight for him to sleep on. This was great, because he could look up at the night sky. Under this bed-shelf was his desk, and more shelves for his collections of old bottles, key-rings and wooden animals. The wall opposite the window was covered with his posters – a mixture of old and new, from Snoopy and an early Beatles, to the 'Police' and a funny, rude one about a flasher who gets caught in a lift. In pride of place were two large photographs of Iroquois chieftains that he'd found in magazines. Neither of these Indians looked remotely like Little Bull, but they appealed to Omri just the same.

His clothes were stored on the landing, so his room wasn't cluttered up with those. That left quite a lot of space for his beanbag seats, a low table (he'd sawed its legs half off after seeing a photo of a Japanese room), his cassette radio, and his most recent acquisition – an old chest.

He'd found this in the local market, coated with dirt and grease, bought it for two pounds after bargaining, and borrowed a marketeer's barrow to drag it round the corner to Hovel Road. He'd cleaned it with a scraper and some sandpaper in the back garden, before hauling it up to his room.

It had 'come up a treat', just as the man in the market had promised. The wood was oak, the hinges iron, and it had a brass plate on it with the name of its first owner. Omri had hardly been able to believe it when he had cleaned the layers of dirt off this plate and read the name for the first time. It was L. Buller. *L. Buller* . . . Little Bull! Of course it was pure coincidence, but, as Omri thought, *If I were superstitious* . . . He rubbed up the brass every week. Somehow it, too, made him feel closer to Little Bull.

The chest was not only interesting and beautiful, but useful. Omri used it for storage. There was only one thing wrong with it. It had a lock, but no key. So he piled cushions and other objects on it and pretended it was a bench. That way nobody who happened to be prying about in his room (it still happened occasionally, mothers cleaning and brothers poking about 'borrowing') would realize that it contained a number of interesting and private objects.

Omri knelt by the chest now and shifted to the floor a pile of cassettes, a bullworker (he was bent on developing his muscles), some cushions and three copies of *Mad* magazine, among other bits of junk. Then he opened the top of the chest. It, too, was untidy, but Omri knew where to burrow. On their way down the left-hand side in search of the folder containing his prize-winning story,

Omri's fingers touched metal, and paused. Then, carefully, he moved some other things which were in the way, and eased this metal object out.

It was a small white cabinet with a mirror in its door and a keyhole – an old-fashioned bathroom medicine cupboard, in fact. He stood it on the Japanese table. The door swung open. Apart from a single shelf, it was quite empty – as empty as it had been when he was first given it, a rather odd birthday present from Gillon, just over a year ago.

Omri sat back on his heels staring at it.

How clearly it all came back. The cupboard. The strange little key which had been his great-grandmother's, and which had mysteriously fitted the commonplace lock and turned this ordinary little metal box into a time-machine with a difference. Put any plastic object – an axe, an Indian tepee, a quiver of arrows – into it, close the door, turn the key – and those things became real. Miniature but real. Real leather, real cloth, real steel. Put the plastic figure of a human being or an animal inside, and, in the time it took to lock them in, they, too, became real. Real and alive. And not just 'living toys', but people from another time, with their own lives, their own personalities, needs and demands . . .

Oh, it hadn't been all fun and games, as Omri had naïvely expected at first. Little Bull was no toy, to submit tamely to being played with. He was for all his tiny stature, a ferocious savage, warlike and domineering.

Omri had soon realized that if any grownups found out about the cupboard's magic properties they would take it, and the Indian, and everything else, away. So Omri had had to keep it secret, and look after, feed and protect his Indian as best he could. And when Patrick had found out the secret, and sneaked a Texas cowboy into the cupboard so that he, too, could have a 'little person', the trouble really started.

Little Bull and Boone were natural enemies. They came close to killing each other several times. Even their respective ponies had caused endless difficulties. And then Adiel had taken the cupboard one day, the key had fallen out of the lock and been lost, and Omri, Patrick and the two little men had been faced with the dire possibility that the magic was dead, that these minute and helpless people would have to remain in Omri's time, his 'giant' world, and in his care, for ever . . .

It was this, the terrible fright they had all had from this notion, that had finally proved to Omri that he would have to give up his Indian friend (for friends they were by then, of a sort), and send the little people 'back' – back to their own time, through the magic of the cupboard. When the key was found, that's what they all agreed on. But it was so hard to part, that Boone (who was shame-fully soft-hearted for a cowboy) had cried openly, and even the boys' eyes were wet . . . Omri seldom let himself think of those last moments, they upset him so much

When they'd reopened the cupboard door, there were the two groups: Little Bull and the wife Omri had found him, Twin Stars, sitting on Little Bull's pony, and 'Boo-Hoo' Boone on his white horse – only now they were plastic again. Patrick had taken Boone and put him in his pocket. And Omri had kept the Indians. He had them still. He had packed them in a little wooden box which he kept safely at the very bottom of the chest. Actually it was a box-within-a-box-within-a-box. Each was tied tightly with string. There was a reason for all this. Omri had wanted to make them difficult to get at.

He had always known that he would be tempted to put Little Bull and Twin Stars in the cupboard again and bring them back to life. He was curious about how they were getting on – that alone tormented him every day. They had lived in dangerous times, times of war between tribes, wars aided and encouraged by Frenchmen and Englishmen who were fighting on American soil in those far-off days. Boone's time, the time of the pioneering of Texas, a hundred years after Little Bull's era, was dangerous, too.

And there'd been another little man, Tommy, the medical orderly, from the trenches of France in the First World War. They'd magicked him to life to help when Little Bull was kicked by his horse, when Boone was apparently dying of an arrow-wound . . . Tommy might, just might still be alive in Omri's world, but he would be terribly old, about ninety by now.

By putting their plastic figures into the magic cupboard, by turning the magic key, Omri had the power to recall them to life – to youth. He could snatch them from the past. The whole business nearly blew Omri's mind every time he thought at all deeply about it. So he tried not to think about it too much. And to prevent his yielding to temptation, he had given his mother the key. She wore it round her neck on a chain (it was quite decorative). People often asked her about it, and she would say, 'It's Omri's really, but he lends it to me.'

That wasn't the whole truth. Omri had pressed it on her and begged her to keep it safe for him. Safe . . . not just from getting lost again, but safe *from him*, from his longing to use it again, to reactivate the magic, to bring back his friends. To bring back the time when he had been – not happiest, but most intensely, dangerously alive himself.

Chapter 4
The Sweet Taste of Triumph

When Omri came downstairs again with the copy of his story, his brothers were both back from school.

Noticing that their parents were fairly gibbering with excitement, they were both pestering loudly to be told what had happened, but, being decent, Omri's mother and father were refusing to spoil his surprise. However, the moment he entered the room his father turned and pointed to him.

'It's Omri's news,' he said. 'Ask him to tell you.'

'Well?' asked Gillon.

'Go on,' said Adiel. 'Don't drive us mad.'

'It's just that I've won a prize,' said Omri with the utmost carelessness. 'Here, Mum.' He handed her the folder, and she rushed out of the room with it clutched to her bosom, saying that she couldn't wait another minute to read it.

'Prize for what?' asked Adiel cynically.

'For winning a donkey-race?' inquired Gillon.

'Nothing much, it was only a story,' said Omri. It was such a long time since he had felt this good, he needed to spin in out.

'What story?' asked Adiel.

'What's the prize?' asked Gillon at the same time.

'You know, that Telecom competition. There was an ad on TV. You had to write in for a leaflet.'

'Oh, that,' said Adiel, and went into the kitchen to get himself something to eat.

But Gillon was gazing at him. He paid more attention

to ads, and he had remembered a detail that Adiel had forgotten.

'The prizes were money,' he said slowly. 'Big money.'

Omri grunted non-committally, sat down at the table and shifted Kitsa, who was still there, on to his lap.

'How much?' pressed Gillon.

'Hm?'

'How much did you *win*? You didn't get first prize!'

'Yeah.'

Gillon got up.

'Not . . . you haven't won three hundred quid?'

Adiel's face appeared round the kitchen door, wearing a look of comical amazement.

'WHAT! What did you say?'

'That was the first prize in each category. I thought about entering myself.' Excitement and envy were in Gillon's voice now, making it wobble up and down in register. He turned back to Omri. 'Come on! Tell us.'

'Yeah,' said Omri again.

He felt their eyes on him and a great gleeful laugh rising in him, like the time Boone had done a tiny, brilliant drawing during Omri's art lesson and the teacher had seen it and couldn't believe her eyes. She'd thought Omri had done it somehow. This time was even more fun, though, because this time he *had*.

He was sitting watching television some time later, when Adiel came in quietly and sat down beside him.

'I've read it,' he said after a while. His tone had changed completely.

'What? Oh, my Indian story.'

'Yes. Your Indian story.' There was a pause, and then Adiel – his ten-O-level brother – said very sincerely, almost humbly. 'It's one of the best stories I've ever read.'

Omri turned to look at him.

28

'Do you really like it?' he asked eagerly. Whatever rows he might have with his brothers, and he had them daily, their good opinion mattered. Adiel's especially.

'You know perfectly well it's brilliant. How on earth did you dream all that up? Coming from another time and all that? It's so well worked-out, so . . . I dunno. You actually had me *believing* in it. And working in all those real parts, about the family. Blimey. I mean it was terrific. I . . . now don't take this the wrong way, but I can't quite credit that you made it all up.'

After a pause, Omri said, 'What do you mean? That you think I nicked it from a book? Because I didn't.'

'It's entirely original?'

Omri glanced at him. 'Original? Yes. That's what it is. It's original.'

'Well, congratulations anyway. I think it's fabulous.' They stared at the screen for a while and then he added, 'You'd better go and talk to Mum. She's sobbing her eyes out.'

Omri reluctantly went in search of his mother, and found her in the conservatory at the back of the house watering her plants. Not with tears – to his great relief she was not crying now – but she gave him a rather misty smile and said, 'I read the story, Omri. It's utterly amazing. No wonder it won. You're the darkest little horse I ever knew, and I love you.' She hugged him. He submitted briefly, then politely extricated himself.

'When's supper?'

'Usual time.'

He was just turning to go when he stopped and looked at her again. Something was missing from her general appearance. Then he saw what it was, and his heart missed a beat.

'Mum! Where's the key?'

Her hand went to her neck.

'Oh . . . I took it off this morning when I washed my hair. It's in the upstairs bathroom.'

Omri didn't mean to run, but he couldn't help it. He had to see the key, to be sure it wasn't lost. He pelted up the stairs and into his parents' bathroom. The key was there. He saw it as soon as he went in, lying on the ledge beside the basin with its silver chain coiled around it.

He picked it up. It was the first time he'd held it for a year. It felt colder and lighter than he remembered. Its twisted top and complicated lock-part clicked into place in some memory-pattern. And something else clicked at the same time, something which had been hovering in his mind, undefined, since he'd read the letter.

His story *was* original. Adiel had relieved his mind when he'd used that word. Even if you didn't make a story up, if *you* had the experience, and *you* wrote about it, it was original. So he hadn't cheated. But the story wasn't only his. It also belonged to the little men – to Little Bull, and Boone, and even to Tommy, the World War One soldier. (It belonged to Patrick, too, but if Patrick had decided to deny it ever happened, then he'd given up his rights in it.)

And suddenly Omri realized, as he looked at the key, that his triumph wouldn't really be complete until he'd shared it. Not just with his parents and brothers, or with the kids at school. No prize, no party, could be as good as what he was thinking about now. This was his reason – his excuse – to do what he'd been yearning to do ever since that moment when the cupboard door closed and transformed his friends back into plastic. Only with Little Bull and Boone could he share the secret behind his story, the most exciting part of all – that it was true.

He turned, went out of the bathroom and up the remaining stairs to his attic room.

Not for long, he was thinking. I won't bring them back

for long. Not long enough to cause problems. Just long enough to have a good talk. To find out how they are.

Maybe Twin Stars had had a baby by now – a papoose! What fun if she brought it with her, though it would be almost too tiny to see. Little Bull had made himself a chief while he was with Omri, but when he returned to his own place, his father might still be alive. Little Bull wouldn't like being an ordinary brave again! And Boone – the 'crying cowboy' with a talent for art, a deep dislike of washing, and a heavy thirst . . . It made Omri grin to think of him. Writing about the little men and their adventures had made them so clear in his mind that it hardly seemed necessary to do what he was going to do.

Chapter 5

From Dangerous Times

With hands that shook, Omri probed into the depths of the chest till he found the box-within-a-box-within-a-box. He eased it out and closed the lid of the chest and put the boxes on top. Reverently he untied the string on the largest box, opened it, took out the next, and repeated the operation.

In the last box, carefully wrapped in cotton wool, was the plastic group consisting of a brown pony, an Indian brave, and an Indian girl in a red dress. The brave's left hand was upraised in farewell, his other arm circled the girl's waist and held the rope-rein. The girl, her long brown legs hanging on each side of the pony's withers, had her hands buried in its mane. The pony's head was alertly raised, its ears almost meeting above its forelock, its feet braced. Omri felt himself quivering all over as he stood the tiny figures on his hand and stared at them.

'You're coming back,' he whispered – as if plastic could hear. But they wouldn't be plastic long!

The cupboard was ready. Omri stood the figures, not on its shelf but on its metal floor. Then he took a deep, deep breath as if he were going to dive into a cold, uncertain sea. He fitted the key into the lock, closed the door, and turned it.

Let it still work. Let it . . .

He barely had time to think his thought before he heard the tiny, familiar sound – minute, unshod hooves drumming and pawing on the metal!

Omri let his breath out in a rush. His heart was thumping and his right hand shook.

His fingers were still round the key. In a second he had turned it back and opened the mirrored door. And there they were . . .

No. No!

Omri's fists clenched. There ~ ′as something terribly wrong. The three figures were there, all right. The details of life, which the dull-surfaced plastic blurred, were there again. The shine on the pony's coat, the brilliance of the red dress, the warm sheen of brown, living skin. But . . .

The pony was right enough. He was prancing and stamping his hooves, fretting his head against the rope. As Omri opened the door and the light fell on him, he pricked his ears again and whickered nervously. On his back sat Twin Stars. But she was no longer in front. She sat back, almost on the pony's haunches. And before her, but lying face-down across the pony's back, was a limp, motionless form.

It was Little Bull. Omri knew it, although he couldn't see his face. His head and arms hung down on one side of the horse and his legs on the other. His buckskin leggings were caked with earth and blood. Omri, against his will, forced himself to peer closer, and saw to his utter horror where the blood had come from. There were two bullet-holes, almost too small to see, high up on his back.

Omri's mouth was wide open with shock. He looked at Twin Stars. She was holding the pony's rein-rope now. Her other hand rested on Little Bull's broad shoulders as if to steady him and stop him sliding off the pony's back. Her face was frenzied. She had no tears in her eyes but they were so round Omri could see the sparks of light in the whites. Her tiny teeth were clenched in a desperate grimace.

When she saw Omri, she started like a fawn with fear, but then the fear faded from her face. Her hand left Little Bull's back for a moment and reached out toward Omri.

It was a gesture of frantic appeal. It said *Help us*! clearer than words. But Omri couldn't move or speak. He had no notion how to help. He only knew that if he didn't, if someone didn't, Little Bull would die. Perhaps – perhaps he was dead already! What could he do?

Tommy.

Tommy's medical knowledge was not exactly up to date. How could it be, when he had only been a medical orderly in the First World War? But he was the best idea Omri could come up with, shocked and numbed as he was.

He beckoned Twin Stars forward with one hand, and while she was guiding the pony over the bottom edge of the cupboard, Omri reached back into the smallest box. The plastic figure of the uniformed soldier was at the bottom, complete with his bag with the red cross on it.

As soon as the cupboard was empty, the horse and riders clear of the door, Omri slipped Tommy in and closed it again, turning the key forward and back in a second. That was all the magic took.

'It'll be all right,' he said to Twin Stars, as she sat on the pony on top of the chest near his face. 'Tommy will fix him.' Then he opened the door again eagerly, and reached his hand in.

The bag was there. And the uniform, neatly folded, with the orderly's cap upside down on the top of the pile. And the boots. And the puttees, the khaki bandages they wore round their legs in that war, neatly rolled, inside the cap. Nothing else.

Omri let out a cry. He slammed the cupboard door to shut out the sight of that neat little pile of clothes, empty of their owner who no longer needed them. He knew, instantly. He knew that Tommy didn't live to be an old man. That one of those big German shells he had talked about, those 'Minnies', or perhaps some other weapon,

34

had got him. His snubby, cheerful face, his bravery and his gentle hands were gone, with so many thousands of others, into the mud of the trenches.

Omri had never experienced death at close hand. No one he knew well had ever died. An uncle had 'jumped the twig', as his father called it, last year, but in Australia. A boy at school had been killed in a car crash, but he wasn't in Omri's class.

The realization of Tommy's death – even a whole year after he had last seen him – came as a ghastly shock. He had no one to share this with – and in any case there was no time. Standing at his elbow was the pony, tossing his head as if in impatience, heedless of anything which delayed attention to his master. Twin Stars' bright, staring eyes were fixed on him. Waiting. Trusting.

Later. He would think about Tommy, and mourn for him. Later. Who would understand better than Tommy that you have to look after the wounded before mourning the dead? Rubbing his hand across his mouth, Omri looked around helplessly, and then he faced Twin Stars.

How much English did she know? During her brief time with him, before, he had never spoken directly to her – she had only spoken to Little Bull, in their own language. Now he must make her understand.

'No good,' he said slowly. 'No help.'

She looked blank, although the shining hope faded a little from her face. To make matters plain, Omri opened the cupboard again, and took Tommy's plastic figure – which had come back, replacing the pitiful little pile of his uniform – and stood it before the Indian girl. She slipped from the pony's back and, holding the rope, touched the figure.

She seemed to realize at once that there was no help to be looked for there. She turned swiftly back toward Omri.

'Help. You,' she said in a clear, silvery voice.

Omri felt sheer desperation clamp down on his heart, already heavy with sadness. He followed Twin Stars' pointing finger at the lifeless-looking body across the pony.

'We must lay him flat,' he said at last. It was all he could think of. But it could not be all he could do. He must think. He *must* think!

He watched Twin Stars struggling to lift Little Bull's heavy body off the horse. He helped as much as he dared, terrified his big, clumsy fingers would damage him, but at least he could make his hand into a kind of platform to lower Little Bull to the ground. With his other hand he pulled his box of tissues toward him and made a makeshift mattress out of several of them. At least they were soft and clean. Soon Little Bull was lying stretched on his stomach.

Omri had been through something like this before – when Little Bull had shot the cowboy, Boone. That time, Tommy had been brought in to help. He had had some tiny instruments, dressings and medicine. Crude as his old-fashioned methods were, they had worked. Omri felt poignantly the absence of an old friend, as one does – not just missing the person, but missing his skills, his role in one's life. For a moment, he felt almost angry with Tommy for being dead when he was so badly needed.

Twin Stars, who was kneeling beside Little Bull, looked up. She said something. It was some Indian word. Omri shook his head. Twin Stars wrung her hands. She pointed to the two bullet-wounds, and said the word again, louder. It must be some special Indian remedy she wanted. And for the first time, Omri thought, *She might be better off where she came from. She'd know what to do there*.

But at least he could clean the wounds. He knew how to do that much. He had some mouthwash, horrible stuff his mother made him gargle with when he had a cold. The bottle was on his shelf. He jumped up and fetched it. His head was spinning. He was beginning to realize how insane it had been to start this business again. He was remembering the awful sense of responsibility, the anxiety, the unending succession of problems to be solved . . . and this time he didn't even have Patrick to give him occasional support or good ideas.

Patrick . . . But Patrick was useless. He didn't even *believe* any more.

Omri flooded a bit of the cotton-wool from the box with the disinfectant and handed it to Twin Stars, making swabbing gestures to show her what it was for. She caught on quickly. With light, delicate strokes she cleaned the blood off Little Bull's back. No more seemed to be coming from the holes. Omri, remembering that injured people have to be kept warm, and noticing that Twin Stars was shivering, snatched up one of the gloves he'd worn to school and recklessly cut the little finger off it with some scissors. The Indian was soon inside the woollen finger, which was like a sleeping-bag. Omri and Twin Stars looked at each other.

'How?' Omri asked. 'How did it happen?'

Twin Stars' face grew hard.

'Soldier,' she said. 'Fight. Gun.'

'In the back?' Omri couldn't help asking. It was hard to imagine anyone as brave as Little Bull getting shot in the back.

'Horse fall,' she said. 'Little Bull lie. Ground. Soldiers shoot.' She pointed an imaginary weapon, a rifle, or a musket, gestured *one*, *two*, then waved her hand sharply to show the soldiers had run on, leaving Little Bull to die.

'You saw this?'

She nodded fiercely. 'Woman see. Soldier come village. Braves fight. Soldier make fire in house. Kill many. Take prisoner. Braves chase. Out, out – far! Twin Stars hide.

See Little Bull fall. See soldier . . .' She mimed shooting again. 'Twin Stars run, catch pony, bring Little Bull home to village. All fire! Dead brave. Woman cry. I shut eyes, not see. Whoosh!' She made a strange noise like a rush of wind. Opened her eyes – and pointed at Omri with a look of acted surprise.

'And suddenly you were here.'

She nodded. 'Spirits bring. You save.'

Omri gazed at her. He had not the very faintest idea of what to do, and here she was, trusting him.

'Don't you think you'd be better at home – in the village?' he suggested helplessly.

She shook her head violently.

'Village all fire. Dead – dead!' She pointed everywhere on the ground. 'No help. Omri only help Little Bull brother.'

Brother! Yes. Little Bull had swopped drops of blood with him in that last moment, making them blood-brothers. He must, he *must* find a way to help! But how?

At that moment, Little Bull stirred and groaned.

Instantly, Twin Stars crouched beside him. Omri, whose eyes had begun to get used to focussing on minute detail once again, noticed suddenly that she had grown fat. Could it be that . . .? But Little Bull was groaning and muttering. His legs were twitching. Omri forgot about Twin Stars' new shape for the moment.

'What's he saying?'

'Say, "Omri, Omri",' reported Twin Stars. There was more muttering, and then she said, 'Now say, "brother".' She looked up at him with a look he couldn't bear.

He stood up.

'Listen,' he said hoarsely. 'I have to bring help. I need something . . .' He looked at her. 'Lend me your moccasins.' He pointed to her feet. Bewildered but obedient, she bent and took off the soft shoes made of bead-embroidered animal hide, and gave them to him. He wrapped them carefully in a twist of paper and put them in his pocket.

'Take care of him,' he said. 'I'll be back.'

Chapter 6
Going for Help

Omri locked his bedroom door behind him and went downstairs.

It was Friday night (luckily, or he'd have had homework, which he wouldn't have been able to do). His parents and Gillon were watching television. Adiel had gone out with friends.

'Mum, d'you remember Patrick?' He spoke very casualy.

'Of course I remember Patrick.'

'He moved to the country.'

'I know.'

'I saw him last week.'

'Where?'

'Outside school. He said his mother had come back for a visit.'

'To her sister, I expect.' His mother turned back to the set.

'Her *sister*? I didn't know Patrick had an aunt!'

'Don't be silly, of course you did. She lived three doors down from our old house.'

Omri frowned, remembering. 'With those two revolting little girls?'

'Tamsin and Emma. Bonkins or something. Donkins. They're Patrick's cousins.'

'D'you think Patrick might be *there*?'

'You can soon find out. I've still got her phone number in my book. It's on the hall table.'

Three minutes later, Omri heard Patrick's voice in his ear.

'Patrick? It's me. Omri. I've got to see you.'

'When?'

'Tonight.'

'*Tonight*?'

'It's very important.'

'Can't it wait?'

Omri sensed the reluctance in Patrick's voice. He understood it.

'No.'

'I'm watching a horror film.'

'The horror film doesn't start till 11.30,' Omri retorted. There was a silence.

'You're not going to start up with all that rubbish about . . .'

'I'm coming,' said Omri shortly, and rang off.

He slipped out of the back door and was soon running down Hovel Road for the station.

Some of the shops, as well as the amusement arcade, were still open. So were the pubs. Their glass doors let out a friendly glow and lots of loud voices as Omri dashed past. In the amusement arcade the skinheads were banging away at the space invaders, not noisy and comradely like the pub-goers but grim, intent, each bent over a machine. They didn't notice him. Omri ran swiftly on, with a feeling of relief. This horrible street was actually safer by night.

Sometimes you had to wait ages for a train, but tonight Omri was lucky, though the journey – only three stops – seemed to take for ever. At the other end he began to run again, but he wasn't scared this time. He found the house of their old neighbours and rang the bell. Patrick opened the door and stood looking at him in a far from welcoming way.

'Well, you'd better come in now you're here,' he said.

It was a small house, and looked just like their old one,

even to the bicycles crowding the narrow hall. Omri's mother had said, only half as a joke, that the reason she'd wanted to move to the new house was so they needn't ever have bikes in the hall any more. Patrick led the way upstairs without a word, into a small back bedroom with a pair of bunk-beds, everything pink and frothy.

'My aunt makes me sleep in this pouffy girls' room,' he said. 'Glad I'm going home tomorrow.' He sat down on the bottom bunk, leaving Omri standing. There was a brief silence. Patrick glanced up at Omri. His mouth was pinched. His eyes said. 'Don't talk about it.' He was silently begging Omri not to. But Omri was ruthless.

'Why are you pretending it never happened?' he asked sharply.

'What?' said Patrick. He had a sullen, stupid look, like those skinheads.

'You know what.'

Patrick stared at the floor. He didn't move.

'I brought them back,' said Omri.

Patrick stood up so suddenly, he hit his head on the top bunk. His face had gone white. He swore under his breath. Then he said, 'I don't believe you.'

'I'm telling you. I put them in the cupboard and the same thing happened. It . . .' (he didn't like to use the word 'magic' somehow), 'it's still working. Just the same. Only . . .' Patrick was looking at him now, frowning, incredulous, as if he'd woken from a dream to find the dream was still going on. 'The terrible thing is, Little Bull's been shot.'

After a pause, Patrick muttered something under his breath. Omri leant forward. 'What?'

'It's not true. None of it's true. We just . . . made it up,' Patrick half-whispered.

Omri took his hand out of his pocket and held something out to Patrick. 'Look. And stop kidding yourself.'

Almost as if he were fighting fear, Patrick slowly looked. He blinked several times. Then he put out his hand and unwrapped the twist of paper. He stared for a long time at the tiny beaded moccasins.

'They're real,' breathed Patrick.

He turned away to the window and stood looking out into the darkness. Omri let him adjust. When he turned round, he was the old Patrick again. Older, but basically unchanged.

'How did it happen?'

Omri had a mad impulse to hug him. Now at least he was not alone with the problem.

'Some French soldiers shot him. I suppose they were French. You know the Iroquois were fighting with the English, and the French were against them. We've got to find a way to get the bullets out, or the musket balls, or whatever they are.'

'Easy,' said Patrick. 'Get Tommy back.'

Omri swallowed.

'He's dead.'

Patrick's mouth fell open.

'*Dead?*'

'He must have been killed in the war. He said – last time, when we were sending him back – that he could hear a big shell coming over. I bet it was the one that got him.'

Patrick stared at him aghast.

'D'you mean if we hadn't sent him back at that minute . . .'

I don't think that's how it works. His – his real, big body – that must've still been there, in his time, lying asleep in the trench. The shell would have killed him anyway.'

Patrick pushed his hand through his hair.

'And you say Little Bull's hurt?'

'Yes. Twin Stars is with him. She thinks the spirits brought her to me to help save his life. I've got to do something. And I don't know *what*.' Omri checked the shrill edge of desperation in his voice.

Patrick sat still, thinking.

'What's happened to all your old plastic people?' he asked at last. 'The ones we used to play with.'

'I think they're up in our loft.'

'Mum threw mine away.'

'Threw them away?' asked Omri unbelievingly. 'Without asking?'

'I hadn't played with them for ages.'

'Why, anyway?'

'Look,' said Patrick. 'We've lost Tommy, but the magic still works. If we could find a *modern* doctor-figure, he'd be even better.

This disloyalty to their dead friend struck both of them at once, and Patrick flushed.

'I didn't mean . . . Tommy saved Boone's life, I know that. But we've got to be realistic. There've been a lot of advances. New drugs, new techniques. Haven't you got anyone in your collection who might do?'

Omri thought, and then shook his head.

'All mine were cowboys and knights and soldiers. Stuff like that,' he said.

Patrick stood up.

'But there *are* modern ones. I've seen them. I've seen them very recently.' His face changed. He almost yelled: 'Wait!' and rushed from the room. A few moments later, he was back. 'Look!'

In his hand was a large, flat cardboard box of brand new plastic figures. They weren't soldiers, or Indians. They were ordinary people from the present day. One look told Omri what sort. *Professional* people. There was a judge in a long wig, and several lawyers. There were

44

businessmen with briefcases, one in a bowler hat. There were scientists in laboratory coats. There was a nurse. And – Omri let out a shout – there were doctors. Two of them, to be exact. One was an ordinary doctor with a stethoscope round his neck. And the other was a surgeon, in a green gown and mask.

Almost gibbering with excitement and relief – he felt as if he were looking into Aladdin's cave – Omri peered closer. The man was bent over an operating table. Yes! What Omri had been hoping for was there. Instruments – trays of them – all part of the same group. Little Bull was as good as saved.

'That's it,' he cried. 'Come on, let's go!'

But, incredibly, Patrick was hesitating.

'What's *wrong*?' asked Omri impatiently.

'They're not mine.'

'Oh, so what? Whose are they?'

'My cousin's. She got them yesterday, for her birthday.'

'We'll give them back!'

'Tamsin does her nut if you touch her things. She's sure to notice it's gone.'

'But Little Bull may be *dying*.'

Patrick gave a shrug. 'Okay. Better wrap them up.'

They found an old Safeway's bag and dropped the whole box in. They were on their way downstairs when a door opened and a girl Omri remembered only too well came out into the hall. Patrick stopped dead like a burglar caught in the act.

'Oh God, it's her,' he muttered. 'See you later . . .' But he didn't turn tail. They just kept on going toward the front door.

Tamsin barred their way. She was a big girl for her age with a pronounced jaw and scowling brows.

'Where're *you* off to, Paddywack?' she asked tauntingly. She ignored Omri, although she recognized him. They'd never been precisely pally.

'I'm going out for a bit.'

'Does your mum know?'

'I was just going to tell her.'

'I bet.'

'I was. *Excuse* me.'

As he brushed past her, some possessive instinct must have warned her. She grabbed the bag. Patrick hadn't expected this, and let go of it. In a flash she had opened it and peered in. The face she raised was suddenly flushed with fury.

'You're stealing my present!' she said, slowly and menacingly.

'No, we're not! We were only borrowing it for the night.'

'For the *night*! Are you crazy? I wouldn't let you borrow it for five seconds.'

Something was boiling up in Omri's head. There went everything they needed to save Little Bull. That wretched girl was clutching it to her as if they were trying to part her from a bag of gold.

'We were going to ask you!' he babbled untruthfully. 'Please lend them to us!'

'*No.*' Her face and voice were of stone. He knew she would never give way. An impulse born of desperation seized him. He reached out and tried to snatch the bag back from her.

She held on, and screeched. The bag tore, the box fell out and its lid came off. There on the floor lay the whole array of figures, held firmly to their backing by elastic string. Omri didn't hesitate. He simply fell on top of them, his fingers under him, clutching and wrenching. Tamsin fell on top of him, clutching and wrenching *him*. He felt his ear being nearly wrung off, his head being

46

pounded, and his ankle kicked, sharp as a dog-bite, by Tamsin's pointed shoe. As they writhed, first one bicycle and then a second crashed down on top of them.

A moment later a door slammed and an exasperated adult voice roared:

'Have you kids gone mad? Stop it this instant! *Tamsin*!'

She, and the tangle of bikes, were hiked bodily off him, putting a stop to the immediate torture, though aches lingered.

'They're nicking my present! They're nicking my models!' shrieked the dangling Tamsin, threshing all her limbs in the air like a monstrous spider.

'*Patrick?*'

But Patrick was already at the front door and Omri was scrambling to his feet.

'We don't want her models,' he muttered. 'It was only a joke!' And before more could be said, they were outside.

Patrick's mother appeared in the doorway, crying after them: 'Where do you boys think you're going?'

Patrick yelled back, 'I'm sleeping at Omri's!'

'Come back!' called his mother. 'You haven't got your toothbru-u-ush!' But they were already round the corner.

Chapter 7
Matron

Under the first street-lamp, Omri pulled up. His heart was hammering.

'Well?' asked Patrick eagerly. 'Did you get it? Let's look!'

Omri had *something* in his hand. But he knew it wasn't what he'd wanted. It wasn't the surgeon – he would have been able to feel the square shape of the operating table. It was a single figure. He held his hand closed round it, afraid to look. What if it were only a lawyer, or that idiotic bowler-hatted businessman?

Slowly, in an agony of suspense, Omri uncurled his fingers. Both boys slumped with despair. Omri gave a deep groan.

Then Patrick rallied.

'It could be worse. Nurses have to know *something*.'

'They can't operate. They're not trained.'

'It's better than nothing.'

They walked on, Omri sunk in gloom. Patrick kept trying to cheer him up.

'Listen. If he can hang on till tomorrow, we can go out and buy anything we like. At the model shop they'll have the same set. Meanwhile at least the nurse will be able to tell us how bad he is.'

'If she doesn't drop dead when we bring her out of the cupboard,' said Omri. He was cursing himself for not managing to grab the surgeon. He would also, incidentally, have liked to jump up and down on Tamsin's stomach until she yelled for mercy. He was bruised all over.

Patrick, of course, had never seen the district where Omri now lived. As they came out of the station, he paused, glanced down Hovel Road and said, 'Blimey. This is a bit rough.'

Omri said nothing. They began to hurry towards his house.

'What are the kids like around here?'

'Well, you have to stand up for yourself.'

They were passing the amusement arcade – on the other side of the street, of course. It was just closing. The proprietor, a surly-looking Sikh, was urging everyone out. There was a good deal of swearing, jeering and shoving. A scuffle started. A rather small skinhead jostled an older boy, who reacted by hurling him unceremoniously into the road, where he was narrowly missed by a passing car.

'Hell!' exclaimed Patrick. 'Did you see that?'

'Yes, and it'll be us next if they spot us,' said Omri. 'Come on!'

Omri's mother opened the door to his knock. She was furious.

'Where on earth have you been? Don't you ever go out again at night without telling me. I've been frantic! Oh. Hallo, Patrick. Fancy seeing you. Are you planning to spend the night?'

Patrick looked daunted, but Omri had no time to pacify his mother. After a brief 'Sorry, Mum!' he dragged Patrick after him up the stairs, deaf to her enquiries about where he'd been and where Patrick would sleep.

As soon as they had the door of his bedroom shut behind them, Omri switched on the main light. He'd left his bedside lamp on so Twin Stars wouldn't be in the dark. Patrick cautiously approached the chest, his eyes wide, as if his disbelief had come back to him. The sight of the living, miniature people struck him afresh as incredible. Twin Stars had jumped to her feet as they came in. She recognized Patrick at once and raised her hand to greet him.

'Hallo, Twin Stars,' he said softly. 'How's Little Bull?'

She stepped aside and pointed. Little Bull's eyes were open. They were big with pain. He fastened them on Patrick, and then saw Omri. He didn't speak, but a look of joy came over his face. He closed his eyes.

'Omri help now?' asked Twin Stars beseechingly.

'We're going to try.' He wanted to tell her not to be too hopeful but he couldn't. He brought the figure of the nurse out of his pocket. He and Patrick examined it again.

'She's wearing one of those weird, high hats,' said Patrick. 'I've seen them in films. Nurses with those sort of hats were important. All the others scurried about when they came into the ward.'

'Maybe she's a matron?' said Omri who, though he hadn't ever been in hospital, did not watch TV for nothing.

'Yeah, something like that. Come on, let's do it.'

No matter what the circumstances, this was always a thrilling moment. Into the cupboard went the little female figure in its blue uniform dress and white apron and elaborate cap. Would she be old or young? Awful or nice? Above all, how would she react when she saw them?

In the past the little people they had brought to life had been superstitious enough, or drunk enough, to accept the fantastic situation. Even Tommy had been easy to convince that he was dreaming. But a modern person might have much more trouble accepting the facts.

A quick turn back and forth of the key, and instantly a severe voice could be heard calling from inside the cupboard:

'Nurse! NURSE! Phone through immediately and tell Maintenance there's been a power-cut in Ward 12! No need for alarm, ladies, just a little electrical failure, we'll have the emergency generator working in no time!'

Omri opened the cupboard door.

'Ah!' cried the voice. '*That's* more like it! Now, what was I . . .'

And it stopped.

Omri swung the door right back. The matron stood there on the shelf where they had put her, her hands coming slowly away from her hips. She looked at the two enormous faces for a few seconds. Then she covered her eyes, rubbed them, shook her head briskly, and looked again. Then she said, 'What's this, then, boys, some kind of trick? Put the mirrors away and get back to your beds!' Then, when nothing happened, her face suddenly went as white as her cap. She did a kind of spin on one heel and fell straight backwards off the shelf.

Omri just managed to catch her. He'd been half-expecting something of the sort. She lay in the palm of his hand in a dead faint. Omri marvelled at the feeling of her tiny warm limp body, in its crisp starched clothes, alive. He transported her gently to the chest and showed her to Twin Stars.

'White woman dead?' she asked, aghast.

'No, no. She's just had a fright. Make her sit up and put her head between her knees.' He showed her how. Twin Stars wasted no time. After a minute or two, the matron showed signs of reviving. The first thing she did was reach up to check that her cap, which was like a white organdy castle with flying buttresses and banners, was still in place. Miraculously, it was.

She scrambled to her feet and stared round her. She was middle-aged, Omri guessed from her face and voice. She wore glasses and no make-up and looked formidable. He was glad that he was not a patient in her charge. At the same time she did look as if she knew her job – if only she were not too terrified to do it.

He cleared his throat.

'I know it's hard to believe,' he began, 'but you've come through a magic cupboard which has made you very small. Please don't be frightened. You can think it's a dream if you like, or some kind of trick, but there's nothing to be afraid of. After you've helped us, you can go back to your – your normal life. Would you mind telling us your name?'

The woman opened and shut her mouth several times like a goldfish. Then she managed to say, very faintly, 'You may call me Matron.' Then she swayed and put her hand to her forehead. 'I must be going mad!' she muttered. And she looked as if she might fall over again.

'Please! You're not mad. Don't faint!'

Matron stiffened at once and lifted her chin.

'*Faint? Me?* Don't be absurd, I've never fainted in my life!' She straightened her splendid cap and stared at them haughtily. 'Matrons don't faint! The very idea.'

Patrick opened his mouth, but Omri nudged him into silence.

'I beg your pardon,' he said.

'Not that I wouldn't be grateful for a strong cup of tea,' she remarked severely. 'Especially if there's any work to be done.'

'There is!' Omri exclaimed eagerly. 'I'll get you some tea later, but could you please look at a patient for us?'

Twin Stars was already almost pulling Matron over to where Little Bull was lying on the ground.

'Dear me,' murmured the Matron. She adjusted her cap and her glasses and knelt down beside Little Bull's prone form. After a brief but efficient examination, she rose, looked over her glasses at Twin Stars, evidently decided that she was innocent of any crime, and turned her accusing gaze on the boys.

'This man,' she announced, 'has been shot in the back.'

'Yes, we know,' said Omri.

'He needs an immediate operation to remove the bullets.'

'We *know*,' said Omri, and added kindly, 'only they're not bullets, they're musket balls. You see . . .'

'He must be taken at once to the nearest hospital. I recommend my own – St Thomas's.'

'Matron,' said Patrick.

'Yes, young man?'

'We can't. You see, St Thomas's is our size, and he is your size. They wouldn't be able to help him. Everything would be too big for him. Don't you see?'

Matron closed her eyes for a moment, swayed visibly (Omri stretched out a hand to catch her), and then righted herself with an effort.

'This is exceedingly peculiar,' she said, 'to say the very least. I don't profess to understand what has happened to me. But still . . . press on! What do you suggest?'

'Could he hold out until tomorrow?'

She pursed her lips and shook her head. 'Most unwise.'

Omri's heart sank.

'Couldn't – couldn't *you* do it?'

Matron started violently.

'*I?* Perform the task of a surgeon? Such a thing would be unthinkable. The etiquette of the medical profession absolutely forbids it.'

'But if it didn't?'

'What do you mean?'

'I mean – *could* you do it, if you were allowed to?'

'"Allowed to"! It is not a matter of permission.'

'Well, then? You see,' Omri said, and now the same

imploring note crept into his voice as had been in Twin Stars' eyes. 'There's no one else.'

Matron turned and stared down at Little Bull for a long moment.

'But I have no equipment,' she said at last.

Patrick threw back his head with a groan. 'That's true. Of course! No one can operate without instruments! Why didn't we think of that?'

'I did think of it,' said Omri. 'We've got instruments. Sort of.'

Patrick turned to gape at him. 'Where?'

For answer, Omri reached again for the plastic figure which had once been Tommy. Silently he put him back into the cupboard and turned the key. When he opened the door, there once again was the neat pile of clothes, the boots – and the bag with the red cross on it.

Chapter 8
The Operation

'You're *brilliant*,' breathed Patrick, as Omri delicately picked up the tiny object. With his free hand he turned one of the boxes, in which the plastic figures had been stored, upside down, spread Kleenex on it, and set the bag in the middle.

Matron bustled over with a swish of starched apron. She started a little at the sight of the battered old bag, but not half as much as she did when she opened it. She positively reeled back.

'Are you seriously suggesting that I pull bullets out of a man's back with this antiquated collection of museum-pieces!' she almost shrieked.

'Are they so very different from what you use today?' asked Omri desperately.

Matron gingerly plucked a tiny hypodermic syringe from the bag and held it up like a dead rat betwen finger and thumb.

'Look at it! Just look. I ask you . . .'

'Matron,' Omri said earnestly. 'You don't seem to understand. *That's all there is*. It's the best we can manage. If you can't do it, he'll die. Our friend. Please! All we ask is that you try.'

Matron gave Omri an old-fashioned look. Then she took hold of Tommy's bag and briskly emptied it on the padded table. All sorts of microscopic things came out. The boys could just make out the rolls of bandages, dressings, dark bottles, and instruments packed in flat cases. She examined these very minutely and then straightened up and said, 'Of course this is some kind of nightmare. But even in nightmares, it is my policy to do my best.'

Omri and Patrick clutched each other.

'You mean, you'll do it?'

'If you can provide me with an operating table, a bright light, some disinfectant, and a strong cup of tea.'

Omri could, and did, provide all those things. By this time it was one o'clock in the morning and the whole household was fast asleep, but he tiptoed downstairs and fetched proper disinfectant, cotton wool, some clean handkerchiefs, and an electric kettleful of boiling water. He also detached the cap from a tube of toothpaste and washed it out. That was for a mug. Then he made some tea with a tea-bag and added milk and sugar. He hoped she took sugar. He carried all this on a tray up the stairs very quietly.

When he returned to his room, Patrick had fixed up the box as an operating table. Omri's bedside lamp, which had a flexible neck and a 100-watt bulb – his mother had a thing about reading in a bad light – had been moved on to the chest. The light shone straight down on to the table, making no shadows. There was Kleenex spread everywhere. It looked very hygienic. Little Bull had already been laid on the table, and Matron, armed with a tiny pair of scissors, was soon cutting up a handkerchief to make a surgical gown for herself and an operating sheet for Little Bull.

'I shall need an assistant,' she said briskly. 'What about the Indian girl?'

'She doesn't speak much English.'

'We'll see. She looks bright enough.' She beckoned Twin Stars who was instantly at her elbow. 'How!' she said in a loud voice. Twin Stars looked puzzled. 'When I point – you give,' Matron went on. Twin Stars nodded intently.

'You say. I do.'

Omri was directed to pour a drop of disinfectant and some of the boiling water into a small tin lid Patrick had unscrewed from the bottle of gargle. The water turned white. Matron dropped the instruments in, and after some moments, poured off the liquid into another lid. Meanwhile, Omri was dipping up a few drops of tea into the toothpaste cap.

'Ah! Thank you, dear,' she said when she saw it. She seemed quite cheerful now. She picked up the cap in both hands. It was, to her, almost the size of a bucket, but she drank most of it at one go, and smacked her lips. 'That's more like it. What spinach is to Popeye, tea is to me. Now then, let's get on with it.'

The boys saw very little of the operation itself. The light shone straight down on the white-covered table. Matron stood with her back to them, working silently. Every now and then she would point at something on the tray. Twin Stars would swiftly pick it up and hand it to her. Only once or twice did she fumble, and then Matron would click her fingers impatiently. For a long time there was not a sound except the occasional stamp of the pony's hoof or the click of metal.

Then Matron said, 'I do believe we're in luck.'

The boys, who had been afraid to come too close, though Matron had made them both tie handkerchiefs round their faces, leant forward.

'One – er – ball went in one side and straight out the other. Missed his lung by a hair's breadth, I'm thankful to say. I've patched that up as best I could. Now I'm playing hide-and-seek with the other one. I think it's lodged against his shoulder-blade. Not far in. I – think – I've – got it. Yes!'

She made a sharp movement and then held up a minute pair of tweezers. Whatever they held was far too small to see, but the tips were red and Omri shuddered. Matron dropped the bit of metal into the tray with a ping. Suddenly she began to laugh.

'Whatever would St Thomas's surgical staff say if they could see me now!' she gurgled.

'Will he be okay?' Omri asked breathlessly.

'Oh, I think so. Yes, indeed! He's a very lucky lad, is your Indian friend.'

'We're all lucky to have found you,' said Omri sincerely.

Matron was stripping the wrapper off a large field dressing. 'First World War dressings,' she was murmuring. 'Amazing how they've lasted. As if they were made last week!'

She indicated to Twin Stars that she should help her apply the dressing to Little Bull's back. Then they bandaged him between them and after that she wiped her perspiring face on a scrap of cotton.

'You can turn the light off now,' she said. 'Phew! I'm hot.' Her towering cap was collapsing like an ice-palace, but she didn't seem to care. 'Any more tea? What an experience! Wouldn't have missed it for the world. Always thought I could do simple ops as well as any of those fat cats . . . Oh dear, what *am* I saying?' And she chuckled again at her own disrespect to professional etiquette.

After swigging down another bucket of tea and making sure Twin Stars had some too, she checked Little Bull's pulse, gave Twin Stars some simple instructions, and then said, 'Gentlemen, I think if you don't mind I'd better be getting back to St Thomas's. Goodness alone knows how they're coping without me! I'm afraid the unthinkable has happened, and I have fallen asleep on duty . . . I will simply never live it down.'

She shook hands with Twin Stars, and then gave her a pat – not on her shoulder, oddly, but on her stomach.

'Take care of your husband,' she said. 'And take care of yourself, too.' Twin Stars looked shy. 'You'll have a nice surprise for him if he doesn't come-to very soon!' Then she waved to the boys, straightened her wilted cap and, hiking up her skirt over her black stockings, clambered back into the cupboard.

When she'd gone, Omri watched Twin Stars settling down at Little Bull's side. He was still lying on the table, warmly wrapped up and sleeping soundly.

'What did she mean about a surprise?' he asked Patrick who was yawning hugely.

'Oh, come on! Didn't you notice?'

'Notice what?'

'Her big belly. She's going to have a baby.'

'A baby! Wow! That'd be great.'

'Are you nuts? That's all we need!'

'Indian women manage by themselves,' said Omri, who'd read about it. 'They don't make any fuss. Not like our mothers.'

'I should think any mother'd make a fuss if she had to have you,' said Patrick. 'Where do I kip?'

Omri was beginning to feel exhausted too, but it seemed heartless to go to sleep.

'Do you think we should?'

'She said he'd be quite okay. She told Twin Stars what to do. There's not much we can do, anyway. Look, can I just put these cushions on the floor? I'm knackered.'

In three minutes he was flat out.

It took Omri a little longer. He crouched by the chest and stared at Little Bull and Twin Stars. She must be tired too, especially considering . . .

'Do you need anything, Twin Stars? Something to eat?'

She raised her tired eyes to him and gave a little nod.

'I'll get you something!' he whispered.

Down he went once again. He didn't turn on lights this time. The reflection from the kitchen light could be seen in his parents' bedroom. He had no desire to explain to anyone what he was doing up at such an hour. The light from the street lamp was enough to show him cake, bread, butter.

What was that? Something had gone past the window. He'd seen it out of the corner of his eye. He froze. He could have sworn it was a man's head. When he unfroze, he went to the window and looked out.

All he could see was Kitsa sitting on the sill. That would have settled the matter, except for one thing. Her head was up, her ears were pricked – and not at Omri, but in the other direction.

Omri climbed the stairs with the food, feeling more than a little uneasy. It seemed to him, on reflection, that the head he had seen had shone in the street lamp as if it had no hair.

Chapter 9
A Good Luck Piece

Little Bull's recovery was little short of miraculous. The operation was a complete success. By the next day he was sitting up, demanding food and other services, not particularly grateful for his deliverance and, in general, very much himself as Omri remembered him.

He was unable to hide his delight at seeing Omri again. He tried to conceal his feelings behind a mask of dignity, but through his wooden expression his black eyes gleamed and a grin kept twitching at his stern mouth.

'Omri grow much,' he remarked, between slurps of a mug of hot instant soup. (There was a distinct shortage of toothpaste tops throughout the house, which Omri's mother was to remark on.) 'But still only boy. Not chief, like Little Bull.'

'Are you a real chief now?' Omri asked. He was sitting on the floor beside the chest, gazing in rapture at his little Indian, restored to him, and, almost, to health.

Little Bull nodded impressively. 'Father die. Little Bull chief of tribe.'

Omri glanced at Twin Stars. How much had she told him of the tragedy which had overtaken their village? Clearly he remembered nothing. She seemed to understand his thought and signalled him quickly behind Little Bull's back. Omri nodded. Much better not to say too much, until Little Bull was stronger. He hadn't asked any questions yet.

Patrick had stayed for breakfast and then, reluctantly, phoned his mother. He came back up to Omri's room looking bleak.

'She says I've got to come back,' he said. 'We're leaving today. I asked if I could stay and come back later, but she said I have to leave here in an hour.'

Omri didn't say anything. He didn't see how Patrick could bear to leave. To make matters worse, Omri's parents had particularly asked if he could stay for another night. They were going to a party that evening and would be home late. Adiel and Gillon would be out, too. There'd be a baby-sitter of course, but she was a stodgy old lady and Patrick would be company for Omri. Omri thought Patrick's mother was being entirely unreasonable, and said so. Patrick was inclined to agree.

Meanwhile, they had this hour. They decided to spend it talking and doing things for the Indians. The first thing Little Bull asked for was his old longhouse, built by himself when he'd been with Omri last year. Fortunately, Omri still had it, or what was left of it. It had been made on a seed-tray packed with earth, but this had dried out in the interval, so that several of the upright posts had come adrift, and some of the bark tiles, so carefully shaped by Little Bull and hung on the cross-pieces, had shrivelled and dropped off.

When Little Bull saw his derelict master-work he had to be forcibly restrained from leaping out of bed immediately to repair it.

'How Omri let fall down? Why Omri not mend?' he shouted wrathfully.

Omri knew better than to argue.

'I couldn't do it like you can,' he said. 'My fingers are too big.'

'Too big!' agreed Little Bull darkly. He stared at the longhouse from his bed. Omri had spent the early hours, before anyone was awake, making him a better bed from two matchboxes, giving him a bed-head to sit up against. His mind was roving in all directions, thinking of ways to make Little Bull and Twin Stars more comfortable. He still had the old tepee . . . As soon as the Indian was a bit better, he would probably prefer to use that, for privacy. Omri had fixed a ramp leading on to the seed-tray, and Twin Stars had begun to go up and down it carrying bedding into the tepee, like a little bird making its nest. A plump little bird . . . Omri wondered, watching her stagger to and fro, how long it would be before her baby was born.

He was busy giving her a water supply. It was a sort of pond. The container was the lid of a coffee jar, sunk into the earth of the seed-tray near the tepee. He was now making a proper bucket out of one of the toothpaste caps, by piercing two holes in the sides with a needle heated red-hot in the flame of an old candle he'd found, and threading in a handle made from a bit of one of his mother's fine hairpins. That would make it easier to carry. Of course, that was just the beginning of all the things that would be needed, if they stayed long.

Twin Stars vanished into the tepee and Little Bull, who had been watching her too, beckoned Omri closer.

'Soon I father!' he said proudly, and hit himself on the chest. A flash of pain crossed his face.

'Yes,' said Omri, 'so you'd better rest and get well.'

'I well!' He shifted restlessly about on the matchbox bed. Suddenly he said: 'Where other brother?'

'What do you mean – my brothers?'

'No! Little Bull brother! Blood-brother, like Omri.'

It occurred to Omri and Patrick at the same moment who he meant.

Patrick had also been busy. He had gone outside earlier and dug up a very small turf of grass from the garden – a piece of living lawn about six inches square, a paddock for the pony to graze on. It was to have a fence round it, which Patrick was making out of twigs and string and glue. Now he looked up from this with an unreadable look on his face.

'When your mum threw your models away . . .' began Omri slowly.

'Yeah?'

'Did she get rid of – all of them?'

'As far as I know.'

'You really are the *pits*,' said Omri between his teeth.

'Me? Why?'

'I suppose you just threw him in with the others and left him for your mum to chuck in the dustbin!'

'What are you talking about?'

'You know damn well! *Boone*.'

Patrick dropped his eyes. Omri couldn't tell what he felt. He seemed almost to be smiling, but Omri felt suddenly so furious with him that this only made him angrier.

Though they had spoken quietly, Little Bull's sharp ears had caught the gist.

'Who throw Boone? I want! Want see blood-brother. Who throw, I kill!' he roared.

Twin Stars emerged from the tepee at the first roar and darted to his side. She forced him to lie on his back and pinioned him to the bed by main force until he calmed down a little and evidently promised her to behave. Then she hurried to the edge of the chest with a gleam in her eyes that boded no good at all.

'Where Litle Bull brother?' she demanded. 'Little Bull want! No good him get angry! Omri bring Boone. Now.'

Omri's insides seemed to be churning up with an anger no less strong than the Indian's. He turned on Patrick.

'You must have been mad to let your mother throw him away! Just because for some idiotic reason you wanted to pretend none of it ever happened! I'm going to kick your head in, you dim wally!' And he made a move towards Patrick.

Patrick didn't step back. He stood with his hand in his pocket.

'He's here,' he said.

Omri stopped short, jolted as if he'd stepped up a non-existent step. 'What?'

'He's here. In my pocket.'

Slowly he withdrew his hand and opened it. Lying in the palm was the crying cowboy, on his white horse. Boone – as large as life. Or rather, as small.

Omri uttered a shout of joy.

'You've got him! You had him all the time!' Then his grin faded. 'Are you mad? Why didn't you say so in the first place?'

'I'm not exactly proud of the fact that I still carry him everywhere,' Patrick said.

'So you hadn't stopped believing?'

'I don't know. I wanted to. I tried to tell my brother about it once, and he took the mick for a solid week, saying I was a nut case, telling everyone I believed in fairies. It really got me. Of course I couldn't prove a thing, not even to myself. So I decided it never happened. But I . . . I just kept Boone in my pocket all the time, like – well, sort of for good luck.'

Omri had picked up the figure of Boone tenderly and was examining it. The horse's legs had become a bit bent, and Boone's beloved hat was looking decidedly the worse for wear. But it was still, unmistakably, even in plastic, Boone. It was the way they had last seen him, sitting on his horse, in his ten-gallon hat, his hand holding a big red bandana to his nose, blowing a trumpet-blast of farewell.

'*Ah cain't stand sayin' goodbye. Ah jest re-fuse t'say it, that's all! Ah'll only bust out cryin' if Ah do . . .*'

'Come on, Boone!' whispered Omri. And he put him without more ado into the cupboard and turned the key.

He and •Patrick bent over eagerly, bumping heads. Neither of them brought to the surface of his mind the deep fear they both shared. Boone, too, had lived in dangerous times. Omri knew now that time worked the same at both ends, so to speak. A year had passed for him, and, in another place and time, a year had passed for his little men. An awful lot (and a lot of it awful!) could happen in a year.

But almost at once their fears were laid to rest. There was a split second's silence, and then, on the other side of the cupboard door, Boone began battering and kicking it, and a faint stream of swear-words issued through the metal.

'Ah ain't puttin' up with it! No, sir, it ain't fair, it ain't dawggone-well right! Ah ain't bin drinkin', Ah ain't bin fightin', Ah ain't cheated at poker in over a week! Ain't no law kin sling a man in jail when he's inny-cint as a noo-born babe, never mind keepin' him shut in a cell so dark he cain't see his own mus-tash!'

The boys were too fascinated to do anything at first, even open the door. They just crouched there, grinning imbecilically at each other.

'It's Boone! It's really him!' breathed Patrick.

But Boone, all unaware, and getting no response to his yells and blows, now decided no one was listening, and his voice began to quaver.

'They done up and left me,' he muttered. 'Gone plumb away and left ol' Boone alone in the dark . . .' There was a pause, followed by a long nose-blow that shook the cupboard. 'T'aint funny,' he went on, his voice now definitely shaking with sobs. 'Don't they know a man kin be brave as a lion and still skeered o' the dark? Ain't they got no 'magination, leavin' a fella ter rot in this pitch-black hell-hole?' His voice rose on a shrill tide of tearful complaint.

Omri could not bear it a second longer. He opened the door. The light struck through and Boone instantly looked up, his red bandana dropping to the floor between his knees. He jumped to his feet, staring, his mouth agape, his battered old hat askew on his ginger head. The horse backed off and snorted.

'Well. Ah'll be e-ternally hawnswoggled!' Boone got out at last. 'If it ain't you-all!'

Chapter 10
Boone's Brainwave

'Yes, it's us all! I mean, it's us!' said Patrick excitedly. He capered about, stiff-legged, unable to contain himself.

Omri too, was over the moon. 'It's so good to see you, Boone,' he cried, wishing he could wring the little man's hand and bang him on the back.

Boone, who must have fallen off his horse at some point, now scrambled to his feet and dusted himself off. The horse came up behind him in the cupboard and nudged him forcefully in the back, as if to say, *I'm here, too*. Omri could just about stroke its tiny nose with the tip of his little finger. The horse bunted it, nodding its head up and down, and then exchanged whinnies with Little Bull's pony on the distant seed-tray.

'And it's mighty good t'see you fellas!' Boone was saying warmly, as he scrambled out of the cupboard. 'Bin more'n a mite dull without mah hallucy-nations . . . Wal! Waddaya know, if it ain't the li'l Injun gal!' Twin Stars had taken a few steps toward him timidly. He raised his hat. 'Howdy, Injun lady! Hey, but whur's th'other one? That redskin that made me his blood-brother – after he'd half killed me?' He looked around the top of the chest, but Little Bull's matchbox bed had its back to him. 'Tarnation take me if'n Ah didn't miss that dawggone varmint when Ah woke up that last time . . . Or "went back", or whatever ya call it.' He rubbed his shirt-front reminiscently. 'Mah ol' pals thought Ah'd gawn plumb loco when Ah tried t'tell 'em how Ah got mah arrow-wound!'

'Are you okay now, Boone?'

'Me? Ah'm jest fine! Y'cain't kill Boo-hoo Boone s'easy, even if'n he does look a mite soft. So whur's Li'l Bull? Lemme shake the hand that shot me, t'show thur ain't no hard feelin's!'

Twin Stars didn't understand much of this, but she heard Little Bull's name. She took Boone by the arm and drew him over to the bed. When Boone saw the prostrate figure of the Indian he stopped short.

'Holy smoke, whut happened t'him?'

'He got shot, too. By Frenchmen,' Omri added in a low voice, and signalled to Boone not to ask questions. But Boone was not the most tactful of men.

'Jee-hosophat! Never did trust them Frenchies. Got one runnin' our saloon. Some day someone's gonna run *him* – right outa town! Waters the whisky, y'know,' he added confidentially to Twin Stars.

At the word 'whisky', Little Bull opened his eyes (he had dropped off to sleep) and tried to sit up. When he saw Boone bending over him he let out a cry of recognition, and then fell back again with a hand to his bandaged chest.

'Gee, the pore ol' savage!' said Boone, shaking his head. He sniffed. 'Not that he probably didn't deserve it. They're allus up to no good, but all th'same Ah cain't stand to see a man in pain.'

He wiped away a tear.

'He's much better now,' said Patrick. 'There's nothing to start crying about.'

Boone blew his nose loudly and plonked himself down on the bed.

'Tell me th'whole thing,' he said.

'Not now,' said Omri hurriedly.

'Why'n thunder not? I gotta hear sometime. C'mon, Injun. Or are ya ashamed o' somethin' ya done to them Frenchies t'make 'em take a shot at ya?'

Little Bull lay on the bed and stared up at Boone. There was suddenly tension in the air as they all – Twin Stars too – waited for him to remember. To ask.

Slowly he raised himself on to his elbows. His eyes had gone narrow, his face taut and scowling. Suddenly he opened his eyes wide and let out a wild cry.

'Aaiiiiii!'

Twin Stars put her hands to her face, turned, and fled up the ramp and into the tepee.

'Whut got into her?' Boone asked, looking after her, puzzled.

But another anguished cry transfixed them all.

'Little Bull remember! Soldiers come – burn village! Burn corn! Many, many . . .' He opened and closed his hands rapidly, holding up ten fingers again and again. 'Iroquois braves fight – but not enough – not got guns – horses . . . Enemy break – burn – steal. Kill . . . kill . . .'

His voice cracked. He stopped speaking.

Another man might have broken down and wept. But Little Bull just stared, wild-eyed and frozen-faced. His mouth was shut in a straight line, like a knife-cut in his hard face. Only his hands quivered at his sides, and his fingers became hooks.

'Gee whiz, fella,' muttered Boone at last. 'That's too bad.'

There was a long silence. Nobody moved. Little Bull lay on his back, his eyes open. He seemed to be neither fully awake, nor asleep. Omri passed a finger back and forth in front of those staring eyes. They didn't respond. Omri, Patrick and Boone looked anxiously at each other.

'What shall we do?

'Nuthin',' said Boone. 'Pore guy's had a shock. Happened t'me once't. Came to after Ah got knocked out in some kinda ruckus . . . Couldn't remember a thing. Started in talkin' and drinkin' jes like ever'thin' was normal, when all of a sudden, it come back t'me. *A lynchin'*. A mob o' coyotes jest strung a fella up for somethin' he didn't even do. Most horriblest thing Ah ever saw. Ah jest laid there, seein' it all over again. Took me a danged long time t'git over it. An' that wasn't s'bad neither, as what he's a-seein' now, pore critter . . .'

Tears of sympathy were streaming down the cowboy's leathery cheeks.

'Them rotten Frenchies . . . Mixin' in . . . Sneakin' up on 'em that-a-way an' skeerin' thur wimmenfolk an' all. Gee. Ah sure would like to help them pore folk, if'n it hadn't a-happened s'long ago!'

This showed an extraordinary change of heart for Boone, who had been absolutely down on Indians when they'd first known him. Omri said, 'If we sent them back now, it would be all still going on. If you wanted to help, maybe we could send you back to their time. If Little Bull just held on to you, you'd all go back together.'

Boone, who had had his face buried in his red bandana, froze for a moment. His eyes slowly appeared above the red spotted cloth.

'Me?' he said in a quavering voice.

'Well, you said you'd like to help. You've got a gun, after all. And you don't like Frenchmen. Maybe you'd like to shoot a few of them . . .'

'. . . before they shoot me!' finished Boone. 'That's a great idee, thanks a lot. Things is tough and dangerous enough whur Ah come from, Ah mean, *when* Ah come from, without goin' back a hundred years t'when things wuz ten times worse. Come t'that – what's stoppin' *you* from lendin' a hand t'the redskins if'n yor s'crazy about 'em?'

Patrick and Omri looked at each other, startled.

'We can't go back!' Patrick exclaimed. 'How could we? We can't fit into the cupboard!'

Boone looked at them, looked consideringly at the small bathroom cabinet less than a foot high, and then back at the boys again.

'That's true,' he said grudgingly. 'Ah reckon Ah cain't argue 'bout that. But thur's still a way Ah kin think of, that ya could help 'em, if'n you'd a mind ter.'

'How?' they asked at once.

'What's that, down over yonder? It's s'danged far away, Ah cain't see properly, but it looks to me like a whole bunch o' folks layin' in a heap in a box.'

The boys looked where he was pointing. Down on the floor was the biscuit-tin full of Omri's collection of plastic figures. He'd gone up to the loft that morning to fetch it. He lifted it and put it on the chest, the top of which was now getting rather crowded.

'Lift me up and lemme look,' ordered the little man.

Patrick put his hand down close to him. Boone heaved himself on to it as if he were scrambling on to a horse without a saddle. Patrick 'flew' him over the box. He lay down flat and peered over the side of Patrick's hand, hanging on to his precious hat.

'Lookit that! Whatcha think ya got down there, if'n it ain't all kindsa men with all kindsa shootin' irons? If'n you could stick 'em in the cupboard and bring 'em to life and then send 'em back with the Injuns, they'd come out th'other end and send them Frenchies scooting back to France as fast as greased lightnin'!'

Omri and Patrick looked at each other.

'Would it work?' breathed Patrick, his eyes alight.

Omri could see that it was not just the possibility of helping the Indians that was getting him excited. From the very beginning, Patrick had wanted to experiment with the cupboard. Omri had barely been able to prevent him from stuffing dozens of soldiers in, bringing whole

armies to life and making them fight . . . This looked like
being just the excuse he'd been wanting.

The idea had a strong appeal for Omri, too. But he was
more cautious.

'We'd have to think about it,' he said.

Patrick almost slammed his hand, with Boone on it,
down again on the chest.

'You're always *thinking*!' he said disgustedly. 'Why don't we just try it?'

Omri was frowning, trying to imagine. 'Listen.' He picked up a knight in chain-mail with a big helmet, and a shield with a red cross on a white ground. 'If we put this one in, for instance, he'd come to us from the time of

Richard the First. He wouldn't know a thing about Indians. He'd want to go off to Palestine and kill Saracens.' He put the knight down and picked up a soldier in a flat cap and khaki shorts. 'This one's a French Foreign Legionnaire. We couldn't even talk to him, let alone to an Arab tribesman or a Russian Cossack. They were great fighters, but they wouldn't just agree to be in an army fighting Frenchmen in America on the side of the Indians. They're not *toys*. Every one of them's a person – I mean, if we brought them to life. We'd have to explain everything. Half of them wouldn't believe it, others might think they'd gone crazy . . .'

But Patrick interrupted in high impatience.

'Oh, what are you on about? Who's talking about soldiers with swords and axes and old-fashioned popguns? What about *these*?'

He dug his hand into the tin and came up with a fistful of British soldiers. Some had self-loading rifles, others had sub-machine guns. There was a howitzer, a 37mm anti-tank gun, three rocket launchers and a variety of grenades. Omri stared at the fire-power bristling out between Patrick's fingers. They had an army there, all right!

Patrick was already moving toward the cupboard, ready to thrust in the handful of soldiers.

'No,' said Omri, as he had once before. 'Stop!'

'I'm going to do it!' said Patrick.

Just at that moment, they heard footsteps coming up the stairs.

As one man, they turned and sat on the very edge of the chest, facing the door, forming a human screen.

Omri's mother put her head in.

'Patrick, your mother just rang. Your cousin Tamsin has had a nasty fall off her bicycle and your mother's going to stay and help your aunt, so you won't be going home today.'

Patrick's face lit up.

'Great! That means I can stay the night here.'

'I'm sorry about your poor cousin,' said Omri's mother.

'I'm not,' said Patrick promptly. 'I hope she broke a leg.'

'Really, Patrick! That's not nice.'

'Nor is she,' said Patrick feelingly.

Omri's mother was looking at them curiously.

'You do look odd, sitting there like Tweedledum and Tweedledee,' she said. 'Are you hiding something from me?'

'Yes,' said Omri. It was always better to be quite frank with his parents if possible. Luckily they didn't expect to be in on everything he did.

'Oh, well,' she said. 'I hope it's nothing too awful. There'll be a bite of lunch in a little while. I'll call you.'

And she went off.

Patrick slumped with relief.

'She's just not normal, your mum,' he muttered. 'Mine wouldn't have rested till she'd had a good look . . .' He brought his hand from behind his back and opened it and looked at the soldiers. The uncontrollable impulse to put them in the cupboard had subsided, but he still wanted to very badly. Omri could see that.

Chapter 11
Target Omri!

Twin Stars was calling them.

She had come to Little Bull's bedside again, and was now helping him to struggle into a sitting position.

'I don't think he should sit up yet,' said Omri anxiously, adding, 'Not – sit – up.' Twin Stars looked very worried, but Little Bull brushed her aside, gritting his teeth.

'Little Bull sit. Stand. Go back and fight!'

'No. You can't. You're not strong enough.'

'I strong enough! I chief. Chief not sit in far place when tribe in trouble! Omri put in box. Omri send back! Chief Little Bull say.'

But Omri was adamant.

'You're not going anywhere till you're better.'

He looked into the Indian's face. He understood very well how he must be feeling: like a deserter, even though his being shot, and finding himself here, was no fault of his own at all.

Once Omri had been away on a week's school trip and when he got back he found that while he'd been gone, his mother, alone in the house, had cut herself very badly on a broken bottle. With her hand pouring blood she had managed to get to the phone, an ambulance had come, and she was soon in hospital and safe. None of all this was any fault of Omri's or anyone's. But he felt terrible – really guilty – about having been so far away.

So it wasn't hard to imagine how strongly Little Bull felt the need to get back to help his people. After all, he was their chief; he was responsible for them. Who knew what was happening at the Indian encampment at this very moment? Twin Stars was thinking about it, too. She was torn, Omri could see, between wanting to keep Little Bull in bed and wanting him to go back and do what he had to do.

'Let's tell him about Boone's idea,' suggested Patrick. It might take his mind off going back right away himself.'

'Yeah! Ah had me a idee, all right!' chimed in Boone. 'Say, why don't we all have us a bite t'eat, not to mention a swig o'likker? And talk my idee over? Ain't nuthin' like whisky fer helpin' yer brain work, ain't that so, kid?'

So Omri crept downstairs and extracted a small glassful of whisky from his parents' drinks cupboard, and some food from the table which his mother had laid for lunch. She was not much of a fancy table-layer and all there was, for the moment, was Ryvita, butter and some rather tired-looking olives, but that was better than nothing. He grabbed a bit of each, and hurried upstairs again.

He should have known better than to leave the room.

As he opened the door, he was greeted by a noise that sounded like a loud chattering of teeth. Then there was a distinct pop, and something went *ping* against the glass of whisky he was carrying.

His eyes flashed to the cupboard. There, on the shelf in the middle of it, were five miniature soldiers, raking the room with machine-gun fire. On the chest below were several more. They were manning a small but lethal-looking artillery piece.

Omri had no time to think. Dropping everything, he threw up his hand to protect his face and dashed forward through a hail of tiny bullets that bit into his palm like wasp-stings.

Patrick was standing aghast, too stunned, it seemed, to do anything. Omri fell on the little men in their khaki uniforms, scooped them up, weapons and all, and, shoving them back in the cupboard, slammed the door. He heard another couple of rounds, and the muffled boom of an exploding hand-grenade against the inside of the door, before he could gather his wits and turn the key.

Silence fell in the bedroom.

Omri's first act was to glance over his shoulder to check that Little Bull, Twin Stars and Boone were all right. There was a line of bullet-holes through the top of the matchbox bed-head, but, mercifully, Twin Stars must have persuaded Little Bull to lie down just before the shooting started, and he was okay.

Twin Stars was holding the two horses, who were in Patrick's paddock. They were rearing and plunging with terror, letting out shrill neighs, while Twin Stars hung on to their reins.

Boone was, at first glance, nowhere to be seen, but then Omri made out a tiny pair of cowboy boots and spurs sticking out from under the ramp. He must have dived for cover when the attack began: not particularly heroic, but certainly by far the most sensible move open to him at the time.

Next, Omri gave his attention to his hand. Half a dozen droplets of blood oozed from as many tiny breaks in the skin. Remembering when Patrick had had a bullet in his cheek from Boone's gun once, Omri quickly started squeezing out the bullets, lodged just under his skin, between finger and thumb-nail. He didn't say a word to Patrick. What was the use? Some people just never learn.

But Patrick had something to say, and in a voice that shook.

'I could've got them all killed.'

Omri bit his lip. The bullets were actually just visible, minute black specks. It hurt, getting them out, but it was rather satisfying, like squeezing a blackhead.

'I just wanted to see what would happen,' Patrick went on pleadingly.

'Well, now you've seen. Thanks a lot.'

'Sorry.'

'You're always bloody well sorry when you've done something thick.'

Patrick didn't argue. He bent down and pulled Boone out from under the ramp by the feet.

'It's okay, Boone. They've gone.'

The little man was gibbering and shaking from head to foot.

'Who in tarnation were those guys?' he managed to ask.

'Soldiers.'

'From when?'

'Now. Approximately.'

'Boy! Am Ah glad Ah'll be daid before *that* kinda shootin' starts!' he said fervently. 'Did they getcha, kid?' he asked Omri anxiously, as a drop of blood splashed on to the chest beside him.

'Only a bit,' said Omri, pressing a wadge of Kleenex to his hand.

'Did ya git any of the hard stuff?' Boone asked eagerly. "Now Ah *really* need some.'

'Oh – I must've dropped it!'

Boone's face fell. But when Omri went to the door, he found that although the glass had fallen to the floor, spilling most of the whisky, it hadn't broken, and there was still a little left in the bottom. He offered the glass to Boone, who promptly heaved himself up over the rim and dived in head first. Hanging on to the rim by his boots, he started lapping up the dregs of whisky like a puppy.

Omri couldn't help laughing.

'Oh, come on, Boone! You can't be that thirsty. Remember, you're supposed to be civilized.' And he hiked him out and poured the last drops into a toothpaste-cap mug. 'Save some for Little Bull.'

Boone looked shocked.

'Ya cain't go givin' likker t'Injuns, don't ya know that? Drives'm crazy. They just ain't got the heads fer it. Anyways, ya couldn't give *him* any. He's too sick.'

'When you were wounded you said whisky made you feel better.'

'Yeah, guess Ah did at that.' He gazed sorrowfully down into his mug. 'Wal, if'n you're ready t'risk it – only don't blame me if he goes loco. Here . . .' He handed the mug to Omri, who passed it to Little Bull. He was sitting up again, examining the bullet-holes in his bed.

'Boone sent you some whisky, Little Bull.'

'Not want,' said the Indian at once.

'Why not? I thought you liked it.'

'Firewater for feast. For make happy. Take from trouble. Little Bull must keep head. Must think, then act. Give fire-water to Boone. He not need think.'

Boone received his drink back without reluctance. Omri picked up some bits of Ryvita and olive from the floor and soon the little people were all munching, though their opinion of olives was evidently not high.

'So ma idee could work,' Boone remarked after draining his drink. 'Ten fellas like them, with guns like that, an' those Frenchies would be on their knees, if they had any left, beggin' the redskins to make pow-wow.'

Patrick, who had been standing at the window, turned round. 'That's what I was thinking,' he said.

Omri felt quite exasperated. How could they both be so stupid?

'What do you think, Little Bull?' Patrick asked eagerly. 'What if we made lots of soldiers like that real, and then joined them all to you somehow and sent you all back together to your village? They could fight the Frenchmen for you.'

Little Bull grew still. His black eyes moved under his

scowling brows from one of them to another. For a moment Omri feared he would jump at this tempting solution. But then, reluctantly, he shook his head.

'No good,' he said gruffly.

'Aw! Why not?' said Boone. 'They'd jest shoot 'em to mincemeat in two minutes, and ya'd be rid o' them for ever. They'd never dare come back to bother ya no more!'

'Now-soldiers not belong,' said Little Bull. 'They not fight for Little Bull's people. They fight on side of French soldier.'

'If at all,' said Omri. 'Much more likely they'd just sit down and refuse to fight anyone, once they realized they weren't where they ought to be.'

'We could explain to them,' said Patrick.

'You try explaining to a whole bunch of soldiers who're probably in the middle of World War Two or in Northern Ireland, that they're not to fight the Nazis or the IRA, they're to go off and shoot eighteenth-century Frenchmen in the middle of Virginia!'

'Well, who *could* you explain it to?'

And that was when Omri had his brainwave.

'I'll tell you who! *Other Indians.*'

Little Bull's head came round. He saw the point at once.

'Yes!' he cried immediately.

'What?' asked Patrick.

'Whatcha mean, kid?' asked Boone.

'Listen, listen!' cried Omri excitedly. 'What we have to do is go out and buy loads of Indians. Iroquois, like Little Bull. He'll tell us what sort of clothes and things to look out for – though I think I know, anyway. Then we'll bring them to life, and Little Bull can talk to them, and we can send them all back together when Little Bull's better, and . . .'

'Send back now! Most soon! I well, I better *now*!' Little

Bull shouted. Twin Stars came running to calm him but he wouldn't be calmed. He began shouting at her in their own language. She seemed very excited, and clapped her hands and looked up at Omri with the shining eyes that had given her her name.

'Spirits know Omri save,' she said. 'Save village too!'

But Little Bull had something else on his mind.

'Now-guns,' he said.

'What?' Omri asked, not understanding.

'Now-soldiers no good. But now-guns *good*. Get Iroquois brave, plass-tick, many, many, then give brave now-guns like one make hole in bed.'

Chapter 12
The Troops

The boys ate lunch downstairs so as not to arouse suspicions though it was sheer agony to leave the attic bedroom when so much was going on. Little Bull was in absolute torment, they could see, and though Omri, for his part, was in no hurry to send him back, he felt they must do something as soon as possible to further the plan.

Omri's parents talked of nothing but the party they were going to that evening. Adiel and Gillon wanted to see a film, and were arguing fiercely about which one. Gillon was carrying on a side-argument with his parents about the desirability of hiring a video, which, he assured them, would save far more than it cost in the end. Parental reaction to this excellent idea was, as usual, automatic and negative.

All this seemed ridiculously trivial to Omri, with so much on his mind.

Patrick and he had been out to the model shop before lunch. Omri had taken along one of his books on Indians, and tried to find the ones who were dressed in the distinctive Iroquois clothes – floppy leggings with feather decorations, moccasins gathered round the ankles, a sort of sporran-thing hanging like an apron from the waist, turkey-feathers in a headband round the forehead. Only there weren't many like that. It was extraordinary what a variety of Indian costumes there were, and the model shop had what appeared to be representatives from a dozen tribes.

Omri knew how bitter the hatred between warring tribes could be. The Algonquins, for instance, were the

Iroquois' mortal enemies. It would be no use bringing any of *them*. But since there weren't anything like enough that he was sure were Iroquois, Omri had bought some others he wasn't sure of, in the hope that Little Bull would recognize them as belonging to some friendly Indian nation who would agree to help the Iroquois in their hour of trial.

Patrick, book in hand, was at another shelf, looking at English soldiers of different periods. He wanted to find some who might have fought the French in America. Omri wasn't keen on bringing any white men into it, but Patrick said they were in it already.

'I bet they'd handle modern weapons better than a bunch of primitive Indians, anyhow.'

Omri told him not to be so racist, but when Patrick found some which looked right, according to an illustration in the book, Omri made no objection to buying four foot-soldiers and even one mounted officer. The horse, a handsome black, made him much more expensive.

The whole lot – about fifty assorted Indians and five soldiers – set them back over ten pounds, which for Omri was more than three weeks' pocket-money. Patrick chipped in, though he hadn't brought much.

So now they had this bagful of potential allies for Little Bull, and the boys couldn't wait to get started. As soon as lunch was over, the rest of the family scattered, and the house became quiet. On the way upstairs, Omri said, 'Do you think we dare bring them outdoors?'

'I want to start putting things in the cupboard,' said Patrick.

'So do I! But let's bring the cupboard out, too. Then if any shooting should start, it won't be so dangerous.'

'Why should it be less dangerous outdoors?'

'I don't know . . . It just feels as if it would be safer.'

'Well, okay. But what if your father or anyone comes out in the garden?'

'Dad's painting in his studio. Anyway there's a hedged-off bit down at the bottom which is just shrubs. He never goes there.'

They found the little people waiting for them anxiously.

'Where Omri go so long time?' Little Bull demanded at once.

'Calm down, we've been getting the men.'

Little Bull sat up straight, his eyes glowing.

'Show!'

'In a minute.'

Carefully Omri lifted the matchbox bed on to the seed-tray. 'Twin Stars, cover him up warmly. We're going outside.'

She put the glove-finger round Little Bull to the armpits while Boone ran up the ramp, pulling it up behind him. The two ponies were munching grass in their fenced-off paddock. Omri picked the whole thing up, while Patrick carried the cupboard and the bag of new men. As an afterthought he slipped Matron in his pocket. Omri did a quick recce to see that nobody was around. Then they cautiously trooped down the stairs and out of the kitchen door into the back garden.

It was a really lovely place, far better than their old garden. It was not just a rectangle of lawn with a few flowerbeds. It had nooks and crannies. Omri headed for his favourite corner, a shrubbery with a patch of grass in the middle, where rhododendrons and other tall bushes kept prying eyes at bay. The sun was high and the place was sheltered from the wind. Still, Omri suggested Little Bull should be put into the longhouse to keep warm.

'No! Not want! Want be in sun! Sun give *orenda*.'

'What's that?'

Little Bull looked baffled.

'Not know *orenda? Orenda* for all men. Life strength. Sun give. And rain. *Orenda* in animal, plant, all thing. Master of Good make. Now Omri be Master of Good! Make brave, many, fight for Little Bull people.'

Omri felt a cold shiver. He didn't like the idea of playing God. But it was too late to back out now.

They laid the seed-tray and the cupboard on the grass. Boone at once put the ramp back in position, saddled his pony, tested his lassoo which he kept coiled round the pommel, and set off for a ride. It was rough going, as the grass in the shrubbery was not often mowed, but he didn't seem to mind.

'You fellas settle things. Ah'm goin' for a gallop!'

'Keep us in sight,' said Patrick.

'That's the same as sayin', keep the Rocky Mountains in sight!' laughed Boone. He waved his hat at them and went racing off between the grass-stems shouting 'Yippee!' in the approved cowboy fashion. One of the most satisfying things about Boone was the fact that he always behaved exactly as the boys expected. This helped to balance Little Bull. They never knew what to expect from him.

The boys now began to set out the little men they'd bought in lines for Little Bull to inspect. Even though the Indian was well aware they couldn't see him, he seemed to feel ashamed before them, lying in what he called 'white man bed'. He made Twin Stars help him off it and on to a stack of rhododendron leaves he ordered to be laid on the earth. It looked very grand, like stiff layers of shiny dark green leather, but not very comfortable, Omri thought.

Little Bull sat cross-legged and stared narrowly at the Indian figures one by one. Several times he demanded that one of them be brought and laid before him for closer inspection. Some he discarded with an imperious wave of his hand. Once he uttered a deep growl.

'Why bring Algonquin enemy?'

'Sorry,' said Omri, hastily removing the offending figure. 'I thought he was a Mohawk. He dresses like one.'

'Mohawk part of *Iroquois* nation. Omri not see difference? Stupid. Big eyes not best.'

About three-quarters of the men they'd bought were eventually approved. Then Little Bull turned his eyes to the British soldiers.

They were rather splendid in their white breeches, scarlet coats, and three-cornered hats, but Omri didn't think they looked very businesslike. The white bands crossed on their chests and backs made an ideal target. But perhaps the brilliance of their uniforms was intended to intimidate the enemy. Anyway they were all armed with muskets tipped with fearsome-looking blades. Omri bent one easily with his finger, thinking how sharp and lethal they would be when the cupboard had done its work and these bayonet-swords became gleaming steel.

'These no good,' Little Bull pronounced abruptly.

Patrick and Omri were astonished.

'What's wrong with them?' said Patrick. 'Are they from the wrong time?'

'Right time. Near right. English soldier like that fight French in big battle soon before. French win.'

'Oh! Why?'

'Fight better. But also English dress stupid. This . . . this . . .' He pointed contemptuously to the red coats and white trimmings. 'Catch sun. Call eye of French soldier. Gun point. Pshooo!' He made a shooting noise. 'No good if soldier proud. Must dress so enemy not see.'

'How do the English soldiers dress – er – now?'

'More like Indian. Earth colours. Like leaf. Shadow.

More good for hide. Jump out on enemy. White man learn much from Indian.'

'Now who's proud?' Patrick whispered to Omri.

'LITTLE BULL HEAR THAT!' the Indian roared. Really, he had ears like a bat.

'Well, anyway, so you don't want us to bring these men to life?' said Patrick hurriedly.

'Not need. Enough with braves and now-guns.'

The boys exchanged glances. This was tricky. Little Bull *was* proud and he wouldn't like the suggestion that the white men might be better with modern weapons.

'Listen, Little Bull . . .' Omri began coaxingly.

Suddenly they froze. Omri heard his mother's voice calling him from the house.

'Omri! *Omri!*'

'What?' he called back, getting quickly to his feet.

'Darling, Kitsa's caught a bird! Or a mouse or something. Anyway, she's playing with it on the big lawn. Can you . . . ?'

Omri's mind seemed to blow hollow like an egg. He stopped hearing what his mother was saying. But Patrick was up and off in a flash, charging through the bushes like a madman. Omri came behind him, the branches smacking him across the face.

On the main lawn was Kitsa, her blackness and whiteness beautiful, sleek and deadly in the sunshine. She was crouched and concentrated; her tail-tip just twitching, all else about her perfectly still.

There was something small and helpless and alive in the grass in front of her.

Chapter 13
A Death and a Healing

'*KITSA!*'

Omri screamed out her name. Startled, she turned her head. Both boys were belting towards her. Furious at the interruption, she turned back and with one quick wiggle of her hips, she pounced. At almost the same second Patrick reached her.

Without time to think, he kicked her, or rather, kicked at her. She started to jump away at the same second, so his foot, though it did just about connect with her, merely accelerated her flight through the air. With a yowl of outrage, empty-mouthed and thwarted, she fled.

Omri and Patrick fell to their knees on the spot Kitsa had so hastily vacated.

· The white horse was lying on its side. Its legs were moving but it was obviously hurt. It kept raising its head and whinneying and then letting its head drop back again. Boone was lying half under it. He didn't move.

Patrick very gently shifted the pony until he could lift Boone clear. Suddenly Boone shot to his feet and shouted, 'Am Ah daid? Did it kill me?'

'You look okay to me,' said Patrick. His voice sounded to Omri like the voice of a complete stranger. It was deep and gruff like a man's. Boone was looking around in a daze.

'What was it?'

'A cat.'

'A *cat*! It was the biggest danged critter Ah ever seen in mah en-tire life! It jest come from nowhere. One minute Ah was ridin' along, mindin' mah own business, and suddenly . . .'

Then his eyes fell on his horse. It raised its head again and whickered softly, as if asking him to help it. There was a terrible moment of silence. Boone crouched by the horse's head, stroking it, running his hands over it. He unbuckled the saddle and lifted it clear, and very gently ran his hands over its white side.

Then he took off his hat. It was a strange gesture. Omri had seen men do it in films when they heard of someone's death. A gesture of respect, of something stronger than respect. He stood up.

'Ribs is broke,' he said. 'Have t'finish him.'

'*Oh, no!*' Omri heard himself say in a desperate voice.

'Ain't no use keepin' him alive t'suffer. He's mah pal.'

His voice, which cracked and dissolved into tears at the least thing, was now perfectly steady.

Slowly he reached for his revolver.

Omri couldn't bear it. 'Please, Boone! Don't! Surely we can save him!'

Boone shook his head. 'He's too far gone. I gotta do it.' He looked up again. His face was strained but dry-eyed. 'You boys turn yer backs. This ain't fer kids to see.'

Omri turned his back. Patrick didn't. Boone bent down. He whispered something briefly into the horse's ear. Then he put his revolver to its head. Omri didn't see this, but he heard the shot. Tears spurted from his eyes. He couldn't check them. He wiped them hard and furiously with both hands.

Why should he, who hardly ever cried any more, cry over the death of Boone's horse, when Boone, who cried all the time, was so controlled? Turning round, seeing Boone standing quietly beside the horse's body with his hat in one hand and his smoking revolver in the other, Omri tried to feel ashamed of his own weakness, but he couldn't. It was his fault, partly, that this disaster had happened. They had been so preoccupied with the Plan and the exciting prospect of bringing more little people to life that they had let Boone ride off into a monstrous wilderness, full of deadly dangers. That it should have been Omri's own beloved little cat who had done this, just made everything worse.

Irrational fury seized him. He crouched down.

'I'll kill her,' he ground out between his teeth.

Boone looked up at him.

'Don't you kill nuthin', kid. Th'critter wuz only follerin' its instincks. Ya cain't blame a cat fer *bein*' a cat, even if'n it do fall on a fella as fierce and sudden as a Texas hurricane.'

'I'll – we'll get you another horse.'

'Yeah, you do that. Ah'll git to be pals with it, same as I wuz with this'n. Some day. Ah guess. A man ain't whole without a hoss.'

He replaced his gun in its holster. 'Jest now kin Ah have a shovel?'

Patrick swallowed, cleared his throat and said, 'We'll bury him for you, Boone.'

'Thanks, son, Ah'd be obliged t'ya.'

Omri fetched a trowel from the greenhouse and dug a small hole in a flowerbed just under a nodding chrysanthemum. Boone took the bridle off the horse, and laid the saddle over his arm. Then Patrick picked up the body. It was still warm, and strangely heavy for its size. He laid it in the hole and Omri covered it up and made a little mound. They stood for a moment. Then Boone settled his hat back on his ginger head.

'C'mon then,' he said 'We'd best be gittin' back t'th'others, before somethin' happens to *them*.'

Patrick carried the cowboy back through the rhododendrons.

There was no sign of Little Bull and Twin Stars and, for a moment, Omri's heart seemed to leap into his mouth. But then Little Bull walked – actually walked, though slowly and unsteadily – out of the ruined longhouse.

'Where you go? Why leave?' he demanded.

Patrick stopped and opened his hand so Boone could step out on to the seed-tray. As far as Omri could judge, the cowboy looked as always; but Little Bull seemed to know at once that something had happened. He even guessed what.

'Where horse?' he asked Boone.

'Daid,' Boone answered shortly.

No more was said, but the Indian touched Boone briefly on the shoulder before turning back to Omri.

'Now we put braves in box.'

But this time it was Patrick who had been doing some thinking.

'Just a minute, Little Bull.'

Little Bull turned to him. 'What minute? Do now!'

'Okay, so say we bring forty Indians to life. Then what? I mean, what will happen right away? Because you can't go back and start fighting the French right away.'

'I go back ry-taway! Why no?'

'Because you're not well enough. No, Little Bull! You can't be. So we'll have forty other people on our hands. We'll have to feed them and look after them until you're ready. That might be days – weeks.'

'Who weak? I strong!'

'Seven days,' said Patrick, holding up seven fingers. 'That's a week.'

Little Bull glowered. 'No week. No wait. If stay here, not help tribe, they make new chief.'

'I tell you what,' said Patrick. He reached into his pocket. 'We'll get Matron back. See what she says.'

'May Tron?'

'Yes.' Patrick held up the formidable little figure in her tall cap.

Little Bull pulled a face.

'What use white woman with face like old beaver?'

'She saved your life, so you'd better not be rude. She's like a doctor.'

Little Bull looked shocked. 'No woman doctor!' he exclaimed.

'Well, this one is. She took the metal out of your back last night. If she says you're healed enough to fight, okay, we'll get started on your army. If not – we'll wait.'

And he put Matron in the cupboard.

When he opened the door, she was standing blinking in

the sudden sunlight. She had a newly-starched cap perched on her head.

'Ah-ha!' she cried when she saw the boys. 'I thought as much! The more I thought about it, the more certain I was you'd need me again. So, do you know what I did? I just popped a few things into my apron pocket, just in case.'

She hitched up her skirt and climbed over the rim of the cupboard.

'Think ahead,' she said. 'That's my motto.' Then she saw Little Bull standing before her with folded arms and uttered a shriek, but it was not of terror.

'What on *earth* are you doing out of bed! Are you trying to kill yourself?'

'Not kill self,' said Little Bull calmly. 'Maybe kill you.'

She bore down upon him.

'Nonsense, my good man, you're delirious, and no wonder. This is absolutely outrageous, twenty-four hours after – ahem! – *major* surgery and here you are, on your feet instead of flat on your back – I mean, on your front. Lie down *at once*!'

To the amazement of the boys, and no less perhaps to Little Bull's own surprise, he found himself obeying her commands. Clearly it never occurred to her that he wouldn't. He lay down on the pile of leaves and she knelt to examine him. Twin Stars ran to help her. Together they took off the dressings. Matron peered closely at the wounds, then she sat back on her heels.

'Unbelievable,' she said. 'Fantastic! If I didn't see it, I would never credit it. Beautiful. You know,' she went on as she took a tiny bottle and some cotton-wool from her capacious pocket, 'the trouble is, *we* live an entirely unnatural and unhealthy life. Eat the wrong foods, don't exercise enough . . . Look at this man. Just look! Superb specimen. Not an ounce of fat on him. Bright eyes, perfect teeth, skin and hair gleaming with health – splendid! And if something does go wrong, his magnificent, well-oiled defence system springs into action, and hey presto! He's practically healed.'

She washed the wounds, then took out a hypodermic needle, and squirted it briefly at the sky.

'Just to be on the safe side,' she said. 'Trousers down!' And before Little Bull could grasp her intention, she had pulled his buckskins down and plunged the needle into his bottom.

Little Bull had borne a lot of pain without a flinch but this humiliation was too much. He let out a roar as if he'd been gored by a buffalo.

'*What* a silly fuss. There! All over!' said Matron brightly, withdrawing the needle and rubbing the spot briskly with the cotton wool. 'Just in case of infection, but really there's little fear of that. He's practically as good as new. What a constitution! Of course,' she added modestly, 'I didn't do a bad job on him, if I say it myself as shouldn't.'

'Would you think he'd be well enough to – well, to do something pretty active?' Omri asked.

'Try stopping him,' said Matron. She rose to her feet and dusted the earth off her knees. 'Personally, if he were on *my* ward I'd say bedrest for another day or so, but a body like his knows its own business best.'

'Could he ride, say?'

'That's up to the horse!' quipped Matron, laughing rather horsily herself. 'Well, I must be off!'

Meanwhile, Little Bull, who had scrambled hastily to his feet, now growled, drew his knife and threatened her with it. But Matron, not at all alarmed, wagged her finger at him.

'Tsk, tsk, naughty man! That would never do at St

Thomas's.' She turned her back on him without a qualm. Baffled, he lowered the knife. 'Astonishing, these primitives,' she remarked to Omri as she strode to the ramp. 'Perfect control over the body – none at all over the emotions.'

Back in the cupboard she offered Omri her hand, and then burst out laughing again.

'Aren't I silly? How could we shake hands? Oh, but do try! I'd just love to shake hands with a giant, even if it is all a very convincing dream.' Omri took her tiny hand between finger and thumb and solemnly shook it.

'Cheerio! Do call on me in any future hour of need!'

'We will,' said Omri, closing the door.

He turned from the cupboard to find Little Bull's eyes fixed on him.

'Old white she-bear say I good,' he said. 'Now Patrick, Omri, keep word.'

The boys looked at each other.

'Right,' said Omri, taking a deep breath. 'Let's get started.'

Chapter 14
Red Men, Red Coats

Bringing forty Indians to life sounds quite an undertaking, but it took a remarkably short time to accomplish. They did a few first, just to be on the safe side; but when the first half-dozen had clambered out of the cupboard and were at once greeted by Little Bull, who regaled them in his strange language which they all seemed to understand, Omri and Patrick didn't delay further.

'Let's put all the rest in at once!' said Patrick excitedly, and this time Omri made no objections.

Soon the seed-tray was jammed with men, milling around, sitting on Patrick's fence, admiring Little Bull's pony, exclaiming in dismay at the ruined longhouse, gazing covertly at Twin Stars, and examining the paintings on the side of the tepee. One or two tried to enter this, but Little Bull barred the way. Boone was in there. None of them knew how the Indians might react to him, so they'd decided to hide him.

The new Indians didn't pay any attention to the boys at first, or to anything in what, to them, was the distance. Everything on the seed-tray was in scale with them, and soon they settled down in rows, cross-legged, to listen to what Little Bull had to say.

He dragged the matchbox bed into position before the tepee and stood on it, making it a platform. From there he addressed them in a loud, commanding tone for several minutes.

Omri and Patrick sat well back, shaded by bushes.

'It was a good idea of yours to be outdoors,' whispered

Patrick. 'Seems more natural, and there aren't huge bits of furniture and so on, to worry them.'

Omri didn't react to this praise for his idea. If they had stayed inside, Boone's horse would still be alive.

They watched. After a while, Little Bull stopped speaking and beckoned imperiously to the boys, who crawled forward on their knees till they hung over the seed-tray. Little Bull pointed to them dramatically and all the little Indians turned to look.

Their reaction was curiously unsensational. Some uttered muted cries; one or two leapt to their feet, but then sank down again after glancing at Little Bull and seeing him unafraid. Evidently he had given them some explanation for the presence of giants in their midst which they had no difficulty in accepting. The 'Great Spirits' business, no doubt. Omri couldn't help smiling at Little Bull's obvious pride in having such beings at his command. It obviously gave him a lot of prestige in the eyes of these tribesmen he was hoping to lead into battle.

After a few more words to his audience, Little Bull turned to the boys.

'Make now-guns,' he ordered.

They knelt, irresolute. Omri had never really taken to the idea of Indians running amok with machine-guns, hand-grenades and artillery. Anything could happen, especially if they got overexcited. But Little Bull was scowling horribly at their hesitation.

'Make now-guns *now*!' he thundered. 'Little Bull give word to braves!'

'Oh, dear,' said Patrick ironically. 'That does it, then. I'd better fetch them.'

He jumped to his feet. Omri said, 'While you're in the house, ask my mum to give you something for us to eat. For *them* to eat.'

'Anything else you can think of?'

'Yes. Bring some horses for Boone to choose from.'

'One thing at a time,' said Patrick. 'Boone'd better stay out of sight.' And he pushed off through the bushes.

While he was gone, Omri thought he ought to have a word with Little Bull.

'These now-guns, as you call them, are very, very powerful. And they're complicated. They can't be used without special training.'

Little Bull curled his lip in scorn.

'I see what soldier do. Point gun. Pull trigger, like gun French, English soldier use fight with Indian. But kill more! Shoot many, many!' Little Bull made a noise like the chatter of a machine-gun. The other Indians reacted with excitement.

'But the bigger ones . . .'

'Omri show how!'

'You don't think *I* know, do you? As you keep reminding me, I'm only a boy.'

Little Bull frowned. The rows of seated Indians below him seemed to sense his doubt, and began murmuring to each other uneasily. Little Bull raised his hand to silence them.

'Omri put now-soldier in box. Him show.'

Omri considered. There was actually no option to bringing the modern soldiers to life, however briefly, because their plastic figures were attached to their weapons. Omri's plan had been to do as he had done once before, when he'd wanted a bow and arrows for Little Bull. He had brought an old Indian to life and taken his weapons from him, meaning to transform him at once back into plastic. But he had promptly dropped dead of a heart attack. Omri thought that some artillery sergeant might be made of sterner stuff. Perhaps it would be worth a try.

'And what about these?' he asked, holding up a soldier

from the time of George the Third (who, according to a verse Omri recalled from somewhere, 'ought never to have occurred').

'Try,' said Little Bull tersely.

Feeling a bit guilty at doing it without Patrick, Omri put the five scarlet-clad soldiers into the cupboard. At once the clattering of metal on metal announced that the soldiers and their mounted officer were ready to emerge.

'Little Bull, you'd better go in there with them. Better if you talk to them first, and decide if you want them.'

'Good!'

Omri opened the door a crack and Little Bull slipped over the edge of the seed-tray straight into the cupboard. Omri put his ear to the opening at the top to listen.

Little Bull began at once to harangue the British officers in his broken English. Omri heard the word 'French' and the word 'kill' but he couldn't make out much more until the shrill bark of an English voice cut him short.

'Who do you think you are, giving orders to an officer of His Majesty's 20th American Regiment, you filthy savage!'

There was a deathly silence. Then Little Bull shouted:

'I no savage! I Iroquois chief! Iroquois fight at side of English soldier! English happy have Indian help, braves spill blood in English quarrel. Now I ask help from English! Why redcoat give insult?'

There was a brief pause, and then the English voice said, with icy contempt: 'Insolent bounder! Kill him, Smithers.'

Omri put his hand on the door to slam it shut, but another voice spoke.

'Is that wise, sir? After all, we have used them in the past.'

'Plenty more where he came from.'

'But if he's a chief, sir . . . Might lead to trouble.'

'Of course, Smithers, if you're squeamish, I'll do it myself! Here! Come back, you blackguard!'

But it was too late. Little Bull had already slipped silently over the bottom rim of the cupboard, and was throwing his weight against the door. Omri was very happy to assist him, and in short order the arrogant British redcoats were reduced to their plastic condition again.

Little Bull, his eyes slits of rage and every tooth in his head bared, gave Omri a look of reproach. Omri felt he was being blamed just because he was English too.

'Surely they're not all like that,' he muttered.

'Some English no better than French,' was all Little Bull had to say. 'Braves fight alone.'

Just then Patrick came crashing back through the rhododendrons. He had a tray in his hand, on which were two glasses of milk, two packets of salted peanuts and a couple of red apples. Also a paper bag containing the now-soldiers. Omri only hoped they might do something to redeem the character of the British Army in the eyes of his Indian.

There was a pleasant interlude while they fed the Indians. They crushed some of the nuts between two more or less clean stones and served the bits on platters made from the round leaves of a nasturtium. Patrick bit a piece off one of the apples and broke it up small, while Omri filled and refilled the toothpaste caps which were passed reverently from hand to hand along the rows of seated braves. Between them they drank nearly half a glass of milk.

Boone, who had been peeping from behind the flap of the tepee, sent a private message with Twin Stars, suggesting a bit of 'the hard stuff' should be added to the milk, 'to put fire in belly', as Twin Stars solemnly explained. Boone evidently felt it would be no bad thing if these Indians did go a bit loco. But Omri and Patrick agreed that everyone ought to keep a clear head.

Then it was time to bring the modern soldiers to life again and see what could be done about guns.

After consultation with Little Bull, they began with a hulking Royal Marine corporal, kneeling behind his machine-gun. He was the one who had sprayed Omri with bullets, so Omri had a sort of warped affection for him.

'We can't risk Little Bull again,' said Omri. He had told Patrick what had happened with the eighteenth-century soldiers. 'A modern soldier would probably be just as unbelieving about an Indian as he would about finding himself tiny.'

'We'll just have to hope he can accept it somehow. After all, he's seen us once, the first shock's over. Come on. No good putting it off.'

Patrick slipped the corporal into the cupboard.

Chapter 15
Corporal Fickits

'We'll have to watch it. Last time I did this, they all just started shooting like mad the second the door opened.'

So they opened the door the merest crack at first, and Omri put his mouth to it and said, 'Don't shoot! We want to talk to you.'

A very ripe soldierly oath answered him which was followed by: '. . . I've gorn off my trolley again!'

'Just don't shoot. Okay?' And Omri slowly swung the cupboard door open.

The corporal had stood up. He gazed around. The machine-gun gleamed in the sun, oiled and ready for action.

'Blimey, now I'm outdoors! What the 'ell is goin' on?'

Omri went into his spiel.

'Of course it must seem incredible but the fact is, for the moment, you've become small. You can tell your grandchildren about it . . . And it's going to get even more interesting. What we want is for you to tell some friends of ours, who are your size, how to work your machine-gun.'

'And 'oo are they planning to shoot wiv it, if it's not a rude answer?'

'Well, you see . . .' But it was too complicated. Omri looked helplessly at Patrick.

'Who do you shoot with it?' Patrick cut in quickly.

The man gave a barking laugh. 'The Queen's enemies and anyone else who looks sideways at the Royal Marines.'

'And are you an expert on guns – I mean, all kinds?'

'You could say so. We're trained to 'andle just about anything. And anybody.'

The boys gave each other a quick look. This suited them.

'Right,' said Patrick briskly. 'Here's your chance to prove it. I'm going to put you and your machine-gun in front of a bunch of men. And you're going to demonstrate how to use it. You'll go through it once, and then let some of them try it. Only be careful, we don't want anybody hurt. This is only a training exercise.'

The corporal's face had gone rigid and he stood at attention while Patrick spoke. Then he gave a smart salute.

'Sir!'

'What's your name, Corporal?'

'Fickits, sir, Corporal Royal Marines, Willy Fickits.'

'How much ammunition have you, Corporal?'

'Three 'undred rounds, sir.'

'Don't waste any.'

'Sir!'

'Now don't be scared when I pick you up.'

The corporal's adam's apple jumped as he swallowed, but his face didn't change.

'Sir!'

Patrick carried the man, stiff as a tiny pencil, between finger and thumb and set him down, still at attention, on the platform. At the sight of him there was a buzz of astonished interest among the Indians, most of whom leapt to their feet. The corporal allowed his eyes to rove briefly across the mass of half-naked Indians. His adam's apple did a jig in his throat, and his eyes popped. Then his rigid expression came back.

Meanwhile, Omri had carefully lifted the machine-gun out of the cupboard, and set it beside him. The nearness of his weapon seemed to restore him.

'Begin, Corporal!' said Patrick, who found he rather liked giving orders he knew would be instantly obeyed.

'Right, men!' Fickits barked. 'Pay attention! I am about to demonstrate the workings of this 'ere weapon, a marvel of military science. I will first break it dahn and put it back together.'

'Never mind that, Corporal,' interrupted Patrick. 'Just show thcm how to shoot with it.'

The corporal instantly changed tack.

'I will first demonstrate the method of firing.' He dropped to one knee, aimed over the heads of the crowd, and fired off a short but noisy burst. Bullets whistled through the air and caused a flurry among the rhododendron leaves.

The Indians watched this impassively. They didn't seem to grasp what had happened. But Little Bull leapt up beside Fickits and shouted something. He must have told them that each bang represented a bullet, or, with luck, a dead enemy. At that, the Indians jumped up and started yelling excitedly and pushing towards the platform. Almost at once a fight broke out among those wanting to be the first to try the gun. Corporal Fickits stared at the scrum in dismay.

'You'd better give these blighters some orders, sir!' he shouted at Patrick above the uproar. 'Goin' on like that, it won't do, sir!'

'It's your gun, Corporal. *You* give the orders!'

'*Me*, sir? Ain't there an officer about, sir? Or at least a sergeant!'

The scrum below was getting wilder. One burly Indian had already laid two others out cold and was scrambling up on to the platform.

'You're in charge, Corporal! Go on, tell them to behave. They'll listen to you!'

After a baffled moment, Fickits saw that the Indian had

laid hands on his gun and was swinging the barrel wildly in all directions. This galvanized him into action.

'TAKE YER 'ANDS ORF THAT GUN!' he bellowed.

His voice was not that of a corporal but of a regimental sergeant major. All at once the howling mob of Indians fell silent. Even Little Bull looked impressed. The Indian at the gun found himself hiked upright by his hair (all Fickits was able to get hold of) and flung off the platform.

'Nah then, you bunch of 'orrible little men!' roared Fickits. 'You touch this 'ere weapon when *I* says you will touch it, and NOT BEFOWER. DO YOU UNDERSTAND THAT? Or you will find yourselves wishin' that your mothers 'ad never met your fathers. IS THAT CLEAR?'

There was a profound silence. Even the birds in the bushes seemed stunned.

'Wow,' breathed Patrick. 'That's telling them.'

Corporal Fickits proved a godsend. He knew a great deal about military hardware, not only machine-guns. As fast as Omri put the soldiers into the cupboard, made their weapons real, removed them from their owners and placed them on the matchbox platform, Fickits instructed his now obedient students how to work them. Soon they had two field guns, ten hand-grenades, three bazookas, two more machine-guns and a small pile of automatic rifles. The Indians appeared to like these best. When they discovered that they could actually run while firing them, it took all Corporal Fickits' new-found authority to keep any kind of order, and even so it was a miracle that no one was hurt during the training. The boys set up stripped twigs and round pieces of trimmed bark as targets, but as there was a limited amount of ammunition, every Indian was given only five rounds to practise with.

Fickets was uneasy about the larger guns.

'Firing artillery, sir, ain't something you do any old

how. Any 'alfwit can blast off with the 'and-guns, sir, or throw a grenade, but if you'll take my advice you'll leave the ordnance pieces out of it. You need a properly trained crew for artillery, sir. Not rabble like this lot, sir.'

'If that's your advice, Corporal, we'll follow it,' said Patrick.

Corporal Fickits' expression did not change, but he seemed to swell up inside his uniform like a miniature pouter-pigeon.

'Thankysir!' he said, making it all one word.

Little Bull was growing impatient.

'Braves know shoot now-guns,' he said urgently. 'Time go back!'

Omri had been, he now realized, secretly dreading this moment. There was his Indian, not yet fully recovered, no matter what anyone said, about to be plunged into a life-or-death situation.

But he knew there was no way to avoid it. However, that didn't mean Twin Stars had to put herself in danger.

'Can you leave Twin Stars here?' Omri asked.

'Yes,' said Little Bull. 'Leave wife. Omri take care. Bring old white she-bear when time come for Little Bull son. But no let stab with claw in backside!'

Omri and the Indian looked at each other for a moment.

'Good luck,' said Omri.

'Need help from Great Spirits. Then fight well, win against French, Algonquin enemy.'

'Did the Algonquins help attack your village?'

'Algonquin lead. French follow. Now go back. Take vengeance.'

'I wish I could see it,' said Omri.

'And me,' added Patrick, who had overheard.

It took some time to assemble the now heavily armed Indian troop and prepare them to leave. Twin Stars directed Omri to bring her some flowers, which she crushed in her hands, producing a coloured pulp with which she smeared Little Bull's face in streaks. Others were decorating themselves with mixtures of mud, as well as some other colours they had had with them.

Every time a bird flew overhead they all looked up apprehensively. Omri thought they were afraid it might attack them (as indeed it might have, had the boys not been there to guard them), but Little Bull, after one such overpass, said:

'Bad omen is shadow fall on braves before battle.'

The last Indians were leaving Twin Stars' pool, smearing patterns of mud on their torsos. Omri looked at the now murky water in the coffee-jar lid. It had a reddish look where the sinking sun caught it. He turned away, glad that *he* didn't believe in omens.

Chapter 16
If'n Ya Wanna Go Back . . .

Corporal Fickits marched his troops into the cupboard and formed them up in two ranks in the bottom of it. The machine-guns were lifted in. Fickits saluted Patrick. 'Trainees drawn up and ready sir!'

'Thanks, Corporal. You've done a good job.'

'Thankysir.'

'Now you're going back where you came from, Fickits. Don't forget how it feels to give orders. You'll be a sergeant in no time.'

Fickits permitted himself a grin. 'Yessir. Thankysir.'

Omri told Little Bull to instruct his men each to put a hand on the shoulder of the man beside or in front of him, so the whole group was physically linked. 'And they must all be linked to you, Little Bull, so you'll take them back with you.'

Little Bull was in the paddock, fetching his pony. He had to get Twin Stars to give him a leg up. He bent over and put his hand on her black head. She gazed up at him, her eyes sparkling, this time with tears. She seemed to be begging him for something, but he shook his head. Suddenly she reached up, seized his hand, and pressed it to her cheek. Then she turned and ran into the tepee.

As she entered, Boone's face appeared at the flap.

'Hey! Psst! Injun!'

Little Bull, who was riding toward the ramp, turned his head.

'Give those Frenchies hell!'

'I give.'

He waved at the boys, rode down the ramp and,

catching the reins up chest-high, galloped to the cupboard. His pony jumped the bottom rim and swerved to a sudden stop to avoid the ranks of Indians. Little Bull barked a command. All the Indians put their hands on each other's shoulders. The nearest brave put his on the pony's rump.

'Omri shut door, send!' ordered Little Bull. His stern face was burning with impatience.

Omri gave himself a second to take in the group. The painted braves in their double row looked proud, ferocious, eager. They were obviously looking forward to the coming battle without a trace of fear. The weaponry caught the sun and glistened with readiness to do what it had been made to do. For a moment, Omri was swamped by doubts. It was like . . . like *posting death*. Why should he help to kill people? But he was caught up in the whole drama now.

'Go on!' urged Patrick 'Send them!'

'Wait – Fickits!' said Omri. He picked up the little corporal who was standing at attention just outside the cupboard, and set him by himself on the shelf. Then he shut the door firmly and turned the key.

For a long moment they didn't breathe. Then Omri opened the door. His hand was shaking and he jiggled the cupboard a bit as he did it. Two or three of the Indian figures, now plastic, fell over. It was like dominoes, each knocking down another until most of them lay tumbled across each other on the floor of the cupboard. Only Little Bull and Fickits and a couple more were still upright.

The boys stared in a dismay they couldn't control at the scene. Boone, who had crept to the edge of the seed-tray and was leaning over to look, voiced their feelings.

'Looks like a massacree, don't it?'

'Don't be stupid, Boone!' Patrick almost shouted.

'They're just plastic now, they fell over because Omri jogged the cupboard.'

'Sure,' said Boone hastily. 'Sure, Ah know that! Ah wuz jest sayin' . . .'

'Well, don't!'

'You ain't superstitious, are ya?'

'Of course not!'

Now there was a feeling of intense anticlimax. There seemed nothing they ought to do. It was getting chilly. They sat for a bit, but that became intolerable because of what they were all imagining.

'Let's go in.'

Again Patrick took the cupboard, with its contents, and the bag of weaponless British soldiers, and Omri took the seed-tray.

Twin Stars and Boone retreated into the tepee, just in case they met anyone on the way back. upstairs, which was just as well, because as they passed Gillon's bedroom on the first floor, the door opened and out he came.

Omri and Patrick started guiltily. They couldn't help it.

'What's all that?' Gillon asked, not because he particularly wanted to know but just out of idle curiosity.

'Just some stuff we've been mucking about with,' said Omri. He tried to push past, but Gillon stood in his path.

'Oh, it's that fantastic little house you made last year,' said Gillon. 'And the leather tepee. Often wondered what had happened to that. Never seen one like it in the shops . . .' Before they could do anything, he'd picked the tepee up to examine it.

It was one of the worst moments of Omri's life. There was nothing he could do. There were Twin Stars and Boone, crouching on the earth, exposed – discovered. Everything seemed frozen. Neither Patrick nor Omri could move, and the little people sat absolutely motionless. Omri's eyes were fastened to them helplessly. They were so obviously alive – so vulnerable! He waited, as a condemned man waits for the axe to fall on his neck, for Gillon to notice them.

Gillon, however, was looking only at the tepee in his hands.

'This is really a mini-marvel,' he said. 'I love the paintings. Has Dad seen these?' He peered even closer. 'This little beaver – and the porcupine . . . They look dead *genuine*, like those cave paintings we saw in France. And the way the poles are attached, inside, it's really a work of art.'

With that he plonked it carelessly back on the earth, nearly knocking Boone's head off, and swung away down the stairs singing a pop song at the top of his lungs.

Patrick did a perfect imitation of Matron, spinning on his heel and falling in a mock faint on the landing. He lay there with the cupboard on his stomach and his eyes wide open and crossed. After a second he sat up.

'Hell, that was close!'

Omri was still rooted to the spot. Boone was lying half in, half out of the tepee on his back. His eyes looked crossed, too – quite genuinely. After a few moments he wriggled all the way out and stood up, wiping the sweat off his face.

'Jeez, son,' he complained, 'd'ya have t'skeer a fella like that? *An'* the li'l lady . . .'T'ain't right, with her bein' the way she is, skeerin' her that-a-way. Might bring somethin' on.'

Omri put his face down and whispered through the flap. 'Are you okay, Twin Stars?'

There was no answer. Cautiously Omri lifted the tepee again. Twin Stars was sitting perfectly still, her face down on her knees.

'Twin Stars? Answer me!'

Patrick had stood up and was peering anxiously over Omri's shoulder.

'What's wrong?'

'I don't know. Let's get up to my room.'

They went up. Omri carried the seed-tray very carefully. Inside, they locked the door and put the seed-tray and cupboard down on Omri's desk and turned on the lamp.

Twin Stars stood up. Her face had a greyish look under the brown.

'Son come now,' she said clearly.

'Ah knew it!' said Boone. 'Git that ol' bat in the white headpiece back.'

'Twin Stars need no one. Need water. Knife. Omri bring, then leave.' She signed that he should put the tepee back to cover her.

'Are you sure, Twin Stars? Little Bull said . . .'

'Little Bull go fight. Twin Stars make son. Go.'

Though very uneasy, Omri obeyed her. He fetched some boiled water, cleaned out the pond and refilled it. Boone carried a bucketful of water to the flap of the tepee, and laid his pocket-knife beside it. 'That's t'cut the cord, y'know,' he confided. 'Animals bite it through, but Ah guess th'Injuns is beyond that.'

After a short time, Twin Stars' hand came out through the flap of the tepee, and took in the bucket and then the knife. Then she fastened the flap firmly shut and all was quiet.

There seemed nothing to do but wait. Omri knew that with white people, anyway, the first baby often took a long time to be born. His mother had been half a day producing Adiel, she'd told them. Perhaps with Indians it was different.

Patrick was uneasy.

'If anything happened to her, Little Bull wouldn't ever

forgive us! I wish he'd taken her back with him. Shouldn't we bring Matron?'

'Twin Stars said not to. Matron's awfully bossy. Maybe she'd just upset her.'

'Well I think she'd be better off back in her own village.'

'I *wish* I knew what was happening – back there!' Omri burst out.

'Yeah! If only *we* could get back somehow.'

They sat, the three of them, the boys on chairs, Boone on the 'couch' of rhododendron leaves where Little Bull had sat. Every now and then Boone stood up and paced the ground outside the tepee. He kept biting hunks off a block of tobacco, and chewing at it and then spitting it out. He was obviously very worked up.

Finally he stopped.

'Ah shoulda gone with 'em,' he said. 'Ah knew at the time Ah shoulda.'

'That would've been crazy, Boone,' said Patrick. 'Someone would have shot you just because you look different, and you're white.'

'Mebbe Ah coulda stayed in the tepee and shot the Frenchies from cover. Ah coulda done *somethin*'. Thet Injun's mah blood brother. His fight oughta be mah fight!'

'We need you here, Boone.'

'What fur? Ain't no use here!'

'Well,' said Omri, 'you can help with the baby.'

Boone stopped pacing.

'*Me*? Watcha take me for? Babies is wimmin's bizness!'

Just at that moment, they heard a little cry from inside the tepee. It wasn't a baby's cry. In a flash Boone was crouched at the flap.

'Lemme in, lady, ya cain't be alone in thur. Ah'll help ya! Ah brung a dozen calves into the world, *an*' a foal once't, an' they're a lot bigger'n a baby. Ah know whut t'do!'

There was a pause, and then a slight movement at the tent flap. Boone grinned a rather wobbly grin over his shoulder at the boys.

'Ya see? She trusts me,' he said. 'Don't fret, now. Li'l Bull'll be glad he made me his brother, you wait.' The flap was loosened and Boone started to crawl in. But just before he disappeared, he turned once more.

'Ah wuz thinkin'', he said. 'If'n ya really wanted to go back, and watch the battle . . .'

The boys looked at each other, then leaned forward incredulously to listen.

'Wal, whut Ah wuz wonderin' wuz . . . Does it have t'be the cupboard? Mebbe it ain't the cupboard so much as that thur fancy key. Did ya ever try the key in somethin' bigger? Like that great big box, for instance, that we wuz all on before.'

Another little cry, more of a gasp, came from inside the tepee.

'S'long, boys – wish us luck!' Boone said, and crawled the rest of the way, leaving both boys in a ferment of excitement at the possibilities of this amazing new idea.

Chapter 17

As Far as You Can Go

'Would it work?' Patrick asked.

'How do I know?' answered Omri. 'I never thought of it.'

'We never asked ourselves whether the cupboard was part of what makes it happen. Maybe he's right. Maybe the cupboard's just a cupboard, and the magic thing is the key.'

They turned both at once to look at the chest.

The top of it still had scattered bits of Kleenex, boxes and other things on it. Omri went over to it and swept all this off. Then he opened it. It was full of his private stuff.

'It's not big enough to hold both of us at once.'

'We couldn't both go together anyway, you wally.'

'Why not?' Then he realized. Of course! Someone would have to stay behind or there'd be nobody to turn the key.

'Who'll try it first?' Patrick was asking.

Omri looked at him. 'Are you serious? You really want to try it?'

'Of course! Don't you?'

Omri looked round the room. Despite irritations he was happy with it, with his life. He wasn't eager to risk losing either of them.

'Have you thought about the dangers?' he asked.

'Coward!'

'No, I'm not. You're rushing in like you always do. Just stop and think a bit. First, if it does work at all, how can you be sure you'd go back to Little Bull's time, to his village, and not somewhere else? You could find yourself anywhere. And any *when*.' Patrick looked mulish. 'Apart from that, what about size?'

'Size?'

'Yes. If *they* reach *us* small, we'd reach them small. Wouldn't we? Of course there was no plastic then. We'd have to be in dolls or – totem poles or something. I don't think it's cowardly not to like the idea of waking up in an Indian village two hundred years ago, at the top of a totem pole.'

For answer Patrick knelt down by the chest and started lifting things out of it. 'Give me a hand with all this rubbish,' was all he said.

Omri helped him silently until the chest was empty. Then he said, 'After all that, probably the key won't even fit this lock.' His heart was pounding. He knew he hoped it wouldn't.

Patrick got up and fetched the key. Without closing the lid of the chest, he put it in the lock and turned it. It turned easily. The lock-part clicked. Patrick removed the key and looked at it.

'My guess is that this key fits pretty well any lock,' he said slowly.

Omri took a deep breath. Once again he was caught up in something he felt overwhelmed by.

'Who'll go first?'

'I will,' said Patrick, without hesitation.

'Wait a minute!'

'What *now*?'

'You've got to have something with you, something of Little Bull's. Otherwise you haven't a hope of finishing up in the right place!'

Patrick stopped. 'What have we got of his?'

'The longhouse.'

'That's no use. The longhouse was made here, he didn't bring it from his time.'

'Then there's only the tepee.'

They looked over at Omri's desk. The tiny tepee stood up from the seed-tray, its poles sticking through the top, its beautiful bold animal designs on its cone-shaped panels.

'That came from somewhere else. The Iroquois didn't have tepees. They had longhouses. Besides, we can't move that. Twin Stars is having her baby in it.'

Patrick said slowly, 'If I took *her*, I'd be sure to go back to the right place. She'd take me.'

'Patrick, you can't! Take her back into the middle of a battle?'

'Listen, it's her village, it's her place. If not for the accident of you bringing them when you did, she'd be there now. I bet it's where she'd rather be, if you asked her. Didn't you see how she was begging Little Bull just before he left?'

'But he wanted . . .'

'Listen, shut up! You're always arguing. I've made up my mind. I'm not going to miss this chance. I want to see the battle. Don't let's have a fight over it or somebody's sure to get hurt. And it might not be one of us.'

He went to the desk and fetched the seed-tray and brought it back and laid it carefully in the bottom of the chest. Omri watched, feeling terribly agitated. He wanted to fight Patrick, but that was impossible now. He should have done it earlier. Now if they started struggling something awful could happen to Boone or Twin Stars.

His mind was racing. *I'm the one who'll have the key*, he thought. He would have control. He could send them for five minutes, or one minute, or less, and then, just by turning the key in the lock again, he could recover them. That was how it worked. What could happen in such a short time? And he couldn't help admiring Patrick's courage. Omri admitted to himself that he would not have been willing to go first, and not just because of Twin Stars, either.

Patrick climbed into the chest, and crouched down.

'Here,' he said, handing Omri the key. 'Close the lid and send me.'

'Touch the tepee with one finger,' said Omri.

'Okay, I am. Now.' Patrick's voice was trembling a little, but not much.

'What about Boone?'

'He said he felt bad and wanted to help. Send us, will you, before I lose my nerve!'

Omri closed down the lid, put the key in the lock, and locked the chest.

It was such a simple action. What had it caused?

After a moment he unlocked the chest again, and, with icy cold hands, opened it. He didn't know what to expect. Would Patrick have disappeared?

Patrick lay inside it. At least, his body lay there. Omri reached in and touched him. He felt cold.

'Patrick! *Patrick*!' But he was not really expecting a response. Patrick was as far away as anyone can be who isn't actually dead.

Down in the bottom of the chest, near Patrick's unconscious head, was the seed-tray. Patrick's limp hand was resting on it. Everything else on it was the same – the grass patch, the longhouse, the pool – except for one thing. The tepee was made of plastic. The paintings on it were crude, mass-produced; the poles were pink and moulded in one with the tent. Gently Omri lifted it. What he saw underneath gave him the biggest shock he'd had yet.

The plastic figure of an Indian girl lay on a pile of cotton bedding. A cowboy was kneeling by her on one knee. In his arms was a tiny naked plastic baby, smaller than Omri's little fingernail.

Omri gasped. On an impulse, he reached in and lifted the seed-tray and its contents out of the chest. Then he slammed down the lid and turned the key. About half a minute had passed since he had 'sent' Patrick. At once he heard him moving inside and threw back the lid.

Patrick raised his head. His face was white and dazed.

'Don't!' he gasped.

'What happened?' shouted Omri.

'I'd hardly got there! It's fantastic – listen – I was part of the tepee!'

'Wha-at!'

'I can't explain! I was in the tepee – not in it – I *was* it! I was on the outside of it – I could see everything! The place is – it's – I hadn't time to look properly, I could just . . . Send me back, will you? Send me back *now*!'

He reached up and tried to pull down the lid. But Omri braced himself against it.

'Get out. It's my turn,' he said.

'You didn't even want to go!'

'Well, I do now.' Omri was almost unable to speak for excitement. He was trying to drag Patrick bodily out of the chest.

Patrick, resisting, grated out: 'Leave off! Listen. I heard a baby crying in the tepee . . .'

'I know. It's Twin Stars', Get *out*, will you?'

'Listen, it's not fair, let me go back, let me stay for a bit, you hardly let me . . .'

'I've got to see!' Omri said frenziedly. 'Let me just look! Give me five minutes, by your watch, then you can have five, I swear . . .'

'Patrick gave way. He changed places with Omri.

'You'd better take the tepee.'

'The tepee won't work now, all that will happen is, you'll bring them back. I've got her moccasins in my pocket. Those ought to do. Go on, get on with it.'

'Five minutes!' said Patrick, and locked the chest.

There wasn't a second in which to catch a breath or even feel scared. Omri, curled in the dark innards of the chest, heard the lock-catch click, and then, immediately, he felt sunlight shining on him. He tried to open his eyes but found they were already open – at any rate he could see. And he could hear. That was all he could do. Not only couldn't he move, he couldn't try to move; but he didn't feel uncomfortable or as if he were tied up. He just had nothing to move *with* and that was that.

Spread out before him was a ruined Indian village. It was evening. The sun was a red ball sinking behind the rocky edge of a hill. The village was in a clearing in a forest of pine and maple trees. The maples were all the colours of fire. It was as if the fires in the village, which had now burned out, had kindled more fires in the surrounding woods.

There were few longhouses left standing. Many had been burned to the ground. They had stopped smoulder-ing, but their blackened ruins gave the view a look of desolation. A number of women were moving about. Some were carrying water, some were cooking, others were helping injured men. There were Indian children of all ages, and quite a few dogs. Hardly any young men.

Omri could see no signs of anything resembling a battle. What had become of the troop of well-armed Indians they'd dispatched less than an hour ago? Had they got lost on the way?

Suddenly he heard a sound from behind him. It was unmistakably the strange, chuckling cry of a newborn baby. Omri tried to look round but found that he couldn't. Whatever he was, he was stuck to the outside of the tepee and that meant he couldn't see in.

A very queer and comic thought came to him. *I wonder if I'm the beaver or the porcupine?*

126

He didn't have time to consider this before he heard Boone's voice.

'He sure is a fine li'l fella,' he said. His voice was choked with emotion. 'Ever'thin' jest whur it oughta be. Now you give him a swig o' milk, an' Ah'll go ask the boys fer somethin' fer you, t'give ya back yor stren'th.'

There was a movement to Omri's left and Boone came into view, blowing his nose and wiping his eyes. Amazingly, he was full size. Or, no, of course that wasn't amazing at all.

'A fine li'l fella,' he was muttering to himself, sniffing and shaking his head. 'Gee whiz, ain't nature wonderful! Ah kin hardly . . .'

He stopped dead and stared round him in horrified astonishment.

'Holy jumpin' catfish! Whur am Ah?'

Omri was aching to tell him but he could no more talk than he could move. However, Boone was no fool. He realized soon enough what had happened. After a few seconds spent taking in the scene, he turned and dived back into the tepee. Fortunately no one seemed to have seen him.

'Hey, li'l lady, do you know whur we're at? Ah do believe we're in yor village! No, no – now don't you go gittin' up. Gee, I shouldn't oughta've told ya . . .'

A moment later, Twin Stars emerged, her baby in her arms. She looked tired and a bit bedraggled, but otherwise fine. Indeed, she was beautiful. Omri, who had only seen her tiny till now, had never appreciated how beautiful she was.

An Indian woman was passing. She noticed Twin Stars, and reacted to the baby. She called to others. Soon there was a crowd of women round Twin Stars, much chattering talk, and a lot of pointing westward toward the setting sun. Omri hoped Boone would have the sense to stay in the tepee, and he did. After a minute or two, Twin Stars moved to go back in. Several of the other women wanted to come with her, but she sent them away.

Now Omri strained to hear the conversation in the tepee behind him.

'Whut's goin' on?' asked Boone as soon as she re-entered.

'Woman say, strange thing happen. Little Bull come with many braves. Go to hills. Wait for new attack.'

'Whut attack?' asked Boone in alarm.

'Soldier maybe not come back. Algonquin come. Take women, food, furs.'

'They didn't git any loot when they come last time?'

'No. Iroquois fight, drive off. Algonquin burn, kill some, get nothing. Now village wait. Little Bull wait in hills. Algonquin come back when sun go.'

'But the sun's almost gone now!' said Boone, his voice going squeaky.

'Yes,' said Twin Stars quietly.

After a moment, Boone's voice said, 'Ain't ya skeered? With yer baby an' all?' Twin Stars didn't answer. After a while she said, 'Little Bull near. And Great Spirits. No bad come.'

Omri's eyes – or the porcupine's, or the beaver's, whose eyes he was looking through – were fixed on the sun. It was sinking behind the rocky hillside so fast, he could see it move. Only a jagged slice of it was left. Darkness was coming, and his five minutes was more than up. Why hadn't Patrick taken him back?

Chapter 18
Algonquin

There was an air of fear about the village. As twilight fell the villagers seemed to be preparing to decamp. Such men as were left – mainly old, plus some wounded or unfit ones – were giving orders, and the women were running here and there, packing things into bundles. Others came with buckets of water and put out the few cooking fires that were burning, removed the cooking pots, and rounded up the children. A few dogs were dashing about, barking excitedly, sensing something in the hurrying and the anxious voices.

Omri watched all this in growing alarm. The minutes were ticking by. Being apparently nothing more than a picture on the side of a tepee he couldn't see how he could be in danger himself, but he was desperately worried about Twin Stars, Boone and the baby.

After a while one of the old women came round the tepee into Omri's sight. She was hobbling along as fast as she could, gazing up at the tepee with gaping mouth as if it had dropped from nowhere (as indeed it had). She bent at the flap and called to Twin Stars. Twin Stars answered. The old woman hobbled away again, her white hair glowing in the deep twilight. The tall pines around the camp now stood out black against the darkening sky.

Omri heard Twin Stars in the tepee say to Boone: 'Village leave now.'

'Whut's that? Leave fur where?'

'Hide in wood.' There was a pause. Then she said doubtfully, 'Boone come?'

'No. Ah cain't.'

'Why no? Here not safe.'

'*There* not safe! Not fur me. Ah don't fit in, gal. You know that.'

Twin Stars said no more. There was a pause, then the tepee flap opened and she came out with her baby wrapped up in some hide torn from her skirt. She turned in the opening. There was a very soft look in her eyes as she looked, presumably at Boone, standing out of Omri's sight inside. Then she hurried away, mingling with the knot of other Indians in the centre of the village.

Soon they were forming into a rough procession. It was almost too dark to see now, but Omri could just make them out as they silently made their way out of the circle of ruined and half-burnt buildings. Even the dogs were quiet as they trailed along after the villagers. One of them, lingering, passed the tepee. He paused to leave his mark against the side of it, and for a moment he looked up, straight at Omri. His lips drew back over teeth which shone white in the darkness and he whined uneasily, the hair on his back standing up straight. Then he tucked his long tail between his legs and shot off after the others.

Soon the last rustles and murmurs subsided and there was a deep silence, broken only by the call of a single owl. Bird – or a signal?

Omri had never known real fear. All he could compare this with was walking up Hovel Road and knowing he had to pass the skinheads who were waiting for him. That seemed to him now like nothing at all. What was the worst they could do to him, after all? A black eye, a few bruises? This was in another category of fear altogether.

Yet what was he afraid of? Nothing could happen to *him*. At any second now Patrick would turn the key in the lock of the chest and recall him to his body, to normality, to the utter, blissful safety of his own life which he had never thought about before, far less appreciated.

So what was this icy feeling which could only be terror?

Perhaps it was for Boone. Boone was behind him in the tepee, no longer a tiny figure but a full-sized man, out of his place, out of his time. Visible, solid, vulnerable, and quite alone. Omri could hardly imagine how Boone must be feeling as he waited in the tepee for some unknown thing to happen.

And suddenly it did.

It began with another hoot from the owl. Omri saw a swift movement to one side of him, close to the edge of the clearing. Then again, on the other side. A man's figure, crouched low, scurried past him. And abruptly the whole clearing seemed to be full of moving men.

They were not Frenchmen, of course. They were Indians. Little Bull's men, returning to defend the place? Omri strained to see them. All he could make out were glimpses of leggings, of a head-feather – the flash of an axe-head catching the starlight. Then he saw that several men were raking wood from the cooking fires into one heap in the centre of the ring of longhouses. Shadows began to spread from a lightsource in the midst of the men. Suddenly a flame leapt high, and another. The fire had been lit. And at once Omri could see clearly.

These weren't Little Bull's men! Their clothes were different. Their heads were half-shaved. Their head-dresses – even their movements, were alien. Their faces, too. Their faces were wild, distorted, terrifying masks of hatred and rage.

They were Algonquins, come to sack the village.

In the light of the central fire, they ran to and fro, dozens of them – scores. It took only moments to find out they had been outwitted, that the village was empty and there was nothing to steal, no women to carry off. Their anger burst out in howls and yelps. Through this outburst

Omri heard a smothered groan below him. Boone! The cowboy must be peering out at the awful scene.

Now the Indians were dipping branches into the big fire to make torches. They were dancing and shouting and leaping. Several of them were running to the few unburnt longhouses. And suddenly Omri knew.

He knew what he had feared. They were going to burn the tepee. And he was part of it!

The tepee was on the edge of the clearing. There were other things to set on fire first. But they would get to him! They were coming closer, their howls fiercer, their torches swirling in clouds of smoke above their half-naked heads.

Omri screamed silently.

Patrick! Patrick! Do it now! Turn the key, bring me home, save me!

He saw an Indian making straight for him. His face in

the torchlight was twisted with fury. For a second Omri saw, under the shaven scalp decorated with a single scalp-lock, the mindless, destructive face of a skinhead just before he lashed out. The torch went back with the man's right arm, there was a split-second pause and then it came hurtling through the air and struck the panel of hide just beside Omri.

It slithered down to the ground and lay there, its flame chewing the bottom edge. The Algonquin licked his lips, snarling like a dog, and ran back to the fire.

Omri had not realized he could smell as well as see and hear. Now he smelt the smoke, the stench of burning hide. It was dry and it caught quickly. In helpless horror Omri watched the burnt area growing up beside him like the letter A edged with flame. He hardly noticed another Indian approaching from the other side with another blazing brand until suddenly, out of the daze of fear he had fallen into, Omri heard a loud bang.

The Indian left the ground briefly. His fingers jerked open. The torch fell. Then the man did the same. He dropped like a stone and lay motionless on his back while the branch burnt harmlessly beside him.

All the others stopped dead, their grim faces turned toward the tepee.

The shot had come from below. Omri saw the tip of a revolver barrel poking out of a slit in the hide just beneath him. And as the whole pack of Algonquin began to run, howling and yelling, towards the tepee, their monstrous shadows sliding along the ground ahead of them, more shots rang out, and two, then three more Indians fell.

The others hesitated, then scattered. The fire burnt clear in the centre, unattended. The fire that was eating the tepee burnt, too. Inside, behind him, Omri could hear and even feel Boone frantically beating at the licking flames with something – his hat, perhaps – and cursing. But it was useless. The fire was spreading.

Get out, Boone! Run, Boone, run into the forest, save yourself!

Smoke flowed past the painted animal Omri was inhabiting and blinded him.

Chapter 19

The Terror of the Battle

From the dark heart of fear, Omri heard a new sound.

He could see nothing now. But through the snapping of the flames which were already licking at him, came a sudden deafening rattle. Then isolated bangs. Nearer and nearer. With no other warning, something exploded almost under him. The tepee crashed to its side. Omri felt it on top of him. The fire noise stopped and so did the smoke, though the smell was still there. The falling tepee had put the flames out. There was a sensation of heaviness, then of threshing, and he could hear Boone's rich cursing as he struggled to get out of the crumpled, half-burnt folds of the tent.

In his struggles, he rolled the whole thing over. Now Omri was staring up at the night sky. He could see the stars, with smoke drifting close above him, and the reflection of the central bonfire on a few pine-tops.

A cowboy boot loomed for a second against the starlight, and came down, narrowly missing Omri. Boone stood above him, astride him, firing into the surrounding darkness once, twice. 'Take that, ya fleabitten coyote!' he yelled. Then a click . . . Omri found he had been counting. That was the sixth and last bullet.

The rattle came again, closer, and Boone flung himself down on the fallen tepee – on Omri. Omri could smell his sweat now, feel how his heart was thundering through his shirt, hear him muttering a mixture of curses and prayers. The machine-gun bullets whizzed overhead. There was the numbing crash of another hand-grenade exploding somewhere near the big fire.

Now, to the noise of explosions was added shrieks and screams of terror, and other shouts, war cries, as Little Bull's men emerged from hiding to attack the hapless Algonquins. Omri heard the thunder of a single pair of hooves drumming on the ground beneath him. Boone rolled aside and, at almost the same moment, the stars were blotted out as the pony cleared tepee, Boone, and all, in a wild leap. As it galloped on, Omri caught a glimpse of Little Bull on its back, waving a rifle above his head, riding down three fleeing Algonquins.

The noise of the firing was now continuous and deafening. Omri could see the flash of large and small explosions in the dark. The tide of the battle swept to and fro chaotically. Twice or three times small groups of Indians – whether friends or enemies Omri couldn't tell – raced across the fallen tent. One tripped over Boone and went flying. His bare foot scraped Omri's face.

It was the nightmare to end nightmares. Utterly powerless, unable to move, escape, fight back or even close his eyes and ears, Omri had long ago stopped hoping that some miracle would save him. He had totally forgotten Patrick, forgotten his other life. He was a helpless witness to the chaos and carnage of war, part of it, yet not part of it. It seemed it would go on for ever, or until some kind of oblivion engulfed him.

Then, in the tenth part of a second, it ended.

The noise, the smoke, the cries – the terror – the helplessness. Gone . . .

Silence.

He lay curled up in darkness on something hard. He could feel his body, his wonderful, three-dimensional body. Light fell on him, and warm air. And he heard Patrick's voice, with panic in it, calling his name.

He lifted himself slowly. One hand clutched the edge

of the chest. The other went to the right side of his face. Patrick was staring at him, aghast, as if he saw a stranger.

'Omri! Are you all right!'

Omri didn't answer. The side of his head felt funny. He took his hand away and some black stuff was on his fingers. Something was odd about his nose, too. He felt something running out of it. He looked down. There was blood on his sweatshirt.

'What's happened to you? You look – your nose is bleeding, and your hair . . . !'

None of that mattered. The blood, and the singed and blackened hair, meant nothing. They didn't give him any pain or any fear, at least none that he would call fear now. Stiffly Omri crawled out of the chest, trying to get his mind back together, to clear it and to adjust.

Patrick was babbling something about Omri's mother.

'She just came in, I couldn't do anything, she made me go downstairs to the phone, and then she wouldn't let me go up again. She kept asking where you were. She delayed me. I was going crazy, she wouldn't let me go . . . Omri, I'm sorry. Hell, you look terrible, as if you'd nearly been killed or something. What happened? Is it over? Should we bring the others back?'

Omri had a pad of something pressed to his nose. His head, where the fire had licked, was beginning to sting. It was awfully hard to think. He remembered what Boone had said about Little Bull, and kept repeating to himself: *Pore critter's had a shock. Pore critter* . . . The 'poor creature' was himself.

The others . . . He turned suddenly.

'Get Boone back!'he shouted. 'Not the others, but get Boone! Hurry!'

Patrick snatched up the plastic tepee, and Boone's figure from under it.

'Don't forget his hat!' Omri said idiotically. Patrick

scrabbled about in the earth of the seed-tray, and almost threw it after the figure and the tent. He slammed down the lid of the chest, and turned the key.

'If only he's not dead . . .' breathed Omri. His head was beginning to ache piercingly from the burnt side. Patrick threw up the lid again.

They looked down into the belly of the chest. The tepee was a crumpled wreck, twisted and blackened. Boone lay on top of it. He was very still. For one horrible moment Omri thought a stray bullet or the blast from an explosion must have got him. But then he raised his red head and looked up at them.

'Is it over?' he called.

'It's over for us, Boone,' said Omri.

Gently he lifted him out.

'Wuz you there too? Whur was ya, son?'

'You were lying on me part of the time,' said Omri.

Boone didn't try to puzzle this out.

'Dang me if'n it wuzn't the most fearsomest thing Ah ever bin through in mah en-tire life!'

'Me, too,' said Omri soberly.

Patrick was staring at them.

'Have I missed it? he said. 'Is it over?'

'I don't know,' said Omri.

With a sudden movement Patrick leapt into the chest.

'What are you doing?' cried Omri, although he knew.

'Send me back! I've missed everything, and you've seen it! Send me back!'

'No.'

'You've got to! It's only fair.'

'Never mind *fair*. You don't know what you're talking about. It was . . . Never mind that you missed it. You're lucky.'

'But . . .'

'It's no use. I wouldn't send you now for a million pounds.'

Patrick saw he meant it, and when he looked at Omri's face, brave as he was, he couldn't really be sorry.

He climbed slowly out again. 'Tell me about everything,' he said.

Omri told him, with Boone chipping in. Boone had accounted for three, possibly four Indians before he ran 'plumb outa bullets'.

'You'd better do something about that burn,' Patrick said at the end.

'Yeah. What, though?'

'You're going to have to let your mum see it sometime.'

'How'll I explain it? And my nosebleed?'

Patrick said the nosebleed was nothing. 'We could have had a fight.' The burn was the problem. Half the hair on that side of his head was gone and there was a big red blister.

'Well, you don't have to worry about explaining it now,' said Patrick. 'They've gone out.'

'Who?'

'Your lot. Your parents and your brothers.'

'Is the baby-sitter here?'

'Not yet, she's late. Can you cope till morning?'

Omri didn't know. He supposed so. He was ashamed to admit how his heart had sunk when Patrick said his mother wasn't in the house. Suddenly he wanted her. He wanted to tell her everything and let her take care of it, and him. Well, he couldn't; that was all. Just as well, perhaps.

Boone, exhausted, flopped down in the longhouse for a sleep, after flinging back the last of the whisky. Patrick and Omri slipped down to the next-floor bathroom and found some ointment, which Omri rubbed on his own head. The sight of himself in the mirror scared him silly.

His face was white, red and black. He felt he could do with some whisky himself, but he only took an asprin.

'What about the others?' asked Patrick.

'I don't know.'

Omri felt the whole thing had gone well beyond his control. Having seen Boone, Little Bull and Twin Stars full size he could no longer think of them in the same way. Some part of him – until the battle – had still thought of them as 'his', not toys exactly, but belonging to him – within his orbit. This illusion was now gone. What was happening back in the village? Whatever it was, he was responsible for it. He couldn't avoid the realization that he had sent devastating modern weapons back into time and that they had certainly killed people. 'Baddies' of course . . . But who were baddies? If Patrick, a year ago, had made him a present of some other plastic Indian, it might just as well have been an Algonquin, and then the Iroquois would have been the baddies. Suddenly Omri felt the nightmare was not there, but here.

'I think we should bring them back,' said Patrick.

'Bring them back if you want to,' said Omri, who suddenly felt tired to death. 'I've got to sleep.' He started back up the stairs to his room, and stopped. Not up there. He wanted – neutral ground. He turned and went down again.

'Where are you going?' asked Patrick.

'Down to the living room. I'm going to sleep on the sofa.'

'What about when the baby-sitter comes?'

'Shove her in the breakfast room.' He stopped, and met Patrick's eyes. 'Don't do anything stupid,' he said. 'I can't cope with any more.'

'I'll take care of everything,' said Patrick.

Omri went on, his feet like lead weights. In the living room he didn't even put the light on, just threw himself on the sofa, where in two minutes he was fast asleep.

Chapter 20
Invasion

He slept without dreams for two hours. Then something woke him.

He lifted his head sharply. His mother hadn't closed the curtains, so a little light came in from the street. He felt strange, but he saw at once where he was and remembered why he was there. He was by no means ready to wake up – so why had he?

Then he saw there was somebody in the room – coming in, rather. Through an open window, facing the front garden, which shouldn't have been open. It was the sound of it opening, and the draught of cold night air, which had woken him. He was peering over the arm of the sofa, which lay in deep shadow at the furthest end of the living room. He could see the clear silhouette of a male figure stealthily putting first one leg and then the other over the sill, ducking his head under the half-raised window frame: a bare head, which gleamed dully in the diffused lamplight from beyond the high front hedge.

For a second Omri thought it was an Algonquin. But there was no scalp-lock on that shaven skull. It was a skinhead. No – not just one. Once in, the first figure bent and beckoned, and from the shadows outside appeared another, and then another. One by one they climbed silently into Omri's house.

In a flash he remembered last night(was it only last night?) when he'd come down to get Twin Stars something to eat. He'd seen a hairless head go past the kitchen window, and then put it from his mind. They must have been looking the place over, 'casing the joint', making plans for a time when the family would be out . . .

Where was the baby-sitter?

Normally she would be in here, watching television. But the set sat darkling in its corner. The intruders made towards it, laid hands on it. While one unplugged it, and rolled up the cord, the other two lifted it between them. Would they try to take it out by the window? No. They carried it silently to the door. The cord-holder opened it and they went out.

Omri swung his legs swiftly to the floor and stood up, holding his breath. His heartbeat was extraordinarily steady; in fact he felt calm and clear-headed. There was another door to the double-ended living room and it was the one nearest the foot of the stairs. Moving across the carpet without a sound, he slipped out of the room, glancing toward the front door.

It was open. The skinheads were going down the path but they weren't yet ready to make off. They put the television down in the front garden just behind the hedge. Omri knew they would then turn and come back for more. He took two swift steps to the stairs and raced up them silently, two at a time.

He must phone the police.

No, he couldn't. The only phone was in the hall.

He must do *something*. He couldn't just let them get away with it. It was bad enough that they made his life a hell in Hovel Road without invading his territory. But the inescapable facts were that they were older than him, that there were three of them, and that they probably had knives.

He reached his attic bedroom out of breath and opened the door as quietly as he could. He stopped. It was full of strange, small lights and flickering shadows.

The first thing he saw was Patrick, fast asleep on

cushions on the floor. Then he noticed that the cupboard had been returned to the top of the chest, and so had the seed-tray. There seemed to be a lot of activity going on on its much-trampled earth surface. Omri moved forward to look closer.

An astonishing scene met his eyes.

The ruined longhouse had been turned into a sort of scratch hospital. Clean pages, evidently torn from a note-book, had been laid on the floor. In a double row, with a walk-way between their feet, lay a number of wounded Indians. They appeared to have been well looked-after. The ones Omri could see, through the holes in the longhouse roof, were bandaged and covered with warm blankets, made of squares cut from Omri's sports socks – he recognized the green and blue stripes on the white towelling. Twin Stars was there, her baby tied to her back, moving among them with a bucket, giving them drinks.

At either end of the building burnt a small fire of matchsticks and shavings of candlewax, each tended by an unwounded Indian. Around the fires, wrapped in glove-finger sacks, more braves lay asleep.

Omri's eyes went to a bright light at one end of the seed-tray. The stub of the candle had been stuck into the earth and lit. Round it, muttering and chanting, Little Bull moved in a slow sort of dance. His shadow, hugely enlarged, was flung all over the walls of Omri's room, and the thin, weird, wailing note of his chant struck Omri's heart with sadness.

Near the candle was the paddock. It was like a grave-yard. Laid out on the grass were some small, still shapes, covered with squares of white cotton blotted with drops of red. Omri counted them. There were eight. Eight out of forty. And all those injured. How – when they had

ambushed the unsuspecting enemy, with far superior weapons?

It took only a few seconds for Omri to take all this in. Then, out of the depths of the longhouse bustled a little figure in blue and white, with a tall, flowing cap.

'Well!' she exclaimed when she saw him. 'Here's a nice how-do-y'do! Call this a casualty ward? I'd rather be Florence Nightingale. *She* had it easy! Whoever let these poor simple fools loose with modern weapons ought to be shot themselves!'

'What happened?' asked Omri, dry-mouthed.

'What was bound to happen. *They were shooting each other*! From what I can make out from their leader, they encircled the enemy, then blasted off from all sides, never realizing how far the bullets would travel. The shots that didn't hit an enemy were likely to hit an ally coming the other way! I've fished so many bullets out tonight, I could do it with my eyes shut . . .'

She bustled back to work, tutting loudly.

Omri bent and shook Patrick awake.

'Get up. We've got burglars downstairs.'

Patrick jerked upright. 'What!'

'Skinheads. Three of them. They must think the house is empty. They're going to clean us out. Only they won't, because we're going to stop them.'

'We are? How?'

'Where are the guns the Indians had?'

'They're in the cupboard. I think they've damaged a lot of them.'

'We were mad . . . Where's that bag of British soldiers we had in the garden?'

'Here. But you're not going . . .'

'And where's Fickits?'

'He's in with them.'

Omri was frantically emptying the paper bag on to the

chest. He found Fickits at once and almost threw him into the cupboard, remembering just in time to take the jumble of rifles, tommy-guns and machine-guns out first. He locked and unlocked the door and, next moment, Fickits was standing bewildered by the pile of guns.

'Corporal! Check those weapons.'

Fickits, rubbing his eyes, at once came to attention, and then began disentangling what now appeared to be a pile of scrap. Omri meanwhile was putting handfuls of soldiers recklessly into the cupboard. Patrick was at his shoulder.

'You're crazy! You're always telling me not to . . .'

'Shut up and bring me something flat.'

'Like what?'

Omri turned on him fiercely. 'Use your loaf . . . Anything! A tray, a book! My loose-leaf will do. Be quick!'

Patrick did as he was told. Omri closed the cupboard but he didn't turn the key.

'Corporal!'

'Yessir?'

'How much ammo is left?'

'Ammo, sir? More like how many workin' weapons. Them redskins 'ave wreaked 'avoc, sir. Absolute 'avoc. I was afraid of this, sir. These 'ere are precision instruments, sir, they're not bloomin' bows and arrers!'

'Never mind that now. I'm going to put you in charge of a – an operation, Corporal.'

'Me, sir?'

'Not Indians this time. British troops. And they're going to mount an attack on three people my size.'

'Gawd 'elpus, sir! Ow can we?'

'Just do as I tell you, Corporal, and make them do as you tell them. Okay?'

Fickits gulped noisily, then straightened himself.

'As long as most of 'em are Marines, sir, I expect we shall manage.'

'Good man. Stand by to reassure them as they come out.'

'No need for mollycoddling 'em, sir. The light's poor. I'll just tell 'em we're on night manoeuvres.'

Omri turned the key in the lock, and opened the door at once. He was glad the light in the room was dim. Patrick thrust Omri's large, flat loose-leaf book in front of the cupboard, and out on to it poured twenty or thirty tiny, khaki-clad figures. Some of them still had their weapons, others, obeying Fickits' barking orders, began to man some of those the Indians had used. The room filled with the metallic sounds of weapons being loaded.

'Shall we use the big guns this time, sir? Now we've got the crews?' Fickits asked Omri aside.

'Yes. Marshal them all on here, and tell the men to prepare for an all-out attack when you give the word.'

'No trouble, sir. Just don't – er . . .' He coughed. 'Don't thrust yourself forward, sir. They 'aven't spotted anythink unusual yet, if you take my meaning.'

Patrick had caught the spirit of the thing and was feverishly sorting out every bit of hardware he could find in the biscuit-tin and getting the cupboard and key to work on it. Soon the men – armed with light arms, machine-guns, portable anti-tank rockets and even a 'bunker-buster' (a Milan missile), a formidable array about which Omri now felt not the faintest scruple – were in position, drawn up on three sides of a square with their backs to Omri.

'Corporal,' he whispered. 'I'm going to transport you all. When you can see your targets, give the order to fire at will!'

'Sir!'

'And don't worry! Nobody's going to get hurt.'

'You hope,' muttered Patrick as they started down the darkened stairs.

Chapter 21
Rout of the Skinheads

They moved silently down through the darkness. Omri could feel through his hands, holding the edges of the loose-leaf platform, the faint vibrations of life. He could also, for the first time since it happened, feel the sting where the row of minute bullets had pierced the skin of his palm.

On the first landing he nudged Patrick to a stop.

Low down on the bottom flight of stairs was one which always creaked. He heard it creak now. He changed direction and slipped through a half-open door into the bathroom.

He and Patrick stood behind this door. There was another door to this room, which led into his parents' bedroom, and it, too, was ajar. They saw a faint light – the sort made by a pencil-torch – feeling its way about on the landing, and heard the stealthy sounds of the skinheads following it. Then a faint whisper:

'Let's try in 'ere.'

The finger of light vanished, to appear again through the other door. The intruders were in Omri's parents' room. He could hear them moving furtively about, then the soft whine of a wardrobe opening.

'Gaaah – no fur coats . . .'

Omri and Patrick stood rooted, hardly breathing. Omri was almost praying that, in the darkness, no soldier would press a trigger by mistake. Suddenly the torchlight was within two feet of them on the other side of the door.

'Look 'ere Kev!'

Omri set his teeth. He knew what they'd found. A little

oak cupboard with small, shallow drawers in which his mother kept the few bits of jewellery she owned, most of it old silver, inherited from her mother. It was very precious to her, though it wasn't specially valuable. Omri heard the scrape of the wooden drawers, and then:

'We can flog this lot dahn the Portabeller . . . Let's just take the 'ole thing.'

And then another voice, further away but audible because they thought they were safe and were getting careless:

'Ere! I'm going to take a leak on their bed!'

And there was a burst of stifled sniggering.

That did it.

Before Omri could even signal, Patrick had let out a grunt of disgust and flung the door open.

'The light-switch! Beside you!' Omri shouted.

There was an agonizing second while Patrick groped. Then the top light came on, flooding the bedroom with brightness. The skinheads froze in grotesque positions, like children playing Statues. Their ugly faces were turned toward the boys, their eyes popping, their loose mouths gaping.

Omri rushed in like an avenging fury, and stopped, the loose-leaf platform with its contingent of men thrust out in front of him.

''Ere, wot the 'ell . . .'

Then Fickits' sergeant-major voice rang shrill and clear: 'FIRE AT WILL!'

The biggest skinhead snarled and made a dive towards Omri. For a split second he loomed menacingly. Then there was a concerted burst of fire, and suddenly tiny red spots appeared on his face in a line, from the bottom of one cheek, diagonally across his nose to the top of the other. He stopped dead in his tracks, let out a howl of pain and outrage, and clapped his hands to his face.

'I bin stung! It's 'ornets! Get 'em orfa me!'

Behind him, his mate started towards Patrick, hands reaching out to grab.

'I'll get 'em. Little nerds . . .'

But all he got was the miniature equivalent of an armour-piercing shell under his thumbnail.

'OWWW!' he shrieked, and let out a string of curses, shaking his hand and dancing in agony.

The third and smallest of the gang had been gazing at the object Omri held, and he, unlike the others, had *seen*. He now let out a sound that started as a moan and ended in a scream.

'UughhhhhAAAOWEEEE!'

Then he flew into a panic, dashing here and there in short spurts, yelling "Elp! They're alive, I seen 'em, they're alive!'. . .through the crump and crack and chatter of the guns which were firing continuously. The other two also turned and tried to flee, but all sense of direction had deserted them. They bumped into the furniture, the walls and each other, swearing and howling, and giving great leaps into the air every time they were hit in a sensitive spot. Omri and Patrick added to the uproar by shouting encouragement to their little men. Patrick was jumping about as if at a prize-fight or a football match. Omri had to stay still to hold the firing-platform steady, but he opened his throat on a long shout of excitement as the three invaders finally found the other exit and fled through it, pell-mell.

'Cease fire!' cried Patrick.

'CEASE FIRE!' bawled Fickits.

There was a fraction of a second's silence. Then the boys heard the skinheads shoving and swearing on the stairs. One of them tripped; there was a series of satisfying thumps, and then a loud crack as one of the bannisters broke. The boys, hurrying down to the half-landing, saw them fleeing along the path and heard the clatter of their boots receding along Hovel Road, accompanied by sounds of anguish.

The boys turned and hugged each other.

'We did it, we did it!'

'The way you switched the light on – terrific!'

'How you could hold that thing straight? I'd have tipped them all off, I was so excited! Hey! Where is it?'

'I put it on the bed . . .'

They rushed back into the bedroom. Fickits was calmly ordering the men to clear up and cover the big guns.

When he noticed the boys, he left the men and edged to the back of the platform.

'Operation a success, sir?' he asked in a quiet tone.

'Definitely, Fickits. Well done!' said Omri.

'Did I say sergeant, Fickits?' said Patrick. 'I meant a captain.'

'Not me, sir! Too much responsibility.' He coughed. 'Better get the men fell-in and back to quarters as quick as possible, sir.'

'Yeah, right! Thanks again, Corporal, it was terrific.' And he started to carry them upstairs.

'See that everything's all right up there,' said Omri.

'Okay.' Patrick reached the door and stopped. 'I don't mind so much now, missing the other battle,' he said. 'Wasn't this one *fantastic*?'

'Yeah,' said Omri.

He was thinking how fantastic it was, too, that he would never be afraid to walk down Hovel Road again. They would leave him severely alone from now on, and even if they didn't . . . Having seen them off like that, and after all he'd been through tonight, he couldn't imagine them holding any terrors for him in future.

He looked round the room. He was going to have a bit of explaining to do. The glass on a picture was cracked, and there were a number of pinholes, and some larger ones, in the wallpaper and the foot of the bed. Then there was the bannister, and his own injuries . . . Well, he could tell his parents about the burglars, say there was a scuffle. Maybe they'd wear it. He hoped so.

He bent and picked up his mother's jewel cupboard. He'd saved that for her, anyway. Under it was a cheap pencil-torch, still alight. He switched it off and dropped it in his pocket. He might, if he felt like it, just hand it back to that little skinhead, if he bumped into him after school on Monday . . . Be a good laugh, to see his face.

Omri drew a deep breath of satisfaction and went downstairs to bring in the stuff piled in the front garden.

Epilogue by the Fire

When everything was back in place, with Patrick's help, except the bannister rail which needed gluing in three places, they made some hot chocolate to take upstairs, with some cold potatoes and other fridge-cullings. They were both so keyed-up they couldn't feel their tiredness, and were prepared to sit up all night.

'I sent Matron back for some drugs and stuff she wanted,' Patrick said. 'But she made me promise I'd fetch her again in the morning. She says she's going to take a week's leave from St Thomas's. She's enjoyed all this, anyway.'

'Fickits, too.'

'Little Bull hasn't enjoyed it.'

Omri didn't answer. Every time he thought of the Indian battle it took away from his overwhelming pleasure in the one with the skinheads.

'Where's Boone?' he asked suddenly.

'I sent him back, too. He asked me to. Said the odd gun-fight and saloon brawl would be a rest-cure after all he's been through . . . He said he'd like to see us soon, when things have quietened down.'

'What about his horse?'

'Oh, yes. I gave him the one that English cavalry officer was riding.' Patrick chuckled. 'You should have heard him swear when I flicked him off! Boone said the horse was a beaut. Really, he was happy with it. And I bet the horse'll be happier with him than with that snooty redcoat.'

When they reached the room, all was quiet. The candle

had burnt out, so Little Bull had had to stop his dancing and chanting for the dead. One fire was out, the other was burning low. The Indians, including the wounded, were all asleep, except Little Bull who sat cross-legged by the fire. Twin Stars was asleep beside him, the baby in the crook of her arm.

Patrick struck a match and Little Bull looked up.

'We've brought food,' Omri said.

'No eat,' said the Indian.

Omri didn't press him. He just poured a toothpaste capful of hot chocolate and put it beside him with a piece of potato.

The match went out. They sat together in the dark, with just the embers of the fire. The boys drank their chocolate. For a long time nobody spoke. Then Little Bull said:

'Why Omri bring Little Bull?'

For the first time in two days Omri thought of his prize. It had gone completely from his mind. Now it seemed so trivial, he was ashamed to mention it.

'Something good happened to me which was partly to do with you, and I wanted to tell you about it.'

'What good thing happen?'

'I wrote a story about you and Boone and it – well, it was good.'

'Omri write truth of Little Bull?'

'Yes, it was all true.'

'Omri write Little Bull kill own people?'

'Of course not!'

'You write before this happen. Next time write Little Bull kill own braves.'

'You didn't. The now-guns killed them. You couldn't know.'

'Then Little Bull fool!' came his bitter voice out of the dark.

156

There was a silence. Patrick said, 'We were the fools, not you.'

'Yes,' said Omri. 'We should have known better. We shouldn't have interfered.'

'Into-fear? Omri not afraid.'

'We should have left you alone.'

'Leave alone, Little Bull die from French gun.'

There was a pause. Then Omri said, 'You did beat the Algonquins.'

'Yes. Beat Algonquin thief. Not beat French.'

'Yeah, that was a pity,' said Patrick feelingly, 'after all that.'

'Fewer dead the better,' muttered Omri.

'Good kill French!' Little Bull exclaimed, sounding more like his old self. 'Kill French next time.'

'But not with the now-guns.'

After a silence, Little Bull said, 'Now-guns good. Shoot far. Now Little Bull know shoot far. Next time not put own braves where bullets go. Omri give now-guns, take back!'

The embers of the fire flared a little. Twin Stars had risen to throw on another curl of wax. Now she crouched beside Little Bull and looked into his face.

'No,' she said clearly.

He looked at her.

'What, no?'

She spoke to him softly and earnestly in their own language. He scowled in the firelight.

'What does she say, Little Bull?'

'Wife say, not use now-guns. Soon braves forget skill with bow. Woman not want son grow up without Indian skill. She say now-gun kill too many, too easy. No honour for chief or chief's son.'

'What do you think?'

'Omri give now-guns if Little Bull think good?'

Omri shook his head.

'Then what for I fight with wife? Give wife own way. Peace in longhouse, till next enemy come. Then maybe wife sorry!'

He scowled at her. She smiled, bent down and picked up the baby and laid it in his arms. He sat looking down at it.

'When son grow, Little Bull tell that Omri write story. Little Bull live in story even when gone to ancestors. *That* give honour, make son proud of father!'

'He'll be proud of you, Little Bull. Without any help from me.'

Little Bull looked up at him. Then he stood up. The fire put out a sudden flare. He stood there, feet apart, his body glowing, his stern face for once untroubled.

'Omri good,' he said loudly. 'Give *orenda* back to Little Bull!'

Orenda. The life-force.

And he held his son up high in both hands, as if offering him to the future.

The Secret of
the Indian

For Sheila Watson – *sine qua non*

Contents

I

A Shocking Homecoming

When Omri's parents drove home from their party, his mother got out in front of the house while his father drove round the side to put the car away. The front-door key was on the same keyring with the car key, so his mother came up the steps and rang the bell. She expected the baby-sitter to answer.

There was a lengthy pause and then the door opened and there was Omri, with Patrick just behind him. The light was behind him too, so she didn't see him clearly at first.

"Good heavens, are you boys still up? You should have been in bed hours ag— "

Then she stopped. Her mouth fell open and her face drained of colour.

"Omri – ! What – what – what's happened to your *face*?"

She could hardly speak properly, and that was when Omri realised that he wasn't going to get away with it so easily this time. This time he was either going to have to lie like mad or he was going to have to tell far more than he had ever intended about the Indian, the key, the cupboard and all the rest of it.

He and Patrick had talked about it, frantically, before his parents returned.

"How are you going to explain the burn on your head?" Patrick asked.

"I don't know. That's the one thing I can't explain."

"No it's not. What about all the little bullet-holes and stuff in your parents' bedroom?"

Omri's face was furrowed, even though every time he frowned, it hurt his burn.

"Maybe they won't notice. They both need glasses. Do you think we should clear everything up in there?"

Patrick had said, "No, better leave it. After all, they've got to know about the burglars. Maybe in all the fuss about that, they won't notice your face and a few other things."

"How shall we explain how we got rid of them – the burglars I mean?"

"We could just say we burst in through the bathroom and scared them away."

Omri had grinned lopsidedly. "That makes us out to be heroes."

"So what's so bad about that? Anyway it's better than telling about *them*." Patrick, who had once been quite keen to tell "about *them*", now realised perfectly clearly that this was about the worst thing that could happen.

6

"But where *is* the wretched baby-sitter? Why didn't she come? How *dare* she not turn up when she *promised*?"

Omri's father was stamping up and down the living-room in a fury. His mother, meanwhile, was holding Omri round the shoulders. He could feel her hand cold and shaking right through his shirt. After her first shocked outburst when she'd come home and seen him, she'd said very little. His father, on the other hand, couldn't seem to stop talking.

"You can't depend on anyone! Where the hell are the police, I called them hours ago!" (It was five minutes, in fact.) "One would think we lived on some remote island instead of in the biggest city in the world! You pay their damned salaries and when you need the police, they're never there, never!"

He paused in his pacing and gazed round wildly. The boys had put the television back and there wasn't much disorder to see in this room. Upstairs, they knew, chaos and endless unanswerable questions waited.

"Tell me again what happened."

"There were burglars, Dad," Omri said patiently. (This part was safe enough.) "Three of them. They came in through that window –"

"How many times have I said we ought to have locks fitted? Idiot that I am! – for the sake of a few lousy pounds – go on, go on – "

"Well, I was asleep in here – "

"*In the living-room?* Why?"

"I – er – I just was. And I woke up, and saw them, but they didn't see me. So I nipped upstairs, and – "

His father, desperate to hear the story, was still too

agitated to listen to more than a sentence of it without interrupting.

"And where were *you*, Patrick?"

Patrick glanced at Omri for guidance. Omri shrugged very slightly with his eyebrows. He didn't know himself how much to say and what to keep quiet about.

"I was – in Omri's room. Asleep."

"All right, all right! Then what?"

"Er – well, Omri came up, and woke me, and said there were burglars in the house, and that we ought to . . . er – " He stopped.

"Well?" barked Omri's father impatiently.

"Well . . . stop them."

Omri's father turned back to Omri. "Stop them? Three grown men? How could· you stop them? You should have locked your bedroom door and let them get on with it!"

"They were nicking our TV and stuff!"

"So what? Don't you know the sort of· people they are? They could have hurt you seriously!"

"They did hurt him seriously!" interrupted Omri's mother in a shrill voice. "Look at him! Never mind the interrogation now, Lionel. I wish you'd go and phone Basia and find out why she didn't come, and let me take Omri upstairs and look after him."

So Omri's father returned to the hall to phone the baby-sitter while his mother led Omri upstairs. But when she switched the bathroom light on and looked at him properly, she let out a gasp.

"But that's a burn, Omri! How – how did they do that to you?"

And Omri had to say, "They didn't do it, Mum. Not that. That was something else."

She stared at him in horror, and then controlled

herself and said as calmly as she could, "All right, never mind now. Just sit down on the edge of the bath and let me deal with it."

And while she was putting on the ointment with her cold, shaky hands, his father came stamping up the stairs to say there was no reply from their baby-sitter's number.

"How could she not come? How could she leave you boys alone here? Of all the criminally irresponsible – wait till I get hold of her – "

"What about us?" asked Omri's mother very quietly, winding a bandage round Omri's head.

"*Us?*"

"Us. Going out to our party before she got here."

"Well – well – but we trusted her! Thought she was just a few minutes late – " But his voice petered out, and he stopped stamping about and went into their bedroom to take off his coat.

Omri heard the light being switched on, and bit his lips in suspense.

"Am I hurting, darling?"

He had no time to shake his head before his father burst back.

"What in God's sweet name has been going on in our bedroom?"

Patrick, who was hanging about in the doorway to the bathroom, exchanged a grim look with Omri.

"Well, Dad – that's – that's where the battle – I mean, that's where they were, when we – caught them."

"Battle! That's just what it looks like, a battlefield! Jane, come in here and look – "

Omri's mother left him sitting on the bath and went through into the bedroom. Omri and Patrick,

9

numb and speechless with suspense, could hear them exchanging gasps and exclamations of amazement and dismay.

Then both his parents reappeared. Their faces had changed.

"Omri. Patrick ... I think we'd better hear the whole story before the police arrive. Come in here."

With extreme reluctance, the boys went through the dividing door between bathroom and bedroom for the second time that evening.

The place looked terrible. All the dressing-table drawers, and those of the chest-of-drawers, were pulled out, their contents strewn about. The double bed had been knocked askew. A chair had gone flying, the wardrobe door was swinging open. Omri had set his mother's little jewel-cupboard back on its feet but its door, too, was open.

But, with the lights full on, the thing the boys were most painfully aware of was the holes. Little pin-holes made by the tiny bullets, and not so little ones made by the miniature mortars and hand-grenades which had missed their targets and hit the wall and the head and foot of the bed. It seemed ludicrous to Omri now, looking at them, that he'd had even a faint hope his parents might not notice them. They might be a bit short-sighted, but after all, they weren't blind. The room looked pock-marked.

And indeed his father was already running his fingers over the white wall above the bed-head.

"What's been going on here, boys?" he asked in a new tone of voice.

Patrick and Omri glanced at each other, opened their mouths, and closed them again.

"Well?"

It wasn't a bark this time, it was just a question, a question filled with curiosity. After all, from a grown-up's point of view, what *could* make those tiny marks?

At that moment, there was a loud, policemanly ring and double knock on the door.

Omri's father gave the boys a look which said, "This is only a short postponement", and left the room. They heard him running downstairs, and they all trailed after him. Half-way down, he paused.

"Good Lord, did you see this, Jane? I didn't notice as we came up! One of the banisters has been broken!"

Eager to explain something that could be explained, Omri volunteered the information that one of the burglars had fallen downstairs in his hurry to get out.

His father looked up at him.

"You boys must have thrown a real scare into them."

"Lionel," said Omri's mother suddenly.

"What?"

"Shouldn't we – hear what the boys have to say, before the police talk to them?"

He hesitated. The bell rang again, commandingly.

"Too late now," he said, and hurried to open the door to the police.

II

Modest Heroes

As the two uniformed policemen were shown into the living-room, and Omri's mother hurried down to them, Omri and Patrick had a welcome moment to themselves at the top of the stairs.

"You look like a Sikh in that bandage," said Patrick. "Well, half a Sikh."

"Never mind what I look like. What are we going to do?"

Patrick said nothing for a moment. Then he said, "Make something up, I suppose. What else can we do?"

"All right. But what? What, that anyone'd believe for two seconds?"

"We might try saying that the skinheads did the damage to the wall. We could say they had – I don't know – spiked tools, gimlets or chisels or whatever, and just stuck them into everything for a laugh."

"Or, we could say we don't know how they did it. We burst in, they ran, that's it. Leave the cops to figure it out."

"If they really look, they'll find minute bullets in the bottoms of the holes."

"They won't. Why should they think to?"

"Boys! Come down here, will you?"

It was Omri's dad calling, peremptorily. They started to walk as slowly as they dared down the stairs.

"And your burn?" whispered Patrick.

"Maybe – we might say we'd had a bonfire in the garden and that you cracked me over the head with a lighted branch."

"Oh, great! Try saying that and I really will crack you!"

So that was it. They didn't try to explain the little holes, and the police assumed that the skinheads had been vandals as well as burglars and didn't examine them too closely. They went over everything else for fingerprints but said that although there were quite a few, the chances were against them catching the thieves who – technically speaking – weren't thieves after all, because they hadn't actually got away with anything.

Omri told the bonfire story without bringing Patrick into it. He just said – the inspiration of the moment – that they'd used a whole can of lighter-fluid to get the fire going and that he, Omri, had struck the match while his face was over the wood. His parents, who had been positively bursting with pride at the way the boys had rid the house of intruders, abruptly changed their views about Omri's brilliance.

"How could you be so unutterably DAFT as to light a fire like that, you little HALF-WIT!" his father expostulated. "How many times have I told you – "

A cough from one of the policemen interrupted him.

"Excuse me, sir. Were these two lads alone in the house?"

"Er – "

"Because as you no doubt know, sir, it is severely frowned on to leave any young person under the age of fourteen alone in a house at night."

"Of course I know that, sergeant, and we never, never do it. We always have a baby-sitter. Very punctual and reliable. She was due at seven tonight, and when we went out we assumed she was a couple of minutes late ... She's never let us down before."

"And where is this person, sir?"

"She never showed up, sergeant," said Omri's father shame-facedly. "Yes, I know what you're going to say, and you're perfectly right, we are to blame and I shall never forgive myself."

"I dare say you will, sir," said the sergeant levelly, "in time. But it would have been much harder to forgive yourself, if *worse had befallen*." Both Omri's parents hung their heads miserably and Omri moved closer to his mother who looked as if she might burst into tears.

"This is not exactly what you might call a – *salubrious* neighbourhood, especially after dark," went on the policeman. "Only this evening, a lady was mugged at the end of your street – pulled right off her bicycle, she was – "

"Her *bicycle*!"

This from Omri's mother, whose head had come up sharply.

"Yes, madam ... ?"

"Who was she – this – lady who was mugged?"

14

The sergeant glanced at his companion.

"Do you remember the name, George?"

He shrugged. "Some Polish-sounding name – "

Omri's mother and father exchanged horrified looks. "Not – was it Mrs Brankovsky?"

"Something like that – "

"But that's her! Our baby-sitter!" cried Omri's mother. "Oh, heavens – poor Basia – "

" 'Basha'?" inquired the younger policeman. "Is that her name, or what happened to her – ?" And he suppressed a snigger. But the sergeant gave him a stern look and he subsided.

"There's nothing humorous about it, George."

"No, sergeant. Sorry."

"You'll be glad to hear she's not badly hurt, madam. But she had to go to hospital, just for a check-up, like. The muggers got her bag, though."

"Oh, this is terrible! What kind of district have we come to live in?"

Ah, thought Omri. *Now maybe you'll realise what I've been going through, walking along Hovel Road!* They'd never accepted before that it was a horrible area and that he'd been scared.

The policemen took all the details and descriptions of the skinheads.

"Could you identify them if you saw them again?" asked the sergeant.

"No," said Patrick.

Omri said nothing. He knew he would see them again, like on Monday morning on the way to school. Whether he would decide to shop them, or not, he had yet to decide.

Adiel and Gillon came home from their film just as the police were leaving.

15

"And who are these young gentlemen?" asked the sergeant.

"They're Omri's older brothers."

"What's going on?" asked Adiel.

"We've had burglars," said Omri quickly.

"WHA-AT!" yelled Gillon. "They didn't get my stereo! – Did they?"

"They didn't get a thing," said their father proudly. "Omri and Patrick chased them off."

The older boys gaped at each other.

"Them and what army?" asked Gillon.

Patrick stifled a sudden nervous giggle. "Only a little one," he murmured. Omri nearly felled him with a heavy nudge.

There was a lot more talking to do – Adiel and Gillon had to hear the whole story (except that of course it was nothing like the whole story) all over again. They were absolutely agog, and even Gillon could find nothing sarcastic to say about the way Omri and Patrick had dealt with the situation.

"You're a pair of nutters," was the worst he could think of. "Those thugs could've flattened you. How did you know they didn't have knives?" But there was more than a hint of admiration in his reproof.

Adiel, the eldest, said: "Right couple of heroes if you ask me. We could've been cleaned out." And he gazed lovingly, not at his little brother, but at the television set.

It was nearly one o'clock in the morning by the time they'd drained the last of their hot chocolate and been gently shooed off to bed by Omri's mother. She gave Omri a special hug, being careful of his head, and hugged Patrick too.

"You're fantastic kids," she said.

Omri and Patrick looked uncomfortable. It simply didn't seem right to either of them that they were getting all the credit for driving off the intruders single- (or double-) handed, when in fact they'd had a great deal of help.

As soon as they got up to Omri's bedroom in the attic, they locked the door and made for the desk.

They'd had to make a hasty decision, before the return of the parents, to leave things as they were, not to send anybody else back after they'd dispatched Corporal Willy Fickits and his men. As Patrick pointed out, "We don't know how the wounded would stand the journey. Besides, we can't send the Indians back to their time without Matron, we can't send *her* back to hers, without them – and we *certainly* can't send them all *anywhere* together!"

And Omri had agreed. But they'd both been on tenterhooks all the time the police had been in the house for fear they'd demand to see Omri's room. The boys had been very careful to say the burglars hadn't got beyond the first floor of the house.

Now the boys bent over the desk. They'd left Omri's bedside light on in case Matron had had to tend to one of the wounded Indians in the night. She herself now sat, upright but clearly dozing, at a small circular table (made of the screwtop of a Timotei shampoo bottle, a good shape because it had a rim she could get her knees under.) On it lay a tiny clipboard that she had brought with her from St Thomas's Hospital. She'd been making up her notes and temperature charts.

On either side of her on the floor of the longhouse stretched a double row of pallet beds. Each bed was occupied by a wounded Indian. Matron's ministrations had been so efficient that all were resting peacefully. She had earned her little nap, though she would probably deny hotly, later, that she had nodded off while 'on duty'.

Outside the longhouse, beside the burnt-out candle, a blanket was spread on the soil in Omri's father's seed-tray. Curled up asleep on the blanket were Little Bull and Twin Stars, his wife. Between them, in the crook of Twin Stars' arm, lay their newborn baby, Tall Bear.

All these people, when they were standing up, were no more than three inches tall.

III

How It All Started

It had all started over a year before, with an old tin medicine-cabinet Gillon had found, a key which fitted it, which had belonged to Omri's great-grandmother, and the little plastic figure of an American Indian which Patrick had given Omri (second-hand) for his birthday.

On that fateful night, Omri had put the Indian into the small metal cupboard and locked it with the fancy key. There was no particular point to this, really. Thinking back later, Omri didn't know why he'd done it. He'd had a thing at the time about secret cupboards, drawers, rooms; hiding-places, kept safe from prying eyes, where he could secrete his favourite things and be sure they'd stay exactly as he'd left them, undisturbed by rummaging brothers or anyone else.

But the Indian didn't stay as he'd left it. Some combination of key and cupboard, plus the stuff the Indian was made of – plastic – had worked the wonder of bringing the little man to life.

At first, when this happened, Omri – once past the first shock of astonishment – had thought he was in for the fun-trip of all time. A little, live man of his very own to play with! But it hadn't turned out like that.

The Indian, Little Bull, was no mere toy. Omri soon found out that he was a real person, somehow magicked into present-day London, England, from the America of nearly two hundred years ago. The son of a chief of the Iroquois tribe, a fighter, a hunter, with his own history and his own culture. His own beliefs and morals. His own brand of courage.

Little Bull regarded Omri as a magic being, a giant from the world of the spirits, and was, at first, terrified of him. Omri could see he was afraid, but the Indian was incredibly brave and controlled and Omri soon began to admire him. He realised he couldn't treat him just as a toy – he was a person to be respected, despite his tiny size and relative helplessness.

And it soon turned out that he was by no means the easiest person in the world to get along with, or satisfy. He had demands, and he made them freely, assuming Omri to be all-powerful.

He demanded his own kind of food. A longhouse, such as the Iroquois used to sleep in. A horse, although previously he had never ridden. Weapons, and animals to hunt, and a fire to cook on and dance around. Eventually he even demanded that Omri provide him with a wife!

In addition, Omri had to hide him and protect him. It needed only a little imagination to realise what would happen if any grown-up should find out about the cupboard, the key and their magic properties. Because Omri soon found out that not just Little Bull but *any* plastic figure or object would become alive or real by being locked in the cupboard.

But he couldn't keep the secret entirely to himself. His best friend, Patrick, eventually found out about it, and lost no time in putting his own little plastic man into the cupboard. And so "Boo-Hoo" Boone, the crying Texas cowboy, had come into their lives, complicating things still more. For of course, cowboy and Indian were enemies, and had to be kept apart until a number of adventures, and their common plight – being tiny in a giants' world – brought them together and made them friends and even blood-brothers.

Omri bought the plastic figure of an Indian girl and brought her to life as a wife for Little Bull. And shortly after that, it was decided – with deep reluctance by the boys – that having three little people, and their horses, around amid all the dangers that threatened them in the boys' time and world, was more than they could cope with. It was just too much responsibility. So they 'sent them back', for the cupboard and key worked also in reverse, transforming real miniature people back into plastic and returning them to their own time.

Omri hadn't intended ever to play with this dangerous magic again. It had been too frightening, too full of problems – and too hurtful, at the end, when he had to part with friends he had grown so fond of. But as with so many resolutions, this one got broken.

About a year later, by which time Omri's and Patrick's families had both moved house, Omri won first prize in an important competition for a short story. The story he wrote was called "The Plastic Indian" and was all

21

about – well, it was the truth, but of course no one thought of that; they just thought Omri had made up the most marvellous tale. And he was so excited (the prize was three hundred pounds, he was to receive it at a big party in a London hotel, and even his brothers were very impressed) that he decided to bring Little Bull back to life, *just* long enough to share this triumph with him since he had been such a vital part of it.

Unfortunately, things were not so simple.

When Omri put Little Bull, Twin Stars and their pony – the plastic figures of them – back in the cupboard, they emerged much changed.

Little Bull lay across the back of his pony with two musket-balls in his back, very near to death. There had been a battle in his village, between his tribe and their enemies, the Algonquins, together with French soldiers. (Omri had already learnt that the French and English had been fighting in America at the time, and Little Bull's tribe was on the English side.) Little Bull had been wounded. Twin Stars, although on the point of having a baby, had rushed out and heaved Little Bull on to his pony, just as the magic worked, bringing them – tiny as before, but as real as ever, and in desperate trouble – to Omri's attic bedroom.

And thus it was that Omri was launched into a whole series of new and even more hair-raising and challenging adventures.

Luckily Patrick was nearby and was able to help with some excellent ideas. Boone 'came back' too, and they also brought to life a hospital Matron from a much more recent era to help save Little Bull's life. Later, when he demanded to go back to his village, a British Royal Marine corporal, Willy Fickits, and a contingent

22

of Iroquois braves, were brought to life to help take revenge on the Algonquins.

At this point there was a most incredible turn of events.

Boone, the cowboy, suggested that the boys 'go back' to Little Bull's time and witness the battle. Of course they thought it was impossible. How could they fit into the little bathroom cupboard, only about a foot high? But Boone pointed out that the magic key might fit something larger – the old seaman's chest that Omri had bought in the market, for instance.

It worked. Each boy climbed in in turn, the other one turned the key, and each separately went back in time to the Iroquois village.

When Omri got back – terribly shaken after witnessing a horrific battle – his hair was singed and he had a burn-blister on the side of his head.

The boys brought the Indian troop back through the magic of the key, discovering to their horror that the modern weapons that they had given Little Bull's men – Little Bull called them 'now-guns' – had proved too much for fighters untrained in their use. Many of them had been accidentally shot by their own side. Matron had to be brought back to treat their wounds, but eight had been killed.

Little Bull was distraught, but Twin Stars comforted him by putting his new son, Tall Bear, in his arms. And Omri and Patrick took the blame. They shouldn't have sent modern weapons into the past . . . But these worked very well when, later, three skinheads tried to burgle the house. The boys brought some plastic Marines to life and mounted an artillery assault on them just as they were rifling Omri's parents' bedroom, and completely routed them. It was exhilarating while it lasted, but now they were faced with the aftermath: reality, the present, the results of the night's doings.

IV

Dead in the Night

The two boys sat on the floor of Omri's bedroom and conferred in low voices.

"We've got to plan what to do," said Patrick. "One of us must be up here in your room, on guard, every minute of the rest of the weekend. We'll have to keep your door locked from inside. Whoever's not here will have to bring food and stuff, so I'd better stay up here most of the time. It'll look dead odd if *I* start nicking stuff from your kitchen. I don't know what we're going to do on Monday – "

Omri said heavily, "I do. I'll have to go to school, and you'll have to go home."

"Oh God, yes," said Patrick, remembering.

Patrick now lived in Kent with his mother. They

were only in London for a brief visit to his aunt and girl cousins, Emma and the dreadful Tamsin. They'd have been back in their country home already, had Tamsin not fallen off her bicycle and broken her leg, so that Patrick's mother had decided to stay on for a day or two to help his aunt.

The boys sat in heavy silence. Omri could hardly bear the thought of being left alone in this increasingly difficult situation. Patrick could hardly bear the thought of leaving it.

"Maybe Tamsin'll die," Patrick said darkly. "Then we'll have to stay on. For the funeral."

Omri hoped this was only a sick joke. He detested Tamsin but he didn't wish her dead – not now he'd seen death, not with those eight small bloodstained bodies lying under torn-up scraps of sheet, right here in his room . . .

"What are we going to do about – the casualties?" he asked.

"You mean the dead ones? We'll have to bury them."

"Where?"

"In your garden – "

"But we can't just . . . I mean, it's not like when Boone's horse died. They're people, we can't just – stick them in the earth. What about their families?"

"Their families are – are *back there* somewhere. We don't know where they are, or *when* they are."

"Maybe we ought to – to send them back through the cupboard, to their own time."

"Send their dead bodies back? With modern bullets in them?"

"Their people would think they'd been shot by white men. They wouldn't examine them. They'd go through – you know, whatever special rituals they have, and bury them properly – or – or whatever they do with dead people."

Abruptly, Omri felt his eyes begin to prick and a hard, hot lump came into his throat. He put his head down on his knees. Patrick must have been feeling the same, because he squeezed Omri's arm sympathetically.

"It's no good feeling it too much," he said after clearing his throat twice. "I know it's terrible and I know it's partly our fault. But they lived in very dangerous times, fighting and risking death every day. And they went into the battle quite willingly."

"They didn't know what they were up against with the now-guns," said Omri in a muffled voice.

"Yeah, I know. Still. It doesn't help to – to be a Boone."

The weak joke about the cry-baby cowboy made Omri chuckle just a little.

"Where is Boone, by the way?" he asked, sniffing back his tears.

"I told you. I sent him back – he asked me to. Gave him a new horse, and off he went. Look."

He opened the cupboard. On the shelf was Boone, standing beside his new horse, a tall, alert-looking black one. On the floor of the cupboard, Corporal Fickits and his men were clustered together, with their various weapons. Patrick gathered them all up, put the soldiers back in the biscuit-tin, but kept Fickits and Boone separate. Boone went into his pocket, horse and all. He always kept him there, when he wasn't real, for luck. He was actually as fond of Boone as Omri was of Little Bull. Omri put Fickits in the back pocket of his jeans.

"The only thing we can do right now is to get some sleep," Omri said.

27

Patrick settled down on his floor-cushions while Omri clambered up onto his bunk bed under the skylight. He looked up at the stars through the branches of the old elm tree which his father kept saying should be cut down because it was dead. Skeletal as it was, to Omri it was a friend.

"Let's bring Boone back tomorrow," Patrick whispered just before they dropped off. "I don't seem to be able to face things without Boone, whether he cries or not. Besides, I want to know if he likes his new horse."

At dawn Omri was woken by a familiar shout.

"Omri wake! Day come! Much need do!"

Omri, feeling sticky-eyed and thick-headed with tiredness, slid backwards down the ladder to the floor. Patrick was still sound asleep. The grey dawn light was only just creeping through the skylight.

"It's dead early, Little Bull," he muttered, rubbing his face and stifling a series of yawns.

Little Bull didn't hear him properly. He caught only his name and the word "dead". He nodded his hard-muscled face once and grunted.

"One more dead in night."

Omri's throat closed up with a sick feeling.

"Another? Oh, no . . . I'm sorry!" He meant sorry-ashamed, not just sorry-regretful. He felt every dead Indian brave was on his own conscience. He should never have made the modern weapons real, never have sent Little Bull and his braves back in time with them. The trouble was, he seemed *still* not fully to have accepted the fact, which he knew with one part of his brain, that these little people were not just toys come to life. They were flesh and blood, with their own characters, their own lives and destinies. And against his own intentions

28

Omri had been drawn in. He'd found himself acting out his own part in these destinies, which would never have been possible but for the magic of the cupboard . . . and the key.

The key turned any container into a kind of body-shrinking time-machine. His seaman's chest had taken him and Patrick back to the eighteenth century, to Little Bull's time and place . . . Omri had not had time, so far, even to begin to think about the possibilities of that.

Now he scanned the seed-tray and saw that two of the Indians who had not been injured were carrying another body out of the longhouse and into the little paddock Patrick had made with miniature fencing, for the ponies, and which was now a makeshift morgue. Matron followed the sad procession, her face, rather grim at all times, now grimmer than ever.

"I did my best," she said shortly. "Bullet lodged in the liver. Couldn't reach it."

She watched the two braves lay the dead Indian down beside the others. Suddenly she turned to face Omri.

"I know I did that operation on your friend!" she said. "And I operated last night – emergency ops – three of them – but blow it all, I'm not a surgeon! Stupid of me – *conceited* to think I could cope. Can't. Not trained for it. Anyway . . . too much for any one person." Her voice cracked upward.

"Matron, it's not your fault – " began Omri, terrified that this capable, efficient, down-to-earth woman might be about to burst into tears, which would have unmanned him completely.

"Didn't say it was! My fault indeed!" She glared at him, took her specs off, polished them on a spotless handkerchief from her apron pocket, and put them back on her formidable nose.

"Blessed if I know how I got here, what this is all about – now don't you go pulling the wool over my eyes, I know when I'm dreaming and when I'm not – this is *real*. The blood's real, the pain's real, the deaths are real. My ops were real, they were the best I could do, but what is also real is my – my – my basic *inadequacy*."

She suddenly snatched the handkerchief out of her pocket again and blew her nose on it. She wiped her nose back and forth several times and then gave a great, convulsive sniff.

"What we need here is a properly equipped medical team!"

Omri gaped at her.

"If we don't get one – and quickly – more of these poor men are going to die."

After a moment, during which she glared at him expectantly through her spectacles, Omri said slowly, "I'll tell you the truth about you being here, and – all the rest of it. But you probably won't believe me."

"After what I've been through in the past forty-eight hours, I'll believe anything!" she said fervently.

He explained things as well as he could. She listened intently and asked a couple of questions.

"You say any article or figure made of plastic is affected?"

"Yes."

"And objects which might be concealed on the person – my hypodermic syringe, for example, and other things I brought in my pocket from St Thomas's – "

"Yes, they're made real, provided the person had them on him before he was – *brought*."

"Well! Why can't you get hold of some plastic doctors and put them in your allegedly magic cupboard? Only you must make sure they have some equipment – surgical instruments and so forth."

"But all the shops are shut! How can I – ?"

Suddenly Omri remembered. Two nights ago, he had gone to see Patrick at his aunt's house and they had tried to borrow Tamsin's new box of plastic figures, only she'd caught them at it and grabbed it back. Omri had only just managed to hold onto the figure that turned out to be Matron. But there had been others in the set – including a surgeon at an operating table.

He stretched out his foot and nudged Patrick awake.

"Patrick! Listen. There's another Indian dead. And Matron says, if we don't find a proper doctor, more will die."

Patrick scrambled to his feet, rubbing his hair.

"How can we get any new ones on Sunday?"

"What about the ones Tamsin has?"

"What are you saying? That I should go back to Aunty's and nick them when Tamsin isn't looking?"

"It's only borrowing."

"Not when the owner doesn't know or agree! Not when the owner's my little creep of a cousin! She'd have my guts for garters!"

Omri said, with a note of desperation, "Well, what *are* we to do, then? This is a real emergency!" Suddenly he had an idea. "Why don't you try buying them off her?"

"It might work. Have you got any dosh?"

"Not a penny, we spent it all on the Indian braves. Maybe Dad'll lend me a couple of quid."

His Dad did better than that. He gave him a fiver, and not just till pay-day. "You've earned it. Here's one for Patrick, too."

So there was no problem about money.

At breakfast, hastily eaten, the boys sneaked some crispy bits of bacon and quite a few Crunchy Nutflakes into their pockets, and Omri astonished his mother by asking for a mug of tea instead of milk. Matron couldn't cope without her tea.

"I thought you hated tea!"

"I'm coming round to it."

"You'll be hitting the Scotch next," commented his father from behind his Sunday paper.

Patrick nudged Omri. When whisky was mentioned, there was just one person who came to mind. Half-way back up the stairs, Patrick whispered: "Let's bring Boone back to life right now!"

At that moment, the doorbell rang.

Omri went back down and opened the door. Then he gasped. Outside stood Tamsin. Of all people!

How could it be, she'd broken her leg!

Omri looked again. It wasn't Tamsin, it was Emma.

Emma was Tamsin's twin sister. She was the spitting image of Tamsin, and yet she was wholly different. As far as Omri could remember, she was quite a decent sort of girl.

"Hallo, Omri," she said. "Can I see Patrick?"

Patrick dragged himself reluctantly down into the hall. Omri stood aside, waiting. He could feel himself tensing all over for fear there was a car outside waiting to cart Patrick away.

"Hi, Em. How's it going?" said Patrick carelessly.

"Okay. Tam's leg's in a cast and she's better. They sent me here because Omri's phone's busted and your mum couldn't ring you and you're to come back with me."

"Right *now*?"

"Yes."

"I – I can't come now!"

"Why not?"

Patrick dithered helplessly, trying to think of some excuse.

"How are we supposed to get back?"

"On the train of course," said Emma. "Come on."

Omri said, "Did *you* come here on the train?"

"Yes, why?"

"And you walked up the road to here, from the station?"

"Yes."

Omri thought of the skinheads. It was Sunday – even the few who went to school or had jobs, were free and on the prowl on Sundays. He himself never walked down Hovel Road on Sundays if he could possibly help it.

"Did you meet anyone . . . ?"

She shrugged. "A few boys. Hanging around. Real creeps, *gross*. I took no notice of them."

Omri shivered. But then he remembered. There was a pretty good chance he didn't have to be scared of that gang any more. He put his hand in his jeans pocket, and fingered the little penlight the smallest of the burglars had dropped the night before.

As he touched it, he felt something else. It was the key. A sudden flash of inspiration came to him, stiffening his whole body like a bolt of electricity.

"Emma," he said in a queer sort of voice, "would you mind if I had a private chat to Patrick before he – er – goes?"

She looked from one of them to the other. "What's the secret?"

They both flushed.

"Wait here, okay?" Omri gabbled, and pulling Patrick into the living-room he closed the door.

"You've *got* to get out of going home," Omri said. "I can't cope without you."

"What can I do? Break *my* leg?"

"Well . . . if you had the bottle for it, you could throw yourself down the stairs . . . probably do yourself *some* serious enough injury . . ."

"Thanks!"

" . . . But I wasn't thinking of that. Tell Emma you've left something upstairs. We'll go up to my room and you can get in the chest with Boone's figure and I can send you back to his time."

V

Patrick Goes Back

Patrick's face was blank for a moment, and Omri thought: *He's scared, and who can blame him*! But then he saw it wasn't that at all. Patrick simply hadn't been able to grasp the idea at first.

When he did grasp it, not just his face but his whole body seemed to light up with excitement.

"Wow," he said simply.

"You mean you'll do it?"

"Are you kidding? Go back to real cowboy-time, cowboy-country? See Boone full-size? Lead me to it! Let's go!"

He bounded out of the living-room and was half-way up the stairs before Omri had gathered his wits to follow. As he came into the hall he noticed Emma standing much closer to the living-room door than she had been before. Patrick had nearly bowled her over as he emerged.

A suspicion struck Omri.

"Were you listening?"

"Yes," she said at once. "But I didn't understand what you were talking about."

"Ah," said Omri with relief. It crossed his mind that she was a very straightforward girl, at least – Tamsin wouldn't have admitted eavesdropping like that. Not many people would.

He gave Emma a closer look. She was a year younger than him – which was why he had hardly noticed her at school, somehow you only noticed your contemporaries or people ahead of you. But she'd been more or less around for most of his life. Odd that he'd never really looked at her before. Now he saw that she was quite nice looking in a fair, snubby-faced way. She had freckles and large eyes, and was dressed in sensible jeans and a blue anorak. She had her hands deep in her pockets and was gazing at him expectantly.

"What *were* you on about in there?"

"Private," said Omri. He glanced up the stairs. Patrick could already be heard thudding up the last flight, to Omri's attic bedroom.

"Where's Patrick gone?"

"Er – up to get his pyjamas and stuff."

"But he didn't take any last night, he just dashed out."

"Oh. Well – anyway he's – gone up," said Omri feebly, making a move to follow him.

Emma followed at his heels. He paused on the second stair.

"Can you wait down here?"

"Why?"

"We'll be – right down."

"Can't I see your room? You saw mine," she said. "Last night, when you came to our house. Mum moved Tam and me out so Patrick could have it."

"Well . . ."

From above came Patrick's impatient voice. "Come ON, Omri! Don't hang about!"

"You wait in the living-room," Omri said decisively. He turned away from her and ran upstairs.

In his room he found Patrick already climbing into the seaman's chest.

"Go on, I'm ready! Send me!"

But Omri, having come up with this amazing idea, was already having second thoughts.

"Listen, how'll I explain where you've gone?"

"Don't. Get rid of Emma somehow, make her go home, and you can tell your parents I went with her."

"But what when Emma gets back to her place without you?"

"It'll be too late then! I'll just have vanished!" He grinned all over his face with glee.

"No you won't. You'll be in the chest – your body will. What if they start looking for you?"

"Listen, this was your idea, and a fantastic one! Stop making problems. Pile all your junk on top of the chest like before, they'll never think to look there."

"But your mum will be dead worried! She's sure to ring up. Then Emma will say one thing and I'll say another – "

Patrick had been crouching in the chest, looking up at him. Now, suddenly, he stood up. His face had changed. He looked quite fierce.

"I want to go back with Boone," he said. "I've made up my mind. And I don't want you bringing me

37

back after ten minutes either. You had your adventure in the Indian village. I know you had a rough time, but you *saw* it, you saw the battle, you *experienced* it. Now it's my turn, and I don't want to hear any of your feeble objections. Just put the key in the lock and turn it, will you? I'm the one who's taking the risk. All you're asked to do is stall everybody for a few days."

Omri's mouth dropped open.

"A few *days*?"

"It's hardly worth going for less than that!" Patrick retorted.

That he would stay away for longer than a few hours had not been any part of Omri's – as he now saw – idiotic idea.

"But it could be dangerous! What if – "

Patrick made to get out of the chest. "Are you going to do it, or am I going to have to bash you?" he growled.

Omri was not afraid of him. They were evenly matched. He stood his ground.

"You don't have to use skinhead tactics," he said.

Patrick looked sheepish.

"Sorry. You're always trying to hold me back from doing what I want. Listen. We'd better decide beforehand when you're going to bring me back. Time works the same at both ends. So let's say – a week from today."

"You're completely round the twist," said Omri. "A week! Anyone'd think you were going on holiday! All right, lie down. I'll send you. But don't get too comfortable in Texas because you'll be back before you know it, if I get into any trouble about you, which I'm bound to."

Patrick stared at him for a moment, then slowly

took the small figure of Boone out of his pocket. Omri reached out and touched it. He wanted to touch Patrick – shake hands with him or something – but he didn't know how to do it, quite. So he touched Boone instead and said, "Say hallo to him for me and tell him – tell him to take good care of you."

Patrick curled up in the bottom of the chest. Omri, feeling quite calm now that the decision was made, closed the lid. He took the key out of his pocket and stuck it in the lock on the chest. For the moment it hung there, its red satin ribbon hanging from its fancy top. Then Omri turned it firmly.

At that moment he heard a small, shrill voice nearby.

"What Pat-Rick do? Why move longhouse? Very bad move sick men, make fear, make wound worse!"

Omri spun round. In order to open the chest, Patrick had lifted the seed-tray with its precious, miniature complement of Indians, healthy, injured and dead, on to Omri's desk underneath his raised bunk-bed. Omri had, for the moment, quite forgotten them. Now he saw Little Bull standing at the edge of the tray, his arms folded and his face, lit by Omri's desk lamp, a mask of reproach.

"What Pat-Rick do in box?"

Omri crouched till his face was level with Little Bull's.

"Little Bull, Patrick's gone. We agreed he should go back to Boone's time. He's going to stay there for a while. So if there's anything you need, you'll have to ask me."

"I ask, you not fear," said Little Bull promptly.

Omri suppressed a sigh. There wouldn't be much of the 'ask' about it, if he knew Little Bull.

"Start with food. Wife must feed son. Need good food, keep up strength."

"Oh – of course! Sorry, I almost forgot."

Omri reached into his pocket and brought out his collection of cornflakes, bits of bacon and toast, which he'd thoughtfully wrapped in a paper napkin. Of course he'd left the mug of tea downstairs. He'd have to go and get it. Meanwhile there was enough food to be getting on with for all of them.

Little Bull looked at the spread, sampled a chunk of crispy bacon fat and grunted with grudging approval. But then he straightened up, his face once more a mask of seriousness.

"Not leave dead brave long time," Little Bull said. "Send back. Own people find, know what do, obey custom for dead."

"Yes," said Omri. "That's what we thought. When?"

"Ry-taway," said Little Bull, who was beginning to pick up some English expressions.

"We'll put them in the cupboard," said Omri. He felt the cupboard was the right time-vehicle for the little people, the chest for him and Patrick.

The logistics of the thing were solved by Omri putting his left hand palm upward on the soil in the seed-tray while Little Bull and three healthy Indians carefully and reverently lifted the corpses, still covered with bloodstained cloths, on to it. Omri shuddered as he felt their body-weight, the coldness of death against his skin. Then the "burial party" of four climbed onto Omri's hand and he slowly moved to the cupboard which stood on the low table in the middle of his room.

He opened the door. Two Indians climbed off his hand and over the bottom edge of the cupboard, and the other two lifted the bodies one by one and handed them to the Indians who then laid them on the floor of the metal cupboard.

Omri reached over and took the key from the lock of the chest, and inserted it into the keyhole of the cupboard. The "burial-party" climbed out and stood in a line, looking at their dead comrades in silence.

"Little Bull," said Omri, "what about if you all go back now? There's nothing to hang around here for, and there's a lot to do, rebuilding your village. I'm sure Twin Stars would like to get the baby back and get on with her life."

Little Bull turned to him, scowling with thought.

"Good," he said. "Go back soon ry-taway. First you send dead, then take out plass-tick."

Omri closed the door, turned the key and after a moment turned it back, opened the door, and removed the nine plastic figures. He knew they were no use any more – the people belonging to them were gone. He certainly wouldn't ever want to play with them. After a second's thought, he took a piece of white writing paper and, piling them onto it, folded the edges carefully round them.

"I'll bury them," he said to Little Bull. "That's our custom with dead people."

Little Bull nodded grimly. "Good. First we do dance, ask Great Spirit bring safe to ancestors."

Matron had come out of the longhouse, serving as a sort of field-hospital for the injured Indians; and watched the removal of the dead. Now she called Omri over.

"I'm very much relieved that you've dealt with that matter," she said in her brisk way. "Now. Having disposed of the dead, do you think you could give your urgent attention to the problem of those who are still alive?"

Omri felt a little jolt in his chest. Now Patrick had

41

abandoned him, he must solve by himself the pressing problem of getting the medical team.

"Matron, look," he said, thinking aloud more than anything, "it's Sunday. Can't go to the shops. We ... that is, I thought I'd try to get some help from a friend who has plastic figures. Not exactly a friend. She's Patrick's cousin – "

"Who, me?"

The jolt Omri had felt before was nothing to the explosive leap his heart gave at the sound of that voice.

He spun round from his ill-balanced crouch, falling over backwards, and sat gaping at the figure of Emma in the open doorway.

VI

A New Insider

"Emma! What – what – what are you doing there?"

But it was only too obvious what she was doing. She was looking. And listening. The only question left was, how much had she seen and heard?

In a forlorn and desperate hope, Omri swivelled his eyes sideways, trying to see what was visible from her angle. Before, when he'd been crouching in front of the desk, he had blocked her view of the seed-tray. Now he was on the floor, everything was in plain sight. Matron's little figure, standing, arms akimbo, on the edge of the seed-tray. Little Bull's pony, grazing in the miniature paddock Patrick had made. Several tiny Indians, busy about the area, rebuilding last night's fire from the unburned ends of matchsticks and twigs. And the longhouse, rising from the ground in all its minute, hand-made magnificence.

But Emma was not looking as far as that. On the low table which stood between her and Omri was the cupboard, and the five Indians. They were chanting and doing a slow dance round the white paper packet. It was upon them, Omri saw, that Emma's eyes were riveted.

There was nothing to be done. Nought. Zilch. Zipa-dee-doo-dah. *Zero*. And when that's the case, thought Omri in a sudden mood of fatalism, you might as well relax.

"Well," he said, his voice coming out quite steady, "what do you think?"

She stared at them for a long time, her eyes fixed and unblinking, her freckles standing out on a suddenly very pale face.

"They're alive," she said at last, in a doubtful tone, as if he might roar with laughter at her.

"You don't say," said Omri, scrambling to his feet. "And not only those. What about these, here?" And he indicated the seed-tray behind him.

Emma moved cautiously forward, as if afraid the very floor might waver and give way beneath her feet. He noticed now that she had a mug of tea in her hand, the one he'd saved from breakfast – it must have been the excuse she'd given herself for following him up. It tilted in her nerveless fingers and he removed it to safety.

As he poured a few drops into a toothpaste-cap for Matron, Omri watched Emma as she gazed and gazed. He knew that what his father called a "quantum leap" had been taken in the situation, the sort of change which means nothing will be quite the same again, and that was scary. But there was no denying a sort of enjoyment in

44

watching someone else seeing, trying to realise, coming to grips with it.

Emma managed this last feat surprisingly quickly.

"I've always thought it could happen," she said abruptly. "It often nearly has, when I've been playing with my toy animals. Can they talk? – Oh, of course they can, that's who you were talking to."

Matron's voice, little but scratchy as chalk on a blackboard, chirped up. "And pray who might this young person be? I don't believe we've been introduced."

Emma turned a suddenly flushed and smiling face on Omri. "Wow! Omri, what fun! How fantastic! I mean, how *brill* can anything get!"

"Yeah," said Omri somewhat sourly. "Brill. Except that in that little hut there are a number of men who are wounded and who could die if we don't do something. And they're real, and I'm responsible for them, and Patrick's P.O.'d – "

"P.O.'d, what's that?"

"Er – gone. And – "

"Gone? Where?"

Omri took a deep breath. "There's no time to explain everything now. Listen. You know that set of plastic figures Tamsin got for her birthday?"

Emma was one jump ahead of him. Her face lit up another few watts. "Yes! Yes! I got one too! You mean we can make them all come alive – be real, like these?"

Omri grabbed her arm. "Wait, did you say you got the same set of models as Tamsin?"

She shook off his hand. "Don't pinch! No, mine was different, mine was a sort of shop with people with trolleys and check-outs and – "

45

Omri's heart sank. "Not doctors?"

She shook her head. "No. I wanted the doctors and that, but Tam wouldn't swap."

Omri said, "Would she *sell* hers?"

"Got the odd hundred quid, have you?" said Emma cynically.

"I've got the odd *five* quid."

Emma frowned, considering. "She might not be able to resist. She's saving for a ski-ing holiday."

"Patrick's got another fiver," said Omri. "I could – " He turned automatically towards the chest. Then stopped.

"Er . . . Listen, Em. I'm prepared to let you in on most of this – well, you are in on it. But there's a couple of wrinkles I think you might not . . . exactly feel comfortable about, not just at first. So, would you mind going downstairs for a few minutes? Then I'm coming back to your place with you and we'll negotiate for the models with Tam."

She hesitated. "And then come back here, and – do whatever it is you do to make them come alive?"

Omri looked at her. Now she knew about the little people. But she didn't yet know about the magic, how to make it happen. She didn't really know much, when you came down to it. There wasn't a lot she could give away. Not that anyone would believe. And that was the nitty-gritty, not her knowing, but her maybe telling. Could he trust her? Could one trust *anyone* with a secret as exciting as this?

"We'll have to have a serious talk," he said. "On the train. Just now I want you to go out. Please, Em."

They looked at each other. He actually saw her decide to give way, whether to please him or for reasons of her own, he wasn't sure. It didn't matter anyhow. Just so she went.

The second she was outside he shot the bolt, to make sure. Then he rushed to the cupboard, took the key out, stuck it back in the chest and turned it.

Patrick lay curled up as Omri had seen him once before, and he remembered his thought that other time: *As far away as you can get without being dead.* It was tempting to stand there, losing himself in speculation about where the real Patrick was.

But there was no time for such thoughts. Reaching into the chest, Omri fumbled in Patrick's pocket for the five-pound note. And touched something that made him snatch his hand away with a yelp as if he'd burnt it.

There was something alive in Patrick's pocket!

Omri stood there with his heart in his gullet. It wasn't a person, it was a tiny animal of some kind. With his fingertips Omri had felt that much. Patrick must have had something plastic in his pocket when he was locked in the chest, and it had come to life!

Cautiously Omri stuck his fingers into the pocket again. Yes, there it was, something small, smooth-coated and bony.

He took hold of it as gently as he could, feeling it struggle and twist. He drew it out.

It was a very distressed black horse, complete with an old Western-style saddle and bridle.

Boone's horse! His new one, that Patrick had taken from the English soldier. Omri set him down very gently in the paddock on the seed-tray, where Little Bull's pony was tethered with a double-ply nylon thread. It threw up its head as the intruder descended from the heavens, and whinneyed anxiously, but as soon as the black pony's feet were on the ground and it had given itself a good shake, both their heads dropped to graze the turf of real grass Patrick had dug up and laid there.

Omri smiled in relief ... Evidently Boone's pony was all right, though he wished he could take off its bridle and saddle. Boone must have put his old tack on it before Patrick had sent him back –

Suddenly Omri went rigid, his brain fizzing with the shock of the realisation which had come to him.

But how could they have been so stupid!

In all the haste and hassle of getting Patrick 'sent back', they'd forgotten! Forgotten the way it worked! Patrick had had the *plastic figure* of Boone in his hand, not the real, live Boone! That meant –

That meant that Boone, like the horse, would have become real inside the chest!

"Boone!" he called frantically into the depths of the chest. "Boone! Where are you? – Are you okay?"

Silence.

Omri grabbed Patrick's right arm. His hand was tucked under his body. Omri dragged it out from under Patrick's dead weight. The fingers were closed into a tight fist. Sticking out from the top of it was a tuft of ginger hair.

Grimly, desperately, Omri prised Patrick's fingers open.

In his hand lay Boone, the real Boone. Limp. Motionless.

Dead?

Crushed?

"Matron!"

Before she knew it, that stalwart lady had been snatched off the seed-tray and set down, somewhat short of breath and dignity, on the low table.

"Not another patient! I've got more than I can – "
Then she saw. Her voice changed.

"Oh dear me," she said softly. "Oh, dearie, dearie me."

With a doomful look, she fell to her knees beside the supine figure of Boone, and applied her ear to his heart. To his horror, Omri saw her give her head half a shake.

VII

Patrick in Boone-land

Patrick's journey through time and space was swift and painless. There was a strange sort of *whooosh* during which he seemed to feel, for a split second, buffeted, as when two heavy lorries pass close by each other travelling at speed in opposite directions. Then there was heat, silence and stillness.

He opened his eyes to the glare of a harsh sun, and screwed them shut.

He felt around with his hands. There seemed to be nothing directly in front of him. But he felt he was upright, and leaning against something blanket-like, but stiffer, rather like a wall covered with flannel.

Then he found that there was something like a wide, thick cord across his middle, holding him against the soft wall. He opened his eyes cautiously. At first he couldn't see anything but glaring sunlight. But in a few moments he got accustomed to that and found himself staring out across an endless expanse of sand.

"Well," he said aloud, "it's Texas I suppose, so this must be a bit of desert, or prairie, or something."

But where was he? Where – in all this sand – *was* he?

He looked downward. His hands were resting on a thick rope-like thing as thick as his own leg, stretched quite tightly across his waist. Under his feet was something which curved away on either side of him, and curled up several yards ahead of him. It was like standing on the brink of a huge, smooth, pale-brown – and empty – river-bed. Behind him it rose up like the bank of the river, but the bank felt soft to his hand, and suddenly he realised what it was.

"It's – it's a gigantic *hat*!" he said aloud. "I'm tied to the crown of it, and this thing must be the hat-band, only it's a huge leather cord!"

He wriggled down until he was free of the cord, into which he seemed to have been stuck quite casually like a feather, or like the 'flies' that fishermen sometimes stick in their hatbands. Suddenly Patrick remembered that Boone had had some kind of a tiny favour – so small one could hardly see it, except that it was blue, like his own jeans and sweatshirt – in the cord around his much-loved cowboy hat.

Patrick crawled rapidly across the width of the brim towards its curled-up edge.

As he did so he noticed for the first time the utter silence around him, and the fact that the hat was perfectly still.

"I must be on Boone's head," he thought. "Why isn't the hat jiggling about as he rides?"

He reached the edge of the brim, pulled himself up to it and peered over, preparing himself to see an immense drop below.

The sand lay no more than four or five times Patrick's own height beneath him.

He could easily make out the individual grains, which looked to him like the shingle on an English beach, except that some of them were like lumps of yellow glass.

Suddenly he stiffened and gasped. A huge creature, about the size of a Galapagos tortoise, moseyed by on six angled legs. Patrick shrank back behind the rim of the hat, then, realising that it was merely some kind of beetle and that it couldn't reach him, raised himself cautiously and followed its progress off across the endless expanse of sand.

He looked around, as far as he could for the enormous bulk of the hat, which loomed against the sky like a soft-cornered building. There was no sign of anything else alive.

"The first thing is to get down from here," he thought. "Even if it's dangerous. There's no point in staying here."

He considered the problem of getting down to the ground. If the sand below had been his size of sand, he might have risked jumping into it (or then again, he thought, peering down, he might not!) But it would be suicide to jump down onto those big hard stones. He'd have to lower himself somehow.

Patrick, unlike Omri, was athletic. He really shone in PE, and loved climbing and jumping and swinging. What he needed now was some kind of rope, and of course the first thing he thought of was the hat-band.

He followed it round the crown of the hat again

until he found the knot. Luckily, it was old; the leather itself was soft, and the knot loosely tied. By forcing one of the ends back upon itself through the knot, twice, he managed to untie it. Then, with great effort, he managed to drag one end around the crown until he had about half of it at his disposal, and carefully lowered the free end down over the brim.

The immediate danger was that his weight, though relatively slight, would pull the whole thong to the ground when he tried to slide down it, but he had to risk that. Taking a deep breath, he threw his right leg over the stiff brim, embraced the thong with arms and legs as if he were sliding down a tree-trunk, and away he went.

He was down almost before he had time to think, and as his feet touched the stones he felt the rest of the thong fall away from the hat. He just managed to leap aside as it fell, like an immense and heavy snake, onto the ground, missing him by a hair's-breadth.

He took another deep breath and looked around.

The first thing he saw was a huge, impenetrable mass of what looked like fine copper fuse-wires.

He touched one. It was very flexible – it certainly wasn't a wire, it was more like –

Patrick gasped. He suddenly knew what it was. And, knowing that, he knew in a flash that something had gone very wrong.

The mass of wires was Boone's ginger hair, sticking out from underneath his hat.

Patrick started to run. It was not easy, running on the glassy shingle, but trying not to stumble too often he made his way as fast as he could right round to the other side of the huge thing like a promontory – which was actually Boone's head – jutting out of the desert landscape.

When he got there, he stopped, stared, stepped back, stared again. At last he realised that to get the face in perspective he would have to move back still further. He turned and ran away from it for about a hundred paces, then turned again.

Yes. Now he could see it was Boone.

He was lying on his side, the bulk of him rising from the flat desert floor like a range of hills. Though his face was turned to the side, the hat was lying horizontally across one ear as if someone had dropped it there, not as if Boone had been wearing it when he toppled to the ground. On his bristly face was an expression which made Patrick very uneasy.

In the distance, behind Boone, loomed a large desert cactus, the top of which – like Jack's beanstalk – was too high for Patrick to see. It looked as if it were growing out of Boone's shoulder. Patrick narrowed his eyes. He focused on one wicked-looking cactus needle which stuck out against the hard blue of the sky, just above Boone's uppermost arm.

If he were breathing, even shallowly, the shoulder level would rise and the spike would disappear.

It didn't.

Patrick caught his own breath and held it until he nearly burst. He had suddenly realised his fatal mistake.

He had taken a plastic Boone back with him. The living Boone had gone back to England, to Omri's and Patrick's present, in the same instant that Patrick had come here. They must have crossed. That was the meaning of the whooshing sensation of something passing him as he travelled through time and space.

Patrick sat down abruptly, and as abruptly jumped

up again. The glassy stones were very hot. Everything was very hot. He felt dizzy. He tottered back a few yards until he was in Boone's shadow, and sank down again to think.

He must have done something to Boone, who'd been clutched tightly in his hand when he climbed into the chest.

Maybe he'd killed him!

No maybe about it. Boone, in the instant of transfer, had fallen down here in the desert. Breathless. Lifeless.

A terrible guilt, backed up by an overwhelming sorrow, threatened Patrick. But, being a very practical boy, he shoved them both roughly to the back of his mind, and considered instead his own situation.

He was on his own. No Boone to take care of him.

Minute. Helpless. Miles from anywhere. And at the mercy of the sun and the empty desert.

It seemed a fairly safe bet that soon enough, he would follow Boone once again: this time, into the oblivion of death.

VIII

A Heart Stops Beating

The suspense was awful – the worst of Omri's life.

He watched Matron bending over the still figure in the plaid shirt and chaps. Boone – so real, so very much of a person, and yet so vulnerable that Patrick's hand closing on him in the instant of being swung back through time and space could have squeezed the life out of him.

Omri thought what Patrick would feel, when he came back, if he learnt that he had killed Boone. *Killed* him. Crushed him to death. Suddenly Omri knew that it was for Patrick's sake, more than Boone's in a way, that Matron had to breathe life back into that tiny body, as she was now trying to do.

"Matron – "

"Sh!"

She had stopped giving Boone the kiss of life and begun giving him artificial respiration, hands on his ribs, throwing her weight forward and back, panting from the effort she was making.

"Is he – alive?" whispered Omri.

"Yes," she said shortly, between pushes. "Just about."

"What's wrong? Is he – crushed?"

"Crushed? – Of course not! He's been – half suffocated – that's all!" She put her ear to his chest again.

"Where's his hat?" said Omri suddenly.

Matron straightened herself with an exclamation.

"His *hat*?" she said sharply. "What in the world does that matter when his heart's stopped?"

"His heart's stopped!" Omri's own heart nearly did the same. "Then he is dead!"

"Not if we can – Wait! You could do it! He needs a good thump on the chest to get it going again! I just haven't the strength. Come here, do exactly as I show you! Now watch!"

Peering at her, he saw her do something with her tiny fingers.

"What – "

She gave an exclamation of exasperation. "Are you blind? It's a flicking movement – flick your finger out from behind your thumb – "

"Oh – like this?"

"Right! Now do it downward – against his chest! No, not so gently, do it hard, thump him, man, thump him!" she cried agitatedly.

Omri flicked his middle finger hard so that his nail struck against Boone's chest, rocking his body.

"Again!"

Omri repeated the movement. Matron then pushed

his finger out of the way and once more laid her ear against Boone's plaid shirtfront.

"AH!"

"Is it – ?"

"I do believe – I think – I'm almost certain – YES!" She raised a beaming, sweat-glossed face. "You've done the trick! Well done, oh, well done indeed, you've saved him! Now. Bring me something warm to wrap him in while I go and fix him an injection of heart-stimulant. Look – look, he's beginning to breathe normally! What a relief, I was really afraid he was a goner!"

Omri, feeling weak with relief, rushed to hack out another square from his shattered sweater, already jagged-hemmed due to all the miniature blankets he'd cut out of it, while Matron hurried up the ramp onto the seed-tray and into the longhouse. She emerged at once with a hypodermic syringe and an ampoule so small Omri just had to guess it was there. She knelt beside Boone, now warmly covered, and injected straight into his chest.

"Now listen, young man. We've saved this one between us, but the emergency cases in there are still in desperate need of expert attention. You will really have to secure qualified medical aid."

"Om-RI!"

He turned. Little Bull was standing nearby, arms folded.

"What happen Boone?"

"He's had an accident."

"Axe? Dent? Enemy dent head with tomahawk?"

"No, no. Something else ... It's okay, Matron'll take care of him."

"Good." Little Bull bent down, and touched Boone's red hair. Omri felt quite choked up at this tender gesture, until the Indian added, "Sometime I sorry Boone my blood brother."

"Little Bull! Surely you're not still hankering after his scalp?"

The Indian fingered the hair regretfully and grunted. "Fine colour, like sugar-tree leaf . . . very bad if other brave get . . . " He gave Boone's head a sharp, possessive pat, and straightened up. "Dance finish. You take dead braves, plass-tic. Put in ground."

"Little Bull, I can't now. I must go with Emma. Did – did you see her? She – she saw you. I have to make sure she – helps, and doesn't tell."

Little Bull looked troubled.

"Woman tongue stay still like falling water, like grass in wind . . . You go. Keep hand ready stop mouth of Em-A. First put Little Bull back in longhouse with wife, son."

"You don't want to be sent back to the village yet?"

Little Bull, usually so phlegmatic, suddenly twisted his face, threw up his arms and turned his body first one way, then another.

"Very bad, need be two place same time! Want be here, not leave hurt braves! Need be there, with tribe! Very bad, one man heart cut in two!"

This was more than Omri could cope with. He lifted the five Indians, including Little Bull, off the table and deposited them hastily on the seed-tray. Twin Stars came running out of the longhouse with her baby in her arms and Little Bull embraced her.

"We'll decide what you should do when I get back," said Omri. He turned to Matron. "Can I leave you?"

"In a good cause – yes."

"Give me an hour."

✳

59

As he came running downstairs, he sensed at once that Emma had gone.

He felt bereft, though he didn't entirely blame her. Waiting down here by herself no doubt she had suddenly been overcome with the feeling that it was all too much for her, that she wanted to run off home to her everyday life. But he couldn't let her go. Of course he couldn't. He grabbed his anorak and dashed out of the house.

As soon as he turned out of his gate into Hovel Road, Omri smelt trouble.

He saw them half-way down, outside the amusement arcade, a whole crowd of them. He couldn't see Emma, but something in the way the skinheads were crowding round – something in their stance, in the sounds that drifted to him along the street – told him that she was there, in the midst of them, trapped, that they were taunting her – the same bullying treatment he had had from them so often himself. Without his conscious command, his feet drove into a hard run.

He didn't stop to think or give himself time to get scared. He just rammed into them head-on.

A piercing pain blew up like fireworks in his head. He'd completely forgotten his burn! He clutched the place and felt the bandage, and at the same time the circle bent and broke, letting him through, and he saw the faces, first astounded, then twisting into sniggering laughter.

"Cor! If it ain't the old Ayatollah!"

Emma was standing erect and defiant, her lip curled in contempt as she faced the tallest of the gang. Omri recognised him instantly.

"You are just an ugly bullying *creep*!" she threw at him.

"Slag," he sneered. "Nerd – " Then he noticed Omri.

60

His whole face altered. Unwholesomely pale already, it turned the dead colour of putty. His jaw went slack, as if Omri's own fear had erupted and were mirrored in this other face.

"You – " he gasped.

"Yeah, me," said Omri, panting, dry-mouthed. There were so many of them! "You lot leave her alone. Or else."

A concerted jeer rose from the circle.

"Look out, lads! Fall flat on your faces and worship 'im or 'e's liable to start an 'oly war!"

But their leader – the big youth who'd been going on at Emma – glanced furiously round at his mates and the jeering laughter died.

He reached up grimy fingers and unconsciously caressed his face, across which, in a diagonal line, were a dozen tiny raw dots.

" 'Ow you done that?" he muttered, his eyes narrowed as he looked at Omri. "I'd give a lot to know 'ow you done what you done to me."

Omri contented himself with a tight little smile. He took Emma by the arm.

"Come on, Em, let's go."

The tall boy gave a kind of twitch of his shaven head. The circle wavered, then gave way and let them through, though not without murmurings of puzzlement and rebellion.

Just as they came clear, Omri had a thought. He paused and reached into his jeans pocket.

He turned casually back. Could they see how his heart was pounding?

"Oh, by the way – " He held out his hand. "I think one of you dropped this."

He held up the penlight that he'd picked up after the burglars' hasty departure.

The tall skinhead reached for it automatically, laid hold of it, then suddenly let it go as if it were red hot. It fell to the pavement where it rolled into the gutter. Several of the others made a dive for it.

"Leave it!" the leader barked. "Don't touch it! It might blow up in your face!"

Omri stared at him for a moment. That great thieving, bullying lout was really afraid of him. It wasn't entirely a good feeling, but it was better than the other way round, which was the way it had always been before.

Now all the faces looking at him were pallid and nervous. Take away their gang-courage, and they really were a pathetic-looking crew. Omri felt the beginnings of a sneer twisting his own mouth, but it felt ugly even from inside so he was glad when Emma tugged his arm.

They walked quickly down to the station, leaving a defeated silence behind them.

IX

Tamsin Drives a Bargain

By the time Omri and Emma arrived at Emma's house, half of Omri's allotted hour had passed and he was getting panicky.

Emma didn't make things easier.

"What are we going to say about Patrick not coming back?"

Omri liked the way she said "we", making him feel less alone with his problems, but he didn't want to confront this one. How indeed was he to explain Patrick's absence? Perhaps he could play both ends, so to speak, against the middle. If each household – his and Emma's – thought Patrick was in the other one, he might not be missed for some time. But for a really lousy liar like Omri it was bound to be tricky.

Patrick's mother was practically on the doorstep to meet them.

"Well, where is he?" she asked without even saying hallo.

Emma turned to look at Omri expectantly.

"Er – I came to explain," he said. "You see – " He swallowed hard. Her eyes were piercing him. He had to drop his. "We . . . we went into Richmond Park this morning to look for chestnuts. On our bikes."

"Patrick's bike is at home in the country."

"I mean – he used Gillon's. And . . . we were playing – and he got a bit lost, and I got fed up waiting and came home without him. I expect he'll be back soon," he added hastily as Patrick's mother rolled her eyes, gritted her teeth and uttered a kind of snort.

"How like him to do the disappearing act just when I want him! Doesn't he realise we're going home today! What *am* I supposed to do? I *have* to leave!"

"Couldn't Patrick stay with us for a few days?"

"Don't be so silly. What about school? It's *school* tomorrow!" She was obviously infuriated, and Omri couldn't exactly blame her.

However, there was nothing to be done for the moment. Leaving her seething in the doorway, Emma pulled Omri past and into the small living-room.

"Leave Tam to me," she whispered. "She absolutely hates you for some reason."

Omri felt rather hurt, even though it was entirely mutual.

Tamsin was slumped in front of a small television set, watching some middle-of-the-day rubbish. Her leg, encased from foot to knee in a white plaster cast, was resting on a pouffe. She didn't even look up as they came in. Emma coughed.

"Hey, Tam, want to add to your ski-ing fund?"

"Fat chance of ski-ing when I'm like this," she said sourly.

"You could go at Easter. Best snow's always in April."

Tamsin looked up sharply at that. Seeing Omri, her eyes narrowed.

"You look a right nana in that bandage," she remarked. "Did someone give you a clout?"

"Not since you," Omri retorted.

Tamsin had the grace to blush. She turned back to her sister.

"What about my ski-ing fund?"

"Well, you know your birthday models – "

"I already said no," said Tamsin. "I won't swap."

Emma shrugged with wondrous carelessness. "I just fancy one or two of them, that's all. I'd buy them off you."

Tamsin glanced at Omri again. "Is this anything to do with *him*?"

"Who? – Oh! No, of course not. You know I wanted them yesterday."

Tamsin looked beady. "If you wait till tomorrow, you can buy the same set at the model shop."

"I need them now," Emma had to say, though she tried to sound careless.

Tamsin uncurled herself slowly and frowningly. Without a word she heaved her cast onto the floor and stumped out of the room. Omri almost felt sorry for her, but this charitable impulse was soon to pass. Emma nudged him. They waited.

After a few minutes Tamsin returned, carrying the box Omri recognised from last night.

She opened it and displayed the contents. The figures, held to a cardboard backing with elastic string, were dangled tantalizingly before their eyes. Omri's flew to the surgeon in green operating-theatre gear, complete with table and tiny instruments, mere pinhead blobs. There were two other doctors, one in white coat with stethoscope, the other also in green who was evidently part of the surgical team. It was as much as Omri could do to restrain his hand from darting towards them.

Instead he thrust both hands into his pockets and turned away to gaze blindly at the TV set while negotiations between the twins proceeded.

They seemed to take forever. Somehow Tamsin could sense that Emma's casualness masked some urgent desire for the medical models. In the end, though, when the price had reached astronomic heights, several times what they'd have cost in the shops, and Omri was beginning to despair of Tamsin's greed ever being satisfied, the bargain was struck.

The little figures were detached, the better part of Omri's fiver handed over, and Emma and Omri found themselves out in the hall again, tiptoeing towards the front door.

"Where do you think you're going, Emma?"

They stopped cold. Emma shut her eyes. It was *her* mother this time, the sister of Patrick's mother and just such another, it seemed.

Omri thought, *Good, she'll have to stop here and that means I won't have to be bothered about her.* She'd served her purpose, and surely the fewer people who were involved the better. But he glanced sideways at Emma's face, and to his own astonishment he heard himself saying, "Can Emma come back to my place for lunch?"

Emma's mother said, "How will she get home?"

"My Dad'll run her back," said Omri glibly.

66

"Before dark."

"Of course."

"Oh – all right then. I suppose . . . "

They gave her no time to think twice. They were off out and down the street as fast as they could run.

"Now," said Emma as they sat on the train back to Omri's district. "I want to know everything."

Omri groaned inwardly. He'd managed to fend off her questions on the way to her house, but there was something in her voice which told him that no amount of fending would work now.

He turned in his seat to face her.

"Listen, Em. You've got to swear yourself to secrecy."

"Okay," she agreed readily.

"No, not like that. It's not just a game. You don't know how hard it's going to be to keep this to yourself."

"With Tam for a sister, I've learnt how to keep secrets, don't worry."

Omri slumped back against the train seat. He'd have to trust her – it was too late not to.

"Okay, then. You saw them. They're real, they're no dream and no game. There's proper magic in this world, to do with time, and – and souls of people that can travel in time and from place to place, and enter things like toys, and make them come to life. And we can travel too. I mean our – our spirits can. That's where Patrick is. He's time-travelling."

Emma was staring at him.

"Why's it a secret?"

"Can't you see? If grown-ups knew . . . "

"Oh. Yes. Not just grown-ups. If *Tam* knew . . . !"

"We wouldn't be allowed to keep it. It works – I might as well tell you this – with a special key. And a little bathroom cupboard, and my oak chest. All that would be taken away. There'd be newspapers, TV – "

Emma sat up straight, her eyes alight.

"Would we be on TV?"

Omri's heart plummeted.

"Em, you mustn't. You must not think like that. Yes, we'd be on TV, and everything would be *ruined*."

Emma sat back, frowning. He could see her thinking. He had the feeling she wasn't particularly used to thinking seriously, any more than he'd been himself, before all this started.

They hurried along the length of Hovel Road unmolested. The skinhead gang had gone, home for lunch presumably. As they half-ran, Emma said, "Where exactly has Patrick gone?"

"Well," said Omri, "I'm pretty worried about that." And he explained how the key worked, as best he could. "You have to take someone or something real, or alive, with you, if you want to go to a specific place and time. Like, when I went back to the Indian village last night I took a pair of Twin Stars' moccasins in my pocket. Patrick took Boone, but he forgot the rules, and as he *went*, Boone *came back*."

"So he could be anywhere, just – floating about in time?"

"I don't know. The only thing is – "

"What?"

"Well, it's only a slight hope, but I'm sure Boone, I mean his plastic figure, was wearing his hat when Patrick set off. Maybe the hat got caught up in some – some sort of time-current, and attached itself to Patrick, in which case he went to Texas after all, because that's where the hat belongs."

"Complicated, innit?" said Emma in Cockney.

Omri wasn't into accents so he just said feelingly, "You said it." But he glanced at her appreciatively. She was taking it pretty reasonably. And she was fun. And it wasn't bad at all, having someone to help now Patrick had P.O.'d.

As they reached the house, it occurred to Omri as ironic that the whole business with Patrick going back in time had come up in the first place so Patrick wouldn't have to go home – in order that he could stay and *help Omri*.

Huh, thought Omri. *Fine friend*.

But Patrick *was* his friend. And even at times when Omri was fed up with him, like now, he still liked him enough to care what was happening to him.

Omri and Emma hurried up to Omri's room. Omri's first act was to bend over the longhouse and call softly.

"Matron!"

She came out. She didn't bustle quite so briskly now. Her starched apron was soiled, and her magnificent cap limp and askew. She looked very tired.

"Well? What luck?"

"How's Boone?" asked Omri. "How are the others?"

"Your cowboy friend is a bit better, though he's still unconscious. He's breathing normally, but he's badly bruised. The Indians . . . " Her shoulders slumped a little. "One is hanging between life and death. Bullet in the trachea, another in the leg. I need help desperately."

"We've brought you some." She straightened up with relief; even the erstwhile magnificent cap seemed to stiffen a little.

"Well, what are we waiting for! Let's get to it!"

Emma meanwhile had lost no time in consigning the medical team to the cupboard. But just before

69

Omri closed the door, Emma, peering at the seed-tray, suddenly said, "Whose are these sweet little horses?"

"*Sweet little horses*"! *God!* thought Omri, gritting his teeth. But he kept his temper and said, "The brown one's Little Bull's. The black one belongs to the cowboy."

"Can I put the cowboy's one back in the cupboard?"

"What *for*?"

"Well, I want to see how it works in reverse. And you said Patrick might be in Boone's time. Maybe he needs a horse."

"Don't be stupid, Patrick will probably be small, like the little people are here! What use would a socking great horse be to him, he couldn't possibly ride it."

"Still, let me."

Omri couldn't be bothered making any more objections. Emma tenderly lifted the little black horse between finger and thumb and put it in the cupboard.

"Will it go *back* at the same time as the doctors come *forward*?"

"Yes! Oh, do let's get on with it!" said Omri impatiently.

The door was closed on the live horse and the plastic men. The key was turned. Emma, her ear to the mirrored door, grinned ecstatically at Omri: she could hear tiny voices questioning each other in the darkness. Her hand went to the key, but Omri stopped her.

"Listen," he said quietly. "One of the tricky things is when they see us, trying to get them to believe it and not think they've lost their minds. Our best bet with these modern people is to get Matron to explain."

Matron was ready and eager, impatient to get the team out and to work on her patients.

"Leave it to me," she said. "Just let me in that cupboard."

"But what will you say – ?"

"I've thought it all out," she said. "Most men, if you just tell them what to do in a businesslike fashion, will follow directions without thinking about it. One proceeds on the assumption that they'll do as they're told, and they do. However, they may be forced to think a bit if they see you two, so I suggest you keep out of the way." She nipped back into the longhouse, presumably to make sure everything was in perfect order, then hurried out, down the ramp and across to the cupboard.

"Right you are," she said. "Open sesame!"

As she slid through the partly open door, Omri put his hand stealthily in at the top and lifted out the plastic figure of Boone's horse.

"Here," he muttered to Emma. "This was your daft idea, you'd better take care of it."

She took the little figure from him and looked into its plastic face.

"He's happy to be home," she said mysteriously. "Now Patrick isn't completely on his tod, anyway."

X

A Rough Ride

Patrick brooded, his chin on his hands, his elbows on his bent knees. He was sitting in the massive shadow of Boone's corpse (not that Patrick allowed himself to think this in so many words, but he was quite sure in the back of his mind that that's what it was) trying to think, and at the same time trying not to think. The two conflicting efforts cancelled each other out. His mind was a blank. His eyes were unfocussed.

Suddenly they did focus. They focused on something he hadn't noticed before. Heaven knows why, because it was absolutely enormous. A vast black mountain-range on the horizon. *And it was moving.*

It was heaving. It was threshing. One part of it, at the far left-hand end of the range, was rearing itself up.

Up, up – into the sky!

Patrick sprang to his feet and shaded his eyes. The vast black mass was erupting in a series of bounding curves and angular jolts. It was awesome, like witnessing the primeval forces which created the world, throwing up volcanic ranges from the hot laval centre of the earth.

But abruptly Patrick lost his sense of awe and terror. He threw back his head and laughed.

Because now the mountain-range finished heaving and stood upright on four titanic legs, revealed for what it was.

It was a horse!

It must have been lying motionless in what to Patrick was the distance – its spirit, or whatever, somewhere far away in place and time. And now it had come back to itself, and stood up and – "Cripes!" – it was lumbering towards him!

Patrick ran. He ran back towards the sheltering bulk of Boone. He hid himself under a vast flap which was the lapel of Boone's plaid shirt collar, tucked under his bristly chin.

As Patrick ducked behind this flannel "curtain", he heard a strange, almost musical sound, like a wheezing groan. A huge fleshy knob just above the neck-band moved – along – then back, making the shirt collar shiver and shift. At first Patrick had no notion what was happening, but as the groaning sounds went on and the motion of the lump in Boone's throat continued, he suddenly realised.

Frightened though he was – the thundering tread of those colossal hoofs was shaking the ground like a series of earthquakes as they approached – Patrick registered with an incredulous sense of relief that the bristly skin above the shirt was warm, and that the groaning sounds were rasping breaths, and that the lump was Boone's Adam's apple.

"Boone, you're alive!" Patrick breathed, feeling a sudden intense happiness. He almost kissed the Adam's apple as it slid past him. But then he sensed the horse's tremendous head coming down on him and he crouched, trembling, behind the collar.

He felt a rush of hot, powerfully horse-smelling breath which came right through the thick flannel. Then there was a loud sound like the rumble of distant thunder as the horse blew through its lips. The horse was smelling Boone. Next it nudged the cowboy's shoulder with its nose, causing another sort of earthquake which had Patrick rolling over on the stones.

He peered out from behind the flap.

The first thing he saw, vast as it was, was recognisable as a hoof. The sloping horny part was about twice Patrick's height, with a fringe of coarse black hairs hanging over the top of it.

Patrick never knew afterwards what possessed him to take the action he now took almost unthinkingly. He knew he had to get out of this desert unless he wanted to die of heatstroke, thirst or the attentions of wild creatures. He needed to escape. So, instinctively, he acted.

He took a run at the hoof, scrambled half-way up the hard slope on hands and feet, grabbed a handful of the coarse black hair, and hauled himself up to a kind of ledge where the gigantic leg-bone started.

There he almost panicked. The hoof he was on was planted firmly in the sand, but at some stage it would start to move, probably very fast. Patrick looked at the tempting slope to the ground and nearly slid straight back down again to short-term safety.

But then he thought, *No. I must get out of this, and this is the only way.*

He hurriedly took several of the long black hairs of the horse's fetlock, twisted them together, and knotted them firmly round his waist. Then he reached as high as he could and took a strong grip with both hands on more of the hairs, at the same time bracing his trainers on the ridge at the top of the hoof.

He felt surprisingly secure, ready for anything. So he thought. He had absolutely no idea of the terrifying experience that was in store for him when the horse, getting no response from its prostrate master, abruptly threw up its head, turned swiftly, and started to gallop across the desert sand.

Patrick had always loved terrifying rides at fairs, the scarier the better – the centrifugal drum was one of his favourites, and that rocket that spins and plunges and twists and whirls around all at the same time. But no fair-ride ever dreamt up by an ingenious showman could compare with standing braced on the hoof of a giant horse as it races over hot sand.

Over and over again the great hoof would rise in the air, leaving Patrick's stomach far below, and sweep through a monstrous arc which had Patrick dangling high above the sand. If he hadn't tied himself on securely, nothing could have saved him. The hoof would bend and turn in such a way that his body would be twisted and flung almost upside down, before the hoof plunged down again to strike the ground with a sickening jar. The speed alone was enough to make most people faint, but Patrick grimly hung on.

But his hand-grips became weaker and weaker as the crazy, fantastic, nerve-and-bone-wracking ride went on and on. To make matters worse, dust and stones, struck up from the ground by the flying hooves, flew through the air and pelted Patrick all over. He didn't feel these at the time. Every bit of his mind, and every muscle and sinew, were preoccupied with the single task of holding on. He didn't know that his eyes were screwed shut, that his breath was coming in jolts, that with every breath he uttered a cry or a groan. For him, all was sickening motion, whirling blackness, jarring blows, and absolute terror.

By the time it stopped, he was almost unconscious. His handholds had given way, though one wrist was still held by a tangle of hairs. He hung from this, and the tie at his waist, like a rag-doll. His whole body was covered with bruises; his throat was choked with dust so that he could scarcely draw breath.

Gradually he came back to his senses, and straightened up painfully. He opened his eyes with difficulty – they were caked with wind-tears and dust. He peered dazedly around him.

There seemed to be a lot going on. Noise, movement. At his level, near the ground, he could see a lot of other huge hooves moving and stamping. The ground itself was not sand, but packed earth. There was a very strong horse smell, probably dung. He raised his eyes and saw some vast posts and rails, and the heads of a number of horses besides his own. Straight before him was a wooden cliff about six times Patrick's height.

The hoof he was still attached to lifted and made a pawing movement which brought it level with the top of this cliff. Patrick then saw what it was – the edge of a wooden sidewalk. Now he could see gigantic feet, some in cowboy boots with villainous spurs attached, others in lighter footwear all but covered by long skirts, striding past with vast steps which thundered on the boards.

Patrick took advantage of the horse's hoof being, for the moment, planted on the sidewalk, to free himself – just as well. No sooner had he slid down the sloping hoof to the wooden floor, when his horse's head swept down and its giant slabs of teeth, as big as tombstones, bit scratchingly into its fetlock, exactly where Patrick had been tied a moment before!

It was dangerous to try to cross the sidewalk – any one of those mighty thundering feet could crush him on the way. From his viewpoint it was like trying to make it across a ten-lane highway during rush-hour.

But he couldn't stay here. Already the horse was snuffling at him, nearly sucking him up into its cavernous nostril. He ran out of range, and found himself surrounded by feet. He must get out of here! He must find someone to help him!

Just then he saw some boots coming to a standstill right beside him. Curiously, they were not brown or black, but bright red and shiny. One scarlet lace had come untied and hung down to the ground.

Patrick put his head back as far as it would go and looked upwards.

He could see a whole sky of frothy white petticoats and the hem of a red satin dress, a long way above him. It was a lady.

She had come up onto the sidewalk from the dirt road and had paused for a moment. Again he acted without thinking, grabbing the red bootlace and heaving himself up – though he ached in every limb – onto the arched instep where he could find comfortable and safe refuge among the crossed red laces and metal-ringed lace-holes.

"I'm safe!" he thought.

That was his opinion.

Ruby Lou

The feet moved on, across the sidewalk, not along it. This ride was quite pleasantly unexciting after the other. Patrick heard a thud as the lady boldly pushed open some swing-doors. Then she walked inside.

The street sounds – the clopping of hooves, the thudding of feet, the sound of wagons and voices and barking dogs – changed to other sounds, familiar to Patrick from Western films. He knew at once he was in a saloon. There was a piano playing a jangly tune and lots of voices shouting and singing cheerfully. The smell in the air was of alcohol, cigarette smoke, cheap scent, sweat and leather.

The lady who was unwittingly carrying Patrick made straight for the bar. She rested 'his' foot on a rail. It was dark down there, and the smell was pretty bad. Patrick wondered how he could attract her attention, or whether it would be fatal to do so. He could hear her voice among the other voices.

"An' who's gonna buy me a drink, boys? Ruby Lou don't take kindly to drinkin' alone, and she never, never pays for her own likker!"

There was no shortage of offers. Patrick saw men's feet crowding round the red shiny boots and heard the jovial cries of male voices above yelling: "Yea, Lou! I'll buy ya a dozen!" "Good ol' Ruby Lou! Have one on me, sweetheart!"

"Okay okay, don't crowd me now!" Ruby Lou said sharply, and the boots shuffled reluctantly a step backwards.

Patrick could hear the noisy glug-glug-glug of whisky being poured from a bottle, and he could smell it, too. Whisky made him think at once of Boone, and so it seemed a quite incredible coincidence when Ruby Lou's voice suddenly echoed his thoughts.

"Hey, where's my favourite fella?" she cried. "Where's Boone? Boone always makes me laugh!"

"Boo-Hoo Boone? Make ya cry, more like!" jeered one man, and the rest all burst into mock boo-hooing.

Ruby Lou took offence on Boone's behalf.

"Ain't nothin' wrong with a soft heart," she said. "Trouble with you lot is, you ain't got hearts, or if ya have, they ain't got no more feelin's in 'em than chunks o' rock! It don't mean he ain't got guts, neither! Gimme a man with feelin's, even if he do git through two-three of my best lace-edged hankies every time we hear a hard-luck story!"

She shouldn't have said that. The notion of Boone mopping up his tears with lace hankies was too much, even for Patrick. As the crowd of men above him burst their sides laughing, Patrick, below on the red leather, laughed too until, weakened as he was, he slipped.

He felt himself sliding down the side of the boot, and grabbed the red bootlace. This broke his fall, but it gave Ruby Lou's foot a tug.

As he climbed back up to his perch, he saw her huge hand coming down towards him. He crouched low in the opening of her boot. He didn't realise that he was digging his hands and feet into her instep, until he heard her say peevishly:

"I got me a itch on my tootsy. This saloon is turnin' into a real flea-circus!"

And her fingers, with their sharp nails, began to prod around the lacings. Patrick tried to dodge, but suddenly one finger fell on him, squeezing him hard against a metal-rimmed lace-hole so that he thought his back would break and he writhed frantically to free himself.

"Hey! This is some flea that's bitin' me!" she squealed, picked Patrick up between finger and thumb, and the next second he was being swung through the air.

Ruby Lou set Patrick down on the bar.

All at once the noise in his immediate vicinity stopped. The sudden startled silence spread backwards until even the piano player faltered and faded out. Patrick stood ankle-deep in a puddle of whisky (the fumes nearly knocked him out) looking upward fearfully at the semi-circle of enormous faces around him, waiting helplessly for one or other of them to raise a meaty hand and swat him flat.

No one did.

Instead the bartender, who was standing on the other side of the bar with a bottle of whisky in his hand, dropped it. It fell on the bar with a (to Patrick) ear-numbing clunk, making the whole bar jump, and to his horror began rolling slowly towards him, spilling whisky as it went.

Seeing it approach, Patrick raced to get out of its way. He ran as fast as his aching legs would let him, hearing the huge bottle trundling along the wooden bar behind him, nearer and nearer. Surely, surely it must soon roll over him like a steam-roller!

But luckily for him it didn't roll straight. Abruptly he heard the noise stop as it reached the edge. There was a brief pause before it shattered on the bar-room floor.

He stopped running and turned, panting.

The eyes of every person in the saloon were fixed on him, and every bloodshot eye was popping. Vast mouths hung loosely open, bristly faces were paper-white or mottled purple.

"Wh – wh – what IS that?" gibbered one man at last, pointing at him with a trembling finger. "Boys, am I seein' things, or – is – that – a li'l – tiny – ackshul – fella?"

Before anyone could reply, Patrick sensed a quick movement behind him. He spun round instinctively, to find himself staring straight up the barrel of a six-shooter.

"Whatever it is, I don't like it!" growled the owner, and fired.

The noise alone nearly killed Patrick, though the gun wavered at the last second (did a red shiny bulk lurch against the shooting arm – ?) The bullet ploughed into the top of the bar right next to him, splintering the wood.

The next moment, complete chaos broke out.

The barman, who had reeled back against the enormous mirror that reflected the whole room, suddenly and silently sank out of sight behind the bar. This seemed to act as a signal. The giants at the bar just went crazy, bumping into each other, throwing punches, firing their guns at random in a series of horrific explosions. One of the light-fittings was hit and came crashing down, causing total panic.

There was a concerted mass-movement backwards, away from the bar, followed by a rising thunder of boots stampeding on boards, causing massive vibrations which had Patrick involuntarily dancing up and down on the bar. Twenty or thirty men cut a parting through the smoky air as they forced their way out through the narrow doorway.

One little fellow, the piano player, tripped, fell, and was ruthlessly trampled underfoot by the rest. When they'd all gone, he lay there for a moment, winded, before picking himself up. He gave one terrified backwards look towards the bar, cast his eyes upwards as if in prayer, let out a weird sound, and fled, clutching his hat.

The swing doors went whump-whump-whump, backwards and forwards, on emptiness, before coming to a stop.

Patrick gingerly took his fingers out of his ears and glanced round the saloon, expecting to find himself alone. But he wasn't, not quite.

Standing a few yards down the bar, the exact distance that Patrick had run away from the bottle, was a giantess with blond hair and a rather low-cut red satin dress. It was hard for Patrick to judge, but she looked quite pretty. She wore a sparkling necklace of red stones and dangly earrings and a very funny expression as she looked at him.

She reached out suddenly and picked up her small glass, which she emptied down her throat in one gulp. Then she plonked it back on the counter and said, "Well, li'l fella, you sure would make a good temperance preacher! I ain't never seen a saloon empty so fast! Thanks for lettin' 'em buy me a drink first. I needed it!"

She laughed a little crazily, and drank someone else's drink which had been abandoned. Then she beckoned to him.

"Come here, li'l Jack the Giant Killer, come to Ruby Lou! C'mon, I won't hurt ya, I just wanna make sure you ain't something I dreamt."

Patrick walked back along the vast shiny expanse of the bar towards her. His legs were shaking and his feet squelshed in his whisky-sodden trainers. He had no idea whether he would be safe with her or not; but he couldn't manage alone, and who else was there? Anyway, she liked Boone, so she couldn't be all bad.

Ruby Lou's face, brightly painted, came down until it was level with his. He could smell her perfume. Well, it was better than the whisky, anyhow.

"Okay, kid, let's have it. What gives? I ain't drunk, and I ain't that crazy, and you look to me like the smallest human critter that ever was in the length and breadth o' Texas!"

"Actually I'm English," said Patrick, feeling silly but not knowing what else to say.

"English! Is that s'posed to be a introduction, or a explanation? I heard it was kind of a small island, but I never knew the men from there was only three inches tall!"

Patrick blushed. "I'm not exactly a typical English person," he said. "You see – "

"Speak up, kid, that's a teeny tiny voice-box you

got there, and I'll admit it to you, I'm a mite deaf from all the shoutin' an' shootin' that goes on around here!"

Patrick cleared his throat. "Sorry!" he bellowed. Then he shouted, "Listen, I need help."

"You coulda fooled me, buster!"

"Not just for myself. For Boone."

"Say!" Her face lit up. "You a friend o' Billy Boone's?"

"Yes. We're old friends. And he's in trouble."

"Yeah? Tell me somethin' new. When ain't he!"

"He's lying out in the desert unconscious. I think someone should go out there and get him."

"Can you show me where he is?"

"No. But maybe his horse can – it's outside, or it was."

Ruby Lou straightened up and looked around. The saloon was still empty; but peering over the top of the swing-doors was a pair of eyes under a well-pulled-down hat.

"Hey, Reverend! Come in here, it's okay!"

The doors slowly parted and the little piano player who had been trampled on sidled hesitantly in.

"I want ya to meet m'new sidekick – er – "

"Pat," said Patrick, thinking that 'Patrick' sounded a bit of a feeble name for the Wild West.

"Pat – this is Tickle. His real name's the Reverend Godfrey Tickson, and he has a past you wouldn't believe to look at him now, but we call him Tickle cause he tickles the ivories. *Plays the piano*, get it? Plays real good, too, just name the tune, he can play it fer ya! Only, not now, eh, Tick? I got somethin' important fer you to do. Is your buggy handy?"

"Yeah, Ruby," said the Reverend Tickle in a squeaky voice. "It's right outside."

"Me'n Pat, here, is goin' fer a little ride on Boone's

hoss, and you're gonna drive right along behind us. What say?" She patted his chubby cheek.

"Sure, Ruby," squeaked Tickle, nearly nodding his hat off. "If you say so!"

Ruby Lou's white hand with its glittering rings swept Patrick up. Gasping, he felt for the first time how the "little people" had felt when he and Omri had handled them. He hoped he'd always picked up Boone as gently as Ruby Lou did him, but he doubted it, remembering some times when he'd stuffed him in his jeans pocket and not been at all bothered if the cowboy were frightened or uncomfortable.

"Where'd ya favour ridin', pal? Not on my shoe again, eh? My shoulder? Naw, bit slippery . . . Hey, I know a nice safe place!"

And before Patrick knew what was happening she had thrust him into the front of her dress. Which, once he got over his slight embarrassment, was just like being in the front row of the dress circle in a theatre. Or maybe in the bows of a very large ship.

Ruby Lou slapped Tickle's hand away when he reached for one of the abandoned drinks, and swept out of the saloon with Patrick just ahead of her like a miniature figurehead on an old-fashioned galleon. She got him to point out Boone's horse, and before you could say "Howdy" she had stuck her high-heeled boot in the heavy stirrup and in a flurry of petticoats and red satin, swung herself into the saddle.

Patrick found himself at skyscraper-height, with a fantastic view of a street which was somehow familiar. Then he remembered. Of course! It was the street Boone had drawn for them that time in the art lesson at school! There was the jail, and across the way the livery stables, the dirt road with the horses and wagons, and the doctor's sign, and the general store ... The only thing there wasn't, was people, though he thought he saw a few curtains twitch in some windows and the door of the sheriff's office hastily closing.

Tickle meanwhile had hurried to where his horse and buggy were parked and climbed onto the driver's seat, picking up the reins and giving them a shake.

"Praise the Lord, I'm ready t'go, Ruby!" he called in his squeaky voice.

"Okay, fellas!" She kicked the horse, who reared up a little, giving Patrick a fright, but Ruby sat her mount as steady as a rock.

"Git on there, hoss! Find Boone!" cried the intrepid Ruby Lou. And the next moment they were galloping down the empty street leaving Tickle to follow in a cloud of dust.

XII

Caught Red-Handed

Boone came to that afternoon.

Matron had been exceedingly busy since the surgical team came. She hustled and bustled them across to the seed-tray, chatting to them all the time in an isn't-this-interesting-and-also-perfectly-normal sort of voice, and before they knew it they were doing their stuff in a makeshift operating theatre with the aid of a powerful torch and relays of tiny containers.

It was Emma's job to keep these coming, though she gave them to Twin Stars to carry in to the team. One lot contained boiling water with a few drops of disinfectant in it. The other lot contained boiling water with tea, sugar and milk in it. (On one occasion Matron apparently mistook the one for the other, and a great deal of coughing and spluttering ensued.)

As Boone didn't need an operation, he had been established in a bed, which Emma, under Omri's guidance, made of a large Swan Vesta matchbox filled with neatly folded Kleenex and a small pincushion pillow, set up in a far corner of the seed-tray out of sight of the longhouse and its occupants. He was watched over by Twin Stars, and occasionally visited by Little Bull, who would stray near the bed as if by accident and peer at Boone's face scowlingly before stamping off again with a grunt of disfavour.

But at last Twin Stars called to Omri and Emma, who were just returning from the garden after conducting a brief burial service over the paper packet of plastic figures. (Omri's family were not churchgoers, but Emma managed a prayer of sorts and even thought of putting some tiny flowers on the grave.)

"Boone wake!" Twin Stars said, shifting her baby's slight weight from one arm to the other. Her face was wreathed in smiles. She was very fond of Boone, since he had stood by to help her during the birth of her baby.

Omri and Emma leant close to the matchbox bed, and saw that sure enough, Boone had opened his eyes and was trying to sit up. When he saw Omri looming over him, his ginger-bristly face broke into a soppy grin.

"Hi there, pardner," he said rather croakily. "Whut happened t'me this time? Did that there sneaky redskin varmint shoot another arrow into me, or whut?"

"I'm afraid it was Patrick," confessed Omri. "He didn't mean it, he just squeezed you too tight."

"Yeah? That'd explain why m'ribs feels like they're broke."

"Well, they're not, just bruised, but you nearly suffocated."

Boone paled.

"Suffocated! Ya mean, like when they string you up? Geez, that's allus bin m'worst nightmare, kickin' the bucket that-a-way! Never woulda thought of ol' Pat bein' so dawgoned careless! Whur is the kid, anyhow? An' who's this?" he added, suddenly noticing Emma.

"This is Emma, Boone. She's a friend of ours. Emma, this is Boone. He's a cowboy from Texas."

Emma stretched out her hand and Boone solemnly took hold of the nail of one finger and shook it.

"A real privilege, Ma'am," he said courteously. He stared at her for a moment. "Y'know, with that fair hair o'yorn, and them eyes blue as the midday sky, ya sure remind me of a lady o' mah acquaintance ... A'course, you're a mite younger'n she is ... " He stared a while longer, and then shook himself and said brightly, "Hey, Ah'm feelin' better every minute. Y'know, thur ain't nothing like bein' close to a beautiful female fer bringing a red-blooded dyin' man back t'th'land o' the livin'! Unless it's ... " And he gave a meaningful swallow.

Omri sighed and glanced at Emma.

"You want a drink," he said resignedly.

"Jest a li'l shot," Boone wheedled, indicating the minutest possible portion between finger and thumb. "Best cure there is fer suffocation."

"Oh, okay," said Omri, laughing. "I'll fetch you some. Emma, you chat to him, tell him where Patrick is, that ought to keep his mind off his thirst."

Omri went downstairs to the living-room where the drinks cupboard was. His father was no drinker, but he always kept a bottle of Scotch and some wine and beer handy, together with glasses of the appropriate sizes and shapes. Omri chose a tiny liqueur glass and was just pouring a small portion of Scotch into it when his father walked into the room and caught him red-handed.

"Omri? What on earth are you up to?"

The question was not angry, merely incredulous. Omri stood there with the whisky bottle in one hand and the tiny glass in the other, the very picture of guilt.

"I – I – I . . . I'm pouring a drink."

"That's the wrong glass for Scotch," said his father, as if he couldn't think of anything else to say. He walked across, took the bottle out of Omri's hand and replaced the top. There was a silence and then he said, "Well, you've poured it, you might as well drink it."

Omri stared at the brown liquid in the glass. He wanted to say, "It's not for me," or "I don't want it," but he knew that if he did, more questions, unanswerable questions, would be sure to follow. So he took a deep breath, and, with a feeling like despair, he swallowed it in one gulp.

The stuff was *horrible*. It seemed to stick in his throat, making him choke. His eyes sprouted tears. When it finally went down it burnt all the way and hit his unsuspecting stomach like a small depth charge.

He was aware of his father, watching him curiously.

"You're evidently not really into hard liquor," he remarked, looking at Omri's scarlet face and teary eyes.

Omri said nothing.

"Just an experiment, was it?" his father persisted in a man-to-man tone.

"Sort of," croaked Omri.

"Well, try anything once, that's my motto too. *Just* once, in this case, okay?" And he put the bottle away firmly.

Omri moved towards the door, trying to get rid of the filthy taste in his mouth. Just as he got there, his father said, "I think it's time I drove them back."

"Who? – Oh! Emma, you mean."

"And Patrick."

"Patrick?" repeated Omri, startled.

"He is up in your room, isn't he?"

"Er – yes. But he's – asleep."

"What do you mean?"

"He was dead tired and he fell asleep and – well, I thought he might stay the night," gabbled Omri.

"Is that okay with his mother?"

Omri mumbled something and then said, "I'll tell Emma to come down."

Later, Emma made a secret phone call to Omri from her home, to say that she'd told Patrick's mother that Patrick had returned safely to Omri's after his 'bicycle ride' "so tired he'd fallen asleep right away." And that, though annoyed, she'd resigned herself to staying in town for another night.

"I'll just give him tonight," said Omri. "What he said about staying a week is ridiculous. I'll bring him back in the morning."

Emma said nothing for a moment, and then said, "I *hated* having to leave. I don't want to miss anything. Will you please give my love to Boone and Twin Stars and Little Bull. And the baby. And Matron."

"Matron wouldn't appreciate it," said Omri. "She's above all that." But something in the intensity of feeling in Emma's voice pleased him. "I'll see you at school tomorrow," he went on. "And don't forget. Not a word to anyone. No exceptions. Promise."

And Emma replied, "I already did promise," but just the same, Omri hardly slept all night.

XIII

Mr Johnson Smells
a Rat

Next day was Monday. School.

Omri got up very early after a restless night. Little Bull didn't have to wake him, for once.

The first thing he did was open the chest. Patrick was exactly as before – chill-fleshed, but breathing shallowly. Omri crouched on his heels, staring in at him. He knew what he should do. What he must do, really. Anyway he was dying to hear what had been happening in Texas – if indeed that was where Patrick had wound up. It was just that he didn't want to interrupt a great adventure, if there was one going on.

Nevertheless, he closed the lid, and put his hand on the key with its red satin ribbon.

"Young man! I need some assistance."

It was Matron in her most commanding mood.

"Could it wait, Matron?"

"No. Some of these men are so much better they can go back where they belong. They're just taking up beds, not to mention my time. Come along, I've marshalled them outside that cupboard of yours, now send them on their way."

Omri stood up. The Indians, about nine of them, many with bandaged limbs or heads, one on crutches made of matchsticks, stood near the door of the cupboard. Little Bull and Twin Stars were with them.

"Is it okay if they go back, Little Bull?"

"Good go back. In village, much need do. Each brave have work, enough for many."

"Do you want to go with them?" asked Omri with a heavy heart.

Little Bull looked up at him.

"I think much of go back or stay. I wish this and this. So I choose. You send Little Bull back now. Then when sun go, you bring back. I see village. Then come back see hurt braves."

"Great idea, you can almost be in two places at once! Will you take Twin Stars with you?"

"Yes take wife. Take son. Take horse. Omri bring Little Bull back when sun go."

Omri felt a bit confused about the logistics of all this, but he nodded and he and Little Bull touched hands.

He opened the cupboard. With some help from Matron and each other, the Indians scrambled over the bottom rim with the horse. Little Bull helped Twin Stars in. She cast a tender look back at Omri and waved to him.

Omri then "borrowed" the key from the chest and

dispatched them. Why did he feel sad about this parting which was to be only for one day? He consigned the plastic figures to the safety of his pocket.

Matron gave a sigh of satisfaction.

"We're not going to lose any more now," she said. "The others are all on the mend."

"What did the team think of it all?"

Matron permitted herself a smirk.

'Well, as the Bard says, 'Conscience doth make cowards of us all'! I think each of them thought he'd probably had too much to drink, and none of them liked to admit it to the others, so they just got on with the job as per my orders. I mean, suggestions."

"I suppose you were up all night, after we sent them back?"

"Let's say I didn't get a lot of sleep. Never mind. All in a night's work."

"You're wonderful," said Omri sincerely.

"Pish, tush, and likewise pooh," said Matron dismissing the compliment, but he had seen a blush of pleasure spread over those craggy features. "What about a cuppa? Can't start the day without my tea."

"An' Ah cain't start mine without mah cawfee!" chimed in Boone's voice. Omri had fixed him up with a little "house" made of Lego and put it out of sight behind the cupboard, so Boone could get a good night's sleep, away from the seed-tray with all the hospital-like hustle and bustle.

Now Omri lifted the roof off. Boone was sitting bolt upright in bed, looking ready for anything. 'Ah'm more'n a mite hungry, too, so as Ah been de-prived of m'likker, don't you go forgettin' some powerful vittles!" Omri had had trouble with him the night before when he'd returned without any whisky.

He hurried down to the kitchen and fetched as many 'powerful vittles' as he could readily lay hands on, while boiling the kettle for tea and coffee. He wished Emma were here. He felt beleaguered, having to do everything himself. He wasn't sure he'd got his priorities right, seeing that everyone was fed before he did anything about Patrick. As he tiptoed back upstairs he thought he'd see to that as soon as he was dressed.

But hardly was he back in his room when he was alarmed to hear footsteps rattling up the attic stairs.

"Hey, Omri! Wake up, you're on the news!"

It was Gillon, banging on his door. Omri hastily heaped some junk onto the top of the chest and opened the bedroom door a crack.

"What are you on about?"

"It was on my clock radio. Radio London. They just announced the winners of the story competition!"

Omri was speechless. He'd forgotten about winning the prize.

"I wish I'd heard it," he said at last.

"Too bad, it's over now," said Gillon, thumping down the stairs again in his pyjamas.

After that, there just wasn't a minute's peace. His parents had both heard the announcement and were clamouring for Omri to come down for a special bacon-and-egg breakfast to celebrate. By the time that was done with, it was too late to go back upstairs because his train wouldn't wait for him. Luckily he'd given the food to Matron to distribute, giving a special, large (so to speak) portion to Boone in his little house.

Omri just had to go off and leave Patrick where (ever) he was.

There were no skinheads to make trouble in Hovel Road and Omri got to school in good order, though feeling highly uneasy. He was dead worried about Patrick. What would his mother say when he didn't show up? And what if he were in some appalling danger, as Omri himself had been in the Indian village, and was waiting on tenterhooks to be brought back?

He put his books and stuff in his locker and then went in to Assembly. Mr Johnson, the headmaster, was already on the stage, clearing his throat for silence. More than the usual number of teachers were there too. Several hundred children were seated on the floor.

Omri crept in and sat down near the main doors. He craned his neck looking for Emma but he couldn't see her. Had she not come to school? He was still looking for her anxiously when Mr Johnson began to talk; Omri didn't take in what he said, until suddenly, with a shock, he heard his own name.

Everywhere in the auditorium, people turned their heads to look at him. Omri sat up straight, alarmed.

" . . . very proud indeed," Mr Johnson concluded. "Omri, stand up and come forward."

Utterly bewildered, Omri rose to his feet.

"Me – ?"

"Yes, yes!" beamed Mr Johnson. All the teachers on the stage were smiling and as Omri moved forward, everyone started to applaud.

Omri found himself being helped onto the stage, and, turning, saw he was the focus of hundreds of pairs of eyes. What was all this – ? If only he'd been listening!

"Now, it just so happens," said Mr Johnson, in unfamiliarly genial tones, "that I have here a copy of Omri's story, which had to be kept by the school when Omri entered it for the competition. And what I thought would be really nice, is if Omri would agree to read us his winning story as this morning's Assembly Feature."

Omri's mouth fell open.

Mr Johnson was handing him a typed manuscript which he well recognised – he'd typed it himself, 'Hunt & Peck' system, in three copies. One he'd sent in to Telecom for the writing competition, one he'd kept, and this one he'd had to hand in to the school office. Across the top was typed the title: *The Plastic Indian.*

He clutched it till it creased, swallowed hard, and looked up at Mr Johnson imploringly.

"Now, now, Omri, no false modesty! Telecom has notified the school that you have won first prize in the intermediate age-group – three hundred pounds! What about that, you people?" There was an impressed and envious gasp from the assembled crowd below and Omri heard murmurs of, "Three hundred quid! Wow – Get old Omri, then – millionaire-time! Blimey!" And they burst into applause all over again.

"Stand here in the middle of the stage," Mr Johnson said, manoeuvring Omri by the shoulders. "Now then! I haven't had a chance to read this myself yet, so I'm just going to sit here and enjoy it. Well done, Omri! Off you go!"

Omri dithered for a moment or two and then thought, *Hey, this isn't half bad, I've dreamt of this happening!* So he began to read.

The story was based on his first meeting with the Indian, a year ago when he'd first discovered the cupboard and the key's magic. It was a great story and he'd done his best to write it well. At first when he began to read it, he was nervous, and stumbled over the words, but after a paragraph or two he hit his stride and began to read with feeling and expression. He did Little Bull's gruff voice, and had a stab at Boone's Texas accent; when he said something funny, the whole auditorium erupted with laughter. During the exciting bits, everyone sat poised to catch what came next. It was very satisfying, and when he finished the story and the applause broke out again, with some cheering, Omri felt this was a great moment in his life, one that he'd always remember.

In fact he was feeling extremely pleased with himself – not at all a sensation he was accustomed to at school – when he suddenly became aware that Mr Johnson had stood up behind him and was looming over him in a distinctly sinister manner.

Before the applause had died away, Mr Johnson bent down and whispered something in Omri's ear that made his blood chill in his veins.

"I want to see you in my office immediately."

Omri turned to look at him. He was appalled to see that all geniality had been wiped from the headmaster's face which had gone the colour of a wet sheet.

"That story," pursued the grim voice in a hissing undertone meant for Omri's ears alone, "was supposed to be an invention. I have reason to believe that most of it, incredible as it seems, may be true."

XIV

A Strange Yellow Sky

Doc Brant put his old-fashioned stethoscope back in his bag in silence.

Patrick, peeping through the frill of cotton lace around the top of Ruby Lou's dress, saw Boone lying on her bed on a bright-coloured patchwork quilt.

At least he wasn't lying out on the hot desert sand any more, though it had not been so hot by the time they had finally found him – it had been getting on for dark, and Patrick had been scared they'd never find him at all.

The horse had been pretty useless – it became clear quite early on that it hadn't a clue where it had left Boone. But Ruby Lou had been absolutely determined to find him. Luckily Tickle's many and varied talents

100

included amateur tracking. With his help, they had finally found the place where the horse's tracks had rejoined the main trail into town. This had been made possible by the fact that the horse was wearing some very unusual horseshoes.

"Like someth'n from a bygone age," Tick had remarked.

After that, it had just been a matter of following them, and when they lost them on some hard ground Patrick had noticed – silhouetted against a magnificent desert sunset – a tall cactus sticking up on the horizon which he recognised. Soon after that, Ruby Lou and Tickle were heaving Boone's unconscious body onto the back of Tick's wagon.

"Sure must have had a crack on the head or someth'n," squeaked Tick. "He's out colder'n last week's beans."

Doc Brant said nothing about last week's beans. He was a man of few words. He just packed his stethoscope away and prepared to leave.

"Well, Doc?" cried Ruby Lou anxiously.

The old man shook his head. "Cain't find nothin' wrong with him. Head's okay. Ain't got fever. Ain't bin shot. Nothin' but a bit o' bruisin' on the ribs, mebbe from when he fell off the horse. Seems like he plumb don't favour wakin' up."

"God pardon sin, Doc – mebbe he's drunk?" asked Tickle piously.

"Look who's talkin'," muttered Ruby.

The doctor shook his head. "No likker on his breath. Cain't explain it. Just better leave him lay."

When he'd gone, Tick said he'd mosey over to the saloon to tickle the ivories for a while to soothe his nerves.

"You be okay here alone, Ruby?"

"I ain't alone," she replied promptly, and patted her bosom. "Pat and me'll keep each other company and decide what t'do about Billy, here."

Tickle suddenly drew himself up to his full height of five feet, and intoned, in an unexpectedly deep, commanding voice: "Don't you go believin' everythin' you see. There's a lot of devil's work in this world! I know it, account of I ain't free of sin myself!" And he cast his eyes to heaven before closing the door.

"D'you hear that? There's a bit of the preacher left in him, even though he ain't held a service since the Dead-Eye Gang went through and burnt the church down in '81. That's how he learnt trackin' – trying to chase 'em."

As she spoke, Ruby lifted Patrick out between finger and thumb, and set him on a table.

It was covered with a rich – and, from Patrick's point of view, colossal – assortment of feminine fancies: a tortoiseshell-backed hairbrush, elaborate bottles of perfume with rubber spray-bulbs netted in silk, a number of sepia-tinted photos in heavily worked silver frames, an ivory comb ... Patrick could easily have sunk and suffocated in the scented powder in a cut-glass bowl, and the mirror in its bright enamel frame, above which he could only just see his head, was the size of a reflecting skyscraper. The copper hairpins scattered about were as tall as himself.

"Okay, Pat, let's hear from you," said Ruby Lou.

"Who, me?" said Patrick, startled.

"Don't string me no line now. You know what's up with my pal Billy Boone, don't ya." It was not a question. Her blue eyes were narrowed as she looked at him, though her wide red mouth was smiling knowingly.

Patrick sat down cross-legged on a white swansdown

powderpuff. "Yes, I do, as a matter of fact. But you won't believe me if I tell you."

"Try me."

Patrick told her. "Boone's left his body behind and gone into the future."

There was a pause while she took this in.

"Supposin' I say I believe ya. An' I just might, 'cause he told me some such tale himself once. Will he come back?"

"Yes. But only if my friend Omri turns the key at – at the other end."

"Into the future, huh? Is that where you come from?"

"Yes."

"What year?" she asked, as if that would catch him out.

Patrick told her.

She straightened up. "Holy snakes! That's almost exactly a hundred years from now!"

She walked about the room for a bit. Patrick watched her. Of course she was rather gaudily dressed and he supposed she was a lady in name only, so to speak, but when she was at the far side of the room, so he could see all of her, it was obvious that she was very pretty. She was clever, too, cleverer than all those crazy men in the bar who had started shooting and fighting at the sight of him.

And she was brave, and tough. The way she'd ridden that horse, the way she'd stuck to the search, the way she'd lifted Boone's big body onto the tail of the wagon . . . Patrick admired her. And she liked Boone, she liked him a lot. Patrick wondered if he liked her.

She stopped pacing. "What's it like – in the future?"

"It's okay. We've got a lot of gadgets and stuff, for making life easier. You get about in cars – that's like, horseless carriages, very fast, and we've got flying machines. We've got moving photographs which you can have in your home to entertain you. And doctors have found out how to cure lots of diseases, so people live longer."

"Gee. Sounds great! Any drawbacks?"

She *was* clever.

"Well, yes. There are too many people really. They make a lot of mess, and plenty of them are still poor and starving. There's still crime. And there are lots of wars. Not just with guns, and bows and arrows and stuff. There are weapons now – I mean – *then*, I mean – well, anyway, they're much scarier, they could blow up the whole world."

Ruby Lou strolled back to him and sat down. She put her elbow on the table near him (her arm was like a great white marble pillar) and rested her chin on her hand. She fixed her blue eyes on him.

"That's quite a drawback all right. I guess I'll stick around here till my time's up . . . It gets rough at times, but at least we're too civilized to kill more'n one or two at once. Say, they ain't gonna shoot any of them big ones off while Billy's there, are they?"

"I don't suppose so."

"They better not blow up my Billy," she said. And the way she said it showed Patrick that she didn't just *like* Boone.

Patrick spent the night cosily in the pocket of a raccoon skin jacket of Ruby Lou's which she laid out on a chair for him. She spent it sitting by the bed watching Boone.

"Won't you be tired?" asked Patrick as she bedded him down after giving him a supper of a few fibres of underdone steak and a crumb of potato washed down with milk from her sewing thimble.

"Don't you fret about me, pal. I'm used to goin' without sleep."

She turned the oil lamp low so as not to disturb him, and he saw her move to the window. She drew back the frilly curtains.

"Sky's a funny colour," she said, peering out into the night. "Don't like the feel of the air, neither. Kinda tight-feeling. Hope we ain't in for a big blow."

Patrick slept peacefully. In the morning he woke, with the fur tickling his nose, to all the noises of the town: horses neighing, wheels rattling, dogs barking, cocks crowing, people's voices – but behind and around all this was something odd and eerie. A sort of whining, gusting sound.

Ruby was standing where he had last seen her, at the window. Patrick sat up in the fur and sneezed.

"Ruby!" he called as loudly as he could.

She turned from the window, stooped, and lifted him. Her hand was soft, except for some callouses as big as watermelons which must come from riding. It smelt sweetly of soap – and was trembling.

"How's Boone?"

"Just the same. Come here and look at the sky."

She carried him to the window. He rested his arms along the top of her curled finger and looked up. The sky, and indeed the air, was a strange yellowish colour. Below the window he could see giant people hurrying about. The gusting sound was wind, coming in irregular bursts. It caught at the women's dresses and pushed them along. It blew smoke from chimneys away in sudden puffs, like warning smoke signals. It was disturbing the horses, tearing at their manes, flattening their tails to their haunches, making them shake their heads uneasily.

As Patrick watched, a man's big hat was blown off his head and trundled up the dirt street along with several balls of thistles. The man ran after it. Somewhere a door banged and banged, rhythmically, as the wind began to blow more steadily.

"What is it, Ruby?" asked Patrick in a worried voice.

"I'm not sure, pardner. I just hope it ain't what it might be."

"What?"

"Blowin' up for a twister."

Patrick turned to look at her, but all he could see was the underside of her chin. His mouth had gone suddenly dry.

"You – don't mean a cyclone? One of those black funnel-things that – "

Ruby Lou looked at Boone, lying on the bed. She'd covered him with a rug the night before. He looked peaceful and had a good colour. His hat, which Ruby had picked up on Patrick's advice, lay beside him.

"Say, that'd be one for the books!" she said with a sudden strained laugh.

"What would?"

"We was worryin' about what might happen to him *there*. What if your friend turned his magic key and sent Boone back t'here – and the bit of him he left behind'd been just – blowed clean away?"

XV

Interrogation

Mr Johnson kept his hand on Omri's shoulder all the way to his office, as if he thought Omri would twist free and run for it if he didn't hold on to him.

And he might have done, too, if he hadn't been half-paralysed – at least mentally – from apprehension.

He knows! Those were the only words in Omri's head. What was he to do when the interrogation began, as it would in a matter of moments? Lie, deny everything – okay, but what if – ?

Mr Johnson thrust him through the door of his office, followed him in, and closed and locked it behind him.

Then he walked behind his desk. But he didn't sit down. He leant forward and rested his knuckles on the desk and glared hypnotically into Omri's eyes.

"Now Omri," he said in a clear, deep voice which he only used on the most solemn occasions when someone had done something expulsion-worthy, "You know what I have to say."

Omri swallowed and stared at him the way a rabbit stares into a car's headlights as it bears down on him.

"You haven't forgotten that day last year," he said, "any more than I have. The day you and Patrick were sent to my office for talking in class. The day I went home early because I supposed I was ill, having seen something I believed I couldn't possibly have seen. You remember all that, Omri, don't you."

Omri felt his head nod.

"What I thought I saw," the headmaster continued slowly, "was two tiny, living people in the palm of a boy's hand. They moved. One of them was dressed as a Red Indian."

"It's not right to say 'Red Indian'," Omri heard himself say in a strangled voice.

Mr Johnson jerked his head back. "I beg your pardon?"

"They don't like it," Omri pursued helplessly, hardly knowing what he was saying. "You should say 'American Indian' or 'Native American'."

"I have always said Red Indian and I shall continue to say Red Indian!" Mr Johnson was suddenly shouting. "I say I saw a Red Indian, a tiny little one, and another figure as well, and they were alive, and I spent *weeks* trying to convince myself that I hadn't seen them, that I'd been overworking, and in the end I did convince myself. Almost. Until this morning. When I heard you read your story," he went on, leaning even closer so that Omri backed a step, "it all came back to me in a flash, and I knew – *I knew* that I was not imagining things after all! I ought to have had more faith in my strength of mind, I ought to have known I am not a man to imagine things!" His voice dropped and his shoulders slumped. "I must confess, it's a relief in a way. That's what it is. It's a relief." He took a deep breath and allowed himself to sit down.

Omri was left standing in front of the desk. His knees had gone woolly and his face felt cold.

"Now then my boy," said Mr Johnson more calmly, "Let us take a new starting-point. 'There are more things in heaven and earth, Horatio . . . ' "

"Who?" croaked Omri.

" . . . As Shakespeare says. I saw what I saw. They were real. *They – are – real.* That is the truth. Is it not?"

Omri stood dumb. He shut his mouth on lies and truth alike, just stood there, silent.

Mr Johnson was thinking. A year ago, on the day in question, he had browbeaten Patrick into showing him the little people by means of a threat: to telephone Patrick's father. It had worked then. Perhaps it would work now.

"Omri, if you will not tell me what I wish to know, I shall have to get your parents' co-operation."

Omri's eyes leapt to the telephone. His mind, numb before, suddenly burst into activity. He had not locked his bedroom door because he couldn't – it only bolted from the inside. The cupboard was there. Boone was there. Matron was there, and so were a number of Indians. Unprotected and alone . . . Not to mention Patrick, in a deep coma inside the chest. If Mr Johnson phoned home, his mother, or his father, would answer, and the first thing they would do was go up to his room . . . If they believed it.

But they wouldn't. How could they?

Looking at Mr Johnson, Omri saw the same thought come into his mind. Mr Johnson was not a man who enjoyed looking a fool.

"Go ahead and phone them," said Omri.

The trap shifted. It was not Omri who was caught in it now. Mr Johnson drummed with his fingers on the desk, looking at the phone, inwardly rehearsing the conversation . . . No. He must get the boy to admit the truth first. But how . . . ?

Just at that critical moment, fate intervened. The phone they were both staring at began to ring.

They jumped. Mr Johnson, recovering himself, answered.

"Hallo? Yes, the headmaster here . . . " He listened, and his face changed. His eyes flashed to Omri and his eyebrows went up. "Yes. Yes, he is. He's with me now, as it happens . . . " He covered the phone with his hand and said grimly, "It's your mother."

"Wh – what does she want?"

He didn't answer, just handed the receiver to Omri.

"Mum?"

"Omri? *Where's Patrick?*"

Omri's heart plummeted to new depths in his chest. "Patrick – ?"

"Yes, darling, where is he? I've got his mother round here, frantic. Emma's with her." His mother lowered her voice. "She's crying. Apparently she told Patrick's mother that he was spending the night with us, whereas of course he didn't. Now come on, out with it, where is he?"

"I – I'm not sure," stammered Omri. Which wasn't precisely a lie.

There was a silence from the other end. Then:

"Omri, let me speak to Mr Johnson."

Dumbly, Omri handed the phone back, and listened as well as he could for the blood still pounding in his ears.

"Yes? Johnson here ... Yes ... I see ... Yes, I remember Patrick very well." His eyes were narrowed with suspicion as he looked at Omri. "You want Omri to come home? No, no problem about that," he said smoothly. "In fact I'll bring him myself."

"Oh no!" cried Omri before he could restrain himself.

"Oh but oh yes," said Mr Johnson. He hung up the phone deliberately and rose to his feet. "Come along, my boy, my – ahem! Porsche is outside. You can direct me."

Omri directed him to his house. What else could he do? His mind was racing ahead. Patrick's mother – his own mother – probably his father – and now, Mr Johnson. They would all be there, all going at him, going at Emma, breaking down their resistance ... All he could think of by way of consolation was, *Thank goodness I sent Little Bull, Twin Stars and the baby safely back!* Their figures were still in his pocket.

Mr Johnson parked his nice new Porsche, part of an inheritance, it was rumoured, outside the house under the big old elm that had died in the Dutch Elm Disease epidemic some years before but hadn't yet been cut down. It was a good climbing tree and Omri, in his imagination, shinned straight up to the top of it in a trice. If only he could be there, on that branch just above his attic bedroom skylight, he might manage to climb in, bolt the door, get all the little people safely in the cupboard, restore Patrick, all before anyone could get there by the usual route ...

If only! If only! But Mr Johnson's hand was back like a steel vice on his shoulder, the front door was opening even before they reached it, and there they all were, waiting. Waiting for Omri to explain!

XVI

Panic

"Okay, Omri, where have you hidden Patrick?"

"Where *is* he, darling?"

"Where's my son? Just wait till I lay my hands on him!"

Emma's face was actually the one Omri's eyes fastened on. She looked really pathetic. When she saw him looking at her, she gave her head a little shake which he instantly understood to mean: "I haven't told them anything." But they'd obviously been giving her a rough time and Omri felt terrible about that.

The mothers both looked as if they were about to pounce on him; his father simply looked baffled. So naturally it was his father he made for.

"Dad, can I speak to you alone?"

"In my opinion, that would be most unwise," said Mr Johnson.

They all turned to look at him, and Omri saw his father's face tighten. He turned back to Omri.

"Let's go into the kitchen."

"Can I come?" asked Emma in a small voice, as if she thought they would all start up with her again the moment Omri was out of sight.

"Yes," said Omri. "Come on, Em." He really felt sorry for her. She actually seemed to be trembling, and as they entered the kitchen, she dropped something which clattered on the tiled floor.

They both bent simultaneously, but Omri got there first. What she'd dropped was a plastic figure of a girl in red. He thought for a moment it was Twin Stars' figure, but it was just an ordinary girl. Before he could return it to her, his father got between him and Emma, so Omri slipped it into his pocket.

"Now Omri, you'd better tell me at once where Patrick is."

When the brain is pushed to its limits, something always emerges. Even if it's the worst possible thing, in this case the truth.

"He's in my room, Dad."

"No he's not," said his father promptly. "We looked."

Omri closed his eyes and waited, but there was no more. Presumably they simply hadn't noticed, or the little people had 'frozen' into stillness. He opened his eyes again. His father was gazing at him expectantly.

"He's – hiding."

"*Hiding*? What for? Where?"

Omri glanced at Emma.

"In – in the chest."

His father looked incredulous. "Are you having me

on, Omri? He can't have been there all this time!"

"I – I don't know. He was there when I left for school."

"But why? What was the idea?"

"He – he didn't want to go home. Yet."

And then his father said the most wonderful thing.

"Well! You'd better run up and fetch him."

Omri's heart bounded with incredulous relief. Galvanised, he rushed to the door and Emma followed close.

"And I think I'll come too," remarked his father.

Omri and Emma stopped dead.

"No, Dad."

"No?"

"No. I – we'll go by ourselves." Omri turned and fastened his eyes on his father's. *"Please."*

He hesitated.

"This is all very mysterious," he said, not at all lightly. "I hope there's nothing going on that you ought to be ashamed of, Omri."

"No, Dad!"

"Okay. Go on. But remember, we're down here, waiting, all of us, and if you're not back – with Patrick – pretty damn quick, I'll be up there after you."

They raced, past the little knot of adults in the hall, up the stairs two at a time, all the way up to the attic.

Omri's chief fear now was that, after over twenty-four hours, Patrick would have come to some harm, wherever he was. What if when they brought him back, he was hurt, or even – ? But it was useless to speculate. The vital thing was to get him back, but first Omri had to hide every bit of evidence of the magic.

The second they got into the room, he bolted the door and made for the seed-tray.

"Give her back."

He turned. Emma was standing by the cupboard.

"What – ?"

"I'll put her in myself."

"Put who in? What are you talking about?" panted Omri.

"It's the end, isn't it? You're sending them all back now and you won't do any of it again because the grown-ups are near to finding out and it's got too dangerous."

Omri looked at her. Her face froze him. She was Patrick's cousin and now he saw a likeness – she had the same look he had seen on Patrick's face so many times, when he had made up his mind to do something outrageous.

"What are you on about?" he asked sharply.

"I picked out that girl. From my model set. I'm going to make her real, and I'm going to keep her forever."

Omri almost pushed her out of his way. "You're mad," he said shortly. He was still breathless from his run, and from stifled panic – his brain wasn't working well and he couldn't cope with this new threat.

He bent to the entrance of the longhouse. "Matron!"

She emerged. Her headdress was all bent, which only happened when she was thoroughly flustered.

"My dear!" she cried, her hand on her thin bosom as if to restrain her heart from leaping out of it. "I thought you and Patrick were giants, but some people came into the room who were even bigger than you! I think they were looking for something. I ducked back into the longhouse the second I saw them, and ordered all my patients to keep absolutely silent. Luckily the giants only glanced round once and then went out again, but oh, dear me, it was a bad moment!"

"You did the right thing, Matron. Now I have to send you back."

"Not a moment too soon! And I think I can fairly say I'm leaving all my patients well on the road to recovery. How will you send them back – the non-ambulatory cases?"

"Don't worry, I've thought about that." When the chest was empty, he would just put the whole seed-tray, complete with longhouse and occupants, into it; that way he wouldn't have to move the injured Indians individually. But he thought he had better send Matron back through the cupboard in case she wound up in the wrong place.

Matron stepped gingerly onto Omri's hand and knelt down to keep her balance as he air-lifted her to the cupboard. She was looking at him closely.

"My boy?"

"Yes?"

"You look worried. Am I wrong in thinking that something has happened to – change the situation radically?"

"You're not wrong, Matron. You – I'm afraid I won't be bringing you back again."

She stepped off his hand into the cupboard. She cleared her throat loudly.

"I can see there is no time for prolonged farewells." She straightened her uniform skirt and checked her pockets to make sure she had all her bits and pieces. Her hand strayed once to her cap, and Omri thought he saw her furtively wipe her eyes with the tail-end of one of the floating ribbons attached to it. He knew he would have felt tearful himself if it were not for his desperate preoccupations.

"You've been absolutely wonderful. I'll miss you," he said sincerely.

"Oh, pish, tush, and likewise – " But she choked on the last word, and simply put out her hand to touch the tip of his finger which he extended to her.

"You'd better hurry!" said Emma. "Here, let me do it!" And before Omri knew what was happening, she had shut the door with a thump and turned the key. Omri stood silent, his heart beating, feeling the pressure of time, of all the grown-ups waiting downstairs, and realised he was putting off the moment when he would open the chest.

Then he was aware that Emma was standing there with the key clutched in her hand.

"Now I want my red girl," she said.

"You're not going to bring anything to life now," Omri retorted. "I can't let you. If you can't see why not, then – then I just wish I'd never let you in on it."

Emma's hard, almost Tamsin-like look softened. "Please, Omri. Just give her to me. All right, I won't do anything. Just let me have her."

Omri reached into his pocket. "Right. Give me the key."

There was a moment – a bad moment – when he thought she was going to refuse. God, this was scary! The very people you trusted most could become like strangers in their longing for a little person of their own! It was worse than the way people behaved over gold. If Emma could frighten him like this, what would happen if the grown-ups ever –

Suddenly an awful thought struck him and he stiffened with horror.

Mr Johnson! Mr Johnson *knew*. He was downstairs now, and there was absolutely nothing to stop him blowing the whole secret wide open! That was what he had come for, and that was what he would do!

No sooner had this thought surfaced than he heard something.

Emma heard it too. Both their heads snapped round to face the door.

"They're coming up here! All of them!" she breathed.

"Oh God," whispered Omri, closing his eyes in despair. "He's told them!"

XVII

The Big Blow

"Quick! Give me the key!"

She didn't hesitate now, but thrust the key at him, snatching the red girl at the same time from his other hand. Omri stumbled across to the chest.

"Bring the seed-tray – hurry – " he gasped as the thudding of feet on the lower stairway got louder. He could hear their voices, querulous, anxious, Mr Johnson's the loudest, dominating their questions:

" – No room for further doubt – biological phenomenon – saw with my own eyes – "

Wait, wait! No time for two operations – do it all at once – Omri opened the chest, grabbed the seed-tray out of Emma's hands and put it in the bottom next to Patrick's feet – he was aware of Emma, leaning closely over him – and slammed down the lid. His hand was so unsteady – they were nearly at the door – that it took two or three stabs before he could thrust the key into the lock. Then he turned it.

What happened next was something he could never afterwards remember clearly, and yet would never, ever forget.

The main memory, later, was of a stupendous noise, a deafening roar that filled the room to bursting. But the pressure of the sound was not what threw him and Emma right across the room and slammed them backwards against the wall.

The chest . . . He was to remember seeing the end of his chest. It simply lifted into the air as the lid blasted open and then it disintegrated. It simply blew outwards into fragments. One bit of it hit him in the stomach and knocked the breath out of him. At the same time something large and heavy was hurled and tumbled across the floor and struck Emma's legs.

Then Omri witnessed, in a few traumatic, incredible seconds, the total destruction of his room.

The skylight above his bed vanished first, though he was too stunned to see it go – the glass erupting in a puff of sparkling dust as the violent charge that had come out of the chest roared upward through the hole in the roof. But the hole wasn't large enough, nothing like large enough to channel that black tower of pure force which detonated from bottom to top of the little room.

The edges of the square hole bent outwards like plasticine for a split second and then with a tearing, wrenching, screeching sound which could be heard distinctly through the original roaring, the whole slope of the roof disappeared.

At that, everything in the room that could possibly move – all the bedding, the Japanese table, the floor cushions, books, Omri's collections, the clock radio and half a hundred other objects – whirled, in a blinding, terrifying tenth of a second, out into the sky as if sucked by an inhalation from the heavens.

That was it. That was all, inside the room. But the noise had not stopped, simply gone out of the house. They could still hear it outside. A wind to end winds, the most ferocious, destructive blast to hit England for two hundred years, was beginning its career that would make news all over the world.

The first of several million trees it was destined to uproot was the old elm outside Omri's house that should have come down years ago, and now did so, with a demolishing crash, right on top of Mr Johnson's new Porsche.

The wind then proceeded at high speed down Hovel Road, blowing off roofs, knocking down trees, and wrecking the happy haunts of skinheads – a maverick Texas cyclone which the weathermen had not predicted and could never explain, on its way to cause unprecedented havoc to south-east England.

Omri and Emma found themselves lying on the floor on the very edge of consciousness. Omri was clutching the thing that had hit him, something sharp which dug into his hands. Emma was clutching something, too. What she was clutching was Patrick.

He alone did not seem to be much fazed or hurt. As the deafening noise began to fade into the distance, he sat up, rubbed his hands over his face and head and said, "Blimey! Just in time!"

The other two stared at him glassily. He stood up, shook himself, turned – and stopped.

"Crumbs," he breathed, gazing round the shell of Omri's room.

He looked upward into open sky, an angry sky still full of whirling leaves and odd fragments. The broken-off joists of the roof stuck out in silhouette. It was like looking out through the wide-open mouth of a gigantic shark.

"You know what," he said slowly, "I think I must've brought the twister back with me."

"Twister . . . ?" Omri's voice came out thickly and he found his throat was choked with dust. The air was full of it.

"Yeah. A cyclone . . . We saw it coming up the street, whirling like a black funnel, throwing huge things into the air . . . it was just about onto us when – "

His hand flew to his mouth. He turned slowly back to where Omri and Emma were lying.

"Where's Boone?" he asked hollowly. "Where's Ruby Lou?"

Boone!

Omri had, in the panic of sending Matron and the injured Indians back, totally forgotten about Boone.

His brain was working thickly. Boone! Boone had been *here*. Where? Where had he put him? Had he been on the seed-tray? – No. He had been in the Lego house, in his matchbox bed. Omri'd put him somewhere, at his own request – somewhere . . . out of sight. Out of sight, out of mind.

Omri tried to get up. It was a struggle. Every part of him ached and protested when he moved. He put his hand to the ground and dropped the sharp thing that had hit him, the last remains of his seaman's chest – an angle of the lid with an oblong brass plate bearing the words "L. Buller".

As it struck the floor he thought he heard a small extra sound, but before he could register it, it was drowned by a banging on the door, and terrified voices.

"Omri! Emma! Patrick! Are you all right? What was it, what happened?"

The three of them froze, gazing at each other. It was Emma who acted first. She scrambled stiffly to her feet and went to the door.

"We're all right! Patrick's here, we're all here, the roof's blown off but we're okay, and – "

"All right?!" yelled Omri's mother. "You can't be! Open the door!"

"I can't," said Emma. "The bolt's bent."

Omri's eyes raced to the bolt. There was nothing wrong with it. *Brilliant*, he thought admiringly. *She's brilliant. That gives us a few minutes, anyhow*.

"Omri!" called his father in a shocked voice. "What was it? What was that terrible noise? The house shook – like an earthquake – "

"I – I think it's some kind of a freak wind, Dad!" Omri managed to croak. "Did you hear the tree come down? It's gone, I can't see the top branches any more!"

Mr Johnson could be heard to give a cry of anguish.

"Tree? Down? My God! My Porsche . . . !" And they heard him rush down the stairs.

"Patrick! Speak to me, speak to me!" cried Patrick's mother hysterically.

"I'm here, Mum, calm down," said Patrick shortly. He was white in the face.

"Listen, Dad," said Omri quickly. "We're okay, I'll take the bolt off the door, you go and see how much damage there is. We'll be down as soon as we get the door open."

"Right," said his father. "He's right. Come on, let's

go down. Bloody roof's off – my conservatory must be wrecked – " And he shepherded the mothers down the stairs, Patrick's still fussing shrilly.

A silence fell. It was almost too much of a relief to bear, after all the terrifying uproar of the last interminable few minutes. The three of them stood still, trying to get to grips with things. And in that abrupt and welcome lull, they finally heard something which must have been going on for some time.

"Help! HELP! HE-E-E-LP!"

The voice – a very tiny one – seemed to come from above their heads.

They craned their necks. "I don't believe it! Look up there!" shouted Omri, pointing.

Impaled on one of the broken roof-beams was a familiar object. Its mirror was no more, its door hung from one hinge, and most of its remaining white paint had been battered off. But there it was, still there, what was left of it.

The cupboard!

And that wasn't all. Clinging precariously to the bottom rim by both hands, his spurred boots kicking over an infinity of empty air, was Boone.

XVIII

Red Satin

"Help! Git me down! Save me! Ah'm gonna fall! H-E-E-E-LP!"

"How did he – Never mind! Quick, we must do something!"

"Boone! Hang on, we're coming!"

"How?" he squawked. "Y'aint got wings! An' Ah cain't hold on much longer! It's no use!" His voice swooped into a despairing dirge. "Don't bother none, fellas . . . It's too late t'save me . . . Ah'm doomed. Ah accept m'fate. Ah jest wish Ah hadn't lived such a rotten no-good hard-drinkin' poker-playin' life . . . !"

Once again Emma was the first to react sensibly – the boys were running around in circles under the dangling cupboard, bumping into each other in their

126

hopeless search for something to climb on. Emma tore off her anorak and thrust one sleeve into Omri's hand and one into Patrick's. Then grasping the bottom edge herself and pulling it taut like a fireman's blanket, she shouted up: "Let go! We'll catch you!"

Boone let go and dropped what must have seemed to him a thousand feet, screaming all the way.

"Aaaaaaaaaeeeeeccccccooooooowl!"

He hit the quilting with a tiny plop and lay there, momentarily stunned. Emma and the boys laid the anorak gently on the floor.

"Boone? Are you okay?" asked Patrick anxiously.

After a moment, Boone slowly sat up.

"That's all Ah needed," he remarked bitterly, wincing as he felt himself all over. "As if it wasn't enough t'lose mah *hat*, an' git crushed half to death by m'best buddy – " he gave Patrick a dirty look – "I git blown almost up to the Pearly Gates, and instead o' findin' m'self on a nice soft pink cloud, I'm hangin' out there in space yellin' my haid off with not a livin' soul takin' a danged bit o' notice till it's nearly Too Late!" And he wiped away a tear. He scowled round darkly, and then changed his tone. "Say, whut hit this place, anyhow? Musta bin some dynamitin' that went wrong."

"It was a cyclone from your town, from your time, Boone. It came back with me through the magic," Patrick explained.

Boone looked appalled. "Say ... Ah hope it didn't wreck the saloon!"

"If the cyclone came *here*, it couldn't be there at the same time, so I guess your town's safe. And by the way – so is your hat."

Boone's whole manner changed. He jumped to his feet excitedly. "Ya found m'hat? I sure miss it!"

"It's okay, Boone. It's back there, waiting for you. Ruby Lou made sure to pick it up safely, she knows you love it."

Boone stared at him. "You – you run into Ruby?"

Patrick nodded. Boone's eyes began to glow.

"Ya don't say! Now aint' she a great gal?"

"Yes, she is."

"She ain't one o' your prissy, stuck-up kind neither, she's a real pal, and purty as paint too!" He heaved a wistful sigh. "Ah wisht she was here now! Y'know," he confided, "when Ah'm with Ruby, Ah never feels sad nor nuthin', an Ah only cry 'cause she kinda likes me to tell her sad stories. And I kin do without drinkin'. That li'l Ruby gal is as good as likker to a man any day. Better."

"That's the nicest thing a man ever said to me, Billy Boone!"

The sound of this other tiny voice was so totally unexpected they all goggled at each other before turning towards it.

They stared unbelievingly. Standing up on the edge of the bit of the chest lid which Omri had dropped was a tiny figure in a red satin dress and high-polished red boots, with blonde hair piled on her head and her hands on her hips.

Patrick let out a yell of delight. "RUBY! What are you doing here?"

"Search me! But the tables are turned now, eh, Pat? Now you're the big 'un, but I don't care so long as Billy's my size. Who's gonna bring me over to him so he can give me a hug?"

The boys dived, but Emma got there first. She took the tiny figure of Ruby Lou in her hand wonderingly and gazed at her. Then she lifted a shining face to Omri.

"She's mine! It's my red girl! I sneaked her onto the seed-tray just before you put it into the chest! Isn't she – just – beautiful!"

"Ain't she, though!" echoed Boone adoringly as Emma gently set her down on the anorak at his side and they fell into each other's arms.

The freak storm was an absolute disaster for nearly everyone it touched. But for Omri, Patrick and Emma, and for the little people, it was a godsend. In one way.

The destruction it wreaked on Omri's home and the neighbourhood was so extensive that what had gone just before was simply dislodged from the minds of the grown-ups.

To begin with, Mr Johnson's precious car was a total write-off. To make matters worse – or better – just as he was jumping up and down beside it, ranting and raving at its destruction, a sizable branch from the dead elm broke off and descended on his head. After that, of course, though he recovered later, nobody was about to believe any tales he had to tell about little live men. (Incidentally, the insurance company refused to pay up for the Porsche because he had only insured for third party risk. He would have to come to school on a bicycle, a sadder and a humbler man.)

As for Omri's and Patrick's parents, they'd never exactly believed what Mr Johnson tried to tell them just before they came rushing up the stairs. And afterwards they simply never remembered it. The conservatory had been blown to pieces, the tree was blocking the road, their chimney had fallen through the roof next door: the whole place looked as if – well, as if a cyclone had struck it. There was no time even to think about anything else, once they had made sure their children were really all right.

The storm had severely damaged the school, which was closed for several weeks. This naturally caused all those who should have been learning there profound unhappiness. But they managed to make the best of things.

Patrick's cottage in Kent was okay, but his mother's orchard (she had taken to cider-making for a living since her divorce) had been devastated. The problems this caused meant she was only too glad to leave Patrick up in London for a time, while she dealt with them. She never did get around to asking him where he had been during that fateful twenty-four hours when he was missing.

So all that was on the plus side, at least from the point of view of the secret.

On the minus side were the condition of Omri's house, his parents' distress, and one other thing which loomed larger for him and the other two – not to mention Boone and Ruby – than anything else.

As soon as possible, Omri got a ladder, and unhooked the cupboard impaled through its back on the broken roof-joist. He took a hammer and carefully flattened the bent bits of metal back into place until the hole was almost concealed. He measured the space for the mirror and went out and bought another to match and fitted it in. He fixed the hinges and gave the whole thing a rub-down with sandpaper and repainted it, after which it looked a good deal better than it ever had before.

But all the time he was working on it, his heart was leaden, and Patrick and Emma – when they could be there – said very little. Each knew all too well what was in the minds of the others.

What Omri was so diligently, so devotedly working on was merely a memorial, a museum-piece. The cupboard was of no practical use without the key.

And the key was gone.

Emma had taken over Ruby Lou, and – since Ruby refused to be parted from him – Boone stayed with Patrick, who was living in Emma's house with his aunt. Omri was utterly opposed to this, but he couldn't say much – the little people had hardly been proved safe in *his* place. But he lived in abject terror of Tamsin, or someone else, finding out.

Omri was having to share Gillon's room. So in a way he was glad not to have the responsibility of the little people. But there was cold terror in his heart nearly every waking moment – even though Emma and Patrick assured him they were taking every precaution.

It was evident to Omri that, despite the dangers, or perhaps because of them, the other two were having the greatest fun of their lives. Ruby and Boone were living in an old dolls' house of Emma's which, if not quite small enough for them (they had to really *climb* up the stairs, and come down backwards) contained plenty of things they could use – tables, chairs, beds, and kitchen things galore.

What the dolls' house didn't provide, Patrick and Emma did. Patrick had fixed them up with a little wood-stove (complete with stove-pipe) made of a tea-tin which had a hole on top of the right size for a real, tiny frying-pan, and with this Ruby Lou could do some cooking. They used a special little loo, like a camping one, which Emma had arranged, and every day she brought them hot water for baths, and tiny towels (Boone got quite to like washing.) Every day there were new things to make and add. They even rigged up real electric lights which were a wondrous novelty for Boone and Ruby, though the switch was too stiff for them to work alone and they really preferred a miniature, but real, oil-lamp twice as tall as themselves.

All this was fine, for everyone but Omri. He felt very much alone and left out. Visiting occasionally and seeing for himself only made him sadder. He longed for Little Bull and Twin Stars to keep him company. Or even Matron . . . But there was no way. There would never be any way again. It made his heart very heavy. And very frightened when he thought of Boone and Ruby, with them forever, unable to get home, and in constant danger of discovery.

One day, two weeks after the storm, Patrick and Emma came to Omri's.

"Boone and Ruby Lou asked us to bring them," Emma explained. "They want to talk about the future."

The conference was held in Gillon's room, which, even though he was not around, was nerve-wracking. He might walk in at any moment – there was no bolt on this door. Besides, the roofers had at last arrived and were banging and crashing about, throwing down tiles into the front garden where they smashed on the stump of the tree, and beginning to remove the broken beams preparatory to putting on a whole new roof. Every few seconds something hurtled past the window and landed with a crash below. This meant they might not hear Gillon if he approached.

Omri closed the window and the curtains, though it was broad daylight, to help keep out the noise. Then he switched Gillon's desk-lamp on and they all sat round

Ruby Lou and Boone, who were seated on a pouffe made of a large rubber.

"Listen, folks," Ruby began, as they all leaned forward to hear her. "I wouldn't want to hurt your feelin's none, I mean you kids've made us feel real welcome, givin' us that special house and all, but we jest can't settle here. It ain't safe. Every time a door opens I git me a heart attack, and besides, I keep havin' nightmares about them big blowin'-up-the-world things Pat told me about. Now, we wanna git back home, but Billy, here, explained me the whole thing, about the key gittin' blowed away, and it's real bad news. What're we gonna do?"

Nobody knew what to answer. The silence stretched.

As always when things were *really* desperate, Boone was dry-eyed and steady as a rock. "Couldn't we try some other key?"

Omri said, "I have."

The others looked at him.

"With the cupboard. I've tried every key in the house, just on the offchance, but none of them even fit."

"Sure is a pity, with the cupboard lookin' so new and fine – makes me wanna jump right in," said Boone sadly. Ruby put her arm round his shoulders.

"Doncha start now, Billy, or you'll have me bawlin' too!"

"I ain't bawlin'," said Boone. "But Ah sure am gittin' mighty homesick. It could make a man cry to think o' never ridin' the prairies or the deserts agin . . . or even settlin' his favourite hat back on his ears . . . " This did cause him to give a deep sniff. "And another thing. How's me an' Ruby gonna git hitched if'n we cain't git us a preacher? T'ain't right, us livin' in that house together, even in separate rooms, when the knot ain't tied!"

Ruby gave him a look that suggested she might not have worried too much about that, but she glanced at Emma and said nothing.

"It looks to me," said Emma, "as if what we'll have to do is just keep trying keys. Old keys. Just keep trying and trying until we find one that works."

Again they were silent. None of them believed that would ever happen. This business was a one-off and they all knew it.

"And meanwhile – what?" said Boone.

"Just keep on as you are – I'm afraid," said Omri with a deep, miserable sigh.

They had something to eat, and Omri – who had a special tea prepared – tried to turn it into a bit of a party, but it was no use. They were all just too upset and scared about the future to enjoy it. At last, Emma put Ruby into her pocket and Boone, with some assistance, clambered to his favourite perch with a leg each side of Patrick's ear, facing out and well-masked by hair. He said it was the nearest thing to riding.

Omri went out with them to the gate.

The roofers had gone home for the day, leaving the front garden in the most appalling mess. There were tiles and broken bits of wood everywhere. The front lawn and the hedge dividing the garden from Hovel Road were all chopped up and smothered with debris.

"Dad'll go ape when he sees this," said Omri – and then he stopped.

He'd seen something. Something that in the first second he didn't comprehend, because it didn't belong. Not that bright colour . . . He paused to look closer. The others were ahead of him, starting down the road towards the station. Omri reached up his hand to the top of the hedge.

And then he saw what it was.

He didn't shout and jump and cheer. It was too important for that. He simply stood there with his hand raised, touching it, not pulling yet, just feeling, deep inside him, what it meant.

That narrow bit of red satin ribbon, sticking out between the twigs.

Epilogue at a Wedding

It was a marvellous, unforgettable occasion.

They all came.

Matron – they had to send her back briefly, when they'd explained why they'd brought her, to change out of her uniform. ("Not *remotely* suitable!") She reappeared in a smart navy-blue suit, a snow-white blouse with lots of unexpected frills down the front, and a funny little hat like a crooked flower-pot, with a dotted veil. She was even wearing a trace of lipstick!

Fickits emerged with his sergeant's stripes, which his newly confident manner, after the Battle of the Skinheads, had earned him almost as soon as he returned to his company. When *he* understood the occasion, he wanted to go back to recruit a Royal Marine guard of honour, but he was dissuaded by Boone who modestly said he wanted things quiet with "jest m'best friends present."

But of course, his best friends had to include his blood brother, Little Bull, and his family.

Little Bull arrived in full regalia – his headdress, his cloak and all his finery. He had had them on for a celebration of a victory – not a final one, no doubt, but still, a victory.

In the two weeks since he had been back in his village, a great deal had happened, which he related to them during the wedding-eve feast. The Algonquin, having regrouped after the previous battle (which Omri had witnessed) had mounted another attack, and been repulsed.

"How did you do it, Little Bull? You lost so many men last time."

"Wise chief learn not only from victory. Defeat also teach," said Little Bull, virtuously but vaguely.

"It's strange that when you had the now-guns you couldn't beat them, but without them, you could."

"Best use Indian weapons as Omri say." Little Bull's tone was now definitely evasive. Omri was not inclined to press him, but Boone, unexpectedly, was.

"Usin' only bows and arrows, ya beat 'em hollow, eh, Redskin?" he asked.

Little Bull inclined his head.

"Oh yeah? So ya never even used *m'six-shooter that ya stole off me*, huh?"

Little Bull's head snapped up. His eyes narrowed to menacing slits.

"Little Bull not steal white brother weapon!"

"Well, ya did, 'cause Ah had m'eyes open a mite and Ah seen ya do it. One o' them times ya come

137

to look me over when Ah wuz laid thur, helpless,"
he went on, while Little Bull became more and more
uncomfortable.

"Little Bull!" exclaimed Omri, shocked. "You didn't!"

"Not steal!" shouted Little Bull. "Take, but not steal!
Here, I give weapon back!" He pulled the revolver out
from under his cloak and thrust it into Boone's hand.

"Real good of ya, seein' y'ain't got no more use fer
it, now it's plumb empty. Where's all the bullets, Injun
brother?"

Little Bull's earlier discomfiture had evaporated. Now
he drew himself up proudly. "One bullet, one enemy!"
he boasted.

"Whut? Ya downed six of 'em?" He held up one
hand and a thumb. "That's right good shootin' fer a
beginner." He tucked his gun away in its holster. "Well,
guess Ah'll have to reckon Ah *lent* it in a good cause.
And *you'll* have to reckon on goin' back t'th'old ways
next time."

Little Bull scowled.

"Hard go back old ways after new ways," he muttered.

Twin Stars, with Tall Bear strapped to her back, was
also wearing a beautiful dress, covered with elaborate
decoration. She rivalled the bride, until Ruby Lou
thought of a way to dress up even more.

She got Emma to go and buy a model wedding
set which included a plastic bride. Emma was not too
happy about this.

"But what are you going to do when I bring her to
life? Just rip the dress off her and leave her there in her
undies?"

"Nope. Course not! I'm gonna buy it off her."

"Buy it? With with?"

"This!" And she pulled out a minute leather pouch with a drawstring and chinked it against her palm.

Emma's eyes popped. "It's not – gold, is it?"

"Sure is." She tipped the bag a little and something winked in her tiny hand. "I reckon a few gold dollars ought to pay fer a weddin' dress. Jest hope I like it when I see it made real!"

So it was done. Ruby went into the cupboard after the bride had been brought to life, and emerged triumphant with the dress – a gorgeous thing of white silk and a thousand tiny lace ruffles – over her arm.

"Don't tell me she was at the altar when we brought her!" said Emma.

"Naw! She was jest tryin' on. She told me she didn't like the darn thing much anyhow, made her look fat."

"Cain't all have a figure like yorn, Ruby!" said Boone proudly.

The preacher was none other than Tickle. Bringing him was no easy task. There were several false tries. They first brought to life the parson from Emma's wedding models, but of course he wasn't Tickle, he was just a parson, a pallid youth who took one look out through the cupboard door, offered up an anguished prayer and fainted dead away.

So in the end they went to the model shop with Ruby and looked at every plastic figure in the place till they found a Western saloon scene with a little man at a piano and Ruby said, "That's him!" And it was. So they got the piano, too.

Tickle was terrified at first. He insisted the whole thing was devil's work and refused to believe it could be happening. But Ruby and Boone took him aside and persuaded him that it was all part of the Great Design, and what really would be sinful was if he left Ruby and

Boone unhitched. After a few pulls from a hip-pocket flask he happened to have on him, he allowed himself to be drawn to his piano and after practising a few hymns (which he hadn't played since the Dead-Eye Gang had burnt down his church) he gradually worked himself into a devout mood and agreed to play his part.

"He ain't much of a preacher-man," confided Boone to Patrick, tapping his forehead. "He went downhill fast after they burned his church – th'likker, y'know. Ain't everyone's got a haid fer it like me. But he still got it in him t'do whut's right."

"You ought to help rebuild the church, Boone," prompted Emma.

"Who, me?" exclaimed Boone, but Ruby gave him a nudge, and he said, "Uh – yup. Good idee. Mebbe."

The wedding was held in Omri's room. It was rather dark because the hole in the roof was still covered with a big roofers' canvas; and there wasn't any furniture except the built-in bunk. But they spread a sheet over the floor and lit a circle of candles and set everything up the way they wanted it. There was a tiny altar made of a piece of decorative stone, with a single daisy on it, a stained-glass window made of scraps of coloured tissue-paper with a candle shining through it, and of course a feast of food including a miniature wedding-cake that Emma had found in a rather posh baker's. It was still as big as a table to the bride and groom, but Little Bull would help cut it with his knife. They had lots of crisps crushed fine, and hundreds-and-thousands in dishes made of tiny shells from a necklace of Emma's. There was 7-Up for champagne.

The cupboard was nearby, a little to one side. Its door was symbolically ajar and the recovered key stuck in the lock. Emma, who had a feeling for these things, had made a little, triumphal arch of flowers and a Lego step leading up to the bottom rim. No one mentioned it, but they all knew the little people were going home through it as soon as the wedding party ended.

Patrick, Emma and Omri had had a long, fraught discussion about the whole business.

"This has got to be the end of it." It was Omri who said it. Patrick knew it too, but he couldn't come right out with it. It was Emma who didn't accept it, who put up a fight.

"It's all right for you two!" she raged. She was nearly in tears. "You've had it for ages. Last year . . . And you've time-travelled . . . It's not fair, it's just not fair!"

"We've got to, Em. It's just too dangerous for them."

"We could keep them secret . . . We *have*."

"For how long?" asked Patrick quietly. "Before Tamsin finds out? It's been a pretty near thing once or twice already. Or someone else."

Emma was silent. She was struggling with her tears. The boys were uncomfortable. They understood too clearly how she felt, because they felt it too. More than she did.

"But I love Ruby!" Emma burst out. "I can't give her up, never see her again! It's like – telling me I have to say yes to her dying!"

The boys didn't look at each other.

"I've been thinking about the wind," said Omri slowly.

"What do you mean, the wind?"

"The cyclone. It – it's done an awful lot of damage. It ripped down millions of trees. It practically destroyed Kew Gardens and lots of other places."

"So what? What's that got to do with anything? It wasn't our fault."

"Well, I think it was."

The other two looked at him.

"Look. We – we interfered. We felt bad about the Indians dying, and now we've done this. Don't you understand? Everything that happened – Boone being hurt, the cyclone – even Mr Johnson's car – it's us. It all happened because we found out a magic trick and messed around with time."

"Good things happened too," said Patrick defensively.

"Like what?"

"We helped Little Bull defeat his enemies."

"Yeah, well, he'd probably have done that anyway, and now we've shown him modern weapons and you see what it led to – him borrowing Boone's revolver because it made killing so much easier!"

"That's going to happen anyway," said Patrick slowly. He, too, had been doing some reading. "White men coming along, interfering if you like to call it that, changing the Indians' way of life. It'd already well begun in Little Bull's time. He knew all about guns ... We only gave a little push to what was bound to happen."

Omri thought about what he'd read about the way American Indians live now. In reservations, their hunting grounds taken from them, their songs and their gods discredited and lost, many of them alcoholics, beginning only recently to struggle back to their own, old ways and traditions and beliefs. After centuries of bad times ... horrible times.

"I don't want to give that kind of push," he said. "It's got to end."

The other two were silent. Emma gave a deep sniff. Then she said, "But as long as we've got the key, we'll always be tempted."

Omri reviewed the many, many thoughts he had had

about that. He had envisaged himself burying the key, but he knew that wouldn't do. Better to throw it away. Into the Thames, into the sea. He'd tried to imagine himself doing what he knew to be the right thing. But every time, something stopped him. In his imagination he would draw back his hand, the key would be about to fly from it – to sink, to drown, to be lost forever. And he would stop. He could never do it.

The solution he had arrived at was not perfect, but it was the best he could do. It had been born of the deep, long, strong fear he had suffered, and the pain of knowing that they had meddled where they shouldn't and done a lot of harm.

"I'm going to ask my dad to take it from me and put it in the bank. I'll make a secret package of it, with the cupboard. He won't know what it is. He'll tell them to keep it in their vaults and not give it back till I'm dead."

Emma and Patrick stared at him, awe-struck.

"Dead!"

Omri nodded solemnly.

"But who will they give it back to then?"

"My children."

Emma spoiled the moment by giggling. The idea of Omri having children – ! But then his solemn face took her laughter away. She said, "And will they know – ? Will you tell them – what it is? What it does?"

"I'll tell them as a story. I won't tell them it's true. I'll leave it up to them. That way it – it won't be quite lost. Only to us. We've done enough."

The Reverend Tickle played the Wedding March as the bride came up the aisle. Matron was at her side, to give her away. Little Bull and Fickits were best men.

It needed two, to support Boone. At this last moment he was seized by an attack of nerves.

"I cain't go through with it! I ain't good enough for her!" he muttered, his face flushed crimson through his bristles. " 'Sides, a man cain't git hitched without a hat – t'ain't natural! I'm gittin' outa here!"

And he turned to flee. But Little Bull and Fickits laid strong hands on him and held him firmly until his bride reached him.

Ruby Lou in a wedding gown, with her blonde hair down and a lace veil floating round her like mist, was very different from Ruby Lou in scarlet satin. Boone was so smitten at the sight of her that he was struck dumb and his knees buckled. Luckily Tickle had anticipated this, and as he quickly moved from the piano stool to the altar to begin the service, he discreetly passed his flask to Fickits, who gave Boone a restoring swig.

"M'very last!" Boone vowed, but even Ruby, tenderly taking his arm, didn't look as if she quite believed him.

Just near the end, Twin Stars' baby began to cry. Matron tutted and said, "Sh!" But Little Bull and Twin Stars looked at each other and beamed.

"Good omen!" cried Little Bull, interrupting the I-do's. "Baby's voice sign of health, long life! Many hope! Much children!"

And he let out a marvellous baying cry of pleasure which sent a shiver of excitement and happiness through them all.